MW01048211

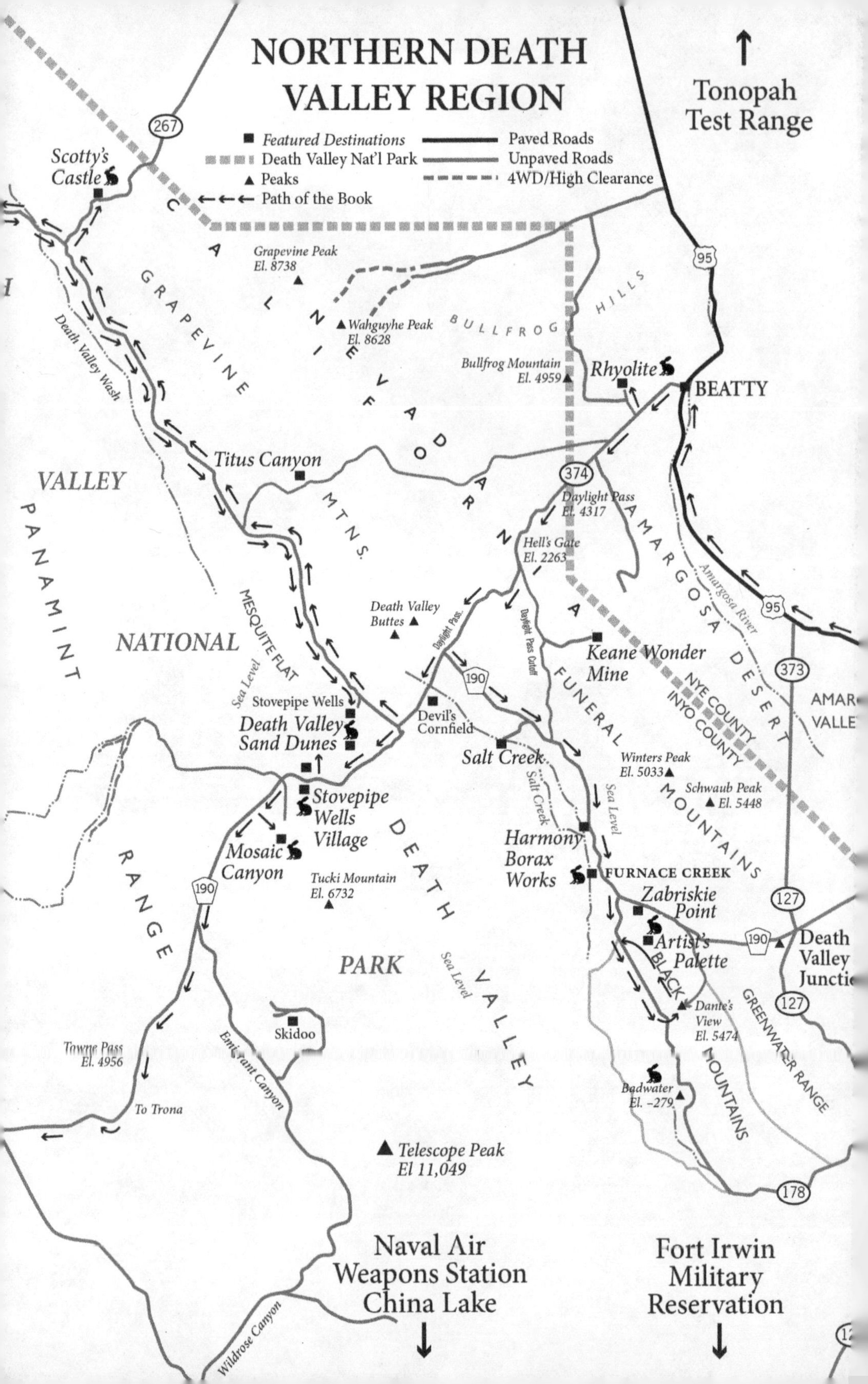
NORTHERN DEATH VALLEY REGION
Featured Destinations
Death Valley Nat'l Park
Peaks
Path of the Book
Paved Roads
Unpaved Roads
4WD/High Clearance
Tonopah Test Range
Scotty's Castle
267
95
Grapevine Peak El. 8738
Wahguyhe Peak El. 8628
GRAPEVINE
CALIFORNIA
NEVADA
BULLFROG HILLS
Bullfrog Mountain El. 4959
Rhyolite
BEATTY
Death Valley Wash
Titus Canyon
MTNS.
374
Daylight Pass El. 4317
Hell's Gate El. 2263
AMARGOSA DESERT
Amargosa River
VALLEY
PANAMINT
NATIONAL
MESQUITE FLAT
Sea Level
Death Valley Buttes
Daylight Pass
Daylight Pass Cutoff
Keane Wonder Mine
FUNERAL MOUNTAINS
NYE COUNTY
INYO COUNTY
373
AMAR
VALLE
190
Stovepipe Wells
Death Valley Sand Dunes
Devil's Cornfield
Salt Creek
Winters Peak El. 5033
Schwaub Peak El. 5448
Stovepipe Wells Village
Mosaic Canyon
RANGE
Tucki Mountain El. 6732
DEATH VALLEY
Harmony Borax Works
FURNACE CREEK
Zabriskie Point
Artist's Palette
BLACK MOUNTAINS
127
Death Valley Junctio
Dante's View El. 5474
GREENWATER RANGE
PARK
Skidoo
Towne Pass El. 4956
Emigrant Canyon
To Trona
Badwater El. –279
Telescope Peak El 11,049
178
Naval Air Weapons Station China Lake
Fort Irwin Military Reservation
Wildrose Canyon

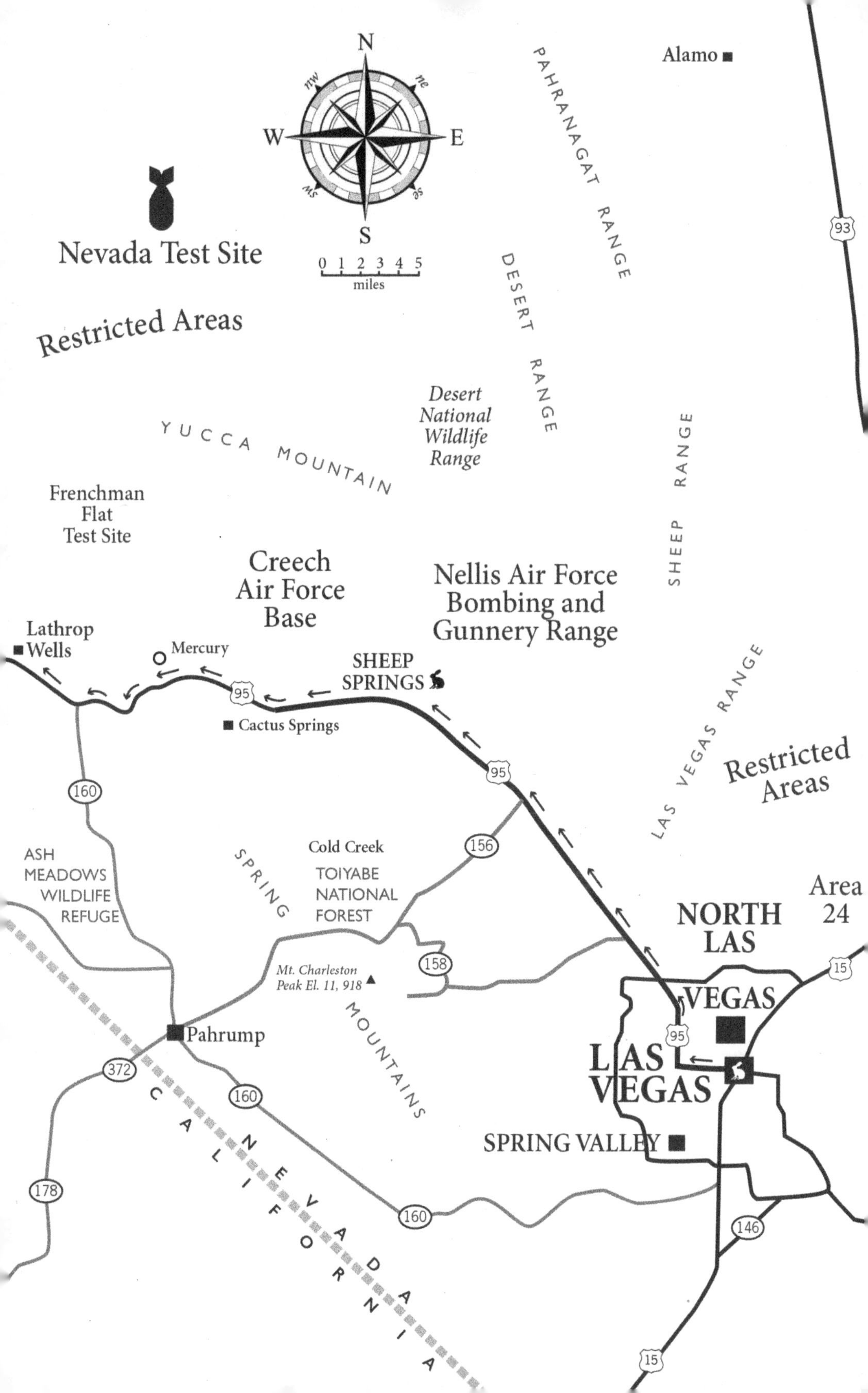

N
S
E
W
nw
ne
sw
se
0 1 2 3 4 5
miles
Nevada Test Site
Restricted Areas
Alamo
PAHRANAGAT RANGE
DESERT RANGE
Desert National Wildlife Range
SHEEP RANGE
YUCCA MOUNTAIN
Frenchman Flat Test Site
Creech Air Force Base
Nellis Air Force Bombing and Gunnery Range
Lathrop Wells
Mercury
SHEEP SPRINGS
95
Cactus Springs
LAS VEGAS RANGE
Restricted Areas
160
156
Cold Creek
TOIYABE NATIONAL FOREST
ASH MEADOWS WILDLIFE REFUGE
SPRING MOUNTAINS
Area 24
NORTH LAS VEGAS
15
158
Mt. Charleston Peak El. 11, 918
Pahrump
LAS VEGAS
372
160
SPRING VALLEY
NEVADA
CALIFORNIA
178
146
93

Death Valley

Also by Susan Perly

Love Street

Susan Perly

Death Valley

a novel

A BUCKRIDER BOOK

Buckrider Books is an imprint of Wolsak and Wynn Publishers.

Cover images: vectorstock.com; timurock, istockphoto.com
Cover design: Michel Vrana
Interior design: Mary Bowness
Maps: Tannice Goddard
Author photograph: Dennis Lee
Typeset in Minion
Printed by Ball Media, Brantford, Canada

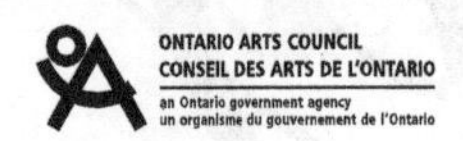

Canadian Heritage Patrimoine canadien
Canada

The publisher gratefully acknowledges the support of the Canada Council for the Arts, the Ontario Arts Council and the Canada Book Fund.

Buckrider Books
280 James Street North
Hamilton, ON
Canada L8R 2L3

Library and Archives Canada Cataloguing in Publication

Perly, Susan, author

Death Valley / Susan Perly.

ISBN 978-1-928088-10-3 (paperback)

I. Title.

PS8581.E7267D43 2016 C813'.6 C2016-900678-6

for Dennis

The harvest is past, the summer is ended,
and we are not saved.

– JEREMIAH 8:20

In other words, through the medium of a camera,
I experienced an encounter with a deeper space-time.

– DAIDŌ MORIYAMA

1

THE ATOMIC AGE

THE CHILDREN WALKED with their necks set up as evolutionary magnets. Who knew that our thyroids attracted radioactive iodine? Who knew that when the iodine flew over grass, flew over cows, flew over furniture, it flew into the bodies of children, it flew into their parents? Who knew that reindeer in Norway had radioactive thyroids from Chernobyl? Who knew that cesium-137 lasts for *centuries*? Who knew that the rocky land we look at from a plane is not done with us yet? Who knew that the radioactive dust from 1957 was still sitting in the rocky canyons below, in 2006?

Vivienne Pink, photographer of war, sat at the window of a plane making its way west, ascending from the sea level city of Toronto on the shores of Lake Ontario. Her final destination was the northern Mojave Desert, where fighter jets began their routine flights to Iraq and Afghanistan, where airmen were trained, and tens of thousands of servicemen had worked and become atomic veterans. Military land, where unions were tough and strong and boldly Western, and the sky took up the top two-thirds of any landscape. Vivienne Pink and her Olympus OM-1, by her side for thirty-three years, were taking a forced break from conflict zones. She was on an assignment to photograph fighting men before they deployed. Men on their last night before they flew out to die. She had made the assignment herself. She had her book half-done. It was December 26, 2006. She had five days to get a bunch of keepers.

She looked down at the Earth, the eyes of the avid hunter scanning over the wing to the canyons rising and falling in their mosaics and tunnels – rust, purple manganese, pale powdery green, mica, iron, gold, silver, red rock, red earth. The skin of the nation. Vivienne got out her camera: crusty patches appeared, white crust sinking into dark cratered areas. A shiny dome popped up beside a deep cut. Maybe it was an industrial cyst. Ahead pale green liquid swirled into red earth, bumps rose in purple and the world looked like a slide under a microscope, a cell with a story. This was the thrill. This was why you sat at the window. The greatest abstract art exhibit was right down there, on the planet. Well, it was the planet itself. Inside her body, similar-looking cells came and went, galaxies floating through her bloodstream.

A neck of rock appeared. She snapped it, seeing a folded part that looked like an ear. The first ear. The last ear of a damaged man. A polished chute. Vivienne looked at her right arm at the window. There was a three-inch white patch on her pink-olive flesh, a white patch with a distinct red rim. Down below she saw the fractal of her arm passing under the wing. Our flesh is the cousin of the earth, with the illusion it is unrelated. The white patch had first appeared after she was in Iraq in 1986 at Samarra, investigating the underground mustard gas facility of Saddam Hussein. She had gone up the famous minaret and shook in the wind going round and round the narrow spire with no handrail, trying to see from the heights if any of the poison gas trucks could be spotted. Nothing. But her skin afterwards had started scaling, and her lungs became more prone to pneumonia, and the Mesopotamian sand she breathed in grated her lung passageways more than it had before. The doctors said her lungs thought they had been placed in enemy territory and so her passageways attacked her body, becoming fiery and inflamed. A cloud tower came to the window and peeked in. She loved clouds as seat companions. This, too, was why you sat at the window: clouds were swell seatmates, they kept silent.

Vivienne kept her nose pressed against the window: the earth was a homeless cell, and still it stood tall and it was a glorious ruined beauty. A billion years was a drop of water.

Nobody sat beside her in the middle seat or the aisle, but on the other side of the aisle three men sat: two with real short hair, one of them in khakis with a pressed crease on the legs. He was looking out the window. The other, in the middle, was in light grey wool pants and watching a movie on the television screen: Sean Penn and Naomi Watts in a car. Naomi's eyes were closed, she was drunk, and Sean Penn loosened her seat belt; Sean the man with a newly transplanted heart, the heart of Naomi's dead husband. It was *21 Grams*. The first time she saw it, bootleg in Fallujah, was with her pal intelligence agent Val Gold in a windowless room in a safe house. Val said, "Imagine another man is using your husband's heart to live. Imagine your body without water. It will weigh only twenty-one grams."

Vivienne lifted her camera, watching the man in the middle as he moved his face close to the tiny screen. His eyes met the eyes of Sean Penn. For a moment the tender emotion the actor brought to the screen transferred to the viewer, who moved his head closer as if to solace the distressed woman in the car. Vivienne grabbed that shot.

The man in the aisle seat had greasier hair and looked too pale for his white skin, like he might smell of last night's beer drama. He had on a harmless checked shirt in non-saturated blues, the shirttails out, giving away that he had buttoned in a hurry – one button off. He scratched his hair and the semi-permanent-looking sweat stains under his arm showed. He had a large backpack that he rested his big white sneakers on, blocking the clean-cut spit-and-polish men from getting out if the plane went down. Vivienne pictured him as a rock climber flying to the Nevada canyons, a guy in a hurry with low blood sugar. And those shoes: way too new. Average height, average weight, Caucasian, late thirties, kept that pack close, afraid to even put it up top. Why? No bombs today, please.

The drinks wagon came by. Vivienne ordered an apple juice, *no ice*. Never trust ice on a plane. Never trust ice, anywhere. The pleasant thin steward put ice in the plastic cup. Vivienne repeated, *No ice*, adding a *darling*, smiling and putting her eyes into the smile. The steward did not mind, he gave a *mea culpa* smile back, dumped the ice out, filled the cup with the apple juice and handed her the can, too. Plane and shadow flew over the empty land. Mountains rose up to meet the wings.

The plane headed right for the side of a mountain, then it tilted and banked over the last mountains hiding the surprise sparkling down in the military valley.

It was their destination, the glittering cup in the desert. Area 24. Also called by its Spanish name, Las Vegas.

Here in the northern Mojave the light was prodigious, it was the beaming of plenty, a wide-open crystal clinic showing how the desert bent objects and bent light itself, how the sky seemed stoned and nutty and bright. Fighter planes rose and fell, shuttles flew men to work at weapons testing areas and jet testing areas and nuclear waste storage areas and war rehearsal areas and explosives practice areas and counter-terrorism and remote drone piloting areas. Men sat in casinos who were third- and fourth-generation locals who had worked the hard land and serviced the hard war work. This had been a military valley for half a century; it was busy and employed, for now the country was in its fourth year of a new big war. And this was a key spot.

Before there was Chernobyl wind, before there was Three Mile Island rain, there were the Nevada Nagasakis, there were the Nevada Hiroshimas. This was the nuclear valley inside the nuclear ranges. And the iodine waited for your neck, that radiation magnet. The wind sought even the birds of flight.

VIVIENNE PICKED UP her hard-shell red suitcase and waited for a cab outside the civilian terminals at McCarran airport. She had her Ray-Bans on. Cheap sunglasses were great if you did not work with your eyes, but even with polarized lenses, she was squinting.

Vivienne Pink, sniper of light, hunter of subjects, late of Baghdad and Kabul and Beirut, rolled through Godzilla Canyon. The Santa Ana winds were blowing in, bending the tall sentry palms lined up on the boulevard, rocking the cab, hurling paper cups and girlie brochures and shards of mystery items against the vehicle's sides and windshield. Desert cities used to be horizontal with miles between short hotels that looked more motel-like and imitated the land, thin strips with tall sky around them. Now the desert burgs had grown vertical and the sky was like cut slices of blue peeking between the concrete towers and tens of thousands of glass windows taking up the space that used to be air. The metastasizing hospitality tumours galumphed across the desert land like Japanese horror movie Godzillas, eating air, eating old radiation, burping up clouds, refluxing forgotten legs and arms in dead elevator shafts, surrounding tarmacs for a showdown, eating the tiny planes, the Jeeps, the tiny soldiers leaving for wars on a map. From drought to drought.

Traffic was light. It was that lacuna between Christmas and New Year's. A seven-minute ride from the terminal and Vivienne was checking in to the Flamingo hotel, she was up in the elevator, into her requested good-luck room 27117, and unpacking her red suitcase with clothes of pursuit, laying them out on the bed. Her clothes were part of the tools of her hunt: khakis, a tight army-green long-sleeved jersey, shiny tie-up patent-leather shoes and her lucky pink leather jacket. She checked inside the right-hand pocket. Good. That Swiss Army knife was still there.

Vivienne liked company in a hotel room so she switched on the TV: there was Humphrey Bogart, getting out of a car at Ed's Gas Station. Vivienne changed clothes, watching Bogart. Love it, she thought, *High Sierra*. Bogart was talking to the gas jockey who was not young; he was telling Bogart, "That there mountain is the highest in the United States, Mount Whitney." Bogart, the ex-con, Mad Dog Earle, on the lam into the Eastern Sierra of California, told the gas jockey he was going to the mountains for his health.

There she was in the mirror. Five-foot-four, one hundred thirty pounds, nice waist-to-hip ratio, that inward curve men liked, set off by the tight jersey, good bra with good uplift for her good breasts, khakis not too tight, black patent shoes polished before she left Toronto. Lizard earrings just limey and shiny enough to attract a man, arouse his interest. On TV, Bogart at Brown's Auto Court was showing the girl with the club foot the stars. "It's always like this out in the desert," Bogart said. "Look…that's Jupiter…that's Venus."

Vivienne leaned into the mirror, applied a wand of black-blue mascara to her lashes, rose gloss to her lips (it had a nice scent), a bit of gloss to her dark, carefully arched eyebrows. Eyebrows were key, eyebrows made the frame for a face. She wet her fingers, messed up her short auburn hair. Done. She left her long neck scar untouched.

She walked back to the bed, picked up the camera and in the reflection of the TV screen showing the manhunt, a white salt playa where the tiny black car of Humphrey Bogart drove up a tiny thread road, Vivienne shot a photo of herself, *Baby Pink, Self-Portrait, December 26, 2006*. She put the camera back on the bed, left the room and closed the door to 27117.

Down the hall, down twenty-six floors in the elevator, across the gaming floor, past roulette, slots, sports book, video poker, real poker, wheelchair men with oxygen tubes, one-eyed men, Vivienne went up the Tropical Breeze coffee shop ramp, past a group of cowboys here for the winter rodeo. A legless man alone was swinging through his crutches, his eyes dead set on Vivienne, his eyes saying *Reconsider me* and he passed on by.

At the entrance to the coffee shop, she scanned the room. Tables and booths full. Then her eyes caught on a white T-shirt sitting one hundred feet away. The back of a man sitting at the far counter. Her gut took a picture of the man's back – good shoulders, nice neck, short buzzed hair. She needed to make real what she had just visualized. Her heart was pounding like a calmly paced athlete, a nice controlled emergency rate. The room of eaters became a soft blur. Her forearms felt hot. The T-shirt man looked around, as if he heard a call. She locked the photographic prey into her sight, moving to him, seeing no seat near him, moving in the steady tunnel pacing, fifty feet, seeing a couple to his right pick up their cheque, moving quickly ahead with purpose, forty feet, twenty, ten and slipping into the one vacant seat. Her hands reached for her camera between her breasts, but of course it wasn't there. Her mind knew it, but her body reacted with muscle memory. No cameras were permitted on the gaming floor. She better work fast to get him to come with her, and pose for her in that white T-shirt. If logic came in, the photograph was gone.

The waitress appeared. DAYSEE by name tag, from San Antonio, Texas. Daysee wore the customary Culinary Workers Union button. Vegas was not only a military town deep in the mountain valley, it was a big union town. Everybody in Vegas was in service.

Mister White T had a newspaper open in front of him.

He did not look at her. He had come to be in a busy coffee shop, militantly alone. It was an urban thing. You could not do it in a small town, where everybody knew you. Urban people liked to be out, watching and ignoring each other. So he probably came from a city. He was super fit, so he worked out or he was in the service. He looked as young as twenty-two or he could be in his early thirties. His cheekbones gave off the micro-glitters of an easygoing but angry man.

He tore one sugar pack, two sugar packs and three. He let the sugar pour into his coffee cup, which was half full.

The waitress asked, "*Algo a comer*? Something to eat, sweetie? A drink? *Café?* Coffee, anything, *mi reina?*" *Por supuesto*, of course, this was Vegas, a Latino-infused town.

"*No gracias, nada a comer*, I'm good," Vivienne said. "No food, maybe later, but *ahora*, right now, *Mamita*, I'd kill for a coffee, *por favor. Sin azúcar, oscurito, por favor, mil gracias.*" Daysee was pouring hot coffee out of the Pyrex pot into the plain white mug by the time Vivienne said *por favor.*

Vivienne sipped her coffee, warming her winter fingers around the mug. Good. Now the white T-shirt knew she spoke Spanish, he knew the sound of her voice, that was key.

He knew what she looked like, what she sounded like, how she talked to service people. How she liked her coffee. Very black, no sugar. Vivienne added for good measure, "*Soy bastante dulce, pues no necesito azucar.*" I am sweet enough as it is, I do not need sugar. Flirt woman to woman with the waitress, use the agency of the waitress to flirt with him, the stranger.

She looked down to see his shoes, because that would tell her a lot.

Some intel men Vivienne knew started with the shoes, profiling the way a Spaniard dresses, from the shoes up. He had on black shoes, laced well, new laces, well-polished.

He stretched his neck, turning it around and around to get the cricks out. It was a good neck, unblemished, muscular. He was a white boy and pale. But he could have been pale in the way intelligence men or men with dodgy titles or State Department men in tropical locales or desert missions are pale. Working in the shadows of sun-drenched places, working at night, working inside, travelling in tinted windows through the revolutions they set in motion. Maybe he put a dark jacket over his white T-shirt in those circumstances. He could be the ensign or he could be a young captain. He might fly for the navy. He might be an airman. There were tens of thousands of them from way up at Fallon outside of Reno and for thousands of square miles down here to Mojave 24 environs. She needed this one. She could already feel the look of his back by a window at dusk, in that white T-shirt. How someone might see the photograph and feel what she felt, the first time she saw him.

2

THE BURNING MONK

VIVIENNE DRANK THE hot black coffee. She looked at her watch. It was fifteen minutes after one in the afternoon. It was winter in the desert. The sun would start to disappear behind the Spring Mountains outside her hotel room window by 4:20, even 4:17 p.m. How to start a conversation with the stranger?

He had a newspaper open to the weather page. "So, how are the temps for Death Valley?" Vivienne asked.

"You going out there, ma'am? Visiting Manson's shack, I suppose."

"Why does everybody say that?"

"Say what?" He turned his head slightly towards her.

"Say, 'You going to see Charlie Manson?' as soon as you say, 'Death Valley.'"

"I don't know, ma'am, I guess they've never been. You here with family? You all going out to have tea with Carla?"

Who was this guy? He was reserved but droll. He had great pale blue eyes.

"No, I'm working," Vivienne said.

"You work in security, then." He smiled. A smile that said, I don't think you do, but I kind of like the idea you might. The Vegas Valley was not only a key military area, it was a global centre for security wonks. In the desert, everybody was watching. Maybe this guy had eyes in the back of his T-shirt.

"Yes, in a way," Vivienne said. "I'm in photographs."

"You model. Nice. Good money, I hear."

"Only for myself. I'm the photographer."

"Sounds interesting. So, no Manson on your agenda. Rock climbing?"

"I came to capture some soldiers," she said.

"Ma'am, you better be careful what you say around these parts. People get in trouble." He used his left hand to flip the paper back to the front page. "You see James Brown died yesterday?"

She hadn't. "Oh boy, another titan bites the dust," she said, leaning over, touching his shoulder, to get a better look at the photograph of James Brown on the front page. The Godfather of Soul in all his glory: bright fuchsia leather jacket with fringe hanging off, his right arm holding the microphone, captured singing in concert only a year ago. The life is short, the night train goes on forever. Vivienne ran her hand over the face of the master.

"I used to listen to 'I'll Go Crazy' day and night in Saigon," she said.

"You're kidding, darling." He swivelled around, his knees touching hers. "Not Saigon-Saigon. You must mean, ma'am, Saigon Elementary, in –"

"In Vietnam," she said. "A lot of James Brown. You know, the bar that opened at three in the morning, in a place that wasn't there, where everybody had conversations that didn't happen, with people who swore on that bible stack they were never there. That bar. That turntable."

"I personally favour 'It's a Man's World,'" he said.

"You left out two 'Man's.' It's 'It's a Man's Man's Man's World.'"

"So, all by your lonesome in Nevada," the stranger said. "You have to be careful. There are all kinds of con artists around."

"Don't worry, honey. I cover war."

He had swivelled back. He was watching the wait staff move in and out of the kitchen area. He was smiling that droll smile again.

Vivienne smoothed out the fold through James Brown's pompadour. "I'd like to take a picture of you."

"Go right ahead, ma'am. I don't mind. I'm leaving tomorrow for another tour of Iraq. Knock yourself out."

"You can't use a camera on the gaming floor," she said.

"So they caught you before? Eyes in the sky?"

"Oh yes," she said. "Once upon another war. I was actually taking pics of the ceiling. They did not like that very much. But then, I did not like how that suited gorilla manhandled my camera very much. That's my living."

"But they let you go."

"I'm here."

"Well thank God's grace for that."

"Will you do it?"

"Sure. Why not?" he said. "Let's go outside. I've got nobody to say goodbye to me, in any case. You could take whatever you need. Then say me a proper adios on the Strip."

"Honey, that isn't what I had in mind. That's not how I work. I don't want a snap of you; I want to make a portrait."

"Oh I see. Fancy."

"No, the opposite. Simple. It just takes a long time to get it plain. To bring out the feeling."

"Ma'am, I wish you all well and good in your enterprise, your *artiste* endeavour, but I am afraid I am not signing on for feelings. Not today."

"Not you. It's the feeling of a moment. I want the moment, I don't want you." He was laughing. "I mean, I would appreciate it if I could but I – You know what? Why not forget it."

"I didn't say no, ma'am."

She put her hand out. "Vivienne. From Toronto." They shook hands. His arms were long, his hands not large but strong.

"Andy," he said, making eye contact. "San Diego. I'd just prefer to leave out the feelings in any picture you took of me. Can you do that?"

"I can. It'll be lousy. It'll be anybody's. When I take a picture, hon, it's another way to have a conversation. That's all. Not scary. Just like we're sitting here."

"I bet you've got James Brown vinyl up in your room. Is that the idea? Get the boys up there and play them some 'Bewildered'?"

"I left all my LPs in Vietnam."

"You weren't kidding. Was your dad in the army?"

"Canada didn't send boys to Vietnam. I was working as a photographer."

"In diapers?" His eyes were flashing light and dark connective tissue to his smile.

"I was fifteen years old when I started working wartime," Vivienne said.

She was sweating. Her hands were getting the memory shakes. She felt the old roiling in her gut, from that May of '69 in Vietnam when the US had taken Hamburger Hill, near Huế, then abandoned it to their enemy. The feeling of useless loss, of war being run by weak watery incompetents, rats with stars crazy in a commanding maze, Nixonitis and his five o'clock shadow, which began to stretch over the land from daybreak, these things had never left her. That summer of '69, when *Life* magazine ran a photo spread showing every single soldier killed in Vietnam, two of the pics were Vivienne's. Nixon on TV, Ho Chi Minh dies, William Calley is charged for My Lai, Tricky Dicky the despised one back on TV, they locate Manson in Death Valley, three days later the massive anti-war moratorium in DC. Vivienne motioned to Daysee the waitress for more hot joe. She drank it so fast it burned her lips.

Andy pulled a pack of smokes out of his Levi's back pocket. The pack was a bright magnetic pink, with black and gold bows, brand name Pink in white letters. He took one, reached for a matchbox, flicked a stick match with the end of his thumbnail, inhaled, handed the smoke to Vivienne, kept the match going, lit one for himself and they sat there smoking. Vivienne was quitting, she had quit, she will have quit someday.

Andy got up, leaving the chair swinging. He walked around the curved counter to the end, where there was an empty seat. He stood drinking the dregs of somebody else's coffee, dropping the cigarette into the coffee cup, looking at her with no smile, thirty, forty feet away now. Vivienne's forearms went into a pain dance; she needed to have a camera in her hands. Andy pushed the coffee cup away. He walked back to her, rubbed her shoulders in the pink leather as if they were old pals and he was just arriving to meet her. He sat down. "Seriously, ma'am. Vivienne. How the hell did you get to Vietnam? You truly must have been in kindergarten."

His face was dry. But his neck and his cotton neckline were soaking, like hers. "I like how you talk," she said, unsure where she was going by saying this. "Your voice would make a good photo." She could picture how the T-shirt would animate his upper body. How she could hone in on the secret life of an object. The T-shirt gave off an air that said, "I've been in fights, maybe even this morning, when I woke up in the wrong bed." If that item of clothing was looking for trouble, it came to the right photographer.

"I'm under a little pressure right now," Vivienne said. "I have a deadline for a book. Could you help me out? It is all servicemen on their way to war, their last night in town. It will only take twenty minutes. We could talk later." He gave her that look: Sure it will, honey.

"Okay, one hour, tops," she said. "You have a great face. I would love to see you in my book. I promise I will send you a copy, over to Iraq."

"I miss shit," he said. "You spend every day over there, 'when will this shit end?' and when it ends you want it more than the girl." He was dancing around her proposition. He might want time. Time she did not have. She could eye the coffee shop, look for another subject. But she wanted him: the white T-shirt on good posture, a straight back, nice shoulders and chin held low, bright crazy-deep eyes, good indigo classic button jeans, dark lace-up shoes, short buzzed fair hair and cheekbones that could, like Elvis Presley, have some Cherokee grandmother in them.

Her sweat was cooling. Okay, the man wants to talk first. Talk to him about Vietnam. Younger men liked to hear about that gone day. The war that knocked America off true, the war that left a generation of homeless vets. The nightmare that still haunted their ancestors, their mommas and their poppas; they had grown up with Vietnam-haunted adults around them. Maybe if she told him a story about photographing in Vietnam she could entice him to come with her to the event horizon. To enter into the gravitational pull of the camera, where the only escape possible was through the lens.

"Okay," Vivienne said. "How did I get to Vietnam? Blame it on Paris. The story: my Auntie Carole wanted to see an old flame from her gap year in Paris, so she says to me, 'You need to see Paris.'" Vivienne held the cigarette to her mouth and inhaled. "Good thing I quit."

Andy chuckled. Vivienne went on: "So, late May 1963, I'm fifteen. Auntie Carole has us staying at this thirty-room hotel in the old medieval quarter, the Mouffetard. Coffee in the morning at Café Delmas, then Auntie Carole takes me on a ten-minute walk to the Jardin des Plantes. She leaves me to go see her old squeeze, André, now a big gallery owner. So I walk around the Jardin and back to the street and there's this big white low building straddling the corner and I go in." She blew out some smoke, kept talking.

"That is it. You walk in. You decide, walk on by or walk on in. It was a mosque. There were, you know, fifty thousand French Muslim soldiers killed in World War One, the Grand Mosque of Paris was built to honour them. I was a nice Jewish girl from Forest Hill, and here I was at the Paris Mosque. I sat by myself on a rose-coloured banquette and had mint tea. The table was a round gold tray. The tea was amber in glasses, not teacups. The glasses had gold rims. They brought a small white plate, it was rectangular with sweets in paper. Things made of almond, pistachio, pale desert colours. There were paintings of the sky on the walls. I finished tea and decided 'I want to see the Louvre.' I was just burning up with a desire for beauty."

Andy flexed his cheekbones.

"So now I am at the Louvre, in front of the *Venus de Milo*. A guy's walking around and around Miz Venus, he asks me how I like the torso, do I like the proportions, the angles. He was an older guy, tall, desert boots, brown cords, beard. He invited me for tea – at the Mosque."

"Did you tell him you'd just been?"

"No way," she said. "He was too cute."

"So you knew your way around men, at fifteen years old?" Andy said.

"I knew my way around something. I guess I was looking for its name."

"So you go for tea with this guy who was how much older than you?"

"Maybe twice as old as me. You know, old. Like thirty-five." They chuckled together. Her younger self was turning into a shared character in a story.

"When I walked back into the mosque courtyard with him, it all felt different. Even from an hour before. He said, 'I want to take your picture.' He posed me for a photograph sitting at one of the blue-and-white tile tables. I was wearing a pink oxford-cloth button-down shirt. That was my thing, then. Button-downs in every pastel. Sleeves rolled up; white jeans; black patent-leather Mary Janes on my feet. When he took my picture it was not the same as anybody ever taking my picture before. I wanted in on that."

Andy was looking at her with listening eyes. "Tell me," he said.

"The light went on forever in Paris in the long white nights of spring. The light felt soft in Paris. Maybe it was the Seine. We had more mint tea. He introduced himself. 'I'm Marty,' he said, 'Marty Hirsch.' So Marty tells me about his grandfather who dealt in silks and textiles, a Jew from the Shanghai Jews who had come to this very mosque café, the textile man in the 1920s. It was a city of Jews and Arabs even then, Marty said. It was Marty who told me that Paris is the city in Europe with the most Jews, and Paris is the city in Europe with the most Arabs. I never forgot that. I did not know Paris was Jewish. I knew nothing. I didn't know North Africa was full of Jews. Who knew Casablanca was a very Jewish city?"

"Maybe Sam in *Casablanca* was Sammy," Andy said.

"You know," she said, moving her coffee cup to clink it against his, "*ojalá*, he could be. Maybe the first draft was: 'Look. Do me a personal favour, Sammila, you should play it again.'" She shook her head. "Nah. You don't have to play Jewish to be one."

"I know," he said. His eyes crinkled, his face was entirely subsumed by the smile.

And so she knew. Jew meets Jew in a desert café.

"So, this Marty character, we'd spent a couple of hours together, he puts his Leica down on the table, and he says, 'Come to Vietnam with me. I'm leaving for Saigon tomorrow. Carry my equipment.'

"Next thing I know I am flying Paris to Saigon, Vivienne Pink, the photographers' mascot. Baby Pink they called me. 'How did you ever get to Vietnam, at that age?' everybody asks. 'Easy, honey, I got on a plane. Paris to Saigon, fourteen hours.' I was not brave, I just took the free ticket."

She put her elbow on the counter, put her chin in her hand and leaned towards him. "Look, I so knew from nothing, I did not know Saigon from sayonara."

His nostrils flared, "Oh yeah, been there. Boot camp ain't Baghdad. It isn't what you think."

"So many maps, so little time," she said, "then you are actually standing in the actual place. How it smells, how low sewer water smells, the rains, the food, meat on the street, smoke and sweet flowers, the wet trees. The sound of rain on a tin roof, how firearms sound. My Auntie Carole said, 'Vivila, you've got moxie. Follow your moxie.' She used to call me Queen Moxie. My parents? They were old rads, they were happy. I skipped two grades so I had two years in my pocket."

This stranger Andy got up again, walked around the counter curve, came back behind her again, holding her chair back. "So what happened to Baby Pink in-country?" he whispered into her left ear.

"It was June in Saigon. A Tuesday. What is it with Tuesdays?" She didn't find the set-up with him odd. How could it be odd, they were in Crazytown, talking about an old Indochina psychosis. "Tuesdays and Elevens. Tuesday, June 11, 1963. I was living with Marty. He gets a call. It was about seven in the morning. 'Come to the corner of Phan Dình Phùng and Lê Văn Duyệt Streets, there will be an event, in one hour, at eight.' The caller did not say what it was but all the news photogs got called. You know, everyone says, *The Vietnam War*, but years before that, the events were going on. The Vietnamese were conducting a war against the Buddhists, the Buddhists were marching pagoda to pagoda in protest. The Roman Catholics running the show were breaking the balls of the Buddhists, but good. Marty told me something I never forgot, 'Before they come for the Commies, they come for the Buddhists.' They come for the religion before the politics. So down we go, Marty and me, to the corner of Phan Dình Phùng and Lê Văn Duyệt Streets. There is a crowd of monks and nuns all in white, white is their mourning colour, behind a grey car that had pulled up. It stopped at the corner. Two men exited the car, two monks.

"They took a can of gas out of the hood. Three other monks get out. Marty has his Leica in his hand, you know holding it like a baby, and a bunch of cameras around his neck as backup. One of the monks places a cushion on the street, and a different monk sits on the cushion, quiet. Marty hands me a camera, saying nothing. He nods to me. I look through the lens –

"One of the monks takes a can of gas and he pours it on the monk sitting on the cushion in the middle of the street in a lotus position in his robe, soaking his robes and his head. I took a picture just as the one monk poured gasoline on the head of the sitting monk. I did not know it was going to go that way, but I was ready. I had never felt anything like that in my life. The lotus monk was sitting in a pool of gas.

"The street filled up with more Buddhist monks who had come in their white mourning robes. I could see ahead of myself, I was elevated, focused. I thought, I want to be in the world, right now. I want to see history. I want to tell the story. I have found my life. The lens was my teacher.

"I could see there was going to be a picture of his body, that I had to be ready for that. I had been called to this. I had walked in the door of the Paris Mosque and that was why I was in Vietnam. I walked in and I did not walk by, and now a camera owned me. I was picturing where his body would fall so the camera could be there; I stepped forward. I still have the image in my head of Marty watching me move away from him, to the picture.

"The lotus monk was not yet on fire and I could see his dead body's position. I felt the immediate future in my fingertips, my forearms were on fire. It was the monk himself, soaked in gasoline, who lit the match to his own robes. It was a sunny day. It was self-immolation."

Still standing behind her chair, Andy reached over to the counter, took the bright Pink smokes pack, lit one, gave it to her, lit another. "Tell me about the monk," he said, close to her ear. She sucked in a long drag of the cigarette, and went on.

"The monk's name was Thích Quảng Đức. He lives on in the photographs of his death. One of the photogs there, Malcolm Browne of AP, took the picture that they say President John Kennedy saw the next morning in the newspaper on his desk, and that he was deeply affected by it. I had walked into one of the most famous photographs in history, sweet Jesus how small the steps, and then boom, you cannot step away from your kismet. It was like love, taking pictures. No second thoughts. What a time. It was early Vietnam days yet, for the Americans. All these handsome stateside boys just spooking around, setting things up in Southeast Asia. Guys going into Operation Rolling Thunder, guys going up the la Drang Valley, guys in their B-52s, all that was later. I was Baby Pink, *pitzel* photographer. I was like a ferret in the wet Asian alleys. I could smell pictures coming as dusk set in. My eyeballs were soaking up the chemistry of the complicated East. I smelled them, then I heard them: the sound of a pic coming. A wing, a clatter, a gun, a motorcycle backfiring. I was jumping out of my skin every day.

"You know what the funniest part is?" Vivienne asked, swirling around. "These new spooks came in, they're asking around, 'Who do we get the gen from, who knows the story on the ground?' And my pals, my mentors, Marty and Co., they would say, 'Ask for Baby Pink. Baby Pink can tell you.' So these tall fit men would come knocking on Marty's and my door – we lived behind a red door, Marty taught me, 'Always have a red door on your house' – and he would answer, 'Yeah? Help you?' in his red bandana and baggy shorts, and they would say to Marty, 'You Baby Pink? Hear you have the word.' 'No, not me, hang on,' he'd say. 'V! Baby Pink, get your sweet ass out here, these handsome lads here want a word.' And out from the darkroom comes me: sweet sixteen in loose thin cotton pants and an undershirt and suspenders. 'Your Mom around, little girl?' 'Listen fartface, you want info or did you come into my home to insult me?' An hour later, we were new best friends, and they were posing for pictures, two photog guys hamming it up on my pink silk bedspread.

I was as young as a Viet Cong guerrilla. Everybody knew me, I was that crazy Canadian coyote with a camera."

"Tell me more about the monk," Andy said, taking his seat again.

"When the fire had burned him and his robe, he fell back in rigor mortis, charred, his arms stiff. They went up like rigor claws, his legs went up like rigor claws, the crowd leaned in. I took that picture, it came out in *Time.* By some magic, I had entered my own life. I set out unknowing. If I had known, I probably would never have gone."

"Amen," he said.

"I have film from that day I have never developed. I have contact sheets I have never made prints from. They talk about Vietnam protestors, they use the word *hippies*. Did you know the first protest against the American presence in Vietnam was organized in 1946 by merchant marines? American merchant marines in *1946?* These sailors were waiting to be shipped back to the States right after World War Two, and they saw American ships being taken from the job of bringing the boys home, their US ships meant to take them – the war vets – back to the States, being used instead to help bring in arms for the French in Vietnam. Like you said, honey, it is never what you think. It is never *when* you thought. Come on up, let me take your picture."

He swivelled on the stool and faced her.

"I am not going to hurt you," Vivienne said.

"A girl like you always hurts a guy like me," Andy said. But he sat there. The dead had cathected onto the photographic paper, their energy had pooled there. She wanted an antemortem photograph of this Andy.

"Would you like to have a picnic in my room?" she asked. Say anything to get the picture.

"You planning on smuggling in the personal vino?"

"It's already contraband in my suitcase." Not true, but hey.

"Sounds promising," he said.

"So, shall we go?"

Andy held his left palm up and made the silent gesture of writing the cheque with his right hand, catching Daysee's eye as he did it. She had the bill ready. Then he silently poured invisible coffee. Daysee brought more hot mud. What was going on? Vivienne thought. First he calls for the bill, then he calls for more coffee. "Is there a problem?" she asked. Now he was pouring three sugar packs and two petrochemical glops into his brew.

"Ma'am, I do not think I would truly be any good for you, right now. I'm on the wrong end of a hangover this morning. And the truth is I'm off to Baghdad tomorrow, so let's say good night and call it a day." His eyes flashed at what he just said. He grinned. But Vivienne could see that his body was rocking slightly with a new weather system coming through. An agitation causing him to shy back.

"Partying hard?" she asked. Trying to revive the moment.

"Ma'am, I –"

"Vivienne."

"Vivienne. Okay. Vivienne, you see, well. I had a bit of a situation over the weekend. Not a good one, by any stretch. My buddy Sean and I were on the road from LA to Twentynine Palms. That wind came at us, blew us off the road. It blew down a palm and crushed our Commander."

"You had a commanding officer with you in the accident?"

"A Studebaker Commander Starlight, 1951. Lemon yellow. A real beauty. The plan was for Sean to take it to the shop. That never happened. That beauty looked like a crashed yellow spaceship sitting under all those stars."

He liked cars, he liked stars, he liked clothes that fit, he liked sweet white coffee, he was at ease in public, he was composed, his eyes were deadly marine blue. "It is so dark, you know, out in the desert."

"We're in the desert now," he said. He had been to the still place. His face showed old geology, old worn harm.

"There's red corpse debris out there all over the sky, you know," she said, and when he smiled at her, she felt her right arm wanting that dear camera in it, badly. "Those stars, they are already gone from us, they are just energy cadavers."

Andy's eyes turned midnight black. "Ma'am, I think I'll just ride it out until morning, thanks all the same." He brought his hand down Vivienne's pink leather-clad arm to her wrist, where his fingers began playing on her wrist bone. Their shoulders were touching. She moved her wrist so her palm opened. His hand did the same. They each drew their fingers back, curling, staying an inch away. He wasn't leaving. Her camera was waiting in the room.

"It could be a quiet spot, upstairs. Quiet conversation," she said.

"Possibly."

She spoke in a low voice, "So, listen, Andy, if you're not doing anything for the next hour or so..."

Andy's eyes had gone off with the ghosts. His body was still there beside her at the counter, but his eyes had travelled to the solo place. Vivienne knew about those micro-blackouts that came after too many shock waves. Temporarily, even without your conscious knowledge, you speak from the grave while being alive.

Andy reached into the back pocket of his Levi's again. He pulled out something crumpled, so old the creases were white. He unfolded it. It was a picture from a magazine, originally in colour. "This is my baby," he said.

Vivienne looked at her watch. 1:35 p.m. Less than three hours to sundown.

Andy pressed the cracked paper with his hand like it was money. "This is my Ford Mustang I have back home in San Diego. It's the prettiest blue you ever saw, some people call it sky blue, some call it robin's egg. You look at that Mustang when it's parked, you can feel the wind blowing through a pretty girl's hair." The talk of being photographed had put him in his own photograph already. "I'd like to redo the interior in a cream channeling. I'm thinking I'll get around to getting it detailed when I get back from over there. I bet you'd like to tool on out to Death Valley in a pale blue Mustang convertible."

"I would," Vivienne said.

"That red hair of yours would get crazy going at speed, real Medusa."

"It grows like weeds."

"Mighty fine weeds, ma'am." He began to stroke her pink leather jacket, her animal hide. That move was okay now, because she could just smooth it along to the elevator, the room, the lens, the shot. Get the man by a window, before sunset.

"The Gorgon was made out of the terror, not the terror out of the Gorgon," she said.

Andy was framing her in that pretty blue Mustang on an open grey road under blue sky. The model was picturing how he could be the artist. This made him the perfect model. The dark kingdom of light was awaiting, the land of light that came after the end of Eden and snakes, the wild light that ran up into mountains through the wind horns of the endemic bighorn sheep and blew down the hard notes of awe into the beds of salt, deep into their ancient cracks. Nothing was settled, nothing stayed in place where the wind ruled the land.

Andy held the salt-white channels of the clipping up to his face. "I'd be sitting with sand right up my ass crack over there in the desert, I'd pull out a picture I used to have of my wife in this very Mustang. I'd stare at that picture the whole night, trying to remember what she looked like."

"And you get home to where she is," Vivienne said, "and there she is, right in front of you and you still can't remember what she looks like. The photograph knows, but you don't."

Andy squinted his eyes like *How do you know what's in my head?*

"It won't take long, honey, I promise. We can be in and out of my room in twenty minutes. Fifteen. How 'bout fifteen?"

"You ever see that movie *Wings of Desire?* Berlin before the wall fell?" Andy asked.

"Black and white; the angels in the archives," said Vivienne. He had taken her to a car crash, a car love and now he was talking Wim Wenders.

"The very one," he said. "One night my wife, Caroline, and I head out to see *Wings of Desire,* but we never made it. A drunk comes out of nowhere and broadsides us. Caroline dies on the way to the hospital. I was blessed I have to say. I walked away with two broken legs." He smiled at the tender idiocy he had just uttered. "Right here," tapping the creased photo of the blue Mustang, "is the car we were in. I got it rebuilt afterwards.

One night, honestly, I can't tell you what channel I was watching on TV. I was back stateside. There's Peter Falk on the screen, at some hot dog stand talking to a guy with wings. It's black and white. How the hell did I know it was the movie Caroline and I had set out to see and never saw? So it's looking a lot like Berlin. The angel's taking a tour of his former life, walking past the Berlin Wall and all. I felt sick with happiness watching it, and I did not know why. This angel goes into a club. Oh yeah, I been there, some sort of German punk band on stage." He drank down the whole cup of sugary white coffee. "But he's invisible. He's back home, but no one can see him. He's listening in on a woman talking Chinese, which he can't understand a word of. He's cracking up with joy at nothing. He's just glad to be back. He's dead and he's glad to be alive. Jesus, ma'am, I'm in bad need of a drink."

Vivienne extended her hand to his forearm. His skin was warm, the hair blond. She stroked his skin lightly. "Let me take your picture."

Andy looked at her, his blue eyes going dark. "You know what, Vivienne, why the hell not? I might not have a face next week. I went to a wedding last year where the groom, a buddy of mine, had half a face. I don't know why I have a face, ma'am. Sure. Take my picture. If it's twenty minutes, what's twenty minutes?" He took her hands. "Baby Pink, you sure are some –"

"Hello, gorgeous, *que tal*?" A tall man with silver hair sat down to Vivienne's right, where there was an empty chair. He pulled at her swivel chair's bottom and swung her to face him. "Having fun, Vivi?" It was Val Gold, who lived with her and Johnny. He kissed her right hand. "How's it going, my darling Vivi? Stepping out on me again, are you?" Val held the seat of her counter stool so her back was to Andy, then let it swing around. "Don't let me interrupt. Go on, rob the cradle, I'll just watch."

Vivienne gave Val a dead-eyed look. "Piss off, you spook buzzard. Piss off, Val, I am working. Can you men ever let a woman get her work done?" Andy looked down into his coffee cup and sucked up the moment. He motioned to Daysee the waitress, and made that writing-out-the-bill pantomime.

"Ain't she cute," Val said. "Oh, I remember now, you used to take pictures, didn't you, Vivi? She used to be a big deal once upon a time, son." Vivienne watched Andy push away from the coffee counter.

Andy gave her a nod and departed. Vivienne swivelled the seat and watched him walk across the room. Her brain was banging around in its skull jelly. The one who got away. Her eyelashes flickered a thousand white T-shirts in one second.

3

PINK LEATHER JACKET

JOHNNY COMA SAT in the hotel garden, reading Genesis on a wooden park bench. The sun shone from the east on his pale face. He had the Holy Bible in a small black classic edition open on his lap. *And the LORD God called Adam, and said unto him, Where art thou?*

And he said, I heard thy voice in the garden, and I was afraid because I was naked; and I hid myself.

Johnny liked that quote. Genesis was good. He liked Genesis. It was a great guide to simple direct writing. Johnny looked down at the Good Book in his lap.

And Cain talked with Abel his brother; and it came to pass, when they were in the field, that Cain rose up against Abel his brother, and slew him.

There you had it, one-two-three, twenty-nine words, the basic Cain and Abel short story. More than a tweet, practically an IM, thirty-four syllables.

And the LORD said unto Cain, Where is *Abel thy brother? And he said, I know not:* Am *I my brother's keeper?*

Syllable count: thirty-four plus twenty-seven. Goddamn, at the sixty-one syllable mark, there is Cain, trying to talk himself out of that one: "How am I supposed know where my brother is?" That's right, Johnny thought, keep it up, Cain. Tell us one we never saw on any *Law & Order.* Detective Bobby Goren on *Criminal Intent* would be head-tilting into you, Cain baby, breaking down that alibi. Yeah, fifty-one sob-sister words. God tested you, brother Cain, God said your crops will fail, Cain you momzer mobster in waiting. Cain whines, boo hoo, Everyone will come and kill me. God takes pity on poor Cain the brother-murderer, God puts his personal protective brand on Cain's forehead so that no one will kill the murderer, the community will treat him as a protected killer. The first skell in history to get a deal, our Cain. God gives Cain immunity.

Johnny flipped to the previous page and counted the lines: sixty lines from the moment Cain was born, through his murder of his brother Abel, through Cain's whining about the diplomatic immunity deal with God, through Cain's going east of Eden to Nod, where Cain meets his wife who is not named, where he has a son named Enoch, and now Cain is let off by God, Cain becomes a real estate developer, Cain did build a city and he called the name of the city after the name of his son, Enoch.

A masterpiece of short story concision. Genesis gives the story of Cain from birth to post-God-parole-business success about six hundred words. Two book pages.

Johnny had received an email, unsolicited, just before he flew here to the desert, which had the erroneous title "Just a Thought on God." The sender, who decided to treat Johnny the Jew to a dissertation on Jesus, decided most cleverly to fold into his piece six pages from Johnny's own 1988 book, *The Spiritual Atheist*, verbatim. Now, that was the gold standard for chutzpah: you plagiarize word for word from a man's own book and send it to him as your own spam and ask his opinion.

The man who sent that email was Danny Coma, his older brother.

Tell me what you think.

I think you should see a shrink, you pinhead. Johnny was finally writing the book he wanted to, a novel set in Death Valley. He was sketching, jotting down a few phrases. Danny's "Just a Thought" email was ninety-three thousand words. Three hundred book pages. When Johnny did not answer him in two days, Danny started sending snide-mails. Cain, the older brother, arrogant, furious that his younger brother, Abel, wrote books and people read them.

Danny was the handsome one as a youngster, Danny was the one with the big dark eyes, Danny was the smiler in the photographs. Johnny was the goofball, Johnny was the kidder, Johnny was the joker.

It was Vivienne who pointed out that even as a teen Danny's smile in photos did not include his eyes. Cover the mouth, the eyes were hoodlum eyes: *I'm getting away with this, you squares.* Handsome Danny announced in high school he was going to be a writer. Johnny the joker announced he was going to be a magician. He did magic tricks for auditoriums. He sought out ladies' silk scarves at the dime store. He spent all his time in his room doing card tricks, playing solitaire. Johnny developed agile hands; Danny went to Harvard, then Cambridge and got hired by maybe Canada, maybe Britain, maybe the States, maybe all three, to do intelligence work. Danny was named as an Economic Advisor. Johnny the magician morphed into Johnny Coma, novelist, while Danny wasn't looking. While Danny was in Bolivia, hunting down Che Guevara, Johnny was in Toronto, conjuring words for the page. When Danny was palsy-walsy with the CIA in Chile, Johnny was prowling Havana with Vivienne, scribbling notes for his 1974 novel, *Cuban Lament.* Then Danny retired, after forty-three years in the shadows as a fixer and began a keyboard mania, babbling, enthusing, bubbling, acknowledging, planning for launches, entering high hypomania, a grand emperor believing life had waited for him, and all he had to do was pick up where he left off as a teenager when he said, "I am, of course, the writer in the family." But when he came to the keyboard for the first time, in his sixties, he was at entry level in a job he had never done.

Johnny opened to Genesis 22. The story of Abraham and Isaac: ninety-two lines. But short ones. Seven or eight words to the line, okay. So call Abe and Ike: ninety-two times eight, equals 738 words. Danny's acknowledgements for his emailed doorstop were five times the length of the Abraham and Isaac legend. (What was dementia, what was dysmorphia?)

Johnny looked up from Genesis to see a bride and groom. The groom was short, stocky, maybe Mayan. The bride was small too, Asian, beaming. She wore a strapless dress, ivory, tight at the waist, rippling in folds at the bottom. Her dark hair was in an updo. She had super-long chandelier earrings on, grazing her bare shoulders. They walked hand-in-hand to the garden waterfall. A woman wearing one large camera came behind them wheeling a baby stroller, which she set to the side. Johnny watched, sketching the scene.

The wedding photographer, in black pants and a black hoodie, adjusted the bride and groom in front of the pouring water, and began to take pictures. Johnny sketched her back hunching into the shots, her elbows akimbo. The baby wasn't in the wedding pictures, but Johnny sketched the baby into his scene. The stroller, the baby's face, the bonnet.

Johnny looked at his watch. It was 11:17 a.m. Vivienne was due to land at 11:45, in twenty-eight minutes. That placed her right now as coming over the Hoover Dam. She loved that view.

He had time yet. She'd be in the hotel lobby around noon. She was on a mission. Johnny was under strict orders to stay away from Vivienne when she was working.

But my oh my, he loved to watch his wife clandestinely. To see her, the foreign correspondent, enter a hotel, to see her the way he had seen her the first time.

The first time Johnny Coma saw Vivienne Pink it was in Old Miami Beach, the first night of his honeymoon. He went out on Collins Avenue for a smoke, wandered down to 15th, took a right for no reason, hit Washington, turned left seeing a clot of lights and street people, got to the corner of Washington and old Espanola Way. He was at the Spanish Village built of pink adobe in the 1920s to house artists in cheap digs.

He looked to his left: through an archway he saw a woman in a red-and-black striped shirt, tight dark jeans, high red heels and a beige trench coat. She had two cameras around her neck. She was at the reception desk of the small Matanzas Hotel. She turned and snapped a photo of him looking at her from the narrow village-style street. The light captured her through the archway.

There she was: his wife. Only problem was the woman he had actually just married was back at the Sagamore on Collins Avenue, waiting.

He walked through the archway. "Got time for a drink?"

"Sure," she said, amused, sending off voltage.

They sat in the February heat outside at one of the Cuban joints on Washington Avenue, where the owner, a guy in a windbreaker sipping thimble-sized Cuban coffees at the next table, greeted Vivienne like a long-lost daughter. Vivienne told Johnny how the café owner was a Havana Jew who had come to the city of Miami Beach on a small plane the night Castro took over. They drank mojitos made with fresh yerba buena, not spearmint, and Johnny spent the first night of his honeymoon not with his new bride, but with Vivienne. They were both twenty-nine.

Things weren't pastel yet in South Beach, they were white and peeling and sunny slummy. Johnny sat with Vivienne, watching her for hours. She spoke a radiant Spanish, flirted with the waiters, knew people on the street, took their pictures, bums from the stucco shadows came out and shook her hand, guys rolling through on no-speed bikes stopped and posed for her.

Johnny never had sex with his one-day wife, she had been whining about her ink allergies for an hour when he stepped out for the fateful cigarette on Collins Avenue, walked over to Washington and fell under Vivienne's sway. Vivienne, by her third mojito, was telling him about visiting the darkroom of the guy who took the original iconic pic of Che in Havana. If he had not gone out for a smoke to get away from his bride… if Vivienne had checked in to the hotel even ten minutes later… Their life together was based on a moment that might not have happened.

Now he had to go spy on her.

The lobby wasn't like the lobbies of old, in those great old films, where the proverbial sneak sits in a lumpy chair (which even in black and white you knew had to be some godawful maroon), reading a lumpy daily, looking for the dame on a tryst or the skell on the lam. The guy could sit all day staring at the same page about bank robbers being hunted up in the mountains or mudslides on the coast or war in the east of Europe.

No, the Flamingo lobby was more like a carpeted check-in area of an airport. Men and women with luggage snaked along between the velvet ropes, then scattered to the individual agents. Off to the side, away from the check-in was the coffee wagon, the portable caffeine delivery system in case you couldn't make it down the hall to the Tropical Breeze (if you name it, they will believe it) coffee bar, or up the hall to the other coffee bar past the three eateries and the deli. Or to the cocktail waitresses circulating the casino floor, serving short squat glasses to tall reedy men, or tall drinks of clarity to round stubs.

It was a noticer's dream: everything open and viewable.

Of course, that meant he could be viewed too.

He located himself at that coffee cart. It was in full view but people coming up the escalators from down below, just arriving, tended to be disoriented, looking ahead not behind them, and as soon as they spotted the registration sign, rolled their goods along to get in line. You could hide in full view by figuring out where people rarely looked. He got a small black coffee. The server looked surprised and pleased. So many workers had been retrained to make coffee with doodads and twirls and sugar syrups like the coffee version of college girls on March break with pretty pink sick-making drinks that when an old school Johnny came by like a trucker at a truck stop and just got a *coffee*, a server just stared, blinked and poured the hot jolt.

Just in time.

Here came heaven in a trench coat.

Vivienne. Vivi. V.

He did not know if Vivienne saw him, or sensed him, when he saw her come up the stairs, making her sweet little hard-shell suitcase heel beside her.

She walked past him forty feet away. He loved her in profile. She had on the grey silky trench coat she had bought in Paris when he took her there for their twentieth wedding anniversary. The trench looked well worn, a foreign correspondent's attire, tied in classic Vivienne style, belted in front, in a studied nonchalance, *très négligée*. Grey collar up. Short red hair, pixie style. Slim black jeans. Her red-striped shirt was the new version of the short-sleeved red-striped shirt he saw her in the first time, in the tropical steam. She had kept the worn-out short-sleeved one and used it as a rag to clean her camera lenses.

Ah, the scarf he bought for her when they were in Paris. Nice, small, with green, pink and orange fishes, tied tight around her neck. Her clothes looked born on her body. The war photojournalist, how she travelled before she changed to her work clothes. She wore her old short pointy mod boots with the gold-tipped toe. They had a gloss under the lobby lights. She must have had them shined at the airport, she liked to get there early, get her footwear polished.

Vivienne was the woman that women noticed sitting easily up at the shoeshine man in airport terminals. She asks Mr. Shoeshine about his work because work fascinates her. She forks over a twenty-buck tip, and they collaborate in a moment. Just a brief square bracket break from the disasters in the headlines.

She got in line at check-in. She fluffed her hair. Maybe she had seen him without moving her head. Vivienne did things like that. It was Vivienne who taught him that hair-fluffing is a tell, that men touch their hair when they see a pretty woman approaching.

He felt elevated just to see her pass on by.

It was the West, Ms. Pink was getting into costume. Vivienne chose clothes that told her body a story. And her body passed along the story to her brain. She arrived in the great silver state of Nevada looking like she had just been to Paris and had come home.

She was leaning on the check-in counter, schmoozing with some lanky Larry who looked like he had been here for the first atomic cocktail of 1951. There she was, no doubt saying to ole Lar there, "Hi, great to see you again. You look good, Larry." Vivienne could read a name tag with an eye sweep, like him she had learned to look, absorb, look away and look back in less than a second. An urban skill, trained as a child on the subways.

"Hello, Miss Pink." – Larry having the same skill, reading her name on the screen in a flash second, talking to her like old pals – "Good flight?"

"Great as always, Larry, always good to be here. I see you arranged for some sunshine for me, I was getting awfully grey around the gills up in Toronto. You've got family there, don't you?"

"Winnipeg, Miss Pink. Well, they used to live in Toronto. Way back."

"Sure they did, I knew it, I could tell, we might be mishpoche, *who knows."*

"At least machatunim," Larry might be saying. Look at her waving her head, talking with her whole body and why not. Life was short, that was Vivienne's motto. Because it was short, she lived it like it was long. Look at her, loosening her belt, as if ole Lar can't *see it* from his side of the counter. Now he's leaning into her, semi-confidentially, no doubt saying, *"Let me see what I can put you in today... Miss Pink, I have upgraded you to our executive floor, I believe you need a desk to work. It's a lot quieter."*

"Lots of mirrors?"

"I think you will enjoy it."

"Larry, you know it's always a pleasure."

She reaches across, that little charmer wife of his, and shakes Larry's hand. Of course, she had a crisp twenty in her hand. She'd seen a lot of things; she tipped.

He had begged her not to go to war anymore. Sweetly, she had said yes. She was a photographer, she was tricky. If you tied her down with guy wires, she'd fly away wearing the whole damn tent. Johnny stayed away – officially. Unofficially, he kept a weather eye out for his Vivienne.

Vivienne moved towards the elevator area. She lit up the spaces she came into. Johnny looked back to old Larry. Larry was watching Vivienne. She paid attention to everyone she was with, how rare. Larry looked like he had a bit of that light on him as the next human came to the desk and Larry snapped back to work.

Vivienne stopped, cupping her camera underneath its body. She moved with her camera even when not shooting as if the camera were a well-fitting nerve-connected prosthetic. The brain sends a signal to the nerve endings that connect chest, shoulder, rotating cuff, elbow, forearm, wrist and eye. A kind of a soul android, Vivienne called it. A neural path engraved in my body after forty years on the job, ten thousand hours. A third breast, a third lung. It was not that a steel extension made a human bionic; it was that the human made the steel breathe. Vivienne stood there, unembarrassed, completely aware of her surroundings, her eyes two sponges.

She emerged from the elevator twenty-two minutes later. It was not yet one in the afternoon. She had four good hours to work in. Oh, five if you counted the blue hour, and Vivienne counted the blue hour. She counted the gold hour, and the mauve hour before the golden hour before the blue hour before the pre-dark, too. Civil twilight, nautical twilight in a land with no sea. There she was, transformed, an actor costumed for her next scene. She knew that her subjects moved differently with different clothes, why wouldn't she?

Johnny was lost in looking at Vivi. If he had stayed married to Ms. Dye Allergy, he would have been safe with a hard-wired kvetcher. Vivienne was hard-wired to kvell from the power of the shadows. Ms. Kvetcher showed him what life writ small could be. Vivienne took the larger canvas for granted, she took misfortune as life's absurdity, even when she had to keep her head still for weeks, had to use a feeding tube after a bomb in the Baghdad booksellers' market sent her flying and dislocated her jaw as she landed on *Tales from the Thousand and One Nights.*

Ah, there she walked: the pink leather jacket she had bought in Buenos Aires, 1982. As Vivienne told the story, it was April, the beginning of Argentina's winter. She was walking along Maipú towards the Hotel Gran Dora where she was living. A white Ford Falcon, a routine vehicle of abduction during the Dirty War, pulled up on the busy Saturday street – a hand reached out a door and grabbed her. Vivienne held her camera high. She fought back. The car dragged her along Maipú. The doorman at the hotel saw her and ran to help her. The kidnappers pulled off her old brown suede jacket. The doorman pulled at her other arm, her foot bent back and twisted, her face hit the car door, the thug inside punched her face numerous times, then the doorman yanked her free and the white Ford Falcon crawled off, stuck in shopping traffic. Abductions in Buenos Aires then were as common as shopping. If the doorman had been on break, Vivienne would have been taken and dropped from a high plane into an ocean.

Limping, she insisted she had to go, *right now*, and replace her jacket. A couple blocks and she was in one of the high-end fashionable leather stores of the day, where, due to the manic depressed economy, smart sparkling clothes at the pricey end of the scale had cost less than bargain basement. For twenty-five American dollars cash, she got a beautiful, fully lined, soft pink leather jacket, still good twenty-four year later. To the world it was a pink bomber jacket. To Queen Moxie, her skin resistance.

Who would think seeing her stride out of the hotel elevator, looking so intriguing, that for years she had slept in that pink leather jacket, with a Swiss Army knife in the right-hand pocket and the blade out just in case? Even home in Toronto.

The jacket had *duende*; it had lived through invisible war, fear, aftermath, visible missiles. That jacket had been to the morgue, it had seen humans shot at point-blank range. That jacket had been to the beach in Beirut, with the ruins of civil war hotels back of it, that jacket had eaten in the desert and the tropics, that jacket zipped up to her glass jaw, that jacket was a prop with certain power. That jacket could talk to her through her skin, transmitting its power. You could put that jacket on a chair and it would tear the hair off a psychiatrist.

She had turned post-traumatic clothing into a power source. Johnny needed her close, or the darkness of his own writing would bring him to places too low to live in.

There she went – her hair red, her back pink, her legs khaki – past the roulette tables, down the stairs to the coffee shop, her pickup spot for men.

And she was his. She'd better be.

4

NEON

NEON IS THE beautiful and rare element found so little on earth, but so much in our universe, a perfect gas for the excitable highway. Neon is younger than photography in use. Neon is about the same age as the movies in commercial diffusion.

Hydrogen, helium, oxygen, carbon, neon. The five most abundant chemical elements by mass. Neon, which stars make in their Alpha genesis moments. Neon, true neon, is red. Red-orange as sunsets and rock planets and hot ranges and firebombs. Any other colour is adulterated neon. Up the neon alleys the rare earth sighting of true neon is in a multiplicity of pleasure to the eye, a kind of pleasure zoo, this red neon.

Neon the new, neon the noble. *Edelgas.*

5

THE BIRDMAN OF PARIS

OUT ON THE wide cosmopolitan boulevard a man in a large bird suit held up a sign: THE SLEIGH BROKE. He was standing in front of Paris Las Vegas and its sky-high replica of the Eiffel Tower.

He twirled a red ski pole, poking the passing parade of desert sunshine lovers. He had not acquired the bird suit's head. It was a man's head and a bird's body. He wore a tiny elf-sized white fedora. Below, he sported a pilly blue Speedo over the bird suit and on his bony legs he wore dusty brown Frye boots. He held out a begging bin: a vintage plastic tub with pink flamingos carrying high stacks of yellow and blue coins.

"The bird is in charge of public safety!" the birdman on the boulevard shouted. "The birdman, not the president. As I myself declared in a recent radio interview, Mister Bush has put the bird in charge of all matters concerning the public homeland. It is the feathered one who shall rise to save the people. The bird will save the banks. Ha." The bird began to sing, "The women were easy, but the money was easier." He put one bird foot and one hand forward, in a Jimmy Durante–style vaudeville move, and continued, "The crooks were on the lam, and the biggest crooks of all were Fannie and Freddie. Oh ho, the women were easy but Fannie and Ginnie were the easiest money of all."

The bird resumed his more deadpan demeanour, sticking his ski pole arm out to waylay the boulevard walkers. "Just a thought on security.

There are no words, yet let it never be said that at the end of the day we must make a new beginning to be able to assume a more confident posture as to who are the bad guys; quite so. When one was busy travelling on matters of some urgency as to the future of, if I may call them that, women in 2040, and so forth. Pursuant to, anything helps. Any change; God bless." Holding out his plastic tub.

A shaven-headed man in a navy blue knit cardigan with a shawl collar, navy velvet pants rolled up at the cuff and low grey desert boots with no socks came up to the birdman on the desert boulevard as the late morning traffic zoomed and idled by in its white and red sedans and pickups through the bright time dust. The man was Johnny Coma.

"What in the hell are you doing here?" Johnny asked the bird.

"Leave me alone," the birdman said, the stentorian tones replaced by a nasal whine.

"There we go," Johnny said. "This man, ladies and gentleman, advised in Vietnam, advised the World Bank, attended the UN sixty-nation Geneva Disarmament Conference of 1963. When did they let you out of the, ahem, facility? I thought you couldn't fly."

Danny Coma had attended a counterterrorism conference at the Bellagio in the spring of 2004. Hotel security found him in the pool area trying to climb an orange tree at two in the morning. He was ejected. He turned up as a character on the Strip. The Birdman of Paris.

"Ha. I walked back the threat. Vet that! Let them try and find me here. This old spook still has a few tricks up his wing." He turned his attention to a red-faced woman, her skin the result of the wind, the sun, the brutal three per cent humidity. "Got a penny, got a nickel, got a quarter, got a loonie, got a toonie?"

"Hey Danny. Birdman, this is the States," Johnny said.

"One has been put in charge of public safety," the birdman said, scratching his thick feathered armpit. "One took risks. Have not commented greatly on your last whoosie as of yet, but from the few comes the – debt! Ha." He did a little time step with his clompy Fryes.

"Could somebody arrest this man for felony stuffed shirt?" Johnny asked the passing paraders, one of whom raised a two-foot-high glass with red liquid in it, sucking the holiday brain-paralysing spirit through a curved straw.

"Shrovlem probeled," the drinker said, "bring him in," and wove down the concrete.

"One shall make the people free even if one has to kill every last one of them," the birdman orated, returning to his baritone preaching. His eyes went away to the high mountains bleached pale ochre in the bright sun, his head looked to the planes lifting up with no identification, and to the planes drifting down inside the valley's impossibly blue dome. "Got a dollar, white collar?" he said to a man tootling by in a motorized chair, legless with not even a blanket to cover his lap and underwear. He wore a red and white trucker's hat with "Save The Painforest" on it. He did indeed stop and hand up a dollar bill to the birdman's tub.

The birdman moved in to Johnny's personal space, whispering from his shorter height to Johnny's neck. "One hears from sources that the big-shot writer Johnny Coma is prepared to blurb the bird's new book, shhh, top eyes-only intel. Down the back-channel pike word has it that Johnny Coma, we are confident, will be recommending very soon in time the passage of the bird's book to the biggest of the New York firms. Shhh. Harper Strauss, keep it under your rug."

It was hard to tell, in the modern times of image anxiety and the vast deserts of life left to go after a life of working, who was a heebie-jeebie pest, who was a panicked desperate, who was a focused stalker, who wanted to write a novel, who wanted to write a novelist.

"My dear avian ass," Johnny said, stepping to the side, fanning the air. The bird suit smelled of old mouldy storage. "In order to blurb a book, there has to *be* a book. Why are you here in Vegas?"

"I came to the high mountains."

"We're in a valley."

"I was misinformed."

The birdman ran out to the traffic on the boulevard, speaking to the cars as they zoomed and braked. The prismatic light bounced off the white cars, and all cars were reflecting surfaces in this town of mirrors.

"The people shall be made secure, above all efforts, this one promises. If one must and so forth to bring freedom, as inferred by x or y degrees in the most recent intelligence partners on various issues, ahem." Like the keynote bird who had a small seizure mid-speech, consider Mister Daniel Coma, late of everywhere in the world and peace treaty conferences, winching himself back up to the vague coherences of his brain.

"Ah, yes, here one is. We in the West..." A circle of holidaymakers had formed. Some took pictures of the birdman with their cellphones. Some dropped coin in his retro Flamingo money tub. Inside the mouldy down, his eyes lit up. "Got an Abe, babe? Anything works." Stabbing a man on stilts in his wooden leg. "Any coin? Spare Rolex? Anything helps. The bird lied for democracy, and look at democracy now." The birdman scratched his feathered breast. A large moth flew out and landed on Johnny's nose. "Scrim, scram; lightness!"

"It's not too late to contend," Johnny said.

"Call Ma, she's waiting. She wants that 1,263 dollars back."

"Danny, Ma's dead."

"I wouldn't go that far."

"She's buried at Mount Sinai."

"In terms of future challenges. On the chance there was some prospect of who knows, I put her mobile in her coffin, just in case her no-good son Jonathon cares to call."

"You put Ma's cellphone in her grave? She didn't know how to operate it when she was alive."

"We have had technical support from the usual quarters. Spare a loonie for the counterterrorism cause?"

The desert at noon shone like the protagonist it had been, before the people. There was a glint in the birdman's cloudy eyes. "I know you. Montevideo. The Columbia Palace. Yes! IMF Anders. The Electrician. Old sod, how's she been keeping?"

Fugue states, then the clarity. Then, in the dry, the mental fog sweeps in.

"Danny. It's me. Johnny. Jonathon, your younger brother. It was Vivienne in Montevideo. I've never been in Uruguay. Please. Do me a personal favour. Say her name. Twenty-five years, you still won't utter my wife's name. Vivienne."

"There was no daylight. We did not have daylight. We didn't know who these people were. Simply guerrillas." Danny Birdman came to Johnny's neck and smelled it. A big smile, unrelated to happiness or joy spread on his face.

"Now, there's a laugh." Johnny stepped back. "I pampered my older brother; I treated the first in command like a baby. I let you run your damn potential into smoking burnout. Vivi? My Vivienne? She went on her own tick to the places you were sent. She stayed in bedbug hotels. She prowled the streets. You lived behind gates, watching the photos Vivi took click by on your plasma screens."

"Don't be ridiculous," the feathered bird said, clomping a feathered tap step. "One simply could not get out ahead of the moving parts."

"What is this?" Johnny picked at Danny's feather suit. A piece of turquoise, an earring stud was stuck in the feathers. Johnny stuck it back in. "You used to be quoted in the articles as 'a source with close knowledge of the situation.' But my wife, whose name you will not speak, was the photographer in fatigues in with the fighters. Say 'Vivienne.' Say her name and we could begin to forgive you. You might even start that novel you've been talking about since Moses hiked the tablets up Mount Sinai."

"Stop picking on me. I have gout. We have to walk the terror stream back."

"If I had picked on you more, told you that you write like crap, you might be a man today in trimmer syllables. Hey, look, you want to come with me to Death Valley? We could make it a family outing."

The birdman clomped up and down in front of Johnny, swinging his ski pole and his feathered arm in a combo of a Peppermint Twist and a latter-day geezer b-boy breakdance. "Bim bam, flim flam, schism shizzle shim Joe Louis, what a man." Punching the air. "Boxing, boxeo, the bird is the word, the bird is a champion contender, to the max. Max Schmeling. Bop! Debt Valley!"

The desert street paraders in visible acts of magical thinking wore the costumes of humid heat their winter minds told them to wear when they travelled to sunshine. Up and down the boulevard they paraded in faux Hawaiian shirts done up in nausea yellows and halucious blues on top of board shorts designed for those who surfed desks, their souvenir Ts saying they were with stupid, their bare sockless legs in squishy pink clogs. The boom was booming, but advisories cautioned: never negotiate a mortgage with a man who wears Jell-O on his feet. The winter Santa Ana winds blew a hard zero degrees Fahrenheit at three per cent humidity. Here and there, with the wisdom of a sartorial satori, a stroller wore outerwear of nubbly sheep, long-sleeved. This was the high-res desert.

The Birdman of Paris spoke: "My younger brother, John Coma, perhaps generally speaking has some renown. Applause please! But one is unaware of the – who is she?"

"Vivienne? Say her name. Vivienne was ten times more known than me. You were too busy lighting the cigarillos of Madame Nhu to be curious about Vivienne. She knew the Nhus, Danny. She took Madame Nhu's picture. It's in one of her books."

"The Nhus! Yes!" The bird brightened in his fugue state. "Big news! Daniel Coma will be blurbed in his new novel by bestselling author Johnny Coma!" Danny was back retailing fake facts about Johnny Coma to Johnny Coma's face. Johnny wasn't buying retail.

"Do you want to come with us to the desert or not."

"One is in the desert, right now," the birdman said. "Hey, buddy," reaching his tub out to a red polka-dotted do-rag man in full leather and a dark beard. "Hey. The bird is in charge of national security, got any spare change to help a poor agency out? Pennies do."

"You tell 'em," the man in leather said, high-fiving the red ski pole, dropping a dollar bill in the plastic tub. "Tell old man Cheney I said hi."

"One will pass it along to one's Dick. Yes, yes. One can see, my dear boy," Danny said to Johnny, this time using a rather more mid-Atlantic tone, somewhere in flight between Houses of Parliament, "the people, to some degree, can be persuaded. A small swim in a river. A small electrical appliance. One had to work without daylight. The mission was blindfolded."

Consider the birdman, late of Washington, DC, and parts invaded, once a government fixer, now a feathered Strip beggar recently escaped from a loony birdhouse. A man who, in the asylum, declared himself the Son of God, though he was, in fact, the son of Murray.

Johnny Coma, novelist, just back from Baghdad, from one desert to another at the same latitude, Iraq to Nevada, Johnny had flown west on the desert belt to another winter crystal. And here was Johnny's only sibling, the once formidable negotiator of all things, the fixer for the Americans, Dan Coma. *Come to Death Valley.* There was a reckoning due.

"Come along, Daniel. We'll talk writing. We'll be brothers. I'll tell you all about how to control your fans." Johnny whispered into the mouldy shoulder. "Get your wife to answer all your fan mail. It's magic – that way the glory hounds are left with nada. Their correspondence was with Vivienne posing as me. Misdirection, Danny, misdirection."

Like all good magicians, while telling the mark how misdirection worked the conjurer was misdirecting him. Flatter the man. Use the way men come to writers to talk away the day, believing writers to be priests, psychiatrists or social workers. But writers are deadpan professional thieves.

Johnny put his arm around the smelly feathers. "Fine. I was ready to talk scribbling with you but fine. Beg money from strangers. We're going to Death Valley in the morning. We're at the Flamingo." He walked away.

"I could come," the birdman shouted after Johnny. Johnny kept walking through fun valley. The sky was filled with planes above, a few of them civilian.

"I'll go to Death Valley," he said to the air.

6

VAN GOGH IN HIROSHIMA

AT THE FIRST of the Flamingo's many blue pools, two figures lay on chaises, bundled in coats, faces up to the sun. Vivienne Pink with her pink leather jacket up to her neck and Val Gold, spy, housemate back in Toronto, with his old Irish sheep sweater were the only ones at the pool.

Val pulled out two postcards from his grey jacket. One the head of Picasso, the other the head of Van Gogh. "Look, this is all you need to know." He tapped the head of Picasso. "Okay, this is Pablo the Spaniard's self-portrait. He paints himself – I mean, I love this, don't get me wrong, but look how he portrays himself – like the primitive art he loved then. He looks African, he looks like a totem, his features erased to a mask. He looks like something iconic you would find in wood, in the Nile region, from prehistory. The open shirt, a blouse really, come on, Picasso's shirt looks like the one in that pic you favour, Vivi, of Walt Whitman, isn't it? The informal guy."

"Do not call me Vivi. That is my husband's name for me," Vivienne said.

"Oh, listen to her, look at this one, 'husband.'"

"If you were married, you would have less time to put a microscope to the names married people use for each other, Val." But she liked what he was saying about Picasso. Val was light years ahead of her in piercing the images. She made them; he could construct their hidden glory.

Val tapped the eyebrows of the Picasso self-portrait. "Look at these eyebrows, he made them long, a line, an entire frame for the face. Picasso got eyebrows, that's for sure, babe."

Vivienne did not like that he was calling her babe either. It was one of their frequent intimate moments, but while she sensed that Val felt it to be love, or the hint that he, The Other Man, might have a chance to step up and be the First in Command, she invariably and exclusively felt it to be a lovely pal-to-pal tutorial. She picked Val's brain and Val felt it to be love. To her it was a platonic thing.

"Look at Picasso's hand," Val said, tapping the crude fist. "The over-blouse in white, the V-neck showing his clavicle, the crude facial features, the high hairline, the hand. Picasso made himself look like a South Seas idol. Look, it's all greys and whites and black. It's severe, it's ridiculously modern."

He put the Picasso self-portrait down and held up the Van Gogh. The paint, even in a reproduction, caught the prismatic desert light around the pool and shone as if the original gloss was evident in the flat card. "Look now at this one," Val said, not tapping but running his finger up and down on Van Gogh's hair. "Look: orange, red, green, the bristling hair of a man, a quiet fire, like Amsterdam. Look at the moustache, the beard. The two portraits could not be more different. I remember seeing this at the Van Gogh Museum; you really can't get it until you have seen how *alive* Van Gogh's paint is. The paint, not the painting. The paint makes the painting but the paint has a life of its own. He painted himself painting, and the man, look," running his palm on the card, "is so focused, so at rest, so in his thing, look at his arm. Picasso painted himself as a found object. Van Gogh painted himself as a man at work."

Vivienne had her eyes closed. Val had tutored her in all things art. She could see the Van Gogh behind her closed eyes as he spoke: "Vincent in the self-portrait has his thumb through the wooden palette hole, and the palette and his arm look one and the same. The first time I saw this, I thought, Van Gogh made a palette prosthetic, he made a warrior's new arm, made up of wood with paint globs on it. A wounded veteran could use his wooden limb as his paint source."

Vivienne opened her eyes. Val put one postcard on each of his legs, his charcoal pants providing a good background. The Picasso on his left thigh, the Van Gogh on his right. "Vivi, you see, Pablo came from the sunny south, he was a Málaga boy. He goes up to Barcelona, he's fifteen, sixteen, all the sunny places formed him. But Vince baby was from the dark north. And he ends up being all about the sunny south. Pablito left the sun and Vince came to it. Vince was consumed by light. Take *The Pigeons*."

"Do not start with Picasso's *Pigeons* this morning, honey," Vivienne said. "No *Los Pichones*."

The *honey* came out of her mouth in love and habit. It was not, however, the love Val wanted. The love he wanted he would not chance to take. The love he wanted was a life with Vivienne as her husband. Still, Vivienne habitually *honey*ed him.

"They reminded me of you and me; we could coo in a pigeon keep, what say?"

"Please," she said.

"Okay," Val said. "But… Van Gogh's stars have emotion. Picasso is warmer than people say. He is my compass, you know that, darling Vivi."

Stop calling me Vivi, she thought, but she did not say it. She liked Val's poolside tutorials. He went on. "But Vince is like some angel down in the engine room, some V8 angel engine. I don't know. But then Pablo comes up with these intentions, he will try anything. Vivi. Listen, you yourself do not know most of the time what your heart's intention is. What your art's intention is. Your stated intention might not be what is going on, subterraneanally. Think about it."

This was why Vivienne cherished Val, why she needed Val in her art oasis. If Johnny had had such marvellous insights into Van Gogh, the truth is he would never have relaxed in a chaise by a pool and entertained his wife's closed eyes as she half-slept with his thoughts, no way, nooo way. Johnny? He would have hied his insights up the elevator to the room and secreted them into his cardboard Moleskine notebook to use in a novel. And that was how it was. Val did not feel the need to put his thoughts into words other than those spoken. Val had no pressing need to put his words into a shaped product to sell to strangers for money, he had a pressing need to charm Vivienne, to compete for her graces. "You never told me any of this before," she said. "Go on. Tell me."

"He wanted Japan," he said, fired up by the nearness of her. "V, listen. Van Gogh's *intention* was – Japan. Not the south of France. You have to know that about a man. What is his intention? It is not what it seems, even what the evidence seems to tell; the evidence is not always the best storyteller. What is your desire, Vivi? Van Gogh's *desire* was Japan. He wrote to his brother Theo and asked why not go to the equivalent of Japan – the south of France. If Vincent had lived he might have scraped together the gelt to get a cheapo trip, actual Van Gogh in actual Tokyo. For all we know, Van Gogh would have gone to Nagasaki to paint the atomic victims. He might have been protean, my Vivi, to their proteus faces; he might never have cut off his own ear, seeing theirs radiated into their cheekbones.

"Van Gogh would have been ninety-two when they dropped Little Boy on Hiroshima if he had lived. He might have been an atomic mutant child portraitist with easy travel. Arles and Saint-Rémy were not his *intention.* He hoped, as he travelled down south, that in Provence he would find the light of Japan he had seen in the great Japanese painters. I remember when I fell in love with that woman with the white cap, and Gauguin's chair, and the courtesan; I did not know why until I went back to Hiroshima that time. It was the light, something about the greens. The acid sparks he infused into those greens, the woodblock air, setting the items forward. He made paint bracing. It was poetry, not decoration. Yes. I think maybe that is it, honey." Val was being easy and companionable. Like old times. But their old times had been so short and so long ago, and they had been feeding off of them for way too long, even when the well ran dry. Now, in a small miracle, the well seemed to have a moment of fresh water, the way it can feel some days with old friends.

She took Val's hand. He went on: "If there had been planes when Van Gogh was painting and Van Gogh had gone to Japan, we might have had *Starry Night over Nagasaki*, he might have done paintings of the atomic victims. He might have shown the neck of a radiated man. He might have done *Night Café in Tokyo*, or *American Sailor in Yokosuka*. Maybe instead of *Woman in a Kimono*, he would have painted a woman suffering full-body burns in Kumamoto. Maybe Van Gogh, instead of giving us rain over a bridge and the small people walking on it, might have painted the exodus after radiation over the bridge in the fallout rain."

Vivienne's eyes stayed closed. Val had a great low voice. He brought her almost to hibernating mode, where she had a mere thought or two, her brain a sleeping bear in winter sunshine. Into the aestivating aesthetic. She was lucid dreaming in the sunshine.

Val lullabied on: "He made us the blossoms of spring three ways. Those peach and white blossoms like flower rain on a wedding day. But Van Gogh was Van Gogh, sure. If he had been alive in 1945, and he had gone to actual Japan, he might have shown us the white rain of the atom. He might have shown us *Atomic Summer*, after the snow and salt blossoms fell. He might have shown us humans like trees, and trees like humans; he might have shown us a mutant piece of meat that was actually a wine bottle melted in the radiation. We do not know. We just don't know, baby. But we know that Van Gogh would have made forever art wherever he went. You can be efficient and you can be learned, but you either have heart or you don't, you either have the juice, the duende, or you don't."

Vivienne kept her eyes closed. High piping light, helium and neon, danced in her eyelids. It was all red light behind her eyes. What was her intention anyway? Her stated intention was to take photographs of men on their way to war, *Soldiers The Night Before They Deploy*, but she could be, as Val was suggesting, like Van Gogh wanting Japan and going to Provence to get it; she could be in Nevada to find something else. Nagasaki, Nevada? Or was it Baghdad?

"If Van Gogh had moved to southern California, he might have painted a plain suitcase at a train station, waiting to be taken on board a train to a Japanese concentration camp up the highway, and it would have moved us as much as his paintings of chives or a chair. He would have found a Japanese woman at Union Station in LA walking through the archway where they collected citizens of Little Tokyo for in-state extradition. A woman whose kimono was in pieces, peeking out of her wicker basket, hidden en route to her new home in the Eastern Sierra, a deportee in her own country. I can picture it, Vivi, there he is on the train at the window, soaking in the California light under the brilliantine mountains. You know, Van Gogh would have been a great photographer. He would have shown us the wild stray dog light of the world. You have the juice, Vivi. Don't dumb down your moxie. Open your eyes. Look at me."

She did. There was a lovely man, Val the silver fox. He looked like an architect or an artist, but he did not desire to be one. No, Val Gold was the rare bird, an intelligence agent, a lover of art and literature who used them to hone his observational skills and to relax his trained body. A man who, unlike so many modern men cluttering up the atmosphere, was an avid consumer of the arts. One who did not ever think that because he loved reading he was, perforce, a secret writer, or that because he loved to go to galleries and museums he was, perforce, a secret painter. This made him first-rate at intelligence.

Vivienne took up a half-lotus position. She trained her eye across the pool. The sky was blue, but it felt red. The crystal clarity of light in the American Western winter? Well, it felt like putting your skull in a prism, and your eyes rotated in this prism that rotated back at you. Light watched you; out here, you were light's delight. Light ate you. Sun was a monster. It drew you in to destroy you and your pictures. Everything was bleached as bones, when the light makes your eyes burn. Van Gogh might have been a cinematographer, bringing us the blinding bent light of the Western sky.

Val handed Vivienne her small director's finder. It was her Cavision model, a nice two and a half inches long, swell for looking through to scope a particular shot. She brought it to Vegas to view stuff when she couldn't use a camera, but she had left it in her room when she came down to the casino floor.

"Where did you get this?" she asked.

"Your room. I broke in while you and Junior were holding hands in the coffee shop."

"You went into my room?"

"You want it or no?" He held out the finder.

"You bet I do." She took it, put the rubber cup to her eye, turned the tiny lens rim and a gold heap beside a chaise on the other side of the pool came into focus. It looked for all the world like a statue, a gold folded lump on display. "You know, honey," she said, moving the lens into the brightness, "Van Gogh wasn't nuts, the light was. It makes your bones weak, all that vitamin D sucks away your calcium. You feel like spring fever every day when the light's so manic."

"Marry me," Val said. "Remember when we were in Amsterdam last month and we got up and turned on the TV and there's Rumsfeld resigning right after the election. So we went to look at the apple blossom paintings at the museum, and it didn't matter. Defence men come and go but the Van Goghs are forever. You and me, Vivi, let's get married." It was an old routine. Art got Val hot. Her view? Val could ask her, time and again, because there was no chance she could say yes. And he knew it.

A guy from the other side of the pool dove into the water, swam and touched the pool edge near them while staying underwater, and swam back. As he lifted himself up on the other side, Vivienne recognized who it was: the young man in the white T-shirt. Her prey had followed her to the pool?

His unadorned torso showed he had a good body, but he had something else. He was, well get that, a damn exhibitionist. The Shy Exhibitionist. He wanted her to take pictures of him. He came to ignore her, to demonstrably say yes. To make her work for her art. All right then. Before Val knew what was happening beside him, Vivienne was up out of her chaise, stripping off her pink leather jacket, her khaki pants, her shiny black shoes and her green T-shirt. Down to her grey-and-black Paris-bought bra and thong underwear, Vivienne dove into the pool and did five fast laps, landing on Mr. White T-shirt's side. She got up out of the pool. He was not there. She wiped the water out of her eyes with her wrists. He was off to the side watching her. He was standing at the towel stand, where there were no towels, it being winter. He had on black trunks and a gold jacket over a bare chest. His hand was radiating like a pink beam.

Vivienne walked over, dripping water. "Got a light?" she said.

He smiled at her. "I do."

She stood like an idiot, realizing she had asked for a light with nothing in her hand. She liked that. She liked looking like an idiot. It was *haimish.* But noir haimish, all the same.

"Do you always ask for a light before you ask for a cigarette?" He was looking at her wet goosepimply body, bold in his up and down. He offered her a cigarette from a bright pink package, the Pink brand that had kept them company in the hotel coffee shop but which was jumping with saturation in the sun. The pink with bows on it, one gold, one black. Party-time packaging.

"Hello, Andy," she said. "That's me. Vivienne Pink."

"They're from out of Okinawa. Japan after the war," he said. "The sailors in their whites, and the ladies who serviced them. I love that expression, *We're in the pink.*"

"And so we are," she said. He did not acknowledge that they had met before. Or that they had traded stories, confidences. She wanted to get that white T-shirt back on him, pronto. She could feel her eye wanting it. The prey was drawing out the hunter. He grabbed her shoulders and pulled her into a hidden green area and kissed her on the mouth, not lightly and not for a short time. Charisma, the gift the gods give so that you might bestow it on others. His kiss in the dry air made her lips spark.

She had sixteen pics of his dead man's stare in her head and there were still 9,984 beats left in a second.

It gave her an extra thrill that Val was watching. Of course he was. He had watched her dive in the pool, get out, talk to the guy from the coffee shop and disappear out of sight while they kissed each other. She knew Val would imagine the kiss. She liked that. But Andy was her intention. She was on the job.

Vivienne ran her fingers down his cheek, inhaling his cheekbones. He was emitting the air of a man who knows the power of a well-timed surrender. "Why don't I come up to your room?" he said. "That is, if you're not doing anything for the next hour or so."

"One sec," she said. She walked back to the chaise, looking right at Val who was looking at her. He was not smiling. She picked up her clothes and returned to Andy. As they walked through the garden back into the hotel, Vivienne scrambled into her pants, leaving only her bra on top.

She slipped the key card in the lock at room 27117 and the door green-lit them in. The TV was still on, there was Clark Gable holding Marilyn Monroe close in the desert cabin in *The Misfits*, his weathered face and her wild cleavage and bare feet dancing. Vivienne wanted a portrait: *Andy, The Night Before He Deployed.* Enter the game with your worthy adversary, Vivienne. Bring your moxie to the man.

7

THE MISFITS

A SHOCK WAVE changes the nature of the medium it travels through. Travelling through air, the wave changes the air, putting it under pressure, building it, making it steroidal, speeded. A shock wave is a propagating disturbance. The wave alters the atoms it travels through; demented, distorted, the air becomes weaponized. The air literally gives you a concussion. Shell shock is not psychological; it is the result of having your brain beaten by air mercilessly pounding your head. Shell shock is a hidden brain injury. Andy and Vivienne had that in common: they shared postwar-concussed brain. And those reverberating brains did come to the high valley city where the nearby atomic tests had mutated the air to attack the place at the speed of a supersonic plane. When you fly into Las Vegas you are not just flying into a military town, a union town, a Spanish city, you are flying into a still-reverberating concussion. What the paperwork called a syndrome, and then called a disorder, and then reified by calling it PTSD, left out the injured brain, the vibrating blur unseen, left out how you do not know yourself to yourself inside your head, left out how the present becomes a place of alien sounds and then the sky begins to rain the fallout rain, in the land of little rainfall.

Vivienne scooped up her camera from the bed. She sat down, motioned for Andy to sit beside her. She held her camera in her left hand, stroking the back of Andy's skull with her right hand. What damage was under there?

They watched Clark Gable watch Marilyn's dress slip off her shoulders in the car, her drunk and resting on his shoulder, him adoring her as he drove the big land outside of Reno.

Vivienne pressed MUTE. Seeing only the black and white images, *The Misfits* felt like a Spanish or Italian movie and one made much earlier than 1961. *La Dura Vita.* Marilyn Monroe looked like a still photograph that kept moving, to its own surprise. A creature who knew, a sylph Aleph, an escapee from the skies of Eden, a sex-charged Golem.

Andy asked, "Do you have wigs?"

"Sure, honey. Always be prepared," Vivienne said.

"Do you have a blond wig?" he asked, a bit guiltily, like a guy shopping for eye shadow in a department store in 1963.

"I do."

"Would you show me?"

Vivienne was up, sliding the closet open, going into her orange props bag. She came back to the bed carrying two wigs, one black and one blond. She put the blond wig on over her short red hair. "I used to have long blond hair like this," she said. "But we Pinks all start out platinum, and age brunette or red." She snapped a shot of the far mirror: a woman with platinum hair, a black bra loosely hanging, beside a man wearing a white tee.

"Wear the black one," he said, holding it in his hands, pulling his fingers through the dark tresses. It was real hair.

"You know, I like the –"

"Wear the black one." Vivienne took it from him, took off the blond wig, handed it to Andy to hold. She adjusted the black wig on her red hair.

"Look at me," she said. "Totally different." She snapped that pic in the mirror. The man who a second ago was with a glamorous blond was now with a black-haired woman who looked like she had left the daylight to enter heaven's troubles.

Andy put the blond wig on his own head. Before her mind thought, her hands took the picture of the two of them in the mirror. A woman with long black hair; a man with long blond hair.

"My wife was a blond," he said. "Make love to me. I want to be the woman who died in the car crash." Changing his voice, he continued, "My husband, Andy, never saw me again. Please love me. If he dies in Iraq, then who will know me. Could you love me one more time? Please, Vivienne, love me. Let me pretend Caroline's here with me. I know you won't hurt her."

He moved her up on the bed, unzipping her pants, removing her bra, cupping her breasts in his hands, sliding off his jeans. Let this, then, be a tender moment in the workplace, when things happen. Let this be stuff. Stuff happens, it was happening down under the duvet, with a soldier and a war photographer. The betrayals moulted off of each of them, the lies of the world high and low. She was experienced; he was tender and knew how to touch her; she had the gift of patience. They made love, listening to each other's bodies. The movie rolled along. They sweat, played, whispered, each in a wig. "I wanted you in the coffee shop," he said.

"I know," she said. "You and my camera needed to meet." The wig's long blond hair lay back on the pillow. He took her hand to stroke his next rising erection. "I needed to get a pic of you, I still need it." Getting him hard.

"Aw, let's go for coffee," he said, teasing.

Vivienne got on top of him, put him inside her. She put her strong small hands on his shoulders. "No coffee. I need to photograph you." What is foreplay in the fields of art? What if the excellent close work, at work, is not the cause of a sexual affair, but the result of it? What if the fine sex leads to the work project bona fides? Art is promiscuous, artists just tag along after.

Andy was enjoying himself, his fingers pinching her nipples; Vivienne was getting adrenalized with intense panic: where were the pictures? She fell forward, the black hair fell on his chest, mingling with the blond. They were soaking wet with sweat and cum. She lay on the pillow beside him. She took off her black wig, threw it on the floor. He tossed his blond hair on the floor too. He kissed her, the way he had kissed her in the shaded corner by the pool, as if he knew her. "It's a man's world," she said.

He stroked her face, "But it ain't nothing without a woman."

"We need to work," she said.

"Just tell me what you need, Sergeant." His ease was scary to Vivienne. A man that at home in his own skin can disarm an entire room. He had shown himself to her, and drawn her to him. There was a dare in the atmosphere: give up something of yourself, dear Vivienne.

"What I need," she said, shy to say it, "is to – adore you." It was true. Photography did not substitute for words. A picture was worth no words at all. A picture took you where words dared not go. On the TV, Montgomery Clift, his head swaddled in bandages, lay in Marilyn Monroe's lap. She was stroking his concussed head. Monty Clift had been the beauty of beauties in the movies, and then driving down a canyon outside LA one night he had crashed his car and become mangled, his delicate beauty gone, his face reconstructed. The beauty is short, the morphine long.

A roped wild mustang was dragging Clark Gable the cowboy across the white salt playa in the high desert.

"They were still setting off atomic bombs while this was being made," Vivienne said, the white duvet up to her chin. "They worked all summer. Summer in the desert, are you kidding me? They were outside Reno, at Dayton, there" – pointing to the TV – "Pyramid Lake is what? one hundred ten degrees. The atomic dust had to be blowing up that way too, plus they're in thinner air at forty-five hundred feet near Reno, plus the Navy's testing its own high explosives at nearby Fallon, plus add in all the damn dust off that dry lake, the two mares, the spring foal, that stallion, Gable, Monroe, Monty, Eli Wallach, Thelma Ritter – their lungs, their skin. Summer, fall.

"I love this movie, you want to know why? Korea was over, Vietnam was not official, everything was flush. But you look at this, a guy trying to figure out how to be a man. The cowboy was looking for a simple manly life, looking for something raw, but men were being dissuaded from rawness. How can a man be his own man, without working for wages? You want to know why I love *The Misfits?*" She put her hand on Andy's shoulder. "Because it's *Death of a Salesman* with cowboy hats. The cowboy wanted attention to be paid to him, but his days of roping the many horses were done. He had the smile, he could sell the horsemeat, but the life was sparse up in the canyons. The Korean War vet was flying planes now to coerce mustangs out of their mountain habitat. The rodeo man was concussed. The aging cowboy had his sales hat... They wanted a home, but all they had was houses. Jack Kennedy had three years to live. Let me shoot your back. Andy, honey." She said his name tenderly, so he could hear her desire for him. If the artist has no desire for her subject, it is simply a road map with no emotion.

Andy gave her a kiss on the cheek. "You sure have soft skin," he said. She put her head in his lap, lying on her side. He stroked her back with little tickles.

"John Huston, they were all inhaling that crap," she said. "Gable has a heart attack two days after they finish shooting, November 6, 1960. Two weeks later he was dead. The bomb dust, the playa in heat, who knows? Less than two years later Marilyn Monroe was dead. When she sang "Happy Birthday, Mr. President" she had forty-seven days left to live. Maybe the film work in the high desert made her brain crazy. Maybe the punch-drunk air at Pyramid Lake killed her. Monty Clift had a bad thyroid. Maybe it was a magnet to the radiation blowing upwind to *The Misfits*.

"They had invited some of the world's top photographers to come and shoot informal pics of the film as it was being made. It was deeply documented, because all these photogs came to *The Misfits* like a desert field trip. They say Arthur Miller wrote the movie as homage to Monroe, who was still his wife then. He captured that empathy, that creature being. And guess what? The next Mrs. Miller was one of the photographers who happened to come to the location to document it, Inge Morath. How like *The Misfits* itself, that the woman who shot a great picture of Arthur Miller's back looking at Marilyn Monroe's back as she looked out of the window in the small hotel where they were all staying, and of the unimpeachable sadness between his unseen face and her unseen face and the high desert mountains out the frame of the window. The woman who shot that picture became the next wife of the man standing with his back to her."

Andy got out of bed and offered his back to Vivienne. He stood naked, reflected in the glass like a goat come down from the high conflict terrain to the lower reaches, to find an oasis before nightfall. Night was beginning the blue hour as the mountains blackened.

"Tell me a story," he said, standing at the edge of the bed, half-erect.

"You have to go," she said.

"Tell me about a place you went. Let me be an ear for a while."

This was not a good idea, Vivienne knew. When the work was done, the work was done. She had grown fond of him, or at least fond of the spell they wove together. He went with the music of hazard. "Okay," she said, "just one, but then you go."

"Yes, boss," he said.

He settled back on the pillow dunes. Vivienne began, "It was 1965, November. I flew down to New York from TO. Marty had a place in Tudor City on East 43rd, at The Hermitage, up the stairs from the United Nations. Marty was in Saigon. I had to stretch my legs, so I took my camera for a walk down by the East River. Down the stairs on bedrock, across First Avenue and over to the UN building.

"So there I am, on Tuesday, November the 9th, 1965, and my camera started snapping and my body was running and I did not know why. There in front of the United Nations, a young man was lighting himself on fire. This cannot be: a self-immolation in New York City? But yes. He was a man in his early twenties; he was pouring gasoline on himself. I came home from Vietnam to see Vietnam in front of the UN."

She jumped off the bed; her body needed to move. She paced a bit in front of the bed as if she were a movie Andy was watching; she got down on her haunches at the foot of the bed, with her chin on the foot of the bed, on the sheets.

"There is a thing today. We have put ourselves in the safekeeping of a thing we hate, an abstract thing that we call *government.* We have never loved it; all we know is our despising of its core and its values. We have never written poetry to it. It is not an onion or an orchid we might write odes to, it is not the true love we lost, it is apart from us, our land has become *them.* We know what we hate, but what do we love? We are like exiles in our own countries, and we blame only the rulers. Even in democracy, we blame the rulers we elected, we are skilled in hate, we are five stars in sarcasm, we have the same skill set in petulance and outrage that we had when we were fourteen. Oh man, honey. I used to fling myself at the world, like an idiot infatuated by democracy. To know it, like a bad crush."

Andy raised his right eyebrow. "Lay off dissing my time, all right?"

Vivienne went from heated to boiling fast. "Look, son. Better vitriol is still vitriol. Do things only *happen* to you? Never being the agency of your destruction is what you are to yourself at nine years old. An immature nine. A nine without eyes or curiousity about the world. Today, all you smartasses are like émigrés to your dry heart state and you hate and you hate and you hate. But, son, you are not heartbroken."

"Don't call me *son*. I bet in your time you were quite the heartbreaker."

"This is my time now, *boy*."

He did not take the bait. "Go on," he said softly.

"When they came to our houses to take our libraries, or to arrest us for our utterances," she said, up and pacing again, "they were taking things we had *loved*. Free speech was not a thing we insisted on because we had come out of our hidey-holes for the first time to march, trash, get arrested and *shoyn*. Oh, you know, *fuck* rights. When they beat the shit out of peace, it was our lover they were beating up. So you want to call me a soppy drip, be my guest. I was covering war when I was fifteen. I was a boomer with feeling, arrest me. So I loved art and life, go on, throw away the key. If we hated capitalism, we loved the co-op. We had songs, we had a soundtrack. Music getting its ghost on, to haunt us in short nights later. I can allocute to the judge. Yes, your honour, I slow danced in all the wrong places. Yes, your honour, I was too humid too young. Yes, I confess, I danced to 'When a Man Loves a Woman,' and Percy Sledge was the damage fur in me, that summer of '66, when a quarter of a million troops was not enough for the US in Vietnam. And I was only eighteen years of age, and I was in my fourth year of wartime. And so I still see their beautiful bewildered faces whenever I hear that song, I still see their faces in the open caskets, and the boys as young as the corpses, folding the flag to honour them with precision.

"How can you fight for antiglobalization? That is *their* language. Why use the language of those you despise? Why not be eloquent in the tear gas, where is the poetry of the resistant tongue? I cannot get excited about the leadership of looters. I get their fury, but I get it for an instant and I pass on."

Andy chuckled. He jabbed the air with his cigarette, a horizontal high-five. Vivienne was at the glass wall of windows, looking down to the garden. A bride in full white walked through dimming greenery like a swan on dry land trailing her tulle feathers. Vivienne turned around to look at Andy.

"Peace was our lover, we were shy to say it, but it was true. Peace was our boon companion." She kneeled at the side of the bed. "We were heartsick at peace's sick condition." She put her hands on the bed, crawling onto it. Andy picked up her camera from the side table, and took a shot of her hands distorted, coming towards him; of her four silver rings, two on each hand, one on the left ring finger. Andy inched down towards her.

"Look," she said, naked, sitting cross-legged. "So I was beating the hell across First Avenue, running, and there was this young man in lotus position in front of the UN, he had doused himself with gasoline. My motor drive was way ahead of me. He was in a peace protest, self-immolating at First Avenue and East 44th Street. My camera was like an animal, let me tell you, it was eating up film." She had her toes up on her knees, and her hands calm in her lap.

"The NYPD, the FDNY, the reporters came. I walked around a while, I got a bite to eat, I swear to you I do not know where I went, I walked through Grand Central Station, I did some grab shots of the Chrysler Building, how could it be lit the same way it was before the young man burned to death five minutes away? Didn't the buildings know what had happened in New York City? I walked over to Park and way down, cut through Madison Square Park and down Broadway through Union Square, then down past NYU into the heart of SoHo, to The Photographers Place on Mercer. I looked at some old daguerreotypes there, and some new ones people were making. I bought a couple photo mags from the '50s, and I walked a minute back along Mercer to Prince and went into Fanelli's to get a beer. True story: I am sitting at Fanelli's bar, flipping through that mag, and lo and behold there is an article by a photog about how he was taken out with a group to see a nuke go off at the Nevada Test Site."

Andy put his hand on hers. She leaned forward. "Man, you cannot get away from the world, it will stalk you at every corner. I went out of Fanelli's. There used to be a nice vacant lot across the street with great yellow and blue graffiti. There was a guy there in a long tweed overcoat and pyjamas and slippers. He was a stout guy with a reddish beard, he could have been an actor, an artist, a bum; life has always been cheap, hon, but back then the rents were more lifelike. He gave me a joint, next thing I knew I was in some theatre with him watching *The Umbrellas of Cherbourg*. Man, the saturated colours. They were singing, the French boy was going off to the war in Algeria, was his sweetheart going to marry the other guy? Mostly I remember the colours and the romance. You really cannot describe how vivid New York City felt in November when the trees were sticks and it was this fucked-up Eden in black and white in 1965. I can still feel the exact shape of the street around me. It felt wet and grey and dour and possible, beautiful in a busy empty way, there was a lot of mix in the city, it was not over yet. I was eighteen. I had a crush on living." She ran her hand through her hair. "Man. But you know what, baby, I will never mock an eighteen-year-old who is embracing the world. There are a lot of eighteen-year-olds who have lived a lot of life. Be wary of mocking your long-ago experienced self.

"I must have walked all the way back to Marty's, because I distinctly remember walking along Great Jones Street in the hustle-jumble of lower Manhattan – you know, trucks loading, idling, people tucking themselves into corners – and then I was on Broadway and Park South and up as the sun set, and how the light just flashed in the slits down the streets as I walked up the avenue. You know, you do not really see the sunset in Manhattan away from the Hudson, the buildings block it, but I was getting these block-by-block flashes off the river as I walked. So I am back at

Tudor City at Marty's apartment, and it's maybe only five o'clock, drive time. So I turn on the radio to one of the local stations and make some coffee and I am in a bit of a trance.

"They were talking on the radio about the man who self-immolated. His name was Roger Allen LaPorte, he was involved with the Catholic Worker Movement, he was twenty-two years old. They were recapping how just a week before another young man had burned himself alive as a protest against Vietnam. Keep in mind, this was 1965. Early days yet. The November 2nd self-immolation had been in Washington. The dead man was a young father by the name of Norman Morrison who had gone to Washington, carrying his baby daughter to the Pentagon. And he positioned himself directly below the office window of Robert McNamara, the Secretary of Defense, and he burned himself alive under McNamara's window."

"I never heard of any guy killing himself in front of the Pentagon," Andy said.

"McNamara looked out his window and saw a person burning alive."

"And the baby?"

"Hang on, hang on," she said. "Man, feature it: Secretary of Defense Robert McNamara looks out his office window and sees an individual dying for peace, by fire. Yeah. He was a Quaker. So the radio guy is talking about this Norman Morrison the Quaker, who had self-immolated exactly one week before, on November 2nd, and now on this day, November 9th, came the young Catholic to the United Nations." Vivienne shifted her upper torso, taking Andy's upper forearm in her two hands. "So here is the part: they were talking about this on the radio, comparing and contrasting the two suicides in one week to protest the war in Vietnam, and saying how the one at the Pentagon was a young father who brought his little baby girl and handed her off to someone standing nearby. The baby's name was Emily. And the way the radio jock said Emily sounded all drawn out like a spook on a phone demanding ransom using a voice distorter. Emmmmilllyyyy. 'Did that joint I took from that guy have acid laced in it?'"

Vivienne let go of Andy's arm and stretched her legs, laughing. "Today,

I might say, 'Did I just have a mini-stroke?' Okay maybe no Purple Owsley, maybe this is a local New York avant-garde radio show, because the guy's voice was getting slower and slower and then it stopped. Oh my God, I thought, did they just assassinate the DJ?"

Andy swept her up to sit with him back on the pillows. He lit two more smokes, saying, "What the hell was going on, babe?" His *babe* was so soft and sweet it could have been local peace on the prowl, purring.

She closed her eyes, seeing the dark of memory.

"All the lights went out in Marty's apartment. I looked out the window: the East River looked mighty dark. The city looked dark. The DJ came back on and said there had been a blackout, that the subways had stopped mid-station, people were trapped in elevators, and... Then he was cut off again and never came back. The city was dark, the radio was dead. You know what it was?"

"Tell me," Andy said, putting her head on his shoulder.

"It was too much, you know," she said. "You cannot bear it, but you know what? You can. They say we use only what is it, ten per cent of our brains?"

"Thirty, maybe," Andy said. "My buddy Sean used to say, 'Like one per cent.'"

"But how much of our hearts do we use?" Vivienne jumped up, went to the hotel room window, looked down to the garden. A man sat on a wooden bench with his head in his hands, leaning forward, his elbows almost at his knees. She grabbed her camera off the side table and took a shot of the posture of grief, unmistakable even three hundred feet up. "Information does not make a heart," she said, with her back to Andy who watched her from the bed. "Information makes a database. A nation is not a database, a nation is a heart. New York was blacked out, and a man had lit himself on fire to claim peace as his true lover just before the lights went out on Manhattan. My brain says they were not connected, but my heart, honey, knew they were. They were connected inside me. War was my kismet, it was my work marriage. I had to go back."

Andy got up, turned Vivienne's chin to him and kissed her with tenderness.

"So out I went into Blackout New York. I walked for hours, and I mean hours, and my camera took pictures of the dark, I mean really dark. A blackout doesn't black out everything, it just brings us back in time. New York was like pictures you see of the 1920s. Like some old George Raft movie, like what's that one with Glenn Ford where he goes into a bar and he's all mixed up with some dame and the music playing is the same music that tormented Glenn Ford in *Gilda*…?"

"The one where Lee Marvin throws the hot coffee on Monroe?" Andy asked.

"I used to think that, too," Vivienne said. "But it wasn't Monroe, it was Gloria Grahame, and he never threw the coffee."

"He did so, I saw it. *The Big Heat.* It's my favourite movie. Lee Marvin takes that coffee pot, like the one she was pouring from downstairs when I met you, and Lee Marvin throws it at okay Gloria Grahame and scars her all up. Yeah, that's right, Glenn Ford is the cop. He's gone on her, he wants to help her after that coffee fiasco."

"You think you see the coffee thrown, you think you see the coffee in the air, you think you see the hot coffee hit her, but none of that is in the movie. It is so brilliantly edited, they make you think you saw what is not there. It's magic, baby."

"We'll get it out sometime. I'll show you."

"I'll show you water in Death Valley," she said.

"Tell me about the dark," Andy said. "Did you meet Lee Marvin ordering a latte?"

"I wish. That soldier can put his stripes on my pussy any day of the week. What is a man? Lee Marvin is a man. He was wounded in war, young, you could tell. Nobody has eyes so blue unless there is a story."

"I have blue eyes," Andy said. "Or so they say."

"So, the blackout. I went into Grand Central Station. There were all these business guys who couldn't get the train home, holed up on benches, trying to sleep. It was like a prophecy of hard times to come. I took a lot of pics of men in overcoats, lines of them talking on the pay phones, sitting in the booths. They say, 'It's never too late.' I say, it is always too late. Who knew these phone booths would be relics in no time? I walked back up East 43rd to Tudor City, my heart was full of the world. Everywhere I went I was having another small lifetime in one day. I was so hungry to live, and I could not stop noshing."

Andy kissed the back of her neck and she did not protest it.

"I was alone, I was always a bit of a solitary bird. I was just eighteen, and I had captured two men in film self-immolating, one the Vietnamese monk in his sixties, the other the young Catholic in his twenties, and I kept walking, and I sat in the Great Northeast Blackout, and I looked at the dark East River. And I thought about Poe and Whitman, and how Whitman came to the soldiers who had been wounded, in the hospitals in Washington, during the Civil War, how the poet came to the most wounded, the most distressed, the men who knew their dressings would not be on a living man in the morning. And how Whitman read poetry to the men all night. He came and sat at the bed of a man who was dying, and they both knew that the poetry Whitman read low in the soldier's ear was the last poetry the young man would ever hear in his short sweet existence on earth. Maybe that is all you can do. I thought of Walt Whitman, living in Washington for a couple of years, and going nightly to the hospitals, and how he was a salve and a balm. I looked out at the East River, and I thought about how poetry might be the twin brother of journalism. And maybe nothing else much matters in this world. You look it right in the face, and you frame it. I thought about how much we need the poet-nurses."

Andy drew her back to the bed. He stroked her hair. He held her in his arms.

"The next day, check it out, I went to the MoMA, and I saw *Guernica* for the first time. My head was exploding. It had been at the MoMA for years, okay? Just an hour's flight from Toronto. But I came to it in just the right time. I had been primed to see *Guernica* by the preceding day. The lies of war you figure out young, but the science of war, the pimp science had become, pimping out humans like rats… I knew nothing, yet, about Franco. I thought *Guernica* was about the Second World War. I did not know when I first laid eyes on the painting that I was in a moment of absolute clarity. I knew *gar nichts*, baby. I did not know that Guernica was a city. I did not know that Guernica was in Spain. I did not know that Guernica was Basque. I did not know that Franco offered to exterminate the people of Guernica as a gift to ingratiate himself with Hitler and Mussolini. Who knew they thought Franco was a pathetic little suck-up wannabe, or that Hitler privately called Franco a pig with verbal diarrhea? But they found Franco useful. After all, he had offered to wipe out one of his own Spanish cities just to impress them. Offering his own people as a test run for World War Two, a lab experiment, the first one in human history, and the experiment was *could an entire civilian population be eliminated by saturation bombing from the air?* Guernica was a sacrifice offered not in the mysteries of faith, but in the creeps of evil. I did not know any of this when I was looking at Picasso's painting *Guernica* at the MoMA when I was eighteen. I sat alone on a bench, inhaling the horses.

"I knew nothing of what it must have felt like to Picasso, a fifty-five-year-old Spaniard, living in exile in Paris, to hear that in his home country, the city of Guernica had been destroyed as a bombing experiment. Picasso was, at that time, facing a deadline: he had agreed, that year of 1937, in March to create a work of art for the Spanish Pavilion of the Paris International Exhibition. Two months went by. Then on April 26th, the Nazis bombed Guernica. Five days later Picasso began *Guernica*. His skilled heart was on fire. He painted fast and large. The painting was ready for the exhibition opening on July 12th. A masterwork in less than three months. I thought Picasso was French. Did it matter? The book learning came later. The painting, in person, destroyed me." Vivienne shivered. She put his T-shirt on.

"I did not know that Picasso's lover when he was painting *Guernica* was Dora Maar. I did not know there were women photographers. I had no role models, boo hoo, so what?" She sat between his legs.

"So in the same room on the third floor of MoMA was a series of photographs Dora Maar had taken of him painting *Guernica*. I did not know that Dora Maar was a celebrated photographer before she met Picasso. Why are women always so damn hung up on how Picasso did the ladies wrong? How come you hear nothing about how Dora Maar was legendary with a camera when she met Picasso? She was Henrietta Theodora Marković, born in Paris, raised in Buenos Aires, Argentina. I did not know that she spoke Spanish to him when they first met, which allured him. Dora Maar, well-known photographer in Paris, teaches painter Pablo Picasso how to use the photographic image in his work while she documents him painting the great *Guernica,* suggesting changes, being his visual editor. You know, none of that is secret information. I do not know why women like so much to moan and groan about how ill-treated the muse is – maybe the muse was the mentor – Dora Maar was. Maar mentored Picasso in the 1930s.

"The man on fire at the UN, New York in a blackout, seeing *Guernica* for the first time, Dora Maar. All of it within walking distance of each other. I was etched, I felt it physically, honey, my future was – SSSSSZZZZed – branded into me. Art was my corner, my safe place. The pictures were waiting. All I had to do was turn up. And always carry a camera."

She turned around, faced Andy, took off the T-shirt and put her feet up on the headboard.

"You want a coda?" she asked. "So there is this beautiful woven tapestry based on *Guernica*. And that homage to Picasso's painting has hung for many years at the United Nations. It has been part of the long-time decor there. So anyway, the *Guernica* tapestry is hanging at the UN as per usual, and it's February of 2003, when George W. Bush is trying to lay down the sales pitch for going to war with Iraq, for the invasion. They're going to make a speech at the UN about this; Colin Powell and John Negroponte are going to talk on TV. So guess what? The White House demands that the anti-war tapestry of Pablo Picasso's *Guernica* be covered up with a white cloth before the cameras roll. Because God forbid someone watching them shill war should be distracted by seeing great art tell the story of a civilian bombing in the background behind them.

'Oh, hey Joe, they're talking about Baghdad, but isn't that the Basque city of Guernica right behind them? Hmmm.' And they did it, they got away with that, too. The UN – what else is new? – caves and covers up the *Guernica* tapestry so Bush can have a white sheet covering up history. A man burns himself alive to show his love for peace, another man covers up great art to sell war. You pick your choice."

"I pick you," Andy said.

"Sorry," Vivienne said. "Love, I am taken."

"I'm all right if you hurt me. I can do that," he said. "Vivienne. Reconsider me."

"Oh, baby," she kissed his cheek. "It's not like that."

But there was something here, he listened to her. He paid attention, he allowed himself to be moved by what had moved her. She felt Andy inhaling her. Her husband, Johnny, was happy if she was in the environs, Johnny was happy if he could hear her footsteps in the house as he went about his business of writing, Johnny was content if he could miss her for dinner and leave her a love note. Johnny did not want to hear about the bad times or the sad times or the damage done. Not in detail. Johnny was family. Family wanted you back, safe, home. Family, in truth, did not want stories. Unconditional love was happy with you just being.

Just being was not enough for Vivienne Pink. The secret, unhidden to her, but hidden to Johnny, her husband, was that she wanted to tell the stories behind the pictures she took. This Andy was her brief companion in solace. Never underestimate the power you have, as a man, if you listen with sincerity to a woman. A woman can tell, and the power is intensely sexual. To be understood, to be heard is the greatest aphrodisiac on this wretched Earth.

Vivienne was in the thrilling vortex that this was not right, this thing, this boy, this man, these feelings. It was not right to remember how it felt to be listened to, and then loved right after. You walk anywhere for this. You walk through the new trails. You bivouac strangely, then in the midnight hour, you leave that safe dark, and you move along where no one has gone, you head up the slope, if only, once more, to see the feeling world. Andy was up out of the bed, putting the T-shirt and his jeans on again. "You want to go get coffee?" he said.

"Are you nuts? Go. You have to go. I'm working." She did not know why she said this. It was not what she felt. It was what she said at other times when things got too heated with subjects. "This can no way happen."

"I've got news for you," Andy said, all cheery, back on the bed, cross-legged. "It's already happened. Enjoy yourself."

"I have to go to Death Valley."

"Come to Life Valley with me." Not a bit of it made sense. He was leaving for Iraq, a different death valley. She was married.

"Kiss me," she said.

"I'm going to think about you every day," he said. "Will you write me every night? I might be able to phone you sometimes, if I can."

She panicked to hear him talk as if there was anything between them. This sudden deep connection made her need to get him away from her. She did not want him to go. And so, he had to go. She had to betray the moment. "You cannot phone me. I will not write you. What happened here was business, work, a mission. I'll pay you money if you want me to. Okay?"

Andy – how could she ever forget it? – did not move to leave. He, instead, unbuttoned his jeans, his back to her, his face at the big glass window. His jeans pooled on the floor. A small pistol fell out of a pocket. You could not carry a camera on the casino floor, but you could carry a firearm. "What is that?" Vivienne said, shooting a pic of the pistol resting on the jeans. Andy walked over to the bedside table. He put the pistol beside the hotel phone. He stood at the edge of the bed.

"The plan, like I said about my buddy Sean, was Seany takes that smashed up yellow Commander to the shop. He gets back to Fort Bliss. Okay. He leaves me a voicemail: 'Andy, they say I'm in Texas. It's a damn trick. It's not Texas. I don't know how, but it's fucking Afghanistan. They kept me up for three weeks, now they're fucking with my mind. The whole thing is bogus, it's a damn trick, I love you, man.' He goes in the shower and hangs himself."

"When was this?" Vivienne asked, reaching for his hand.

"What day is it today?" He got back on the bed.

"Day? Wednesday, maybe Wednesday. I think the 25th was yesterday."

"Yeah, yesterday. Christmas Day. Just like James Brown. Comes the day of reckoning. No way I'm going to let Sean have a pauper's funeral."

Andy's eyes were right in front of her but they were occluded again with the micro-blackouts blowing in.

"And you want to know what the best part was? Sean slept with Caroline," he said, bringing Vivienne into his arms, as if to console her with his own loss. She angled her flesh against his.

"Your Sean? Who hung himself?"

"Yeah – my fucking Sean. Only my Sean was her Sean it turns out. Right behind my back, right in front of my face."

Everything had been betrayed. Everything, everyone. Every baby atom inhaled the air of betrayal. This was the century of betrayal. "Did you tell her you knew?"

"No way. She acted like it was peachy-dory. Her and me – Caroline and Andy – was a lie the day she died. She died thinking I was her fool. You know what?"

"Tell me." Vivienne moved closer to him.

"I was her fool. But him – Sean? My best buddy. We went through missions, then he fucks me."

"Is that why he hanged himself?" she asked. Andy looked at her as if she were an alien.

"Hanged himself – over that? Come on, I thought you were a sharp cookie." He ran a finger down her neck.

"I'm not seeing it."

"Our commanding officer left us with no water, no supplies, shit for vests – a fly could get in that fake foam they call bulletproof. I could look at you and be inside that vest. I don't want to talk about it. Sean saw it before any of us. Those blowhards up on high? They were granting us the divine privilege of carrying out how they did not know a rat's fuck about what they were doing in Iraq. I volunteered to go over there and fight for

Dick Cheney's right to be an ignoramus. When did he ever lay his body on the line? When did he ever band with a group of fighting men? He's got his pedal to the metal. Yeah, Dickie DUI. Driving Under the Influence of Shit for Brains."

They lay back on the bed together, sitting up against the mounds of pillows. Andy lit two smokes, gave one to Vivienne.

"I got a good telephoto shot of Dick Cheney one time when I was working in El Salvador," Vivienne said. "Cheney comes down to San Salvador, hangs out with the head of the Salvadoran death squad, Roberto D'Aubuisson. So, they're having a club sandwich in the coffee shop of the Camino Real hotel. I'm a couple of tables away. That was back in the days when Cheney dressed like the guy who the guy from the used car lot hires to torch the joint: too bright blue shirt, cheap striped tie, light blue sports jacket with the back drooping. He had brown hair then. That was the day the death squad had a contract to kill a bearded US AID worker in the hotel coffee shop. But they came in and executed a bearded Jesuit priest by mistake. I call my pic of Cheney and D'Aubuisson *He may be Murder Incompetent, but he's our Murder Incompetent*."

Andy let Cheney dissolve back into the fog of patriotic lies, and said, "I don't know why my Sean killed himself, at Bliss. Baby, I am feeling kind of abandoned." Andy's eyes went across the latitude line to another desert. "Your buddies over there aren't the war, in a way. It's a place out of time it's so real. You're in the minor chords all the time. I was with Sean in a promise. I'm going to get back home, if I ever get back home, and at least my Sean will know, like you said, my soundtrack. How can the music hang itself? I loved that man. He was better than a brother. I get over there tomorrow, Sean will be gone for good."

Andy threw his lit smoke on the floor. He grabbed her into his body, wrapping her in his arms. He stroked her head. "I could love you. That would be okay."

"Okay's not an option now," she said. There was no *ma'am* anymore. He was abandoning the protocols so he could be at his ease with her. Listening was a form of healing. It might be a form of honour, too. Vivienne had seen how war counterintuitively brought out the compassionate side of men. It had to. If you are counting on your brother warrior to save you, to have your back, then it was a form of love you each had to have, for each other's flesh. The love warriors have for each other is outside of gender or sex; it is eternal love, love for which we have no word. Love in the action towards your closest co-operant saviour. She could feel the wound Andy had, that his saviour-buddy Sean had gone and said the whole enterprise was bogus. And now Andy's Sean was gone.

Andy stroked Vivienne's neck scar. "Let me nurse you," he said. He was wounded, and he kept comforting her. He pecked her the way a bird that has known damage pecks a new damaged arrival. He put his ear to her heart. "Let me take care of you."

"I am not someone anybody takes care of," she said. It was a statement of fact. It had the Baby Pink decree in it. Andy kept his head at her heart.

"Let your feathers down." He was stroking her face. "Here, we'll ease you down, down, fold into me, no more nightmare feathers." He set her into weeping. He folded her in. "Hush now, hush down, the battle will never be won. No one wins. Down, down, ease your wings down."

From her thighs came a weeping up through her pussy, and her ribs hurt, constricted. "I love you, regardless," was Johnny's love for her. But *regardless* made a kingdom of stories jammed up behind her rib cage. Andy made her feel like a bird on a curb, with so many high low songs yet to sing.

"Little one, ease those wings, sleep now. Hush. Girl, lay low, lay low, come to earth, be low in the pillows, hush. Don't go yet, don't make me leave, let me put you down to sleep. Hush your eyes, little one, little dove girl. Would you just give me one more kiss I can stow securely until I see you again?" And she was asleep in his arms, and he fell asleep.

HE WOKE UP, lit a cigarette and stood pulling the curtains closed. Vivienne, still in half-sleep, reached for her camera on the side table, ready to be aimed. Her conflict art was anticipation. She pushed the pistol into the frame, and snapped a quiet pic of Andy, the pic she had been waiting for: Andy cupping his hands around the smoke, the match illuminating his face as if it were the age of Rembrandt and this was a candle casting gold on his skin, a moment caught, a nonchalant last night in town shot, an offhand look of a man fully and entirely aware he was being photographed. A man with the skill set children have, but do not know it, to play unselfconsciously and allow themselves to be photographed, not aping for the lens, accepting it as part of the life.

The man in the photograph on the way to or from undress, at dusk, in contemplation with a cigarette in a room with a side table, a phone, a gun. This was the shot Vivienne had hoped for, even though she planned one of his back. Those ones were good, even excellent, but this photograph she shot while half-asleep was the one, because it had in it the intentionality of the photographer to capture her subject who was being damn intentional in his lighting that smoke and holding that light. It was the detour you adopted as your intention.

"I need to take a shower," Vivienne said.

That was it?

"I could write you," he said.

"Thanks for the photographs." She went into the bathroom, closed the door, got in the shower and wasted water all over her face.

When Vivienne came out of the steam, she heard the door to the room close. Sitting up against a pillow on the bed was the white T-shirt.

8

OVER THE RAINBOW

THEY SAY THAT the infant in his first transitions sees his arms and his legs as lies, in that unformed early perception of himself. He does not understand *self*, he sees only the glimpsed sections of his being as unconnected strange falsehoods. A man torn apart by a woman can feel just like an infant without speech: dematerialized arms, legs, eyes floating in woozy unfocused space. Only the infant doesn't know how crazy it is. The infant is in a Paul Klee painting he's making with pretty little feces. The man is a man saying, "I am in a Paul Klee painting, and I don't know how to get out."

Behold the arrival of the jugglers. They were juggling Andy's body parts. He tapped a plastic bucket sitting on top of a woman's head. "Ma'am, do I have skin? I think I might be burlap."

She took the long straw out of her mouth with which she was sipping a two-foot tall drink. "He's super-cute, don't you think, Artie?" Talking to the magenta-coloured drink, which had a corsage on its rim.

The truths were all in play. Where was the centre? His brain, concussed in an Iraqi explosion, red-shifted and blue-shifted astronomical rays. Andy walked up the sloping hill beside Lago di Como, a ten-acre lake, where the water had been taught to dance to music. At the top of the hill he came to the ochre facade of the Bellagio. Inside, a canopy of glass flowers hung suspended from the ceiling, the artist Dale Chihuly's masterwork *Fiori Di Como,* two thousand pieces of undulating glass blooms in deep blues, verdant greens, scarlet and brilliant sun yellows. Where were the bivouacs if there was no centre? The world was a mysterious affront. He went up the few wide stairs to Petrossian Bar tucked in the lobby with little balustrade railings to look out on the passing parade. His armpits were soaking wet. He ordered a Knockando and knocked it back. An old cat was at the piano, pushing the ivories and ebonies with ease through "Over the Rainbow."

Andy looked at his own long fingers around the copper-coloured liquid. He opened and closed a fist three times. He sat back in the cozy chair, listening. Those happy little bluebirds flew like unmanned drones over the rainbow, making direct hits on the hearts of men. Andy called for more single malt Knockando. He hugged himself tight around the ribs, looking behind him. He got up and walked the periphery of the Petrossian outlook, holding the balustrade railing. He eyeballed the inside bar. He came back to his table. He moved the three other chairs closer to his chair. He sat down, hands open on the table. He looked behind him again.

He was disturbed earth, as disturbed as any blown-up roadside shoulder. But he had organized his disturbances so they did not have to disturb him much. Things were set before she came along, and like intimate psychoanalysis the photographic process of being a subject had moved things around inside him, a feral thing war counted on, but he knew that one, and he did not know this one.

A jolly threesome waved some bills at the piano man and asked for an encore of those bluebirds. The tuxedoed gent, old as the Earth's crust pressed the piano keys with his nicotine-stained fingers. Andy said, "Fuck her. Ah, you know, you gotta love her. Who does she think she is? Sorry if I didn't. Well, screw her, then."

The buxom middle-aged brunette waitress came over to his table. "Can I get you…?"

Andy talked to his empty glass. "And then you know what she did? She made me take my clothes off. Huh. And then she took pictures of me."

"Sir, can I get you another Knockando?"

Andy looked up at her, regaining some poise. "You can, ma'am." Then, slipping back, "I believe it's time to go."

"Sir, was there anything wrong with your drink? I can…"

"Fine, then have it your way. And you know what else? I liked it. That's the fuck of it all. I liked it. She was the enemy and I liked it." He looked at the waitress as if he had just seen her. "Ma'am, thank you very much. You know you could really hide some serious weaponry in those glass flowers. Yeah, fine if you want. Sure. Another Knockando. I'm in Iraq tomorrow."

"Thank you for your service," the waitress said.

She went away. Andy got up and moved the three vacant chairs closer, tipping them forward onto the table. He rubbed his left arm above the elbow. He rubbed his jaw on the left side. He held himself. He closed his eyes. He rocked himself, humming "Over the Rainbow." He reached into his Levi's for his wallet, took out a hundred dollar bill, put it on the table, got up, came back to the table, left another fifty dollars and drifted left along the carpeted promenade, buoyed along by the casino crowds in their forced holiday chatter. He did not appear to notice that Val Gold was sitting in one of the chairs, reading a newspaper. Andy went through the doors to a balustrade lookout over a green dusk garden.

9

CHEMICAL DONNY

THE BELLAGIO GARDEN was a lush Mediterranean oasis. Orange trees and lemon trees, tall cypress spires, cold pools, hot pools, whirlpools, chaises. In the last rags of sundown, hotel guests lay in their sunglasses, sleeping. A woman using a long lynx coat as a blanket lay on a chaise with sunglasses almost as big as her face, bare feet with blue toenails, her hair grey and blond like another fur animal tumbling down into the fur coat. Beside her, a man in an ochre field coat, his bent legs covered by white towels wrapped mummy-style, was asleep with his mouth open, a hardcover book held aloft in his hands. *Hollywood Station*, Joseph Wambaugh.

A man you'd identify to police as average-looking, average height, dark hair, mid-thirties, slid down the side of a big empty swimming pool. He held out a small camera, and with a bright smile he waved at the lens. He put the camera down on the poolside, and he stared across the garden. A lonely traveller with that sad holiday feeling coming over his private face. The civic twilight was disappearing the mountains.

Andy went back through the glass doors. Opposite sat the Bellagio Gallery of Fine Art. Exhibit on today: *Ansel Adams: America*. Andy crossed the lobby. Inside the gallery gift shop, Val watched him from behind the glass walls. Val browsed the art cards and bought one by Matisse, *Pineapple and Anemones*. After Andy had paid and gone inside to see the Ansel Adams exhibit, Val bought a ticket, came to the door of the small exhibit space, looked at Andy's back, the walls of black-and-white photos and the equipment, and left.

Andy stood beside a camera as tall as Michael Jordan. The legend said Ansel Adams carried this very camera up into the Eastern Sierra, into Yosemite, into Death Valley on his photographing trips there. A camera with one of those old-timey capes, a tent you got under to look out on the world.

There was a letter from the great Georgia O'Keeffe to Ansel Adams, handwritten, dated December 22, 1938.

Would you drive down and spend two or three days in Death Valley with me on my way west?...a week or two... It seems this is the time of year for Death Valley... Hastily Georgia.

Georgia and Ansel in Death Valley. December.

Andy came close to Georgia O'Keeffe's handwriting: she wrote the word *two* with such a long crossbar through the *t* that the stroke across was ten or twelve times longer than the height of the *t*. And all her *t*'s were written that way with that extraordinarily long stroke line, flourished across the tiny vertical stick. Like the land where she was living. And what did Georgia and Ansel do when they went to Death Valley? There was nothing on the wall to say. Were they just art pals, visual colleagues or more? Georgia the painter, age fifty-one, invited Ansel the photographer, age thirty-six, to come on an art trip to Death Valley, before the Second World War.

A photograph that looked like whales' backs in a light and dark sea, as Andy came closer, turned out to be: *Sand Dunes, Sunrise, Death Valley National Monument, California, c. 1948.* Ansel Adams climbing like a pack mule with a camera as big as a man, a camera Sherpa with his heavy load climbing sand like mountains, a camera soldier with his painter comrade, two masters of reduction and the holy in the wild, creeping in the dark desert to set up for the approaching adversary: the first light of day.

Georgia O'Keeffe and Ansel Adams...*Dunes...Death Valley...1948...*

Vivienne said she was going to Death Valley tomorrow. Back in ancient days at the coffee shop, she had leaned across him to point the way there on the weather map. Death Valley and Mosul, Iraq, were on the same latitude.

Andy came to another photograph.

A road shining in the late day or early morning, a wide curve, a white road in the middle of outback trees and cliffs. Andy got close: the road had black tire marks in the middle of the white shine; those herringbone marks of a crime scene. Andy stepped to the side and the road became water, the tire marks became ripples in the water. Which was it? Road or river? A canoe could paddle that road, a truck ride that river.

"There are no people," a voice behind Andy said. A piping voice, a bit nasal.

"*Liebe*," a second voice said. Lower, more guttural. "The people are behind the photographs, they have the security watching you. *Komm*, let's eat."

Andy did not turn around. He rocked back and forth in front of the black-and-white photograph of river or road; he felt elevated by his agitation. How did someone make a thing to make a stranger feel so much? Was Ansel Adams courting him from the grave?

ANDY WALKED UP the Strip, trying to turn the night into Somewhere Town.

Out on the dry washes of the metropolis, old boxing champs in striped pyjamas sparred with dust at the corner of spare change and concussion. Bent to unknown music, the street figures bowed to the hidden gods of the pavement. Flightless angels flapped their armpits as if to rise to the night clouds. Who knew that the real margin of America existed right in its dry centre? Who knew that when you enter a plane, they are preparing you for the desert environs, where those dry hands will peel on peeling sidewalks, where your palms will become exfoliated by sunny drought, where your lips will ache in dry furrows and your epidermis will slough off like parchment? Andy felt like paint, like someone was painting him right now, a white sketch on a chalkboard. Vivienne had made him feel like a paradise inhabitant. The kings of empire walked dethroned in tin foil coronas; they wore barbed wire belts; they wore vests of old war headlines. Even the night stars had to peek through the hotel towers; even starlight was homeless these days.

Behold, the jugglers did dismantle sanity.

A man in a rickety wheelchair sat under a green glow by a closed Hertz rental. He wore a piece of rope around his waist. He wore a cardboard apron that announced in block letters: JUNGLE ROT. NO LOOKING. An arrow pointed to his crotch. He had wooden arms, a rough olive-brown pullover, leg stumps. The night was as dry as the inside of a plane.

Andy walked on, past yellow and red discount liquor lettering, past a short building saying ALARMCO SINCE 1950, the time 5:51 beside an iconic Marlboro man. Andy slid down a wall and slept. The underbelly alley was never far from the dark limo windows.

Andy opened his eyes. Why had this Vivienne chosen him? She had tricked him with her camera. She had made him want more of it. She had dark secrets.

High beams came at him.

An indigo Buick Riviera stopped in front of him. A severely white man sat at the wheel. "Son, do me a favour. Get off the street. There's murder police in the vicinity. You'll be safe with me. Climb in."

Andy got in.

They rose up out of the glittering desert valley and left behind the settlement called Las Vegas, glitter in a dark valley. They rose in elevation, coming up through the narrow canyon to reach level ground, flatter, higher and empty as Europe in a long, dark night in wartime.

The severely white man said he was heading up to fix some munitions at Hawthorne Army Depot. He had a job to do regarding decommissioning some of the weapons of mass destruction that had been tested, the mustard gases were his specialization.

"There's Cold Creek," he said, waving over to the west. "Did a long latte there, myself."

The man's cheeks caved in. His fingers were long and yellow. They held on to the wheel at four and eight o'clock. The wheel was glowing. The man wore a shirt in yellow, two sizes too big for his body. His face hung in folds, too. His eyes were set back so far you saw only sockets when he turned to look at you. He had on a brown dusty cowboy hat that he promptly took off: his hair was black and white, a salt-and-pepper wetness, laid stringily on a scaly scalp. It was desert cold, that desert night drop in temperatures. The severely white man had no heat on in the car, but he was breathing heavy and sweating.

"We're heading down, hold on," he said to Andy. They pitched down an incline, Andy holding the dashboard with his right hand. The glove compartment swung open: inside was a grenade.

Andy said, "You're kidding me."

"Don't worry, it's harmless." The car tipped forward on a deeper angle. It was black pitch on black void, the beams lit nothing. An amber dot in the sky came snaking towards them. The light got tall and squeezed-in, flew right at them and passed. A car. Even at night, the bent optics of the desert ruled you. "There's the sand dunes out there if you're interested," the severely white man said, taking his right hand off the wheel and pointing across Andy's body, veering with his left hand around a quick curve in the road. "You're in Death Valley now. Feel like a bite?"

The headlights shone on a green sign with white lettering: SEA LEVEL.

Andy looked at his watch. Liar: it said 8:27. They pulled up beside a double gas pump. It was a couple feet from STOVEPIPE WELLS GENERAL STORE. A tall man in black leather came out, letting the screen door slam. Six more leathered individuals came out. They got on their Harleys and rode off, making a gold-lit chain into the night.

Andy and the severely white man went into the store. "You want an Eskimo Pie?" the man asked, putting his head into a big freezer by a big coffee urn.

"Sure," Andy said. Why not? Down to freezing, no coat, why not get an Eskimo Pie?

"Hey, well if it isn't Chemical Donny," a round woman at the cash said. "You finished getting rid of those WMDs, Don?"

"Not yet, Charlene. I've still got two thousand igloos to dispose of. Today's paper come in?"

"No paper from LA 'til next week. Monday is a holiday, didn't you hear, due to President Ford being buried. So if you want today's news, Don, wait until next Tuesday."

"Fine with me. No news is the same as – news. Take care, Charlene. See you at the next igloo inauguration. You coming up?"

"Not on your life, Don. I got way too sick last time. I think I inhaled what they're hunting down Saddam for."

"I hear he's going to get all hung up on New Year's. Now that's something worth toasting. Have one on me. Tell them Don sent you."

"Thanks, Don. This one of yours?"

"No, this is... What did you say your name was, son?"

"Andy." Why lie?

"Andy, meet Charlene, anything you need, right, sister?"

"My pleasure," she said, extending her hand across the counter. His hand had Eskimo Pie on it, bits of chocolate and wet vanilla transferring to her palm. "See you Don, Happy 2007."

"I'll be up in Deseret come January. There's a ton of nerve gas to burn. It's slow going in Rush Valley."

Andy and Chemical Donny got into the car by the general store and drove across the gravel and the narrow highway road a five second journey and up an incline and parked. RECEPTION said a sign at a storefront-looking spot. To the left up a short incline was a timbered Western-style eatery: WAGON WHEEL. "Come on," Don said. "I could eat a horse."

Inside, benches lined the entry where future eaters, hopeful, sat. Don walked to the podium. A shiny-headed smiling round man stood behind the podium. "Here he is. I thought you forgot me. Hey, Louise, trouble's back in town."

Everybody seemed to know the severely white man called Don or Chemical Donny, congenial in his lankiness, still sweating, but a popular figure in a dark remote night stopover place.

"Eugene, it's been dogs' years," Don said. "How's the husband?"

"Elliot? Elliot's good, Elliot's fine, he's over in Pomona with Mom. He put his back out, she put her back out, I'm supposed to go down Friday and get them. How's by you?"

"The same. Got to go to Utah and light a fire under some of those men there, get that chemical junk burned off before some of those kids blow themselves up. Gene, how's about a table for me and my friend Andy here?"

"In twenty minutes cook is closing the kitchen, we'll call it half an hour." Eugene led them to a curved banquette in a corner. Andy slid in. It was 8:40 p.m. He had met Vivienne only seven hours ago. Don handed Andy a menu.

Here he was in another restaurant with another stranger, in another desert, original desert with a small way station. What was he going to do about tomorrow? Did he even know the loopholes as to AWOL status? Did he care? He had thirty days until he was classified *deserter.* Did he have a determined intent not to return? What was his intention? Once upon a time he might have been classified *undistinguished*, but now they had made a new deserter category, *accomplished*, for those who had suffered a trauma.

"How far is it back to Vegas?" Andy asked Don.

"Back to Vegas so soon, son? I barely got you to Death Valley."

"I don't know. I was wondering."

"I am going over the mountain tonight, I might change my mind and go over in the morning. I was due up to burn off those weapons of mass destruction, but I might go see some guys I know looking into putting some of that mustard gas into cellphones; you sell them to the terrorists, they try and set off the bomb, the phone gases them. Well, anyways, I got some people to see over in Lone Pine, consult about explosive devices. They're doing a movie on the big kerfuffle back there in the '20s, you might have heard of it, when the locals, well when LA stole the Owens Valley water. I used to rope a bit you know with Rex Allen. I was the bad hombre you saw pushing that horse to gallop like the dickens away from that sheriff's posse, then they went back and shot the posse, and it was us, the same guys. They'd shoot us in different hats running after ourselves from the last footage, oh it was fun. Course it was no fun when they kidnapped that water. Those were shoot-'em-ups for real, I'll tell you that."

"*Chinatown*," Andy said. "My favourite movie."

"Mine too. What do you know? I bet you say that to all the girls."

Andy put his palms flat on the table. He pushed his body up. He sat down. Chemical Donny kept talking.

"They came up from Los Angeles, those sons of bitches. They came in, you know, posing as surveyors and guesstimators working in the locals' interest. They cheesed them out of their homes and their water rights. They sucked the valley dry. You talk to anybody there, it began in 1902. Son, it might as well have begun in 2002. That water wound is ever fresh in the Owens Valley." Thin white Don sat back into the leatherette half-booth. "They need me to consult, about how you blow things up without blowing yourself up in the process. They're calling this movie they're making *Water War.*"

"Kind of like drought noir, you might say," said Andy.

10

KING UBU

"AND I WILL tell you something," Don said, "the people of the Owens Valley, they fought the good fight in that water war, and it was one, it was a war for survival. Those crooks from LA bought the land and abducted all the goodness out of her. Years of plentiful water flowed down to LA. The year was 1924. The men of the Owens Valley had had enough. Down they came from Independence; they veered west into the Alabama Hills. There lay the water gates, the Alabama Gates as they were known there. The men walked to the gates and basically opened them, turning the wheels to let the water return to the desert, the Owens River water, like prodigal water returned over land to Owens Lake. They repatriated their own damn water.

"And up from Los Angeles Mayor Mulholland sent armed police to take back the water gates from the Owens Valley men. The local sheriff stood the LA police down.

"Now this," Don said, motioning for the waiter with a head move, his chin up, then a brief hail salute. "This was after the locals had dynamited the aqueduct just to make a point, and after the near-lynching of an LA official the locals had kidnapped from a restaurant and put in a noose. What did they think was going to happen? You steal the water from under a farmer, you steal that farmer's life."

A small man at a far corner table was holding a cardboard sign up to their waiter. Don shook his head, and went on with the water war story.

"What these Freddie Mac and Fannie Mae bums are doing today with their fancy loan packages and promises? Why they're just following suit from their daddies and their great-granddaddies from a hundred years ago. Fabricating real estate lies, dangling cash money, hurting families, closing businesses."

"Greed," said Andy.

"You want to believe it," Don said. "Anyway, it was some time, I grew up hearing the stories of the No Name Siphon when the boys dynamited her. Then they went back and dynamited again – it was June, summertime – a train of LA detectives armed with machine guns and Winchesters. How dare those farmers fight for their water? Oh they set up roadblocks, they searched cars, they had floodlights on the highway, that water war was twenty years old by the late '20s. Talk about the Roaring Twenties, the best gangsters you could find were the government water bureaucrats out of Los Angeles. Oh, that old wound is fresh up there.

"When the farms went out of business, some of those boys who knew something about riding and wrangling made a living in the pictures, which were just coming along. The movie people came up to the site of the water wars and damned if they didn't hire some of those same men who opened the Alabama Gates to be in a Hopalong Cassidy or two. I had a great-uncle got hired for *Lives of a Bengal Lancer,* right there by Lone Pine. I had a cousin of mine, used to grow apples, was out on the Olancha Dunes there as an Indian extra for *Gunga Din.* If that damned Los Angeles had never stolen the valley water, the farmers and ranchers would have been too busy working their land to play extras in the movies."

The waiter came over. Bill, Visalia, CA. "Hey Bill," Don said.

"Hey Chemical Donny," Bill said. "Ready to order?"

"Don's going to have," Don said, "your sole amandine."

"Rice or potatoes?" Bill asked.

"Rice and lots of it," Don said. "And go easy on the broccoli. That stuff'd kill a steer."

"Gotcha," Bill said. "And for you?"

"I'm not too hungry," Andy said. "A glass of house red."

"Eat, son," Don said.

"Do you do a turkey club?" Andy asked.

"I can ask Cook."

"Do," Don said. "Tell him Chemical Donny is here. Tell him we want his special turkey club, lots of fries. You good with that, Andy?"

"I'm good. Thanks." Time was weighing on him. "Hey, remember in *Rawhide* where Jack Elam holds up Susan Hayward's dress against him like he's going to put it on?"

"Sure," Don said. "I liked the part where the other guy, the more dumb one, Yancy, he sits on the bed and tries on her shoes. They didn't make a big deal about it, but those cowboys were fond of women's clothing. Yancy sure had a crush on those shoes."

"The guy who escaped from prison, Zimmerman…Zim out of New Orleans and his mother has, what was it?" Andy said, trying to remember it. "Did Mom kill the mulatto Zim married, or was it just that she disapproved? What was Zim in the clink for?"

Andy's brain was a scramble of timepieces, fragments from old movies, Vivienne.

Bill came with the sole for skinny Don, and well-built Andy got his turkey club, perfectly toasted with good-cut fries. They sat like old buddies eating fast. Men in the army, men in prison, men brought up in households with frugal moms eat fast. They eat fast, gathering their plates close to their bodies. Andy surveyed the room. At a table on the other side of the room sat a small old man. White fedora, a big-sized navy-grey sweatshirt on top, fleshy little legs stretched out under the table, cowboy boots. The little man was using his mouth dramatically to chew on his food. He waved for the female waitperson with his hand up as if he were voting in a Senate count, imperial and elfin.

"Where are we?" Andy asked.

"Where? We're in Paradise, son. We are in God's country. *And Abraham lifted up his eyes, and looked, and behold behind HIM a ram caught in a thicket by his horns: and Abraham went and took the ram, and offered him up for a burnt offering instead of his son.* We're in Stovepipe, Andy. Stovepipe Wells."

The little old elf stood up. "I am the special ambassador to Iraq!" he called to the room, opening his arms wide to receive his minions. Nobody paid much attention. They were used to crazy old guys wandering in from the old miner country in these parts.

"Guess that's the guy who fired Saddam's army," Don said. "I generally head for the hills when you meet some guy's got the word *special* in front of his title. My view? If you're so damned special, you don't need to advertise."

The special ambassador at his table for one waved a piece of meat on a fork at Eugene, who swept a new couple through from the podium and seated them. The special ambassador rose, pushed his table back and, using his meated fork as an aide to communication, began to speak. "I am in charge of public security, not the president."

"Hey, Chief Fema," called out a sturdy woman in a trucker's hat near Don and Andy, "heck of a job, buddy."

The old guy seemed oblivious to the taunt. He put his gesticulating fork down. He braced himself with the table edge, his arms thin and old, brown-spotted. He looked around the room of eaters, the way a king let out of his moated castle might. He beamed, the room was full of his subjects. "Yes, I have been personally put in charge of the public safety. It is me, it is I. I, I, I will be running the security from now on, not the president."

"No doubt," said Andy. Maybe this Dionysius in Depends could get him a deferment.

"Pre-emptive psychosis," said Don. "I've seen it. I was a medic in Laos. Lost in Laos. Yeah, that was the movie they should have made. You saw it. They went in, they came out, the jungle fever subsided, they got paralyzed. You ever read *Ubu Roi*? They go in, and they come out believing they are the puppet man they were hired to play. Ubu is a dog who thinks he is a king. Ubu is a consul who thinks he is a royal. Ubu, I will tell you, young man, is this damned real estate boom. Ubu Heights, Ubu Homes, Ubu SUVs, Ubu Hummers, it's all going to end one big shithole of pardon my French."

Chemical Donny surprised Andy. But why? He himself looked like a construction worker or a soldier – he was both – and he was an educated man, more in the tradition of the men of the GI bill, so why shouldn't this cat be brain cool? So, Chemical Donny was white as a spectre and read Alfred Jarry.

"We read *Lord Jim* at college," Andy said.

"Same difference. Some men are too civilized to take it. The factor of Patusan. The Tuan of Titwaddle. They start putting fingers on the ladies. Now you got eight staff, three of them female, and some Chief Fema comes in and they won't work with him, but they are all I got. How to keep Chief Walking Digits from getting into ladies' underwear?"

He pulled a pack of Three Castles out of his breast pocket. Andy accepted. They were wildly strong smokes.

"What you do," Don said, "is you give the poor bugger a title. Some men will shut up for as long as it takes to get the mission accomplished just because you name them special bugger. I'd rather have some puffball blowing hot air than getting into my girls' matched quim sets, right, son?"

"Lemon meringue or coconut cream?" Bill the waiter had appeared at their table.

"I didn't realize we had Pentagon royalty in the house," Andy said, raising his chin in the direction of Chief Fema.

"He said he was heading to Washington to give a speech," said Bill.

"I am going to London with my cat to meet the Queen," Don said.

"I'll carry your water," Bill said. Don and Andy chuckled.

Nevertheless, Don the severely white man stood up and applauded the special elf to the president. "Good job," Don called out. "Well done, Pepe."

Don sat down. He pulled about half the smoke into his lungs, briefly got more colour in his face than Andy had seen in hours and said, "Nothing changes, does it? Your *Lord Jim* there, son? Conrad wrote that one hundred years ago. Pilgrims off to the hajj, Muslims going to Mecca, nothing much different, won't be one hundred years from now. Abandoning the Muslim ship is going to haunt us." He mashed the cigarette stub into a glass ashtray.

The elder elf took off his white fedora, bowed from the waist, put the fedora back on his head and proceeded to wobble on his skinny pins past the podium to the exit, without paying. His waitress caught him, and Don and Andy watched the gesticulating and wallet removal and card handing over and the signing of the paper. The special elf to the duchy of Stovepipe doffed his hat and set off, perhaps to organize the security of the North Pole, and meet with ambassadors Donder and Blitzen.

ANDY WALKED UP the desert highway alone.

This was real darkness.

A roadrunner the size of Ohio ran across the sky in streaks. He was not AWOL yet. Canada. There was an honourable tradition of escaping to Canada. They did not look down on war resisters there, they welcomed them. The Vietnam War resisters were now grandpa age, zaydes who could give counsel. Could he be a refugee, take refuge with her? With Vivienne? The papers were saying that in the first year of the war with Iraq, more than five thousand US military personnel deserted. Where were they? Was each one alone, bivouacked in his solitude, in cars or private deserts? They said that three years into the Iraq war, eight thousand had deserted.

In the sky, the roadrunner became a roadrunner's tail and drifting head.

The night air, rich with dark dry tinder, put on his lips the electric ghost kiss of Vivienne.

Andy walked back towards the Stovepipe settlement, where only the metal roofing shone in the moon a long way ahead like dots and dashes of tin Morse code.

Love is so short, and the forgetting so long. Brotherly love is so short, and there is no forgetting.

HE WOKE UP in a room with one bed.

He opened the door. The air was fresh and thin. The light was piney, under lacy pale green trees. There was a garden chair by his door: white rounded back, with thick arms, white-painted metal. He walked out on the dirt.

He was at a motel-style length of rooms. He looked at the numbers: 1 to 16. He was at room 15, the number 15 nailed vertically on the post in green patina metal, the 1 and below it the 5. It was dead quiet. He was in his clothes, but barefoot. He walked out to a main building in time to see the Buick Riviera, top down, drive west towards the badlands, severely white Chemical Donny zipping away.

He had been taken over the mountain in the night.

He came back to the white metal chair. It could not be tomorrow. This could not be the next day. If it was, he had made a decision. But he had not made a decision. Had he made a decision of omission?

Had he gone AWOL by accident?

What had happened to the hours between the time he had walked the road at Stovepipe under starlight and now, bright morning? Had tomorrow come and gone?

Could he plead blackout?

Was he up for a court martial? Was he other than honourable? Or this new category: *accomplished* – they who have suffered a trauma. Was Vivienne a trauma?

He went back inside room 15, lay on the bed, turned on the TV. Jack Palance got out of a big blue boat of a car, in the middle of nowhere with white-peaked mountains behind him. An old gas pump sat there, an old guy came out of a shack, "Help you, sir?" "Not many people around," Jack Palance said to the aging gas jockey. "No sir." "What's that?" Jack asked, pointing to the highest mountaintop. "Why that, sir, is the highest point in the United States; that's Mount Whitney."

"I came here for my health," Jack Palance said.

Andy fell asleep on the bed.

HE WOKE UP to the sound of a girl singing in a high little voice, a girl allowed to smoke many cigarettes, singing "The Thrill is Gone." Andy lay there, listening. The voice told the true story: the thrill, supposedly gone, was a haunting. That thrill would not get gone, at all. Andy got up and looked out the door: a large car, a lemon yellow Studebaker Commander, the same model he and Sean had driven and crashed the night before Sean hanged himself. "The Thrill is Gone" was coming from the car. Just like in *The Misfits*, where the car outside the cabin door played music so Monroe and Gable could do that slow jive, age and youth, in Nevada heartache. Andy lit a cigarette. The car kept looping that one song, the singer's voice tiny but nicotined, the voice of a wizened cherub. Ah, yes. It was Chet Baker. Andy's dad, Barry, loved Chet's music, the trumpet, the thrilling man-girl voice. He used to play it on the big stereo speakers in the house.

Andy got off the bed and sat down in the metal chair outside his room. He lit another cigarette off the first. Chet Baker jumped or fell from an Amsterdam hotel room in 1988, and they flew his body back to his home in the California desert, a returned water bird back to the haunted promise. And the musician was gone, and the thrill remained.

Now the Commander Sublime was singing, "They're playing songs of love but not for me," recorded in the early deep of the nuclear era, love in small thermonuclear Chet Baker registers. Through sierras of broken teeth, Chet's cracked mouth went around his beauty horn and offered a radioactive ministry to the lost souls of thirst.

Andy picked a tobacco thread out of his lips and blew smoke into the crackling air. The war is long, the thrill is short, the love is short, you go berserk, because the songs of love were not for thee.

The TV was speaking lines from inside, through the open door. Robert Mitchum, pushing around the who-gives-a-damn with such damn style you could kill yourself. Andy looked back into the room: A sign showing Bishop, north of Mammoth Lakes, north of Mono Lake, he knew that country. He used to drive a pickup truck over the mountain to Bishop for R & R from Deep Springs College, his alma mater, the famously unknown desert college, deep in the empty Deep Springs Valley. He had intended to herd cattle and study Kierkegaard at Deep Springs, to be a cowboy intellectual in the desert. The desert had seduced this San Diego boy. The remoteness had appealed to him. Vivienne made him remember his original intention. A life of the mind, being physical in his body. Things got lost in war. She opened up the desert inside him. The sense that you drove for hours facing vehicle breakdowns to go over the mountain from your college that had only two dozen students, just to see a town, like your soul could again be a pioneer in the possible. Who stewards your soul when you have lost it? The car sang Andy back to sleep, like a little girl lullabying her daddy. He woke up in the chair to more cold morning and the car wasn't there.

Andy put his hand in the pocket of his gold windbreaker, pulling out the Pink smokes package. Something else came out with it – a piece of olive green jersey. Vivienne's. Had he taken it from her room? Did she give it to him? He smelled it. Like sweet oranges, a light citrus, covered with the smell of her he couldn't define. A womanly sweat, something cedar, even chocolate. He lay back in the chair, with the jersey over his nose and mouth. He was somewhere in Death Valley. Let it be. But she would not let him be. She was inside him. If he removed his body, Vivienne Pink would still be with him. He needed to get away from her. He inhaled the intoxication of her. He reached into his left pocket. He took out his pistol. The world dismantles men, and leaves their parts unholy.

11

AUTOPSY ON THE AIR

JOHNNY AND VIVIENNE got deep under the down duvet. He was kissing her neck. They smelled of semen and viscosity. They were heated, sweaty, getting the post-love chills, hair wet, giddy. They were in Johnny and Val's room. Two queen beds. Room 10688. Johnny fed Vivienne strawberries from the room service breakfast at two in the morning: OJ, muffins and croissants, big pot of coffee, berries, yogurt and omelettes. Val had agreed to look for Danny in front of the Eiffel Tower. The Birdman of Paris.

VAL FOUND DANNY at his perch right below the bistro Mon Ami Gabi. "It's time to go to Death Valley," Val said.

Danny twirled his red ski pole in circles. "Fucking A," he said. "You got that right."

"Come along, Mr. Towne," Val said, using Danny's alias from his Montevideo days.

"Thank you, kind sir," Danny said, as Val led him into the Flamingo, across the slots floor, a sharp right down the mini-shopping hallway to the parking garage stairs. Up four flights, Val held the door open for Danny. A couple came through the door, paying no mind to an elderly gent in half a bird suit. At the vehicle, a 2005 white Honda Accord – Val wanted white paint to reflect the sun, Vivienne wanted a car low to the ground for better photos, Johnny wanted a trunk, where he could put his brother – Val said, "Climb aboard, captain," lifting Danny by a feathered armpit.

"Always glad to be of service," Danny said, laying himself down in the trunk space. Val adjusted an oxygen tank already set up beside Danny. "Hey, hey hey!" Danny said. "Dubya W. all the way!" Val slammed the trunk shut.

WHEN IT WAS brighter morning, they drove out of the valley of Vegas into the pariah lands.

On a windy open plateau, Val said from the back seat, "Stop up ahead. At that store. I have to see someone there about a thing."

Vivienne said, "I want to go straight through to Death Valley."

Danny was banging from inside the trunk. "Your brother's calling, Johnny," Val said.

"Vivienne's right," Johnny said. "We can make it to Death Valley in no time. I'm not stopping."

The store appeared off the road on the right. A half-hour from a major metropolis there were no billboards, no turnoffs, a lot of sky, a lot of restricted land. One small store, takeout food, available gas. "John," Val said, "am I not your second-in-command? Besides which, your Vivi can grab some nice pictures. I know the proprietors, Vivi, there's some great desert shots out the back. Lots of areas, what say?"

"Fine," Johnny said, swerving the car fast on the empty highway.

Here, the legendary Thunderbirds had made home base. Here was the area where men and women sat and operated drones for Iraq and Afghanistan. Here, in the Big Nowhere, the planet had been heated beyond Hades. Here, the biggest scandal of the twentieth century had taken place – hundreds of atomic, hydrogen and thermonuclear bomb tests. Here, men heated the globe, and they touched evil, and they liked it. Here, a twirling giant chicken up high asked you in giant letters: WHY SLEEP?

Val led them into the store.

Vivienne stopped at the maps, just inside. She liked the look of all the maps of Nevada, California and Utah lined up by the store window, with the gas pumps outside and the rock desert beyond. She lifted her camera. A short woman with a gravel smoker's cough appeared at Vivienne's armpit. She had on an olive green jumpsuit. In scripty gold writing a pocket said FRED. "No pictures of maps. No can do. Put it away." Vivienne kept the camera up. The gravel-voice said, "Orders of the military."

Vivienne laughed. "You can buy these same maps in any hotel in Vegas. They're road maps."

"I could call the authorities. Or how's abouts I don't call the MPs and we just fit you out with some nice quiet popcorn chicken."

Vivienne was relentless. She was holding her camera in one hand, bouncing it up and down. "Miss," the woman said, "you do happen to know we're at war, don't you?"

"Not me. I'm Canadian."

"Well, la-di-fucking-da, ain't she a party on a plate."

Val walked over and kissed the gravel-voiced woman on the back of the neck. "Gold," the woman said. "You termite, when did you blow into the desert? I got a package for you been waiting what is it, six months? You don't write, you don't call." Coughing and chuckling at the same time.

Val had a cigarette lit for her, "Here, Jolene, we gotta get rid of that cough for you. Vivi baby, Jolene's been servicing flyers since the stone age."

"Are they secure?" Jolene asked. "Are they source-reliable?"

"You can trust them," Val said.

"That is not what I asked, Gold." Jolene pushed back the sleeves of her jumpsuit. She had a risen purple-red scar from her right wrist bone to her elbow. Vivienne took her camera in her own right hand, held it at her hip and took a shot of Jolene's keloidal scar. That Olympus had such a nice quiet shutter.

"I want to check how Simtown is looking, Joley," Val said. "It was pretty damn weather-beaten the last time I was in. We might want to freshen up the kitchen. Maybe refresh the autopsy."

"Gold, the government is out of money."

"Get a loan," Val said. He was all matter of fact. "They'll put up a third mortgage on this place."

"You know as well as I do this is owned by the Feds."

"Good. All the better." He gave her a peck on the cheek. "Now now, Jolene, there's always money for nukes. It's in our self-interest. Iran is looking iffy, Kim Jong-il is looking dicey, Israel is looking dodgy –"

"Let's call the whole thing off," Vivienne said.

"Jolene, meet my girl Vivienne."

She extended her left hand. It had that regular drought look of the desert people, filigreed white pathways all over the skin. It had rained 1.3 inches in the last six months.

"And this," Val said, grinning, "is my girl Vivi's husband. Johnny, meet Jolene. Jolene, this is Johnny."

"So, this is the pair they set you up with," Jolene said.

"What is she talking about?" Vivienne asked. "'Set you up?' We invited you to live with us, after we met you at the draft-dodger counselling."

"No worries," Val said. "Jolene, take the people out back. Is Jack on the premises?"

"Jack's always on the premises, Gold. You know that." She spoke into her jumpsuit pocket. "Three for the EVOC."

Val, Vivienne and Johnny walked to a red door at the back of the store, behind the shelves of cans and tape cassettes. When Val opened the red door, it was an IMAX landscape.

They were in a parking lot full of white, red and black cars. A yellow steam shovel was parked at an angle. Motorbikes were parked there together. There were no people coming or going. Next to the parking lot was a railway crossing, the familiar black-and-white lettering, the blinking lights, the brown boxcar sitting still. To the side, a white Ford Falcon was stopped at a stop sign, two figures inside. Vivienne tried to take in the whole scene: miles of desert all around, open land with far-off jagged mountains lit white with winter snow on top. Into this massive emptiness, the parking lot, the railway crossing, the cars had been placed, as if it were a film set.

"Bring them to the EVOC," a voice said. "They will practice the PIT."

A wheelchair rolled up; a man in the same olive green jumpsuit Jolene had been wearing, with the same name, Fred, on the left breast pocket, waved for them to follow him across the sand.

Johnny said to Vivienne in a stage whisper, "What the hell has your boyfriend got us into this time?"

As they walked past the parking lot, Vivienne took a shot of the white Ford Falcon. The two people inside it were dummies, she could see now. A woman in a white shirt, just like the one Vivienne put on this morning; a man in a black cowboy hat with a wide brim. "Seriously?" Vivienne said to Johnny. Were these the famous mannequins used in atomic tests? Good job they didn't bleed or scream. Stuffing on fire tends to say nothing.

Where the hell had Val taken them? And what about Jolene's comment about Val being placed with her and Johnny? Sure, Val was a spy. But wasn't he their best friend?

Val was up ahead, chatting with the man in the wheelchair.

With thousands of acres of nothing on either side, a simulated city alley lay. The man rolled away. Val waved them forward down the alley. Vivienne walked past cute little piles of "urban" garbage. No rats, no raccoons, no stray dogs, just clean litter. And back stairs all tidy, fresh paint, geraniums in pots. Geraniums, Vivienne thought, snapping pics all the while. What did they think this was, the Costa Brava?

There was a white police vehicle ahead. Vivienne peered in the window, snapping the mannequin in his patrol blues. Fire extinguishers lined up behind each dwelling, neat, tidy, no people in sight yet. Vivienne Pink was born in a city; her people had lived in cities around the world for hundreds of years. No one ever spoke of fire extinguishers lined up in alleys. Was it possible that the big dogs in charge of setting up simulations didn't know what it was they were actually simulating? Vivienne stepped into a puddle. There was no rain. Everything was dry yet there were puddles. At the end of the alley, a mannequin sat on a step, wearing rubber boots.

The voice spoke: "Take them to LASER VILLAGE."

A real white car drove towards them. The driver wore a light grey suit, white shirt, no tie. Vivienne, Johnny and Val got in the back. Across the sand, then pavement began, then they were on a two-lane highway. Everywhere around them the land was a thin strip, the sky was filling Vivienne's eyes. She felt lulled by the bright light. The highway was grey and perfectly maintained and empty. They stopped at a sign that read HOTEL BUILDING.

The front door was off a hinge, open. The man in the light grey suit walked in, and the three of them followed. There was a counter, with a cardboard sign folded on it, RECEPTION. There was an old-fashioned metal bell to ring for service. An orange lazy boy recliner sat in front of the reception sign. Its vinyl skin was torn, with flat stuffing sticking out. The wooden floor, dark and wide-planked, had gold metal rounds of ammunition all over it. A white plastic side table had a big screen TV on it, large and flat with wires out the back attached to nothing.

Mr. Grey Suit said, "Bringing them to the kitchen."

They went past the reception and through a door to a room with a light grey table and metal curved legs. A sign on the table: KITCHEN.

There was a large white fridge covered in graffiti, which looked like the idea of graffiti sprayed by someone who had heard of graffiti but had never seen it except in movies where the graffiti was done by people who had only seen graffiti in movies. JAPAN said a poster on the wall, showing a latticed pavilion with a green mossy roof.

Another poster said, "'I am Temujin…Barbarian… I fight! I love! I conquer…like a Barbarian!' HOWARD HUGHES presents JOHN WAYNE · SUSAN HAYWARD. THE CONQUERER. CINEMASCOPE TECHNICOLOR."

Beside it on the whitewashed kitchen wall was another poster: ONE-EYED JACKS. Marlon Brando was in a cowboy hat, a jacket and a belt of ammunition, lying on a wide arc of sand, a rifle in his left hand, a pistol in his right hand, creased crinkled mountains in the distance and pinched sloping sand dunes closer behind him. "I know those dunes," Vivienne said to Johnny. "That's the Death Valley Dunes; that's our dune, honey. There's Marlon in Death Valley."

"Be good," said Mr. Grey Suit. "Don't talk too much."

The stove in the kitchen was copper brown. A dummy in camouflage clothing lay in front of the stove, headless. Where his head would have been they had stuck a wooden two-by-four and wrapped it in layers of thick plastic. There was a venetian blind on the wall just to the left of the stove to give the illusion of a window. Low-rent *trompe l'oeil* as interior decorating for the fake houses meant to be exploded. Your tax dollars well spent.

They returned to the car and drove on. The highway was clean, kempt. An oil tanker truck lay on its side ahead, on the sand shoulder. They kept driving. A man in a grey suit like their driver stood at the side of the road waving a pistol at an oil tanker truck that had yellow-and-red lettering on it. They stopped behind the long silver truck. The man with the pistol came around to the driver's side window, he pointed the pistol and shot. "You cannot drive to Iran," he said. "You cannot drive to Syria, turn around." He shot into the window again. He got in and drove the tanker truck down the highway himself. They took a side road, where clouds of dust far off showed other vehicles present. A sign at the side of the road read in yellow on black: SOUTH OF MOSUL SIM.

Trucks appeared in great numbers, shining like tin and silver, waving perilously as wind came up, shaking, tipping.

Vivienne's head was hurting. Pain started making its familiar route along her jaw, shattered back in Iraq, from her left ear to her lips. In her own body, she had a real place called Painville. Painville had its own roads, byways, eight-lane pileups. She got out of the car.

Here in the Nevada desert, they were simulating Iraqi highways she had been on, with petrol tankers through the northern Kurdish territory to Turkey, desert winds shaking them crazy. Her facial nerves got in on the glass jaw, and she bent forward, fighting the invasion inside herself, the embedded pain flashes not stopping. She kept taking pictures of mock-Iraq in front of her. Big space was a magnet for the dreams of men.

She got back in the white vehicle. Val had his eyes closed, unworried. Johnny squeezed Vivienne's hand. The driver stopped at a small stucco cube. Over the door, in red neon, it said ON AIR. "Only her," Mr.

Grey Suit said, pointing at Vivienne. Val and Johnny stayed in the car. Mr. Grey Suit took Vivienne into the stucco cube and down a hallway to a glass wall. "Look in," he said. It looked like an operating room. In lit red neon a sign said AUTOPSY ON AIR. On a metal table lay another wooden post with a mannequin head stuck on it. Two mannequins wearing headsets sat on either side of the dummy head. There was a microphone on the table. A knife lay near a yellow pad of paper.

"So," Vivienne said to Mr. Grey Suit as he took her back outside to brightness. "Did all your medical examiners train at Two-by-Four U?"

He wasn't laughing. He opened the back door. "Get in the car." Val and Johnny were down the way, walking across the sand without her.

She got back in the white car, which drove on paving through the sand. A pile of dummies was burning on the side. The car stopped. Vivienne hopped out of the back, her camera up, snapping a man in an olive green jumpsuit kneeling, cutting open something furry. It howled. It bled. The kneeling man put a small dummy, a child mannequin perhaps, inside the still bleeding fur. Another green jumpsuited man standing nearby had an old-school rotary phone in his hand. He twirled it around and back. The real creature with the dummy stuffed in it blew up, scattering canvas arms, canvas legs and fur into the air. "Get in," Mr. Grey Suit said. She did not know why they had taken her, and not the others.

They drove past further fires. Lobo scraps, mouse bits, pack rat portions, jackrabbit ears lay on both sides of the simulated highway, then they re-entered that fake back alley. The mannequin with rubber boots had not moved, the garbage lay undisturbed, the geraniums were perfect. One of the homes was on fire. "Time now," Mr. Grey Suit said to Vivienne. "Get out."

She walked what she thought would be a couple of feet down the short alley to the open sand, but she was still walking fifteen minutes later. She exited the alley finally. Six blocks of salt with nails in them sat in front of her. She walked alone across the sand. Signs she hadn't seen before were lined up: SIMUNITION. DANGER SIMUNITION. NO OUTLET.

The air was blowing sand into her eyes, her nose, her mouth, her shoes. This was forever-sand. Vivienne knew this sand from Iraq. It lived in your armpits, your luggage. It fell out of books years later. She could see that parking lot, that railway line ahead. Where was Johnny? What had they done with her husband? Was it Val? What did that Jolene mean Val had been placed with them?

She had been clear she wanted to drive directly to Death Valley. What was the big deal about stopping here? Wait a minute, she thought, did Val set me up? What is his angle? Am I in an experiment? Has he been a fake friend all these years?

Hundreds of dogs ran towards her. Hundreds of white dogs. They stopped short of her feet. They began to eat sand. Their eye sockets glowed.

Ahead, two blurry figures wibbled in the windy light. Maybe that was Johnny and Val.

A Jeep drove up. A man at the wheel said, "I will take you to Control Point. Come along."

12

NAGASAKI, NEVADA

THIS GUIDE WAS in regular clothes. Pale chinos, a pale blue work shirt. He drove to a lookout. "Down below," he said.

It looked like a little army village. A small barracks by a huge white lake. On the right a set of jutting mountains with a deep road zagging up them, white on dark grey. That led to a small set of lower mountains on the other side of the lake.

In front of the white lake the land was flat, rolling here and there around large white circles. White roads had been cut through the grey-green earth, long flat metal roofing sat with upside-down *V*s over buildings where rows of tiny vehicles were parked. "We'll take you down to see one of the control rooms," the guide said.

THEY STOOD IN a control room that looked like it was a set for a low-budget B movie, a space invasion scare. This was an actual control room for setting off an atomic explosion.

Two old office chairs, vinyl or bad leather, green, metal arms and back, with casters to swing up to the control panel or back to the high wall of blinking lights. Two large lamps hung from a ceiling beam. Harsh lighting, cold metal corners, white flooring. This was a utilitarian space, outfitted for maximum ease in atomic tasking. A reel-to-reel tape recorder, boxy amplifiers, grey drawers with metal handles, the blinking lights. On a separate table, a telex machine, bulky, stolid, on its own pedestal.

"This is where they...?" Vivienne asked.

"That's right, ma'am. Try it out."

Vivienne sat down in one of the office chairs, the guide pushing her right up to the control panel. It had a ledge and tilted back, three sections.

"Go ahead," he said. "Push a button."

She gave him a look. She smelled smoke. She could see Val's reflection in the shiny panel. "What the hell, Val? Where were you?"

Val said, "Hello, Vivi." His cigarette bobbing up and down, stuck to his lower lip. "That's my girl, chief."

The guide raised an eyebrow. "No smoking, sir, regulations. You'll have to step outside." Val kissed the back of Vivienne's neck. He left the control room.

"Just you and me," the guide said. "Go ahead, push the button right there." He tapped an innocuous button on the panel, silver with a black rim. "Go ahead, it's decommissioned, nobody's going to get hurt."

"That's what they said in the old days," she said, giving him more of that bold skepticism in her eyes.

"No, ma'am. If I may, that was never said. Go ahead."

"I think I won't," Vivienne said.

"Then I will." He reached past her left arm and pressed the button. A siren went off, a rising-falling wail. An air-raid siren: someone somewhere, or some thing unseen was coming for them. Vivienne saw no menace, but the siren kept going.

"Where are we?" she asked.

"Oh down by Frenchman Mountain. You'll see Yucca Flat and Frenchman Flat outside the door." They left the control room. The grey and white desert opened up. Val looked far away and also a footstep away. Desert optics are the original high definition. The guide pointed to the white salt playa and the mountains. "This is what they call Area 6."

"How big is Area 6?" Vivienne asked. The siren stopped.

"Oh not too big, ma'am. Maybe eighty-two or eighty-three square miles."

"Manhattan Island is twenty-five square miles."

"You got that right. Now you take your Area 5, where the motels are."

"Motels? You can stay here?"

"No ma'am, we have an excellent selection of motels we blow up. Or, ahem, blew up."

"But you are still doing tests out here, I mean if you are blowing up motels."

"President Bush cancelled Test Divine Strake. No, ma'am, nothing going on, no worries. No preoccupation. Everything's good in the areas. Now Area 2 had seven tests, that was back in the '50s. Now Area 3, well Area 3 is one of the big stars out here. In just six years they did seventeen tests. So you do the math."

Vivienne was trying. Six years, seventeen atomic tests. "That is three," she said. "Call it," laughing, "two and a half or two and three-quarter nukes a year."

"Call it three, ma'am. But that's nothing. How about our Area 9, one of the, if I may be so bold as to say, biggies? Area 9 hosted 113 detonations. You've got your Area 7, which hosted oh somewhere in the nineties of detonations And now you've got your, well ma'am, you've got your underground bunkers, you've got your goat farmers, you've got your bad soil buried, you've got bunks for the men who don't want to commute back home, but if they do, you know we shuttle them by plane back to base, end of day." Sure, all those planes up and down in the sky over Vegas, and some of them were even civilian. Here came Val walking towards them, getting smaller as he got closer. The guide went on, "But now I'm leaving out the tests they did after they signed that Limited Test Ban Treaty. I bet you knew that the treaty was to end above-ground tests. Nothing about testing below. They got good use out of Area 3 then, twenty-five more tests after the peaceniks forced them underground."

"I like peace," she said.

"Who doesn't?" He escorted her to the Jeep.

They drove across the beauty gruel with no horizon. At their vehicle, the guide left Val and drove Vivienne on further into the nuclear land.

There were no outskirts here, everything seemed like an inskirt. Where did you put things, if there were no corners? Did infinite space make you fill the air with conspiracies?

"Come on, Miss Curious," the guide said. "I want you to see something."

The mountains looked to be a fifteen-to-twenty-minute drive away. "How far is that?" asked Vivienne, motioning with her camera, putting it up to her eye, shooting.

"That? Where they set off the Stokes test? That's a good day's drive, ma'am."

"You're talking eight hours," she said.

"I am talking thirty-six hours, ma'am," the nuclear site guide said. "At a minimum."

So. They were driving a flat land where you could see clearly one thousand miles away. You could see from Toronto to Gainesville, Florida, with everything that existed gone. The mind could not comprehend this. But the eye, the reception desk of the body, could see it. Vivienne felt her eye shape-shifting. The desert forced a different order of seeing. A balloon that looked to be a one- or two-minute drive away sat with its nose pointed skyward. "How high is that? How tall?" Vivienne asked. "Ten stories?" She couldn't get all of the nose-coned balloon into her lens. They must be close by now, but the land kept rolling away. She felt panic. She could not see the edges of anything. The world could have disappeared and she would not know it. Nobody would know it.

"The balloon?" the guide asked. "That, ma'am, I am proud to say is higher than the Twin Towers. Ah, I mean than they were. We have maintained it in its original state since the test, quite a success. Men come out and check on her on a daily basis. Proud to say no harm has come to the old girl since '57."

They drove an hour by Vivienne's watch. The balloon ahead was no closer. Inside her lens the proportion of land and the vertical balloon on the massive horizon stayed the same. As they drove closer to it, it got further away. Tiny black sticks in a row stood to the right of the balloon. One, two, four, five, six, maybe fifteen black sticks on the white plain. The Jeep stopped.

Vivienne held up her thumb. The sticks were the height of the white of her thumbnail. She held up her hand. The balloon was the height of her hand, about one hundred fifty times taller than the black sticks. It was grey. It looked like an art project by Christo, like a grey billowing draping over a building. You could pull the drape off and there would be one shining tower in a land with no corners. Vivienne felt more panicked, and took more pictures.

"We met and matched Hiroshima with this one," the guide said. "They changed the name I am proud to say of that range, gave it due respect, named it Stokes Range. The Stokes test was all of nineteen kilotons. Not our biggest by far. Still Hiroshima was only fifteen kilotons."

"You set off a bomb bigger than Hiroshima, here in Nevada?" She knew the answer of course, she knew all about it, but as with Andy back in the valley, she liked to see the face of a man when he thought she was less informed than she was. She could play "little lady" if it got her the picture. Dumb redhead.

"Ma'am," he said. Giving her the look she wanted. Smart white guy, in shape, late sixties, giving her an expansive smile, the kind that welcomes you while keeping you at a distance. Warm, wary, playing that game. That was okay. Her camera around her neck had made her a life-long bluffer. Her camera was up for anything, it lead her, taught her, mentored her, was her lens-sensitive sensei, a gamer. "Ma'am, have you ever heard of Hood?"

"Hood?" she asked.

His eyes came into his smile now. It was not a fake smile; it was an authentic smile of authentic male condescension. Open, friendly, welcoming, *très* American. Looking at her like she's the cute polite Canadian doll. "The stories I could tell you," he said.

She got an excellent shot of his face, the test balloon in the background, his head large against a white shining plain. Weathered, getting leathery in the sere air. The insides of her eyelids felt scratchy. The sky was ten times the height of the land.

"I would love to hear them," she said. "I've got nothing but time."

"I signed papers. No can do. It's public information that Hood was seventy-four kilotons, five times the power of Little Boy."

"Little Boy? You mean Hiroshima."

"That's right, ma'am. I had a feeling you knew more than you were letting on. You probably know all about Operation Plumbbob, summer of '57, we exploded twenty-nine bombs, twenty-seven had nuclear yield. The busy time was June, July. Priscilla yielded thirty-seven kilotons, eleven days later Hood, ten days after that was Diablo, yield seventeen kilotons."

Vivienne was looking at the something going on in his eyes. She lifted her camera and he gave her a hazel-eyed half-squint that could kill a deer at one thousand feet. Tough chin, hollows under that scary squint. "Hood," he said. "I flew a helicopter through the cloud to pick up evidence. You could say we were atomic CSIs. Nineteen of us."

"Nineteen men?"

"Nineteen birds, checking out how bad it was. I was just a pup. Eighteen years old. They never told us we were part of the experiment." He looked around. In a land this vast with no people you felt more paranoid someone had overheard you than in a city restaurant sitting on communal benches. He looked up to the sky. "No one had any idea in those days. We were going in to check on the test results. See what was happening with the detonation. You're married to the weather reports, ma'am, when you're setting off five Hiroshimas."

His hazel eyes were streaked with amber. Out here, the sun forced an intimacy with men's eyes.

The nuclear guide looked over the Jeep's windshield to the hours-away balloon. Vivienne opened the passenger door with her right hand behind her back, holding the camera in her left hand, stepping down, praying it was solid ground, and it was. He didn't mind, or at least say anything. He looked ahead. Good. Excellent.

Vivienne walked backwards, not looking behind her, hoping she wasn't backing into anything. The chances were slim. There was seriously nothing here, unless she walked two days backwards and hit one long snarly dwarf tree. She kept walking backwards hoping for the shot she had been feeling. She wanted the balloon like a mystery and the tiny stick people beside it to be in the right of the frame like a thing the viewer would look at and wonder

"What in the hell is that?" And the guide, a serious military man, with coyote eyes and a stern companionability, he was a guy you wanted to be seated next to on a train. The first hour or so you did not trust him or like him, but you had a long ride ahead and soon you got into coded confidences and good bourbon.

He did not shift his lower torso. Good.

He moved his upper torso around. Vivienne took a chance: she motioned to him, pointing to her chest, wordless, and he got it. He tipped his upper torso towards her. She put her hand under her chin. He lifted his chin. She took her first two fingers and pointed them at her own eyes. He gave her more with his eyes – if that was possible – and she had him in her scope, she could hear the photograph now. He stared her down like an equal. He was confiding the surface. He was working fast, like a pro. Putting his body into his angles, his look.

There were way too many slow-moving shutterbugs obstructing the landscape today as far as Vivienne was concerned. The sight of a camera in their hands made them feel famous. Being near a camera made an untrained person feel the way a fan might feel near a famous person. As if the machine itself was a raja or a king or a VIP or a talent scout or God's representative. As if the machine itself were fame, forgetting that in all of Earth's history, photography is still a baby, in its marvel baby steps, a mere one hundred sixty, one hundred seventy years old. And when photography was much younger, about age ninety-nine, after the Americans dropped the atomic bombs on Japan, they sent soldiers out in the cities of Hiroshima and Nagasaki, to confiscate cameras and film. Also to make sure no one was taking pictures in Iwo Jima, because it was the place from which the B-29s carried the bombs to these places. The story is told that the Americans fought at Iwo Jima in order to secure it as a portal for their atomic bomb planes.

Vivienne snapped six shots of the guide, at a nice easygoing speed of 1/60th of a second each. She nodded, and he pulled out a pack of smokes. Three Castles. He cupped his hands in the wind behind the windshield. A body memory of Andy in the hotel room came back to her. He had cupped his hands just this way. Sand came up in the wind and was blowing hard at them. This changed the game, it was sandstorm time. The balloon became a ghost balloon, a grey tower in front of which the fierce cheer of the blue day became dust in visible air. The human black sticks were now sketchy, the air in the lens looked like fog made of gold granules. The wind percussed sand into the windshield. The guide kept looking in profile at the far balloon, he kept smoking, she got a marvellous shot of him. Without a caption, what does the shot say? *Who was this man? What was he looking at? Why is he sitting alone in a Jeep, smoking a cigarette as an amber sand cloud pours over his body?*

A man wrapped in sand inside a Jeep wrapped in sand, with a white cigarette caught by a shaft of light from below. The picture had mystery, she knew it as she took it. What had stepped out of the frame right before the shot was taken?

The atomic bomb had stepped out of the frame. The man in the gold and white sandstorm caftan was looking at fifty years of history.

He was an atomic war veteran. The picture didn't say this. But like rain or sand it informed the entire photo. He had told her his story, and that informed her arms; she had listened to him, and that informed his eyes. This was why you went, whole, to the broken places, and became part of them. You made things, and then art became your oasis. Vivienne felt the old feeling: I am alive in the world, the world is full of fascination. I came from desert people. I am a Semite. I have desert genes. And it is told: once, in a story, men packed out spices and journeyed in long darkness in indigo robes and gold-embroidered coats across the sand of the desert, seeing tessellations and polygon sunsets. Once, they walked in an exodus across the desert and they did not have cameras. This capture is our new bauble, our new treasure.

She felt for the first time in a long time her intention: to create the feeling of sanctuary in a viewer who might be wandering lost, and who might come across a photograph of hers, and find it became his heart oasis, even in passing.

She got back in the Jeep. "Done?" the guide asked.

"For now," Vivienne said.

He turned out on the white plain where a set of whiter lines marked a road. She was being driven into the heart of lightness. "That pay money?" the guide asked, leaning his head towards her camera.

"Some," she said. "I have eight books out. Enough to pay for my garden habit."

"I have to say I enjoyed the one about the surf squatters in the Canaries. I used to do a serious amount of surfing myself in the San Diego days. I guess I am just not cut out for one-legged surfing. Buddy of mine used to surf there in the Big Canary. Fine Atlantic breaks."

So, he had seen one of her books. *Surf Squats*, from that winter in Las Palmas, Gran Canaria, when she had lived in a crumbling squat painted turquoise, on a hill above the beach, in the days before they pulled the eyehole-windowed squats down and put up fancy condos where ex-pats were more fat than surfing and the view was great, but the dispossessed who surfed in rags with makeshift wood were exiled. So, he knew who she was. Of course. Today, someone announced your name at a gate and the man in the hut had your entire history before you arrived. These were the small powers given to men, now that they were not setting off Nagasaki, Nevada. But this man had served; his lungs and brain had served and been degraded with honour. So where was he taking her? The land went on and changed to time and time changed to space. How had it happened that Einstein took the theory of relativity and its endgame was the death of so many Japanese? Who knew that the desert would be seen as homeless, to be set on fire, to be left scarred and burned? And so did science rage its genius.

13

A SINGLE MUTANT SHEPHERD

JOHNNY COMA WALKED further into the space that kept opening.

A small runty animal approached him. It looked like a sheep, a shorn ewe. An object, like an inside organ lay on the ewe's side. Johnny came closer. The sheep's heart had grown outside its body. He put his hand on the ewe's heart, and indeed it beat outside its body. Another came, wearing lungs up at its neck.

He walked further, the ewe with the exterior heart trailing him, like a single mutant shepherd of humans.

Ahead Johnny Coma saw a small mountain of bones covered with large vehicular wheels. The cadaver of a Jeep was somehow placed atop the unnamed bone mountain.

The land seemed like the physical manifestation of an unslept world. Sleep disruption, disrupted brainwaves. Your rawness, your fears were the physical materials of mountains, sky, rock, dirt.

Inner space had been made outer space by the radioactive fallout, the sick gift that keeps on giving.

Remember when nobody had cancer? Remember when cancer was rare? Remember how when we were growing up everybody had a relative, a distant aunt, a person in the neighbourhood, who had cancer? How is it that today everybody has cancer? How our hearts would dissolve if we thought: To keep the Russians away, we destroyed a North American generation's health. We set the world on fire, and put young heads in the nuclear atmospheric oven.

Remember when brain cancer was rare? Remember when you went to your first funeral for someone with brain cancer, so long ago, so rare? And the bureaucrats and the technocrats and the true nuclear believers did not escape the air, either. They too have deformed grandchildren, they too have lost count of the funerals of their colleagues with cancers and they too lie in their tumorous stained soil in pine.

Johnny walked across the windy cratered land. It was a dried mud and pathology museum. The Earth was a blue tumour in space, too marvellous for words. And the small woolly ewes walked to him in their flocks, born with no wool and their hearts beating, unlike symbols but like ruin, outside their bodies.

14

NUCLEAR PHARAOHS

IN THE DESERT, men set up desks, as men like to do, to receive the data. The hunter-gatherers of the nuclear data came to the desk with their cloud samples, and the men in suits in their open-air offices looked at the clouds on the desks, and other men came with the burned retinas of rabbits. The data men counted the retinas and the cloud noshes, and made neat charts of the atomic fallout. Other men gathered the sheep from trenches and the sheep tied to stakes in the open. It was quite an inbox: rabbit eyes, radioactive cloud samples and sheep still on the stake. To the paranoid, this is all logical self-defence. Keep in mind the paranoid man is the hero of his own story.

They set off multiple atomic and hydrogen bombs in the glory months of June and July. When the heat was scorching before the fireball came, when the nuclear workers' bodies were under severe pressure anyway, even if it were a day off from playing God's servants, or at least the servants of the Nuclear Pharaohs.

The nuclear workers had to don big heavy hazmat suits to examine the pieces of the experimental houses that had been blown off in the bomb tests to see what would happen to houses in bomb time. These workers did not wear hazmat suits as they watched the tests. They put them on after. They examined the highly radioactive houses: the doors, the roofing, the driveways, the parked radioactive vehicles. They examined the sheep that had been bound and set in foxholes, the pigs that had been incarcerated in cages and the cattle placed out on the nuclear range.

But the men whose job it was to tend the test animals, to examine the animals, to brush the radioactive dust off the animals, to exfoliate the hides of the animals or to cut the animals up, these men also most profoundly suffered the blowback, the fiery balls, the dust, dirt, poison. They too became atomic veterans. The chart makers, the cloud pilots, the men at desert desks, the men setting up the living-room mannequins and picking up the dummy families later, they too were in the tests. We tell ourselves the story that the scientist in the lab is not the rat in the cage. But bomb tests are the lab experiment where the scientist and the assistant are inside the cage, also. You can't escape this world you live in. They too lived in the mutations of air; the mutant sky on fire lives above us still, in its own keloidal scars we might call sunsets. Yes, and the photographers too. Just as a reporter in war is *in* that war, so the scientists and photographers and seismic graph men were also poisoned. Original child atom begat the atom generations.

You can't think your way out of the nuclear age. This is the new sick womb we are born in. Our skin has gone inside us, to come up like stealth attacks from invisible hideouts.

The pilots, yes, were told the nuclear clouds were safe to fly their data-collecting planes through. Those men became sick. The words chosen were *test* and *safe*. But a man's body does not know whether the tumour growing inside him came from a test or the real thing, because a test is the real thing. Calling a nuclear blast a test is the way humans use words for inept magic.

They put men out in the blistering desert on dry crackling days, over 110 degrees Fahrenheit in the midday sun's burn, and asked them to observe the test of a bomb. The air started at 110 degrees, which meant the ground temperature could be 135 degrees, or the air started at 135 degrees which meant the ground could be over 200 degrees. That was before the bomb. In the desert on a summer's day, you can get third-degree burns with bare feet on the ground, hiking. You began at third-degree burns and heatstroke, and then they set off the bomb and rushed to see how the fake house doors were doing.

15

THE JACKRABBIT SPOKE

A SHORT PERSON with tight grey curls, wearing that same green jumpsuit with Fred on the pocket took Vivienne, Johnny and Val to the vault. The vault had been loaded on a plane, flown to the desert and dropped right there. What was built to hold securities had been tortured. It had been set on fire, had bombs blown up inside its steel skin and now Vivienne snapped a pic of its steel hanging in bent filigrees of commerce untended. The guide motioned them to walk inside, past the door hanging off its hinges.

The inner sanctum of the vault was like a darkroom. Vivienne was used to the dark cave, used to her pupils dilating, growing large, her eyes seeking out spots of light in darkness. She could see the slightest line of light along Val's Roman nose.

At the doorway, Vivienne saw a figure lit from behind – a jackrabbit. She had seen them before.

The desert hare, *Lepus californicus*, the black-tailed jackrabbit, with that little black tail, the black eyes to go with it, the big black-rimmed ears. Those ears, classic. One-third of the creature was ears. Nothing to do with cuddly little bunny rabbits; jackrabbits were desert creatures, dark buff and black, what they called an agouti fur: fur chiaroscuro. Jacks liked the night. They gathered in big-eared groups by moonlight. The creature's eyes, set back in its head, shone at the doorway, weird, malign, compelling.

But wait. This jackrabbit was a big mother of a jack. Vivienne watched as its big body filled the doorway, its ears were still going where the doorway stopped.

The jack wore a knee-length dress – full at the breasts, with a definite waist, an hourglass figure – and a thin black belt. It was a silky dress, shining in dark blood red and dark moss green stripes. A flattering lace collar revealed a nice swatch of the agouti dark-light fur below the neck. The sleeves of the jack's dress were elbow length, on the left the sleeve led to a foot instead of an arm, on the right the sleeve led to a long pole with a hook on the end of it, a hook in gold.

The hook was at Vivienne's face. The jackrabbit spoke: "You'd better come with me." The jackrabbit's voice was flat and nasal, as if it had been taught to speak English by a human who spoke like a computer, emotion hidden. "Come with me." The tiniest of twitches played around the jackrabbit's mouth, by the facial pads and tufty whiskers. "I am not going to hurt you." The one flat tone made the voice sound terrified.

"Hey Sam," Val said. "Got a smoke?"

"No smoking," the jackrabbit said. "I am not Sam."

Johnny was still scribbling away in his cardboard-backed Moleskine.

"Come with me. All of you. Everybody." The jackrabbit in the proper lady's dress swung the hook through the dark, and paused, backlit in the doorway.

The biggest covert war the US had ever waged was right here, in the Nevada desert. The jackrabbit stood with eyes black as poison plates. "Do not worry. Don't you worry," the giant jack said, tall as basketball heaven walking towards the eastern flats. "No worries."

"Worry," Val said, walking between Vivienne and Johnny behind the jack's red-green-striped sateen dress, its hem blowing in the windy sun. The shine blew around, light being blown by air motion. They walked further into global forgetting.

A set of bleachers came into view, filled with spectators.

Johnny was writing things in his notebook, walking, looking around, keeping his footing, doing thumbnail sketches of the jackrabbit, their feet, the bleachers ahead. "You need to sit here. You're guests of honour," the jackrabbit said. The flat tone made *guests of honour* sound like *guests of death.*

"They're dummies," Vivienne said, lifting her camera. The jackrabbit had made no attempt to take it away from her. The bleachers were filled with dummies holding cameras. They looked like flour sacks with smiley faces on them. Their cameras were soft, made of sewn canvas, with lenses drawn on with Sharpies. Some test dummies had been placed, head on a neighbour's shoulder, in a coy vignette of the photographers, here to witness an event at a test site in the desert.

"Sit down," the jackrabbit said. Those black plate eyes seemed to have come straight from a jackrabbit asylum. But the figure was womanly. In the transformation of genes, creature and beast, fur and pelt, Jill and Jack had become one figure.

Things were things in this bigness; so big even God could doubt religion.

Vivienne was snapping wildly, capturing whatever was on the go. A car came out of the sunny dust towards them. As it came close, you could see the top of it was a woman's body, wearing the same green-and-red striped dress as the jackrabbit. Close at the breast, hourglass to the waist where the steel car began. The woman's hips were the roof of the car curving out to the headlights. She had arms lifted up as if to dance or cheer. On both sides of the car-woman lockstep figures marched in Marine Corps uniforms. As they came close you could see they were all leashed together as if by the Great Dog Walker in the Sky, and now Vivienne saw that the leash holders were other giant jackrabbits, not in dresses, but in black morning coats.

"We blow the balloon tower," said the jackrabbit. "No swearing. No coarse language, discretion is advised, we have young ewes on the premises. Hold your horses."

The sky went dark. The great outdoors went dark as a darkroom.

"Welcome to the Divine," the giant jackrabbit said. "Presenting: Divine Strake!"

AND SO IT was on that day, December 27, 2006, one hour outside the metropolis of Las Vegas, an atomic bomb exploded. All eyes were diverted to Iraq at the time.

Vivienne Pink was a witness. The bomb went off. The bomb test was called Divine Strake.

The neck of the world rose up from the desert, alert to the light and the fissionable extravagance of damage this scientific spree was on; and the neck rose in hot colours, and the colours of hell pushed ground to sky. Hot blues, icy reds, lush oranges on a jag to make Earth an unnatural planet. The spine of Earth rose out of itself in an orgy of atoms. The witnesses, trapped in heat and fire glare, prayed to be released to heaven below as hell enveloped them. Crazy punching winds flailed in nine directions. Thereupon, the brain stem of Earth separated from the neck and rose in a coral twist to the stratosphere, and the supporting foundations rose inside it, all the time pushing the brain matter skyward. The planet's spine split the atoms of its vertebrae, which loosened and flew and became shaken. The silt, the stealth desert sage, animal pelts, human clothing, Jeep steel, bleacher wood and soft cameras became weaponized as the air became weaponized from the shock wave, roaring like desert-based speed-of-sound barrier trials. The air became a tsunami. A rolling thunder of hot punishing air.

This was the harvest of atoms.

This was the play of men. The sucking vacuum, the suppurating sky wound for which there is no suture; the susurration of the woolly sheep, the helpmeet horses as they received the fire onto their manes; the confined squeals of a thousand pigs tied to barbed wire, fashioned in different clothing; the look of the psychotic century no cold war at all but a fiery self-inflicted furnace, a slow centurial suicide by nuclear bomb.

Here was the cradle of global warming. They overheated the Earth hundreds of times. They baked the planet heat-viral.

What Vivienne saw was not the shape of a mushroom. It was that spine, that cervical twist rising to the neck in abasement, scorching higher and higher, until it bloomed like a blunt-force-trauma pounded brain, splitting, blooming with its fiery brain matter. The sky now owned the core, the core was heaving. This the brilliant men made: the evolution of our self-poisoning.

Here was the land of the primary lesion.

The wind lifted Vivienne Pink up and knocked her down. Pummelled her, shook her crazy, dropped her on gravel sand. Vivienne Pink, photographer, predator of light, sat in the smoke rain.

The neck of the world turned blue and burned on.

World, I am afraid there will never be another you.

The ground began to sink, the bleachers with the test dummies began to sink, the land got pocked with sinkholes like new burial grounds in the desert. The Earth's brain matter became hooded in a sky cave of fire. The air became a monstrous x-ray machine. The bones of all creatures glowed; all flesh was made onto itself a skeleton.

Vivienne held up her camera, her arm glowed. With her left hand she took a picture of her right arm. Yes, her bones were glowing. She could see her humerus lit up from the shoulder to the elbow, she snapped that, lifting her arm, showing to herself this living x-ray of her elbow, then down along the ulna and the parallel radius to her wristbones.

"I can see my invisible self," she said. "I can see my own lies."

A roaring train at speed knocked her in the face – the sound of the next shock wave. Sand was crawling in all her crevices. Her mouth was jammed shut with sand. She couldn't hear. Where was Val? There was Johnny, his bald head wearing a sand pyramid. His eyes popped out of his cheeks gone wild in high G-forces. The next shock wave rolled at them, sucker-punched them, smashed their faces. Uppercut, left hook, below-the-belt gut slam.

The test dummies were on fire. The test dummies were still smiling. It was commonplace to dress the female test dummies in white simple frocks, the better to deflect the atomic heat from them.

We could not cage the sky, but we could poison it. We had art, but the world was our toy.

Vivienne watched a Jeep melt down into the sand.

We are the infant planet. What things in early days did we do to the newborn universe? Before its strange beauty was revealed to us, we began to torture it. Because we could.

And so did the newborn universe spread its fallout atmosphere to the baby teeth of the newborn children.

THE JACKRABBIT SPOKE: "*They that did feed delicately are desolate in the streets: they that were brought up in scarlet embrace dunghills.*"

"Is this something you have known?" she asked.

"It is something I have known. It is something I have been. It is something which will come around again."

"Was this just a bomb?" Vivienne asked.

"It was a bomb *test*," the jackrabbit said. "Divine Strake. George W. spoke of it. They that did feed at the breast of fear did not much report it. The president announced a bomb test on home soil, but the flock was busy being shepherded by that toothsome wolf, Dick Cheney. The Pentagon put eyes on Iraq and began to test bombs again, here in the Nevada desert. Those bad boys. It's all misdirection. Government? It's all bad magic."

Vivienne lifted a clump of her red hair from her scalp. Small pieces of thick skin came off with the hair. Her luxuriant tresses were now dry, old. Gone in sixty seconds.

The jackrabbit's eyes were rotating in its head. "*Their visage is blacker than a coal; they are not known in the streets: their skin cleaveth to their bones; it is withered, it is become like a stick.*"

"*Eikhah,*" Vivienne said, using the Hebrew name for the book of Lamentations. "I remember Jeremiah from *cheder.*" The jackrabbit's eyes were focused on her as she spoke. "Eikhah, *How,* the wail. How could they do this, how could they allow Jerusalem to burn, how can I abide this, how can we bear this as a nation, how, how, how. Tell me, Jack, how can we rent and tear our clothes when the A-bomb takes over the favour? We cannot wail anymore, the world is too much with the kvetching."

The jackrabbit kissed her cheek.

Vivienne went on, "We're in the desert. Where is Jeremiah? We studied it, I was just a kid, I mean you're six, seven, you're nine years old, what do you know from Jeremiah? The Ketuvim. I'm nine, I'm wailing with Jeremiah about Jerusalem, Shabbos morning at Beth Sholom; Shabbos matinee I'm going to the Nortown to see Sinatra in *Pal Joey*."

"They shall bring out the bones of the king of Judah," said the jackrabbit.

"Did Judah get nuclear radiation?" Vivienne asked. "Were the princes x-rayed by God?"

The Earth had become the sick hidden basement. The secrets were the world in its open daring. To be a con man was where men went, in the modern. What was a man? Was this desert a radioactive *shul*, was this original awe? And yet here she was, chatting with a mutated black-tailed agouti-shaded giant jackrabbit off Interstate 95, the ribbon through the military test zone.

"I can take you to the bones of the prophets," the jack said. "They are not far from here."

"Where? You're telling me what?" Val's face was coming towards her and the jackrabbit was a bright pink, the colour of flesh on the inside of a body, throbbing, pulsating. Val didn't seem to realize he had a head like a fluorescent disco peach. Vivienne felt super-present in a circumstance. "Come here, honey," Vivienne said. "Jack's seen the bones of kings. She says they're somewhere out here."

"They have a test area," Jack said. "Area 109. We call it Damascus Gate. The bones of prophets are kept there."

"Jack, honey, talk Haftorah to me," Vivienne said.

"I can't cry. My eyes are dried up."

The air around Val changed, his ions re-upped into interest. "Who are you?" Val asked, with the tone that made Vivienne remember he could still pull it out, be the intel man, be soft, be working. "What's your job, ma'am?" Sensing something in the jackrabbit.

"I was one of the first women to come to the tests. I used to ride cleanup. We came on horses in the morning. It was a beautiful place back then. Beautiful horses all over the wild country. I grew up riding in the canyons. Wild manes. I loved to be around horses from the time I was a little girl. I thought I would grow up to be a cowboy. This was my grandmother's dress. They let me wear it. I am a woman from the waist down. A jackrabbit was standing nearby when the test went off. The jackrabbit got blown by the shock wave into my face. When the fire was over and the shock wave, the jackrabbit had a woman's head and I had its face. Somewhere out there is a thing with paws and tracks, with the face of an eighteen-year-old girl. When my hands got severed by the wind, the docs sewed on a foot and put in an old ski pole."

"The docs?" Val asked.

"They were actually women who did laundry. They had some thread. They would not let me have a drink, they said it wouldn't be legal. They did let me drink the ether. You never know, do you? You feel like you are not in the right body, growing up, being a teen, then one day you wake up and you are half jackrabbit, half girl and you are addicted to your five o'clock ethertini. I've seen worse."

Johnny, off on the side, had that adrenalized air of the old reporter he was, in on history, down with the sand beetles in the tsunami shock wave sand, scribbling with his hot paws the eyewitness story. He did not notice his singed fingers, nor how shock and thrill gave the same writerly adrenaline.

Val was on the ground, staring off into the deep blue sea. There was no deep blue sea.

Vivienne walked with the frocked jackrabbit. "Tell me," she said, "how far were we from the bomb detonation? It looked like it was right next to us at the bleachers. Does that mean it was miles away?"

The jackrabbit said, "If it was fifteen hundred feet away, you'll be dead any day. If it was a mile away, you might have a thirty per cent chance of being alive next birthday. Now, if we're talking over a mile distant from the scorching detonation, you'll probably live; I can't speak to the damage. But then, much like the gaming tables, you could be one of the ones who does meet Lady Luck on life's highway. But then, sweetheart, if that bomb was over two and a half miles away when they set it off, you might win at life's penny-ante slots."

"But do you know?" Vivienne asked.

"Anybody's guess, when it comes to the rogue afterlife of radiation."

The jackrabbit then came closer to Vivienne, and began to speak in a lilting whisper. She spoke about how her father was stationed in Okinawa during the Vietnam War when Japan was used as a staging area for American soldiers. About the American base at Kadena, about the fifty thousand and more American troops stationed then in Okinawa, this world of American military, three hundred miles away from main Japan. Vivienne had smoked the Japanese Pink cigarettes with Andy back in Area 24, knew they were from Okinawa, but had not known that Okinawa was an American place in Vietnam War days. "We're in the pink." Smiley, smiley, all over the world. Smiley, smiley, and the invasion nightmare.

The jackrabbit said, "Pop used to say that the word went out that the US had planted nuclear weaponry *in* Okinawa. The Japanese used to buy cigarettes from Pop and tell him that he should tell his superiors the Japanese did not want any nuclear war on their homeland. I don't know if it happened."

Vivienne felt ill. Could it be? You drop bombs on Hiroshima and Nagasaki, and then twenty years later, like some thug let out on probation going back to the crime scene, you get your atomic ducks in a row in, are you kidding me, *Okinawa, Japan?*

Sure, every journalist knew the quote from Ambrose Bierce: "War is God's way of teaching Americans geography."

But what bad dream could lead the US to have positioned nuclear warheads in Japan during *Vietnam*? Was Vietnam the US's last great affair? The one that got away? Was Vietnam the Moby Dick of American military history? The jackrabbit did say it was a story her dad had told. Maybe good old Pops knew a good story, no more.

"He used to sell the locals Lucky Strikes, they used to give him anti-war pamphlets."

Vivienne stood looking south across the thin strip of land, the low fires across the low land and the high sky, singeing out the purples, the acid greens, the pale pinks with fireballs of orange travelling like sunspots, an atomic mirage that was true. The atomic light bulb burned black edges on the sky. This was the end of lamps. This Nevada desert was the original ground zero.

CLANDESTINELY, HUNDREDS OF photographers made thousands of movies and still shots of the mid-century atomic blasts being detonated in the desert. A secret movie studio was formed in Los Angeles for this purpose. The studio compound was known as the Lookout Mountain Laboratory. Its field photographers were USAF airmen of the 1352nd Photographic Group. Between 1947 and 1969 the secret studio on Wonderland Avenue, making films for the Defense Department and the Atomic Energy Commission, was actually the biggest movie studio in LA. The studio developed new camera technology to film the bomb blasts at long distance.

Then, in the same way that they moved soldiers at the actual bomb test sites ever closer to observe and collect data, they sent the secret cameramen out, all with top clearance, to get close and personal at the bomb sites to photograph the atomic bombs going off, and to hide the footage in vaults.

The secret studio compound sat on an LA hill, lit day and night, with thousands of workers coming and going, and nobody saw a thing. (Or did they?)

And the photographers, too, suffered the close nuclear rain; their bodies, too, over the years, felt the workplace damage of the fallout. Their shop floor was the open desert.

THE TRANSCENDENT BLUR of a B-52 lifted its shadowy power above the ghost world. Zigging and zagging a speed stain, its beautiful nose lifted. The American planes at Okinawa so familiar to the local Japanese were tested here in Nevada, their testing grounds also familiar to this citizenry, home and abroad living at the behest of American bases. Their skies looking so much the same, steel birds lifting one by one or in formation from the military aviary below.

The jackrabbit reached into into her bosom and pulled out a small photo: a lanky blond, white, bare chested, skinny, fair faced, crew-cut of the era, baggy silky shorts, tennis shoes, a white gob hat, a pack of Luckies in his shorts' elastic band; a Japanese woman, twice his age, doubled over, laughing, a soft dark pageboy, a pullover sweater, a pencil skirt, high-heeled pumps, glasses with winged jewelled frames. They were standing, arms around each other's waists in front of the Club New Formosa. Off to the side, two young American sailors in uniforms and white gob hats. "This one here," Vivienne said, tapping the face of one of the young sailors, "this one looks like an old flame of mine. He was Navy. He shipped out of Brooklyn to San Diego. He went to Japan during Vietnam."

"It could be," the jackrabbit said. "Stranger things have happened. I cut this out of a book. Tōmatsu, the great photographer. This was the United States in Okinawa."

The stranger thing had happened. The jackrabbit had given up the monotone and was speaking with Vivienne in a poly-tone, speaking like a full human. Had the portal to the Hebrew books been kind to the scorched fur? "Give me a quote I can carry, little Jack," she said. Had a mutated jack at the atomic testing grounds become her provisional rabbi?

"*The harvest is past, the summer is ended, and we are not saved.*"

She said, "Travel safely, have a good trip," and it sounded like old field blues sung by the desert Hebrews.

"We have got to get going," Vivienne said. "We are on a trip to Death Valley. *Hasta luegito, Jackito.*"

"*Hasta luego, Viviennita. Bienvenido al Valle de Muerte.*" The jackrabbit waved her right ear. Her eyes stayed with their black plate menace. She was down on the ground re-ingesting black scat, looking up at Vivienne. She took a photograph of the jack, eyes daring, mouth liquid brown at the edges. A drop fell on the dress's white lace collar. She moved her body up, the red and green sateen shone, and she bounded off to the south. Vivienne was shooting like a mad thing, grabbing at least one keeper:

the jackrabbit, a creature with tall ears, a vision in a Dora Maar frock, high in the air, bounding past sand depressions burning with fire, past collapsed conveyances, and exploded simulation villages. Meanwhile, the adult test mannequins in suits and dresses, and the child mannequins in overalls, and the mock photographers sewn of canvas split apart or smouldered. But since test dummies have no thyroids, and mannequins have no tissue, what could a nuclear test mean?

They were back at their car. They got in. Vivienne pulled the sun flap down and looked in the mirror. Her hair looked like a dusty fright wig. Her fingertip felt a small metal button rising on her scalp. Her eyes were red. She had bruises on her face, and a bump was sticking out on the right-hand side, swollen as if it were filling with bacteria. Johnny at the wheel looked very pale. His eyes stared straight ahead; he was in some mental capsule. He drove with his left hand only, at eight o'clock on the wheel, his right hand held his Moleskine notebook; he was writing with his right hand, and driving with his left. His face looked almost turquoise.

Val, for his part, lay stretched out in the back seat. Vivienne turned around with her camera, hearing small chirps. Val was weeping. Vivienne snapped him. The sky in the back window was black with gold claws. The sky became cement.

Danny was inside the trunk, banging to be let out.

16

THE HAWK MOTH

VAL OPENED THE trunk. Danny lay there, with his bird suit on. "The person of a foreign service agent shall be inviolate," he said. "They shall not profane him."

"Oh, God," Val said. "Here we go again."

"Thou shalt not profane an agent of the person of your country." He smelled to Val like old wet leaves in a northeast rainy season.

"You are not a foreign agent, Danny," Val said. "You carry the water to conference room B. You're a fixer."

"I demand my rights. I demand to be taken to my embassy." His head was small with sweat locks.

"This, you septic excuse for a spy," Val said, "is your embassy. Welcome to sanctuary. You knew all about this bomb test, didn't you?"

Danny stroked his crotch. "So what?"

"You knew this was coming. That's why you stayed in the trunk. You knew they were going to finally test Divine Strake today, didn't you?" He picked up a tire iron.

"No," Danny said. "I did not. Stop accusing me. I want my gofer, I have immunity."

He lay back like an outsize baby bird. "Does anybody know the whereabouts of Johnny? Matters on the ground speak to the immediacy of contact."

"We'll see about that. Don't worry. You will be going to Rhyolite. At Rhyolite, we will take you to the bank. No problem, it's right on the border of Death Valley."

"I demand my gofer." He wrestled with his bottom half, trying to get in to scratch his southern hemisphere, but gave up. "Have you got my mobile? Where the hell is my mobile?"

"No reception," Val said. "You can't use a cellphone out here in the desert. Oh wait a minute, what am I thinking? I have a cell you could borrow. Special issue."

"Very good. I am going to ring through to the president. He will be on you in a minute. I was personally put in charge of public security for the country."

Val pulled an orange cellphone out of his jacket pocket. A special ops issue, unknown to and unavailable to the public. He pressed a white button. A small hawk moth flew out of the cellphone. Val pressed the button a second time. The tiny hawk moth landed on Danny's cheek, right below his left eye. Val pressed the button a third time. The hawk moth sent electric jolts into Danny Coma's eye area. It flew to the back of Danny's head where it joined his body. It flew to his crotch. Sending strong silent electricity at each stopping station.

Danny's whole body shook with spasms, he writhed back and forth, hitting his arms on the trunk's sides. He looked like he was having an epileptic seizure. Val knew from experience that Danny was in what a chromotherapist would call red, the blood speeded up dangerously. Val pressed the white button a fourth time. The hawk moth lifted off Danny and flew back to the cellphone, inserting itself flat against the cell's body. Val put the orange device back in his jacket. Danny's bird body was wet with urine and small bits of blood. His face was pale. "You should've noticed something at the Boston airport on September 11th, Danny boy. We have you on CCTV sitting right across the way from the 9/11 bombers in the pre-boarding area. You never saw a thing."

Danny lifted his head to Val. "They put me in economy. After all I've done. I told the bastards they should be *grateful* to have someone like me offer to tell them how to run their damn departments, but no, not them. You people." He threw up on the bird suit.

"Now look what you've done, Dan," Val said. He closed the trunk.

"I am in charge of national security," Danny shouted from inside.

Vivienne was posing Johnny at the edge of the vehicle, to show his reflection in the hood, all funhouse-mirror melting. The wind blew burnt matter off her scalp. "You coming?" she asked Val. "Val. Baby, you promised you would not go to the orange phone right away."

"I've been watching Daniel Coma coast for years. He doesn't even know that Val Gold is way above his pay grade. He has no idea I am his superior."

"*Vamos,*" Vivienne said.

"He wants diplomatic immunity. Call ahead to the vultures."

17

A BETTER EDEN

THEY DROVE THROUGH the skull of time. Inside the skull, the penetrating light of experiments shone. The skull curved and inside it, dead cows lay with skin hanging. The wool of sheep clung to the wet parts of the skull, floating teeth attached to bone and ate it away, exposing the wire nerves. The world's sand had been heated to glass. They drove along the glass jaw, the flashing nerve highway. This was Nevada, the atomic state.

Vivienne pulled out a piece of something hard sticking out of her jawline. She put it on her thigh, taking a photograph of it against her khakis. White, charred, sharp at the edges, folded in a small hem, with hairs sewn on it. Her bowels and lungs felt tornadic. It is the gas-filled organs that the atomic bombs affect first.

IN 1946, THE United States of America had stockpiled eleven nuclear weapons.

In 1958, the United States of America had stockpiled 9,822 nuclear weapons.

In 1962, the United States, already in Vietnam, had stockpiled 24,111 nuclear weapons.

Over a period of sixteen years, the USA stockpiled 24,111 nukes.

That's fifteen hundred nuclear weapons per year, give or take a nuclear weapon. That is thirty nukes hoarded per week. Crazy Uncle Sam was on a shopping spree. From 1946 to 1962, the US acquired an average of four new nukes every day. When the state is a hoarder, can we blame Citizen Sam for having one house and twenty-four thousand dead cats in the parlour?

By 1964, the USA had 30,751 nuclear weapons stockpiled.

By 1964, the USSR had 5,221 nuclear weapons stockpiled.

AND SO, ON the route between the nuclear testing grounds and Death Valley, Vivienne, Val and Johnny arrived at the ghost town of Rhyolite. On a rise, the skeleton of the Cook Bank stood like Hatra, an archeological ruin in pink stone. Grand and gone. Constructed of the surrounding hills' abundant soft pink rhyolite. They stopped, as travellers do, to rest in the ancient shell of commerce.

Until the year 1904, Rhyolite was unbuilt desert. Then gold was spotted. In 1905, Rhyolite had ten thousand people. But the boom fizzled. In 1910, Rhyolite had six hundred people. The last mine closed in 1911. The last train pulled out of the station in 1914. Rhyolite was born and died in ten years.

As the town of Rhyolite lay dying, the Nevada-California Power Company had no pity; it removed the electricity from the townspeople. The money people, well, they lived mostly in San Francisco, and they had their 1906 earthquake rebuilding to attend to, and so they pulled their money from the mining enterprises. The financial panic of 1907 panicked more men to pull more money out of start-up Rhyolite.

That panic erupted in the fall of 1907 when big money tried to corner shares of copper mining stock out in Butte, Montana. Money men bought and sold short, using that very phraseology, and other money men spoke of the short squeeze, trying to squeeze the short sellers to pay for their short sells. And the copper cornering attempt brought down the banking of New York City, and Wall Street was filled with panicked men, as banks went bankrupt during a recession. Back when bonds were suspect, when the public lost confidence in banks and trust was lost, and broken trusts and contagion filled the nation with money panic. When J. P. Morgan famously said that before money or property, he considered character when deciding if he would loan a man money. If he did not trust the man, then all the bonds in Christendom would not matter.

The story is told that there was one lone man left in Rhyolite, Nevada, by the year 1922. They sing of the one cow waiting on the train platform for the last train to pull out, but that old last train had long been and gone and nobody told the cow. They say that the bovine skeleton waits to this day on the platform at Rhyolite, Nevada. For the train to take her to a better dust in a better place, somewhere where booms don't go bust every day.

To take her out to San Francisco, west, or back south to Las Vegas, which was already incorporated back in 1905, a desert city older than Tel Aviv.

And yes, in Rhyolite, Nevada, in the midst of the mines and the miners' union hall and the stores and hotels inside the pink buff land, the igneous air, the soft silica, the mains of quartz and alkali feldspar, where volcanoes had erupted, and gold and silver were rushed like mirages in the rock land, in morphic lava and water stops, where the lava had cooled and stopped and made breccias and cooled obsidians, foundries and machine shops once did bloom, and children on their way to school did dot the desert land.

And of the three banks, the Cook Bank was the palace. Standing three stories tall, built of the local rhyolite hills, it stretched impressively along the concrete sidewalk. Or so the ancient photographs do show us. It had magnificent tall showy windows and a grand entrance, where a miner might enter in with wages to the opera hall of capital in the newly hot nowhere.

How fast the showpiece becomes a skeleton, the bones tempting as a location for a movie. The money palace called the Cook Bank of Rhyolite lasted but one year. The child born with weak lungs and a scary cough, who prevailed and lived until she died at age three, lived longer than the bank in the boom town where she was quietly buried.

Val took Danny into the bank bones. Johnny, in his long black coat, and Vivienne, in her pink leather jacket, left them alone and walked up an old mining hill. Val sat Danny down in the currency rubble. Why spoil the holidays by going abroad for your special rendition? Why not be a patriot, and do it at home this year?

18

IN THE KINGDOM OF RHYOLITE

"LET'S GO BACK a couple years to 2004, my friend," Val said, sitting beside Danny. "What were you doing in Burgos?"

"I have never been in Spain," Danny said, not looking at him.

"I did not say anything about Spain."

Val opened Danny's hand and began to stroke the flesh on Danny's palm. Be like the date he wishes he had, who showed curiosity about his life as man.

"I understand you are quite the spiritual fellow. I understand you walked the pilgrim trail to Santiago de Compostela, Danny."

"Who told you that?" A man suspicious of all things will become suspicious that someone knows the very thing he might brag about.

"Oh come on, Danny. Walking all across Spain and into Portugal. I myself would do it if I had half the time."

"Time? I have no time. The wife wanted to go."

"Ah, of course. The wife. She who must be obeyed."

"You've got that right. Don't worry, she kept busy. She was quite the figure in Rio. She whipped those Brazilians into shape."

Nice, Val thought. A little bread crumb about Danny's wife.

Val watched Vivienne and Johnny up the hill. They stopped and kissed. Vivienne arranged Johnny's black coat, pulling the wool collar up, kissing him again. Taking his photograph. The grass is always greener, even where there is only dust.

Danny was at the windowsill of the bank, trying to pet a raven. Val walked over to him. "I hear Burgos is a lovely town on the Santiago walk."

"Burgos, my dear man," Danny said, "is one of the choice medieval towns of España. We stayed at a parador. A parador is an inn that is supported by the government. Subsidized, if you will." Val knew what a parador was. He stayed steady, sucking up Danny's condescension. The raven flew to Danny's shoulder. "High wooden rafters, not my thing. But the missus insisted." Chuckling. Talking like he and Val were on the same team – the put-the-blame-on-the-dame team of men. Val, however, had a different game.

"I'll tell you what I like," Val said. "That Spanish ham."

"Jamón Ibérico," said Danny, who moments ago under the witness of the big blue sky had sworn he had never been to Spain. "Ibérico, the Jamón Serrano is my special favourite."

"How about that sausage?" Val said. "The blood? Love the blood." Switching his voice into a somewhat British musical mode. "I do adore *la morcilla de Burgos.*"

Danny cupped his hand to Val's right ear. "Don't tell anybody, but we discovered this quite marvellous spot, where one can procure possibly the best blood sausage in Spain. A butcher shop, right there in the lovely town of Burgos."

"Right on the Camino? Where the pilgrims walk to see Saint James' bones?"

"The very Camino. On our way to Compostela, we bought the sausage from the butcher in Burgos, and voila! – my word. Simply splendid. Dark. Not with onions, as Don Quixote, if I may say, might have found in La Mancha." Danny rubbed his hands. "That rain-jacket-thing they assured me was waterproof? Not even resistant. We sat down, soaked as ducks, and thanked god for the blood sausage."

"But you do know about the butcher of Burgos, Danny?""

"I just told you."

"You do know he was in the papers."

"Look, you fool. I am trying to keep the world safe, I do not have time to read every local rag in town."

"It was in the *Guardian*," Val said. "The butcher of Burgos. They arrested him in May 2004, in medieval Burgos on the route to Santiago de Compostela. He was the main conduit in Spain for money going to al Qaeda in the Arabian Peninsula."

"That's bull diddy," Danny said.

"Danny. Pakistan…North Africa…that blood sausage, the *morcilla cocida* you bought in Burgos, April '04? The real Santiago trail story? Your foodie find was a terrorist money launderer."

"I was on holiday."

"Terror doesn't take a holiday, Danny."

Danny had that puzzled look of a man so sure he had it covered that he literally could not conceive he had nothing covered.

Val Gold spoke: "The prosecution will be bringing charges of dereliction of duty, lack of professional focus, becoming a 'spiritual person' and being gravely misdirected by a Spanish *chorizo*. Sentence pending."

Danny smirked and fondled himself. "One gives fully frank assurances that, at this point in time, the Camino was no ham-handed stroll, but rather an attempt at the normalization of relations in the bigger picture of the Spanish Street."

Val led Danny back to the bank ruin's floor. They sat.

"So, terror money being washed in Spain," Val said. "Let's stay with Spain and go to that fateful year of 2001. You were on vacation, right? South of Barcelona, at the resort town of Salou."

"I work hard. I deserve it," Danny said.

"Did you know that the men who planned the attack on the Twin Towers were vacationing in Spain in the same town as you, Salou? Same place, same time. They were, our evidence now shows, in Spain in June of 2001, finalizing their September 11th attack. Three months after the Madrid train bombing, the Saudi terrorists were finalizing the details of their intention to fly into the Twin Towers as they lay on chaises at that resort in Spain. The same hotel where you and the missus were switching from your vodka martinis to your cava wine cups, lying back in the hell heat. The Dorada Palace Hotel. The Gold Palace, appropriate, don't you think? Security footage shows you working on your melanoma three feet away from the men making their final plans to destroy New York City."

"Call me a cab, la-la-la-la," Danny said, putting his fingers in his ears. "One must needs return to the scribbling; my novel awaits me! Where is my gofer?"

The desert sand was silent.

"You could have stopped September 11th; you could have stopped March 11th, at the Madrid trains; you could have stopped the June 19th, 1987, ETA bombing in Barcelona; you could have fingered the Butcher of Burgos; you could have prevented the murder at the Bilbao Guggenheim the day it opened; and now you have to face the people's court for it all."

"For things I didn't do?" Danny said.

"In our field, Danny, omission is a sin. The venal sin of incompetence. Your intent was vanity. You trained your pride. You became a B-plus in looking in the normal places. But, Danny, when counterterrorism gets a B-plus, people die."

"Who retired and made you chief of spies?"

"They offered it to me," Val said. That was true. "But you know what, Danny? I kinda like working the field, flying down to Rio a hell of a lot better. I used to go hole up at the Hotel Inglês in Botafogo. Go down when Washington was suffering one of those Rangoon Junes, and it was nice and autumn-like in Rio. On a nice crisp day, I used to take a long walk to Copacabana Beach. I believe I saw a man who looked just like you lying on the sand, oh back in '64. You know, back when the Brazilian military was getting torture training from its American buddies. Was it you there, Daniel? With a small brunette. Very tan, white bikini. You and the missus? Maybe a little bikini volleyball on the Copacabana sand?"

"That wife of mine worked like a demon," Danny said. "They gave her an airless office in a basement out in Leblon, and put her to work, training under the master, Mr. Mitrione. She deserved some time off. Then it was on to Montevideo. Beautiful little city. For my money, the beaches there were preferable. I told her I wanted to retire there."

"You and Gilda."

"Excuse me?" Danny took off his right boot. His leg was scaly.

"Danny. Dear dear Danny. You remember the movie *Gilda*?" Val was still on the track of his intention.

"Ah, yes, Miss Joan Crawford."

Val chuckled. "I don't think so, sonny boy. Yeah, I like it: Joan Crawford in a gown, entertaining at a nightclub? No, Dan. Rita Hayworth as Gilda. She and Glenn Ford get mixed up in that romance on fire. You know the one. Kinda like you and your brother, Johnny. Hate is the emotion so very much like love. But now Gilda is back at the nightclub, doing that dance, inducing Glenn Ford to hate her, while he can't keep his eyes off of her with lust. It was Montevideo. Montevideo in *Gilda* was like romantic, alluring casinos; glamour figures; the Southern Cone –"

"Hello, sweetheart." Vivienne was walking into the bank frame, with her camera at her eyes, saying, "I remember meeting your wife in Montevideo, Danny. 'She who must be obeyed.' The famous Mrs. Coma. Val, ask him about Mrs. Coma, La Doctora. Ask him about when she put the electrodes –"

"Out of order!" Danny said. "If it please the court..."

"Vivienne," Val said. "Not now."

"Ask him," she said, walking over to Danny. Saying, right up in Danny's face, "Ask him about when his wife put the electrical wires around my neck, applied the shock and asked me, and I am quoting verbatim, 'Why do you like cartoonists?'"

"Vivienne. Please," Val said. Johnny was outside the bank, listening.

"And I said to Mrs. Coma, 'Cartoonists are fun. I like cartoons.' She showed me a photograph of me and my buddy, a cartoonist from *El Dedo*, the satirical magazine in Montevideo, the two of us sitting in the Columbia Palace Hotel's coffee shop. 'Yeah?' I said. So she shocked my neck again with the electric collar. No sense of humour, your wife, Danny. She wore a suit. That killed me. A little navy suit, dull black pumps. 'Tell us where he is.' They knew very well where he was. They always know the answers to the questions they are asking you. 'Why are you taking pictures of public buildings?' she asked me. 'Because public means of the people,' I said. More neck jolts. And you know what I remember most about Mrs. Coma? She smelled like booze. Bad enough she was a heart doctor torturing supposed subversives. She was a boozehound to boot. She put her ugly *punim* right up at me, saying, 'Where is the cartoonist?' and her breath smelled like a distillery."

"This is outrageous," Danny said. "Preposterous. Vodka doesn't smell."

"Vivienne," Val said, "I am trying to do my work here."

Vivienne snapped a pic of Danny. "Stop it," he said. She snapped a dozen more.

"It's people like her who forced us to put into effect the Homeland Security Act," Danny said.

"Note the 'us,'" Vivienne said. "Danny got duped by his own role-playing, in America."

"I'd like to resume," Val said. "If you have no objections, Ms. Pink."

Vivienne was camera-stalking Danny. "You know what the best part was, Val? When Betty Coma was putting the electrodes to my neck… Oh, and by the way, Betts called her torture room the executive suite. It was a soundproof room in the basement of her and Danny's capacious home in Montevideo. Gotta love that cork. And while you, Danny, entertained the local military wags upstairs, Mrs. Coma – said to be away on a medical mercy mission – was torturing citizens under suspicion. You know, photojournalists. Witnesses. People with eyes. Me. Then when the guests went home, guess who brought his cognac and cigar down to watch his wife. You watched the good doctora torture me, Danny Coma. You took a little VIP guest turn at the electricity machine. I saw your eyes, Daniel. You thought God was with you."

"This is absurd," Danny said. "I will have none of it." He stood up on wobbly pins.

Val pushed him flat onto the gravel. "The prosecution accuses you of complicity, aiding and abetting the humiliation and degradation of innocent civilians."

"Nothing of the sort," Danny said, looking for help to the amorality of sky.

Johnny stepped into the ruins. "What are you talking about? Vivi, V? Why didn't you tell me, Vivienne?"

"Val knew," Vivienne said.

"You told Val and you didn't tell me?" Johnny asked. He started buttoning his coat.

"You couldn't handle it."

"And you could?" he said.

"You know the answer," Vivienne said. "It was thirty years ago."

"My very point," Danny said.

"He watched," Val said. "Then he wanted to be a player. He stepped up – didn't you, Danny? – to operationalize his need to know what it felt like to apply electricity to a woman's nerve endings."

Vivienne took pics of Johnny's face. "Why, tell me why you didn't tell me," he said to her.

"We were dating," she said. "You were already worried I might get killed, or worse. I made a decision to spare you."

"But you told Val. When?"

"Let it go, Jojo."

"When?"

"One night, in a Sarajevo taxi."

"So, you and Val are off working in Sarajevo, and you go tell him how Danny's wife, Betty Coma, tortured you in Uruguay? But you don't tell me. 'Oh hi, honey. No, I'm fine. Val says to save him some Gigi pizza.' Is that it?"

"About right," she said, crouching down to snap a pic of Danny's rogue Frye boot and the scaly calf.

"All these years I never knew. I was your husband."

"You needed to write your books, honey."

Vivienne came up to Danny. She hated flashes, but she attached one to her camera. In the bright sunlight, standing a couple inches from Danny she kept using the flash. "You know who your wife was? She was the person who would have stepped into *Gilda* and taken Gilda in Montevideo and put her in a basement and tortured her to find out who this 'Mame' was who Gilda kept singing about putting the blame on."

"You were fat," Danny said. "Fat and blond. Now I remember. Don't blame me because you lost weight and changed your hair colour."

"What was it like, Danny?" Vivienne asked. "To be married to the most unkind of women? Is that why you threw her off the cliff in Patagonia?"

"You people are all one and the same," Danny said, putting his bony face right up to Vivienne's. "The wife? She was a damn embarrassment."

Johnny unbuttoned his black wool coat. He stepped up to Danny and brought Danny into the coat. "Chilly, isn't it, Dan? Feeling a bit *freddo*." He kissed Danny on each cheek. He held Danny close inside the coat. "How did it happen, Dan? Two brothers, so different, nothing in common. So now I know. All that talk about writing a novel? It was just a con, to cover what your life really was. You knew my weakness was you, my brother. Your goddamned unused potential. You, the perfect son, hanging out with punks, watching them smash streetlights at night, and you became the perfect shadow man, watching your wife torture photographers. What were the choices you made, Danny, every day of the week, to take you to that soundproof basement?"

"Call Ma," Danny said, inside the long black coat. "You should pay her back the thousand dollars you owe her. You should stop criticizing me. You should be more of a brother. You should do yoga. You should be less judgmental." He stepped out of the coat. "You should never have married – that one."

Johnny grabbed Danny by his bony arm. "My heart goes to my throat, you know, some nights. I think about how much I wanted to be proud of my older brother. And then I saw that all he ever wanted in life was that his younger brother be unhappy. Your intention in life, Dan, was to feel big by making other people feel small. Congratulations. Mission accomplished."

Vivienne said, "To hell with it," and started back up the old miners' hill. Val followed her. She got to the abandoned train station, and sat down on one of the wide wooden stairs.

"You know, from here," Val said, "that bank looks like the old city hall I saw in Hiroshima." Like Vivienne, Val had seen things when he was too young to see them.

"You're thinking about your mother," she said. "Ruth." His mother was a photographer; she had taken young Val on assignment with her.

"I was only – what was it? – seven years old," he said. "And she takes me to Japan."

Vivienne knew the story: Val's dad, Len, had fought at Iwo Jima. He came home with only one leg. He went back to have a reunion with buddies at Okinawa, and he was never seen again. Gone like smoke. Val at age six became the man of the house. The next year, Ruth Gold took little Val along when she went to document Hiroshima, ten years after Little Boy was dropped on the city. Young Val had his Brownie camera. He wandered in the wreckage while his mom took pictures. He emulated her.

"I can still see it," he said to Vivienne. "The gas company building with columns, and the high entryway, and everything is collapsed and bombed. Two and a half stories standing against a ruined atomic sky. Like a Turner-smudge-pot sky. Look down there. That bank looks like the sky fell on it."

Down below, Danny was standing with his back to them, leaning on an old bank counter, looking into blue space. Johnny was on the ground, his head bowed.

"Did I ever tell you about the day my mother met Pablo Neruda?" Val asked.

"I like that story; tell me that story again." Vivienne zipped her pink leather jacket to her chin.

The story went something like this: Ruth Gold's hero was the war photographer Gerda Taro, a redhead called *La Pequeña Rubia*. She was Robert Capa's lover and Capa said she was the braver of the two. Gerda went to the front in the Spanish Civil War and died in combat. Ruth had known Gerda. Friends had introduced them in Paris.

Ruth had told her young son, Val, not only about Gerda, the brave war photographer, but about palling around with Robert Capa. Endre or André Friedmann who had become Robert Capa. How Capa had died covering the Indochina War, in Vietnam in 1954, living to only age forty.

And another photographer buddy in Ruth's circle: Dawid Szymin, who became David Seymour, who became Chim. Chim died when shot by Egyptian gunfire at Suez in 1956, living to just shy of forty-five.

But first, there was Gerda, his mom's role model and hero. Gerta Pohorylle, the Jewish Spanish-German woman who covered war and who had renamed herself Gerda Taro. (Tarō was the name of a Japanese painter she knew in Paris.) Gerda was killed at the Battle of Brunete, during the Spanish Civil War. She lived to age twenty-six.

The French Communists gave her a grand funeral and commissioned the sculptor Alberto Giacometti to make a monument for her grave. And then, in came Pablo Neruda. Ruth Gold was at Gerda's funeral in Paris, and so was Pablo Neruda, and they got to talking.

It was Ruth who told Val that Gerda Taro is considered the first female photojournalist to die covering war. Ruth used to say to Val, "How could this woman on the front lines be unknown when everybody who was anybody knew her?"

The photographers of the Spanish Civil War had been Hungarian, Polish, German. Jews all. And this, too, his mother had told him. (And Vivienne knew that she came from the same tribe, knew she entered a profession where every day you expect to die, knew she had already outlived each one of them.)

And that was their life, Ruth the single mother and her little boy, Val, out to the locations in Japan which his American elders had bombed. Where he saw necks like withered trees, trees like gouged steel, bottles looking like melted animal carcasses.

Val never let on to his mother that, when he was studying acting at Yale in the '60s, he had been approached by the CIA, who wanted to recruit him as an information asset who would move to Toronto, in order to ingratiate himself with art and literary circles for the purpose of gathering intelligence on active individuals. Like photographer Vivienne Pink and writer Johnny Coma. Or that the usual advice – strongly "suggested" – was to not marry, not to become a homeowner, to stay low around the university area, to be ready to return to the States if needed for intelligence work. He could have said no, he could have declined, he could have become an activist for love, he could have made a love plan and acted on it, but he did not. He travelled with writers and artists. He reported back on them. He chose the rat existence.

"Did you spy on us?" Vivienne asked.

"What kind of a question is that?" Val said.

"Did you?"

"I'm not going to dignify that with an answer."

"So answer without dignity. Did you?"

"Vivi. Why torment yourself? What's past is past. Didn't you yourself say that?"

"Do not turn this back on me. It's just chumps and cons, isn't it, Val?"

"What?"

"Everything. Everybody. Well, not Johnny."

Val got up and walked to the end of the train platform. He picked up a dusty chair and brought it back to Vivienne. He stood leaning over the back of it, talking to her. She shot a pic of Val. He looked like an informal professor. "Gauguin's chair," he said. "Ruth took me to Hiroshima's city hall. There was a chair sitting in the bomb rubble. There was a little boy's jacket draped on it, charred, burnt." He ran his hand through his silver fox hair. "When I first laid eyes on Van Gogh's painting of Gauguin's chair, it felt Japanese to me. It was lonely, like Hiroshima. Van Gogh's green. What a green. Vincent wrote Paul a poem in paint."

Vivienne took the shot. Val's eyes were not on the chair or the haunted desert in which he stood. They were in that perfect place: when he was new and young and suffered the ecstasy of how bitterly transformative the world could be. Yet he still had not been able to cross the threshold into marrying her.

Everyone had their default oasis. Vivienne's oasis was making art. Val's oasis was knowing how to speak about art. Vivienne's love oasis was

Johnny. Val's love oasis was picking the scab of his own stasis. The rat highway was a cold, cold place, indeed.

"If you were a widow, would you marry me?" he asked. Vivienne was already walking down the hill. The sun was waning on the bank. The bouncing desert migraine shone on. Van Gogh knew hell was a sunny day. Van Gogh was our monk to the canvas. Van Gogh knew about the burn. Van Gogh spoke to the crows on the sunniest of days.

VIVIENNE AND VAL walked back down to the remains of the Cook Bank building. Vivienne left Val, and walked to Johnny. They watched, as Val restarted the holiday special rendition.

"Danny, let's cut to the nukes. What can you tell me about your time in Spain with the family, Christmas holidays just like now, family time, right? You, the missus, your four kids, you take them down south to Málaga. Correct? For New Year's, January 1966?"

"I have never been to Spain, my dog has never been to Spain, my cat has never been to Spain, my mother has never been to Spain, my father has never been to Spain, my sister has never been to Spain, my son has never been to Spain, my daughter has never been to Spain and I have never been to Spain."

"So, you're in Málaga, but you have work to do nearby. At Palomares. Little fishing village, some market gardening, tomatoes."

"There was no daylight in Spain."

"Now, if it please the court," Val said, reaching into his jacket pocket, pulling out a photograph, serrated edges, black and white: two men in swimming trunks, standing in waves. One man tall, the other one short. "I would like to introduce into evidence a photograph." Val tapped the photo. "This short guy? In the Speedo? That's you, Daniel Coma, only forty years younger." Val showed it to Danny. Then Val passed the photo to Vivienne, who looked at it, and passed it to Johnny, who passed it back to Val.

"This is preposterous," Danny said. "I demand a cab."

"Sorry, Danny, the last taxi left in 1910."

"Call dispatch!" The sight of the photograph had put Danny back into the state he had been in on Las Vegas Boulevard, when he had dressed like a bird.

"Tell me the story of this snap, Danny. You're at the beach. It's the first week in January 1966. Lucky you, you get to be on the Costa del Sol. I think I was in Copenhagen that year. What about you folks on the jury? Did anybody ever pay you to go to the beach in Spain and hobnob with the American ambassador?"

"1966, let me see," Vivienne said. "I think I was... Oh yeah, that's right. I was back in Vietnam. Taking pics of the soldiers, getting in even deeper. The American government had left Crazytown and gone right into the crotch rot of Psychosis Corners."

"Me?" Johnny said. "In '66? I think that was the winter I took that freighter from Havana to Luanda, and I got the light bulb for my book set in Angola."

"I never heard anything about any book about Angola," Danny said.

"No surprises, there," Johnny said.

"Now, now," Val said. "Let's keep our eyes on southern Spain. Sunny days, the beach, coastal seafood, Daniel Coma, fixer-at-large, by special invitation is meeting with the American ambassador to Spain."

"I want to lawyer up." Danny was so used to deniability that even though the photo Val had in his hand had appeared in *TIME* magazine, Danny denied it existed.

Danny maintained that I-am-not-here look. "In Vietnam," he said, "we were looking for peace. We got a ceasefire, you people have no idea. We were trying. Rusk, Pearson, me, we were giving it our all." Danny had left his birdman fugue and rejoined his pissed-off bitter bureaucrat part.

"Giving it your all? No, Danny, you were giving it your *some*. When they upped it to four hundred thousand American troops in Vietnam you were doing US dirty work in Spain. You dare to mention Lester B. Pearson, our beloved ex-prime minister, please. You think you're Lester Bowles Pearson? Since when did you play semi-pro ball and head up the UN, like Pearson?"

"He was the reason I got into politics," Danny said.

"Another category error heard from," Val said. "What you got into was a pair of gloves to leave no prints when you broke into foreign offices."

"Like he said," Vivienne said. "Politics."

"If our Pearson was your role model, Dan, what in the hell happened? He brought in the forty-hour workweek. He's in the Canadian Baseball Hall of Fame. He got us our own flag. He was a fly boy, he went to war, he was a medic and an airman, he crashed a plane, and then, while recovering, he got hit by a bus in a blackout in London and he came home and, next thing you know, he invented peacekeeping. Lester B *invented* it. He *started* NATO, he *started* the UN, he *averted* the crisis in the Suez. For God's sakes, Danny. Wake up, Lester Pearson won the Nobel Peace Prize. I am talking here about a statesman. Our man Pearson. You signed on to be a career sneak. You washed the blood off their words."

"A troll with immunity," Vivienne said.

"Meanwhile, what was your idol Pearson doing? He goes down to the States, and in good old Philly, he gives a speech at Temple University, criticizing LBJ sending more soldiers to Vietnam. Unheard of. Pearson dissed LBJ in Lyndon Johnson's own country. A Thou Shalt Not of diplomacy. Here was a man. Pearson put the diplomatic shiv into LBJ."

Val got up. "Then, as the story is told, Lyndon Johnson summoned Prime Minister Lester B. Pearson from Temple U to Camp David. Whereupon LBJ picks up Pearson by his lapels, shakes him, tells him, 'Don't you dare come in my house and talk to me like that.' Pearson refused to send Canadian boys to Vietnam."

There is the man who shies back and makes no decision. There is the man, exhausted by his options, who just lets his impulse manager go, and picks anything. But Danny Coma was the third man, the man who stays on the shore and invents the lie that he has crossed the Rubicon, and tells it to the mirror, and the mirror says that the man in the mirror has done that thing and the mirror whispers to tell it to the face of those who have made the crossing. You could see the sides of Danny's cheeks chewing themselves.

Val went on. "Okay. All right. A little detour, to speak of what a man is. But now let us stay in the days of Vietnam, but let us travel, once again, to those sunny climes of southern Spain. January 1966. Just after New Year's. Along the coast from Málaga, there in Almería, there in Almanzora, there in Mojácar, there in Palomares."

"So big deal, so I took the kids to the beach," Danny said, not looking at Val, but talking to the far shining horizon.

Vivienne shook her head, questioning, "You took my nieces and nephews to that beach?"

"They are my brother's nieces and nephews," Danny said to Val. "Not hers."

"Danny," Val said. "Let us contemplate the story of that January, as it has come down to us through history. They call it Broken Arrow. The US Broken Arrow over Spain."

And the story goes something like this: On January 17th, 1966, a Monday, two planes, one flying east from inside Spain, one flying west all the way from South Carolina, USA, collided over southern Spain, over the fishing village of Palomares. It was a refuelling mission. The plane from the United States was a B-52G carrying four hydrogen bombs. The mission was called Operation Chrome Dome. The idea was to fly to the European borders of the Soviet Union, and return.

At thirty-one thousand feet, a KC-135 out of Morón Air Base in southern Spain began to refuel the B-52. The story is told that the nozzle of the refuelling boom hit the B-52 fuselage. The planes exploded. The four Spaniards in the KC-135 were killed, and three of the seven American crew were killed. And four H-bombs landed near the Spanish fishing village of Palomares.

Palomares is on the Mediterranean, nine miles from the resort town of Mojácar, and not far from the Costa del Sol town of Almería, a desert land on the sea known to movie lovers as the area where Sergio Leone made his spaghetti westerns.

Now come up a little northeast from *The Good, the Bad and the Ugly*, put your eyes to the sky and there you see two planes explode, two planes catch fire and four H-bombs land on European soil. The United States became the avatar of its own nuclear nightmare.

The tiny Spanish fishing village became briefly world famous, because the story went that the conventional explosives inside a nuke, which normally set it off, did set off two of the nukes. The third nuke was said to have not detonated. A fourth H-bomb was lost at sea. The stories vary.

Danny Coma was sent in to stage-manage this nuclear disaster. The questions began fast: did all the bombs, not just two, in truth, go off at Palomares? Was it two or three? Or was it four, and there was a fifth hydrogen bomb the US was trying to cover up? An H-bomb that no one ever found, leaking into the fish and shellfish, and which sat, nuclear, on the Mediterranean Sea floor, still leaking into the twenty-first century? Might that tasty olive-oiled octopus be radioactive?

That Monday, January 17th, 1966, was a black swan day. As delegates met for nuclear disarmament conferences, the day that could never come had come, the day when you happened to drop hydrogen bombs on an ally. Future doom was already in progress.

The American B-52 carried four hydrogen bombs. Each H-bomb was 1.5 megatons. Each bomb was one hundred times the power of the bomb that was dropped on Hiroshima on August 5th, 1945. You could say that on that January winter morning, the United States dropped four hundred Little Boys on Spain. You could say that the United States hurt its amigo in peace, España, one hundred times more than its enemy in war, Japan. You could say it, because it was true. Japan received a total of thirty-six kilotons, Spain received a total of six thousand kilotons.

The only thing to do with such a monumental sovereign sin was to spin it. Send in the spinners! Ask them to eat nuked seafood out of nuked sea water. Ask them to swim in the blue plutonium sea.

The American ambassador to Spain, Angier Biddle Duke, went swimming in the Mediterranean at the nearby beach resort of Mojácar, to demonstrate to the press that four hundred Little Boys dropped nine miles away meant nothing, left no radiation. The ambassador, at age twenty-seven had been on the cover of *Life* magazine, at age forty-eight he had been in charge of protocol for John F. Kennedy's funeral and at age fifty US ambassador Duke paddled around in radioactive waters to spin the nukes. If a state representative was in exposed skin and swimming trunks in the water, the spin said, wouldn't he be nuts to do that if the water was nuclear?

In the photograph beside Duke was Danny Coma, his arm around the ambassador's shoulder.

Maybe it is not what a nation does in victory, but what it does in *shanda* – in shame – that makes it a nation. Does it shrivel and con, or does it stand tall and make reparation and tell the true story? Do you repent, or do you spin the shanda?

"And you took your children down there," Val said. "In lieu of truth-telling, you'd rather poison your own kids."

"Objection!" Danny said. "Stop calling me names. Look, I will show you the dirt," Danny said. "It's here in my suitcase. It's in the car."

"In the what? Where? You are telling me you put a suitcase with radio-active dirt from Spain forty years ago in our car?"

"You naive youngsters. What did you think we would do? Leave the evidence in the ground? American troops were dispatched, quite handily I might say, to dig up the dirt and repatriate it back to the US."

"Hang on," Val said. "You are telling me to hide it they – what? – flew the Spanish radioactive soil back to the States and buried it?"

"Indeed." Danny scratched his balls.

"Where?"

"How should I know? The funeral was private."

"What? In paper bags, I suppose."

"For your information, it came in coffins. They covered the coffins with flags and kept the dirt hidden."

"So, let me get this straight. You can't today, by order of the president, take photographs of the pine boxes holding servicemen who died overseas, but they could ship the nuclear accident evidence back using those coffins like jokes from a TV show about inept cocaine cowboys?"

"Don't blame me. I smiled and ate shrimp."

"Danny; Danny Danny Danny. Daniel. Dan. Don't you see? You got poisoned."

"I will have you know that was very fertile soil. Legacy tomatoes. Heritage seeds. I made some quite lovely *pan con tomate* out of it, if I do say so myself."

"Am I crazy or are you crazy or am I the only one here who is nuts? You made Spanish crushed tomato bread out of plants that grew in nuclear soil?"

"All I get is criticism."

"You carried that nuclear dirt on planes?"

"More than you'll ever know. My tomatoes had immunity. If you didn't want my dirt in the trunk of your car, you should have let me sit in the front seat. Minding my own business at my posting at Paris, you kidnapped the special ambassador to Rhyolite. I do not negotiate with hostage-takers."

"Just say you are sorry," Val said. "All we want is that you allocute to the court. Tell us how you regret what you did. Tell us, once and for all and finally, that you feel remorse for lying to the public about the nuclear water and the poisoned food chain. That you regret your role in the torturing of the Canadian photographer Vivienne Pink, daughter of Isadore 'Izzy' Pink, former mayor of Toronto. We need to see you feel remorse. We need you to feel sick at heart."

"Perhaps," Danny said. "In due course at the end of the day never let it not be said that in the final analysis, where was I? Ah. Of course. I have it now. Édith Piaf! '*Je ne regrette rien*.' And yes, many salutations for the trigger. Yes yes. Cows." Danny's Speedo had fallen down to his knees, and he urinated on the rocks. He stepped out of his Speedo, allowing his nether brothers a little desert air.

"May it please the court, I would like to introduce, what is, in my opinion, the much overlooked scandal of the blue steak." Danny put his hands behind his back, his head leaning forward, as he walked back and forth in front of Val, swinging the Coma jewels. "Of course, this had been of some concern to the international community on the ground, for an unspecified but notable length of time, not at this point in time, but prima facie, once."

"Get to the meat," Val said. "Show me the regret. Be merciful, Dan, to the damaged."

"Oh, I had to meet with the terrorists. Medical degrees? Sorry, impress me. Art collections. I've seen art. Wives in high leather boots. On and on about their bombs. I sat across those terror *tregua* tables with them, negotiating ceasefires day and night, and I can bring you this information: not one of them knew what a blue steak was." He retrieved his Speedo and pulled it up his bony legs.

Val lit a cigarette. "Danny, the three of us have a room reservation at Stovepipe Wells. We need to leave soon. We're not feeling so well."

"Yes, your honour, with my greatest pleasure. I spent my life telling them, 'Go out and get a cow. Walk the cow through town. When the cow gets in front of the damn restaurant, send the waiter out with a gun to shoot the cow. Then set the kitchen on fire, and rush the cow back to the kitchen door. Let the cow look through the double doors and smell smoke. Then push the cow into the kitchen fire and pull the cow out, fast. Then put the damn cow, bloody and burned on a plate. *That* is *blue*.'

"But oh no. Did they give me a blue steak? No sir, Uncle Sam Siree. People of the jury, do I not deserve your pity? People, I asked for a steak, they gave me small leather goods on a plate, 'here's the horseradish.' I rest my case." Danny saluted. "*Avanti*!"

VAL TOOK DANNY over to the vehicle. Val popped the trunk. Danny took out his little hard suitcase, an old-school one, tan and brown, and he clicked back the metal locks and opened it up, like a travelling salesman. There was his booty: smelly socks, another blue Speedo, a fuzzy grey fleece pullover, a pair of pale chinos crumpled into a ball and a paper bag. He put his hand in the paper bag and came out with a handful of dirt.

"Get that away from me," Val said, backing off.

"This dirt, kind sir, I would like to inform you," Danny said, sifting the gritty mix through his hands, letting some of it fall on the ghost ground. "This is one of our finer clandestine soil batches. A mere culling from the American Broken Arrow nuclear crop. But first impressions..."

Val had no idea what Danny was getting at. That was rare for Val. "What's going on here, Danny? What's all this BS leading to?"

"As fine as your finest Islay whisky," Danny said. "With much the same notes of salt and iodine. But this, my friend, has in it some of the rare dirt gathered from the Vallegrande Airport. The Big Valley. In that excellent year of 1967."

That Val knew. The legend of the killing of Che: First, the men who came to kill Che Guevara were kind and gave him one last pipe to smoke. But one of them took the pipe away immediately, and saved it for a souvenir. Then the executioner posed for a photo with the man he was appointed to execute. Then he executed him. Then they flew Che's dead body to Vallegrande Airport, where they posed for more photographs with the corpse. October 9th, 1967. Then they cut off Che Guevara's hands and posed with the amputations, soon put into formaldehyde in a jar. Then they secretly buried Che at the airport. They assumed they would be known in glory, for the charisma dust that might fall to them, for murdering a legend. But, like wind, a photo op has a life of its own. *Saint Che before the Martyrdom. The Corpse of the Martyr Doctor Guevara Lynch.*

"Talk about incompetents," Val said. "Dead Che might as well have hired Washington to market his image. The killers are *Fulanos de Tal*, little Joe Nobodies. But like a magnetic force we are pulled to the face of Che. And now, Danny Coma, you are telling me you took some of the soil from the Bolivian airport where the botch-up boys interred Che Guevara, and mixed it with the Spanish soil from where the Americans accidentally dropped several nukes near Málaga?"

"It's excessively rare, my son. Antique terroir. We even have some zygote tomatoes." Danny fished down in the paper bag and brought out a small red object. Palm of his hand, pulpy, glowing, zaftig. It looked like a miniature callipygous Venus.

"Don't you worry, little one," Danny said, speaking to the tomato. Diva, or demented, who knew?

"Give me the damn dirt, Danny," Val said, then he pulled his hand back.

"Oh wait," Danny said. "We have one more thing to show the man, do we not, little one?" He fished further down in the paper bag, pulling out a Rolex watch. "Don't mind if I do. The very one," he said, "as you might have guessed. Doctor Ernesto Guevara's wristwatch. Rolex GMT Master. The man had good taste, I'll have to give him that."

Consider the man, Daniel Coma, hearing the silent applause in the shadows. Consider that he scooped up the bird suit from the trunk, and carrying his avian avatar in one hand and a nuclear-execution blend in the other, and wearing the Rolex stolen from the corpse of the sainted asthmatic physician, he bade, "*Hasta Luego!*" while walking back east towards the main military highway.

19

ROOM 214

JOHNNY AND VIVIENNE got in the back seat of the white Honda. Val got behind the wheel. In that early slow sundown, which goes to black quickly, they drove west into light and shadow, descending to sea level.

"You know, I remember having a beer with Che," Val said. "In Ireland on St. Paddy's Day."

"Like hell you did," Vivienne said, checking out Val's laughing face in the mirror.

"True story," Val said. "So I'm doing some checking up on our boys in the IRA. First I had to go to New York, because Che was speaking at the UN. December 1965. Sure, a couple nutjobs had tried to knock Che off in Manhattan: a woman with a knife at the UN, and then some real brainiac who sat in the East River with a badly timed bazooka. So then Che decides to tour the world and check out his Irish roots."

"Che? Irish?" Vivienne asked.

"Absolutely," Val said. "Lynch. In another life he was Ernie Lynch. So, I had a little sit-down with Ernie in Limerick. March 1966. Think about it. St. Paddy's Day in Ireland, and two and a half years later they assassinate him in Bolivia. He had a great low droll voice, Che did. He spoke in that distinct Argentinian Italian-sounding lilt."

"Without the photographs of Che, there would be no worldwide Che," Vivienne said. "Heck of a job, CIA."

THE THREE MUSKETEERS pulled up at the Stovepipe Wells rustic motel. They went up the timber stairs into the motel's reception. The check-in area was about the size of the front seat of their vehicle. Jammed into it were three people, a tall fair-haired man with a shorter woman, pouring coffee from a Pyrex set on a hot plate on a little table, speaking Russian, and a round man in a scarlet short-sleeved shirt and a panama hat. He was at the counter, mid-conversation, saying, "No, that is not right. I was distinctly told I could drive right up to the room."

"Sir," said the tall man at the counter in an Irish knit sweater the colour of the sand outside. "Sir. You can easily drive up to the room. I think you will find there is no problem here, I think you will find there is no disagreement, sir, we are on the same page. You will be able to drive your car right up to the room. The cars back up to the walkway and you will be able to unload right there. I can send somebody with you to help you unload. Sir, the room is as advertised."

It was the way the clerk, whose name the threesome had forgotten, but whose face they knew as that droll gent from years gone by, said *sir* that alerted them to his inner voice saying, "We got a live one here." He had seen it all. But the clerk was in the hospitality industry and he knew it, and so, a modern miracle, he was being hospitable. "Sir, if you want to take your car around, I will send José here right with you." He looked at Vivienne, then at Val, then at Johnny. "Well, look at that. Here they are. Folks, glad to see you back, with you soon as I get my friend here sorted out."

The man in the scarlet short-sleeved shirt took off his panama hat and claimed precious space on the tiny counter. The Russians in their ski jackets stayed in the corner and sipped their coffee from their Styrofoam cups, watching. Val was near the counter with Vivienne slightly behind him and Johnny was at the door, no one else could get in the small space. "No," the scarlet-shirted man said. "That is wrong." He was tapping a brochure for the motel, Stovepipe Wells Village. "Look. Look at this picture." The clerk did not look at the picture. The world over, travellers take the brochure snap as the literal bible and base their true heavenly happiness on a small thumbnail shot, then get to Saint Peter and complain. Here it was: level five loony-tune negotiation.

"No, that's not right," the round man said to the man at reception. "Look." Tapping the tiny snap in the brochure. "This car is pulled right up to the room." The car in the photograph was not pulled right up to the room. It was pulled up, as the clerk said, to the walkway that had a shaded overhang and benches, a walkway about six feet wide. The cars pulled up on the sandy gravel, and then it was smooth carrying across the walkway to the rooms. That was what the picture in the brochure showed.

"I have come from Hawaii; we got off the boat from Hawaii last night in Los Angeles. I have boxes of goods I import from Hawaii – clothing, textiles – I am not carrying those into the room. What do you want me to do with them, leave them in the car? Well I am not leaving them in the car, mister, I can tell you that much, that is for sure. I have important goods I am carrying from the big island, we drove all night to get here, now you tell me I can't drive my car, I can't *back* my car to the door of my room. What kind of place is this?"

"Sir," said the clerk, picking up the phone and dialling. "I am happy to find you alternate accommodation in the town of Beatty. If you prefer I can call Pahrump. There are plenty of places in Las Vegas. It's a three-hour drive; you can be there by seven. Furnace Creek is just down the road an hour. I can call and see if we can get you into Furnace Creek, if you prefer it to our Stovepipe. Party of three?" he said to Val, while trying to find a better place on earth for the round man with the scarlet summer shirt in winter.

"I do not want any of your *alternate accommodation*, I want *this*." Tapping the photograph in the brochure. Sticking with his negotiation at heaven's portal.

"Sir, we have you in the Tucki section."

"Well put me where the back of my car is at the door to the room."

"No such room exists, sir. It's our busy time, you were lucky to get anything at all without a reservation."

"Who do you people think you are? I just got off a ship from Hawaii,

I have things to sell." He waved his hand to the door. Vivienne had not noticed it before, but they had parked right beside an old beat-up station wagon, a woodie wagon stuffed to the gills with green garbage bags, the back area stuffed so the driver couldn't see behind him, the bags coming out the windows. Sitting thin and hunched in the back seat was a pale woman with dark hair, looking stunned and travel-beat herself.

The round man waved again. "At this rate you know what's going to happen? She's going to have to unload the whole damn thing. She had to load it off the boat in LA, and now look what you're going to do to the poor woman. Last time I stop in this place. What a dump. Okay, Becky, I got bad news coming your way."

He pushed past Val and Vivienne, smelling like the sea and mouldy humidity; he flat out pushed Johnny away from the door and made his sour egress. The clerk said, "Merry Christmas, folks. I trust you're all now in the proper New Year's spirit. They'll be hanging Saddam, get out your bubbly."

They all chuckled. The Russians chuckled. They pitched their Styrofoam cups and left. The tiny space felt mansion-like all of a sudden.

Vivienne stepped right up to the counter. "Coma. Reservation for three. Room with a dunes view."

"That's right, the Coma party." The clerk found them in the file. "Room 214 in the Roadrunners," he said. "You'll find maps and the daily weather right there, folks, and menus for the restaurant. There's drinks and appetizers in the saloon, and we have coffee ready at five in the morning, if you're aiming to go out early."

"Oh we are aiming," Johnny said, coming up behind Vivienne. "Aren't we, sweetie?"

"We love going out in the dark," she said to the clerk. "Get some of your fine joe, get a head start on the picture takers. I like to get into the dunes before sunrise."

"Well, good luck to you. You're going anywhere too far afield, you let us know; check in with us, in case you go missing. You can die of thirst in the winter too."

"Gotcha," Vivienne said. He handed her three key cards without anybody having to ask.

They got back in the car and drove from the reception parking to the parking just outside their room. Johnny put his key card in the slot at room 214. They faced east to the dunes, watching the sun pour low from the west through embedded palms, and the small sandstorm at the dunes looked like a golden shower cut ten ways, and then early night green came into the golden storm.

They ate early and well, and slept in steady REMs, Vivienne and Johnny in one double bed, Val in the other.

20

THUNDERBIRD

INTERSTATE 95 RUNS out of Las Vegas, reaching the same elevation as Nellis Air Force Base and the Nevada Test Site and Creech Air Force Base, set up in reaction to Pearl Harbor and used today by combat-ready airmen flying MQ-1B Predators and MQ-9 Reaper aircraft. Here under desert skies air-power innovation took place for the Korean War; here research and special weapons and the famous Thunderbirds had made a home; here there had been staging bases for the delivery of nuclear weapons to the Soviet Union for joint verification tests; here was the home of remotely piloted aircraft being used in Afghanistan and Iraq.

And here a man dressed as a bird stood on the highway, hitching.

He held out a cardboard sign: THE SLEIGH BROKE.

A snazzy pink Ford Thunderbird stopped on the opposite side of the road, heading back north. Danny Coma ran across the highway.

A sharp Thunderbird, a dazzling pink T-bird from back in the day. The woman at the wheel was blond, she wore a turquoise stud in her right ear and her hair was in a scarf laden with metallic thread that sent emerald greens, ruby reds, sapphires of blue electric zizzing in the wind. "Get in," she said, opening the suicide seat door for the big bird. The bird climbed in, sheltering a small hard suitcase from the driver's view. "Hey, honey," she continued, "how ya doing. Whatcha got in the suitcase?"

"Top of the season!" the big bird said, adjusting his bulk into the creamy leather seat. "Wow! Flush out the cowards! There has been some loose talk on these matters…travelling for some time on a variety of, well – Lips zipped." He put the suitcase on the floor in front of him, resting his feet on it like a footstool.

"You said it," the woman at the wheel said. She wore big dark sunglasses. The big bird, who had none, squinted as the rays from the west beamed into his left eye. They drove the empty lane, through protected areas. A permanent sign read: MILITARY EXERCISE IN PROGRESS. Though this was a public thoroughfare and a major roadway, kept up excellently, the citizenry and touristic travellers were not on a government-controlled and government-maintained highway in quite the same way they would be anywhere else. When they drove north out of the metropolis of Las Vegas on the interstate, they were on a highway passing straight through an old nuclear test lab. The cars were vehicular mice in the lab hallway. A pretty woman in a pink T-Bird driving a small man in large feathered suit was the least of the weirdness.

And the big bird carried nuclear dirt from Spain in his suitcase, gathered from the fallout of the bombs developed right there on that highway. The bird examined his red mitt.

"You a salesman, honey?" the lady in the scarf and shades asked. "I'm dying for seafood. They have to fly the octopus here. Hell, they have to put the lettuce in an aisle seat. Cause if that is octopus in your luggage, you know what? I'd pay for some squid. You got squid, brother?"

They passed by the open area where the High Desert State Prison sat, a long, low box on scrub. Grey mountains with a dusting of snow on their peaks sat behind it, against the hard blue sky. A sign came up on the right: NO HITCHHIKING.

"Call me Andres," the big bird said.

"Okay, Annie," the driver said.

"Andres, if you please," he said, scolding her for saying his fake name incorrectly.

The big bird leaned forward, no seat belt, and put his mittened red hand on the windshield, saying, "I come from Viking blood; I fought naked as a Norseman! I sat commando on the prow in Greenland. I walked the Santiago Camino. *Un aplauso, por favor, muchas gracias.* I got that revolution started in Portugal, I was behind it, they call me Mike the front man. Do you know, young lady, that fully 87.3 per cent of CIA plants are called Mike? Oh, yes. I was Mike in Lo Curro when I concocted sarin; I let those Lefties – ha! – have it. Me and Mike, Mike and Mike they called us, we set sarin loose in Chile, we killed that Dutch banker, oh yes, no fear." He held up the red mitten.

She pulled down her shades and looked at him with lime green eyes.

Ahead, there were blue-red ranges below blue-grey ranges. The rock sheers evolved in true slow reportage.

"Call me Daniel," Danny said, introducing himself by his real name.

"You seem more like an Annie to me," she said, alluring by her uncaring, just driving the highway.

"I was young. They put a headset on me: 'Listen to the enemy.' I felt important, honey."

She slowed the car and she beamed those radiant limes at him through the red-brown dust. "You do not call me honey, I call you honey, or you can get out here."

Here was nowhere at all.

Beatty, which led into Death Valley, was about a half an hour away. Mercury, just north of Beatty, was about an hour away. Beatty and Mercury had stayed alive for years as service centres for the staff, the scientists, the military working at the Nevada Test Site, which the pink T-Bird had passed some miles back. Nearly all the land for hundreds of miles outside of Las Vegas was set aside for military purposes and government land management, from Las Vegas through the four hundred eighty-eight miles on up to Reno and beyond. (Imagine travelling north by northwest from Amsterdam to Belfast, and the land and all the water you travel through being military or government, with spookily few civilians.) Nuketopia is with us.

Planes invisible and eyes invisible watched the pink car, the big bird, the lady in a scarf at the wheel.

The big bird said, "We were under orders to get the Left. We kidnapped the Dutch banker, if I do say so myself. We beheaded him, nice job too. Mike was good at that handiwork. We sent him to Guatemala where he did a nice job with those aid workers at the hotel in the jungle at Petén. That was Mike, you know, he came on to them like he was…what is that word you people use? *Progressive?* Sure. In Chile, we called ourselves The Red Group." Danny had had a mental breakdown after he walked out of the ghost town with his nuclear ground blend in a suitcase. His mind, after the interrogation, had skidded back to the things he had done in the name of public safety, money and a hubris skill set.

"I am Daniel," the bird man said. "It was I who ran that Red Group. Bunch of idiots. I will tell you something, honey, you will find incompetents right across the political spectrum. Views?"

"You call me honey one more time and I will personally mount you on my hood, little horsey."

"Ha. Love a woman with a sense of humour. I recall one time in Patagonia, we were on our way to Colonia Dignidad. Right beside that nice eco-park. We are great hikers, the wife and I. Were. She was a little wisp of a thing; she blew off a cliff one day. Don't worry, I was cleared, honey pie." He put his hand on her thigh.

The lady with the lime-green eyes slowed her pink T-bird on Interstate 95 just south of the desert town of Beatty. "Get out," she said.

"Aw, come on. Why finger me? My wife was advising. She advised a couple Germans what questions you use to find out what the children know. She spent nine years getting that medical degree, and then she goes and gets a psych doctorate on top of it."

"Get out, big boy, or I'll get it out for you."

"No."

They were in a dangerous position, stopped on a government highway through the atomic secrets' areas. You do not stop along that road to have a random cheeky fight with a feathered nut who claims to be CIA black ops, especially in a neon pink T-bird.

Unless, of course, you were one of them.

She was one of them.

"Are you getting out?" she asked.

"Aw come on, you can't be serious." The big bird was talking to the pretty lady like she was his wife or his incompetent secretary. She was staying deadpan, hiding a reaction that said, "This feathered yapper will be useful, then I will complain to State. He is insufferable, is there any way we can fire him?"

"Things continue to remain somewhat uncertain," the big bird said, his arms crossed like chubby limbs, a big bird in a fat avian snit. "One had to be prepared for sudden and unexplained changes in the military situation. I had to write their damn memoranda, if I might say, of fucking understanding. Host nations you don't want to know. I had to cover their asses, that was me, thereby clarifying reports made pursuant to advance notification procedures."

This was the place that language was built to cover. This was the location where the *-ations* and *-abilities* were put to frequent use, to cover the plain awe of the spinal cord of earth lifting to the sky, with every vertebra of fire exploded, with every thyroid of every child threatened. Plain speech is the enemy of the bureaucracy. Daniel Coma had twisted his love of language to make meeting about nuclear disarmament, and using the abstract words of meetings at the top levels, a safe thing to touch, to remove the harm from the living by speaking in dead words, to name things best named clearly, best because best for the soul of nations, and to do harm, by naming them in the worst possible way, however on the other hand, named in obfuscation and reification and nuclear capabilities, and here they were. The bombs went off here. The tests were done here. The radiation came from here. The plutonium drifted from this locale. This was the place. This was Atmosphere Zero.

"Leave my vehicle. The military police will pick you up pronto," the lady in the pink Thunderbird said.

"I was put in charge of the safety and security of countries."

"In that?" She put her shades back on. "Come on, old man, get out of my car."

"They gave me a summer job when I was nineteen, at a listening post in Labrador."

"Did you find anything?"

"I found I liked it." Danny closed his eyes, rested his head back on the seat and smiled. "Can you take me to the next town?"

"I could take you to Hell's Gate. There's a nice view from Hell's Gate. You can see all the way down to the Devil's Golf Course. You ever see the movie *Greed?*"

"Can't say as I ever heard of it." Now the big bird was trying on an old-coot Walter Brennan voice.

"It's silent," she said. "Unlike some passengers in this car I could name. If they had a name."

"Oh," he said.

"*Greed?* Erich von Stroheim? The great silent director? Ring any bells?" She looked at him like he was nuts. Cinema was the true international language, after mangled English. How could a modern spy not know how to talk movies? The weather, sports, movies: you pass.

The bird was in a stew, looking out the side of his suicide seat. He did not know how to be at his ease, unknowing.

"*Greed.* Death Valley," she said. "The Devil's Golf Course. The great part in *Greed*, when the two men and the mule are stuck out in the desert. There is this sandstorm and the mule walks off with their water and the one guy hits the other one with the shovel – I think it was the dentist – and they die of thirst in Death Valley. Made in 1924, if I'm not mistaken. From *Greed* to *Sunset Boulevard*, now there's a trip."

"Who the hell cares? You people and your movies, you arty people, you make me sick, you remind me of my brother."

She reached across him and clicked open the glove compartment, taking out a pack of cigarettes: KOCMOC. Dark blue with a sleek white rocket and a red star under it. "Have a Kosmos?"

"You smoke Russian?" Danny said.

"I found them in an old briefcase this morning," she said. "Got them from an old work husband at the UN, the day Khrushchev banged his shoe. October 12, 1960. You know how it is, old-timer. Some days you feel like your Sputnik doesn't fly like it used to. Take one," she said. She lit two. She gave one to Danny. He stuck it in his mouth.

"I never knew what others were bringing to the party," he said.

"Just turn up. Just open the door and walk in. Just have yourself appear."

"Some things seemed of an advantage, others not."

"So you became a spy, because you did not know what to do?"

"I did not know what others were doing."

"Hang on a minute," she said, pressing a button on the radio, pulling a small phone out by its cord. She turned away from Danny. "Yeah, he's here. Apparently he got out of Vegas. Sure, I know, Rocky, you've got the tapes of them walking around the bomb site. Good for the jackrabbit; the wire worked… Fine. I don't know. He was in the scope on the Strip, he seemed okay, at least…" The green-eyed woman pulled the cord further and got out of the car, walking up and down the highway shoulder. "Look: that's what Val told me. Gold; yes. He had him in the trunk. We have verification that Betty Coma was the one. He told that story so many times, yeah, I know, Rocky. I believed him. Now we have the evidence; the bird was Betty's assistant. I know. The girl, Pink, she was the one, Betty came after her. Yes, I just told you. Gold has it on tape, Pink accusing the bird. They're calling him Ambassador. But, we have proof now that 'Mrs. Coma' existed. Yes, Rocky, yes I remember what happened with SAVAK. Okay, fine, look I'll turn around and leave the bird dead on the road. Yes, I do *recall* DINA, the Chileans, Condor, come on, Rocky, please. The Night of the Pencils, don't remind me. It wasn't me, Rocky, who said go kidnap students. We cleaned that up. No, I don't know if he is still a threat. He is off the leash, that's for sure. They're on their way to Death Valley; they've got rooms reserved at Stovepipe. I'll take him there. Val Gold is definitely on the case. Yes, Rocky. I am fully aware. If he keeps talking, he may eventually say something." She wound the black cord around her wrist, got back in the driver's seat, pushed the slim phone back into its hidden spot and zoomed back on the highway going north.

"Timing, schedules, directions, others seem to have the knowledge," Danny said. "I thought if I studied the protocols, I could get by."

"You didn't know what the hell to do. So they put you in charge of the security of nations?"

She turned west on to the bumpy road past Daylight Pass, and on to Hell's Gate. She asked him to pose for a quick photo.

A pale man in his sixties, big deep blue circles under his gaunt eyes, slightly pointed ears, half balding with dark hair and some salt in the pepper on his pate. The bird suit was cheap enough that it was moulting in the dry air on to the dirt at Hell's Gate. They stood and looked down the magnificent fjord-like basin of Death Valley to Salt Creek, down to Badwater, across and up to Dante's View, back down to the river water sparkling white with blue sky in it, travelling in a long meander to its pools of white showing blue sky and grey mountains with their snow peaks in the water, and all of it a mirage. Every fjord river of Death Valley was salt.

She drove the big bird in her beautifully angled pink T-Bird down the incline into the shadows as they approached Stovepipe Wells, dipping down fast to sea level, into the shadows. When they got to the shadow level, the shadows were sand. They drove alongside the Death Valley Sand Dunes, and the walls of light were the Panamint Range. What was negative space from a distance had proven to be positive space up close. This was a kind of poetic physics, much better than science or poetry. This was the animal that science studied, the look that poets bowed their heads in shame to.

SHE TOOK HIM to Stovepipe Wells, right up to the hitching post at reception. "See if they have a room," she said. "I'll wait."

He went up the couple of steps to the tiny one room check-in, with his little suitcase of H-bomb dirt.

A burly guy, bigger than the small man in the big bird suit came to the counter. "Help you? Got your down on? You're going to need it, well below zero tonight. Room for two?" he asked, nodding to the car. These old-school reception guys could spot a blond in a convertible at fifty paces through a half-slit venetian blind any day of the week.

The birdman was mystified. He did not know what she was bringing to the party. Was she bringing him to the party? Was there a party? He was on his own. "Ah, room for one?"

"Dunes view?"

The big bird was further confused. He had been driven past the dunes, but he was unsure what the reception man could mean. All his life it had been laid out for him: travel department, per diem, flights arranged. He had never checked into a hotel by himself. He had never made his own arrangements. He had never just turned up. What did you do?

"Ah, okay."

"I can put you in the 49ers, no wait. Independence cancelled. I can put you in the Roadrunners. Dunes view. How's that?"

"Sounds about right," Danny the bird said.

"I will need to see some ID. A major credit card works."

The big bird had never shown ID in his life. That is, regular person ID. He had shown his special get-out-of-jail-free *laissez-passer* papers, and he had always had special treatment after they saw his papers. Did he have ID? And if so, which one would he use, who would he be?

Did he happen to have anything on him that said Daniel Coma? Daniel Coma, economic and trade consultant? He fished down inside his feathers, saying, "*Moreover I said unto the king, If it please the king, let letters be given me to the governors beyond the river.*"

The reception man came around the counter, and took the coffee pot and went into a back room and refilled it with water and came back and put a new filter and grounds in. "Have a nice nap?" he asked, coming around the counter.

Danny the birdman was still fishing down in his nether feathers. "*That they may convey me over 'til I come into Judah.*"

"Any major plastic works," the man said.

"I used to advise the president," Danny said.

The reception man sipped on his coffee. "Got no phone in the room if that's a problem. I have to go to dinner in an hour, just letting you know. You got a security pocket in that rig, just in case you forgot? Driver's licence works."

"I don't drive," Danny said, smoothing feathers. "I am driven."

The reception man picked up the phone. "What did you say the number at the White House was? I'll call George W., and tell him you don't drive. Sir, when you want a room, you come back and see me."

The birdman found something hard down in his crotch feathers. He pulled out a passport. Michael Towne, American, born Detroit, Michigan, 1931, passport issued Bogotá, Columbia, September 9, 2001. The photo was of Daniel Coma in 1967 with a dark beard. The passport was three and a half months expired. "Fine," the reception man said. "Here's the key to 204. If the sand walls you in, just holler. Room enough for two in that king, if you're inclined."

The birdman went out to the pink convertible to report back.

The pink convertible was not there.

He walked across the highway, which had become as narrow as a residential street, to the general store. No T-bird. No T-bird at the gas pump beside the store. No pink T-bird in sight when he made the trek through open ground, on pale brush, soft gravel, to the rooms. Across the scrub there were tall picturesque palm trees, each one with its own water tap attached at the bottom. You could indeed see the Death Valley Dunes from inside room 204, in the Roadrunners section.

Daniel Coma took off the bird suit, opened the door of the room, sat on a yellow fabric chair at the open doorway and watched the sun turn the sand dunes into a gauzy emerald city.

Night came fast. The room was a beacon light. Daniel Coma opened his suitcase, pushing aside the bag of nuked dirt. He grabbed the too-big grey sweatshirt, put it on. He pulled the baggy grey sweatpants over his boots. He walked the walkway, turned the corner at the drinks machine, walked past the swimming pool – deserted behind a high fence, it being night and winter – and climbed the wide western stairs to the dining place.

He had never before eaten in a public restaurant alone.

21

WALK, AMBLE, TROT, GALLOP AND LOPE

VIVIENNE PINK GOT up in the dark. Her hiking clothes were draped over a chair, prepared. She put on wool leggings, two pairs of wool socks, a long-sleeved navy-and-white striped nautical jersey, her olive green pants and a bright orange boiled wool jacket she zipped to its high neck. Johnny was dead to the world in the double bed closest to the door. Val was asleep in the one nearer the loo. Vivienne slipped her feet into walking shoes, fastened their Velcro orange straps and opened the door. The dark was a form of quiet. She could feel starlight sharpen as it began to die out. She turned left, walked down the walkway, turned left and took the hillside dip to the reception office, shining in the darkness. It was freezing out. Vivienne pulled the slim black silk glove liners out of her jacket pocket and slipped them on her hands, even as she got to the door of the motel office.

The man behind the counter and his sidekick from yesterday afternoon were back on the job. It was 05:29 hours. Vivienne's mission was to be deep into the dunes and set up with all the needed equipment well in advance of her 07:07 deadline. The sun rising from the west hit a particular notch between two particular mountains from the viewpoint of one particular sand dune between five minutes and ten minutes after seven, although ten after was probably too late. If all went well, her day's work would be done by nine a.m. The clerk said, "Well, good morning. Lucky you, I got your coffee for you, just the way you like it, but better hurry, our friends from Moscow look ready for a second cup, they might beat you to it."

Vivienne had not seen the three older gents in the corner, one of them more sparkly and bald, looking like he was from the TV show *Lost.* Maybe they were lost in Death Valley. Vivienne stepped to the coffee pot as the two Russian speakers from yesterday came in the door and, being tall, either did not see her in her shortness or did not give a morning damn. They wedged through and starting pouring coffee into two neat cups of ever-faithful Styrofoam, which they lifted in a toast and drank down, oblivious to Vivienne's hand in mid-air and now without any coffee. The clerk said, "Well, now, José, will you take a look at that, and I was just telling you last night, chivalry is alive and well in Death Valley." He then said something to the man and the woman in Russian, which made the man smile and the woman sulk. The Russian man said something right back to the clerk and they left.

"Better get that coffee going, Pepe, the lady is waiting. She's got a hot camera on the go."

"What did they say?" Vivienne asked, leaning on the counter. Men told her things. Johnny was amazed how often this happened. She leaned in and smiled full face at the older clerk. He gave her a good smile with lots of eye crinkles. Oh, he had seen his day, and the ladies had been there all the way with him, you could see that – another one with great blue eyes.

"They're making the big movie," he said.

"Oh, yeah," she said, "I will just bet they are."

José-Pepe had the coffee coming through the filter to the Pyrex already. "Don't you boys go touching that. That is the little lady's. Good luck, ma'am, out there, it's a morning for the light."

She poured hers black, put two little oil products into Johnny's with a sweetener and walked the coffees back, thinking, It turned out that the big threat to America from the Russians was that they would be big coffee buttinskys in the morning at the motel carafe. The warheads were all lined up, and NATO was all lined up, all in the name of getting those Russians to learn to line up like a mensch and not butt in for the coffee.

She rounded the bend to the Roadrunners walkway. Well, she was Russian, too. It was just that she knew it as an adjective, as she had told Andy. Russian Jew, ignoring her own word, *Russian.* When she was a blond pigtailed pitzel, doing duck and cover from the phantom attacking Russians, maybe she was being taught to be paranoid, a child afraid of herself.

Back at the room, Johnny was sitting up in bed. Vivienne gave him his coffee. He moved quickly, getting ready. They got in the white vehicle, driving in darkness under stars.

They sipped coffee for five miles down the road going east. Johnny stopped the car and turned off the headlights. The road was empty, the world and all its night stars were their stage. Up in the exploding black, infinity danced its stellar equations.

They got out of the car, entering the dark, the rich resource that darkness was. We pollute the dark kingdom with too much light, debasing it by shining artificial light upwards into its onyx secrets. And they entered the dune fields of Death Valley. The first low glow of light came from a curved mystery in the dried-sea horizon. First the early gravel under their feet, then the small resinated bushes brushed their shins, then the sand filled their shoes as they sank into it up to their knees and the dunes looking like warrior encampments became lit in more golden light, low on their tips.

The cold empire of wonder, Death Valley, was all theirs.

They came to a small dune, about six or seven feet high. There were no human footprints. Overnight, the wind had erased all clues. Every desert hiker wants to be the first person on the moon.

It was 06:12 hours.

Vivienne and Johnny walked without talking. The vibrating silence between them was the second language of their marriage. Marriage takes on a life of its own. Marriage is like a desert. Even when it looks like nothing is going on, or nothing is alive, you hunker down, you listen, you close your eyes, you walk in the dark with your eyes open, and what appeared dead and quiet is thrumming with its own live tracks, its beetle herringbone lines, its coyote footpad markings, its holes in the shade, the scant rustling of the midden, where all the precious things have been stored away, hidden and piled up, and the next dune is even higher as the world becomes dusted with the pre-light before the official sunrise.

They walked in the dark desert past ghost trees dry as the petrified gnarled limbs of corpses. The wind blew harder, drying out the largest organ on their bodies, their skin, as the ground lost its trees and its squat bushes. Vivienne reached over to Johnny, touching his face, feeling the lack of moisture on his skin. It was icy. She lifted the hood of his puffy parka up. He squeezed her gloved hand. He had black smudges under his eyes she did not recognize as belonging to him. His face was greyer.

She touched her own face: too smooth, raw, the early days after an atomic burn. Her aching dried fingertips felt something beside her left eye: a blister. It released black matter. Vivienne held it out on her fingers. Johnny took some on his fingers, wiped it on his own cheek. A black lip blister spontaneously exploded on Johnny's lower lip. Vivienne shot a picture of it, a thousand miles of sand behind him. Their faces were layered with grey dust, and the wind sand veil swirling.

They understood that their adventuring time was work time. Art labour is mysterious even to those who do it. The light began to seep from all the curved desert spaces. An intense sense of mutating came over Vivienne. It made her joyful. Who said we had to be smooth, symmetrical, all hairs in place? The world was a wonder we never asked for, yet it wakes us in desert spaces with its grace. Rimy in our abodes, we are the mutant nomads called human. Even on Earth, we miss being earthlings. They were ploughing through a sea of sand. There was sand, and there were mountains, and you could see the immense lack of being told what you were seeing go on and on as one long evolutionary take moving at its own incremental inching. That radiant glow on the top of a dune when you drive by on the road could be the bebop of the saltating grains, a sunstruck flurry like sand fur above the crescent dune. Sand migrates, the minuscule cigar-shaped grains, spheres, disks chipped at the edges bouncing and hopping in the wind.

Laid out before you, in the desert, is Earth's slow thinking.

Johnny got out his Moleskine and sketched some scat: two long corded pieces, each with a black tail. Hairy scat, the flowing tail: coyote scat. Way back on the road, their white vehicle was a dot bouncing the light. They had been walking twenty-five minutes; twenty-eight minutes to their dune.

Worldwide insomnia could be from lack of desert. From too much life in too much verticality, the big tall buildings in cities only allowing slivers of body clock–setting blue. Here in Death Valley the blue was so big it could reset the natural clock of all Earth's wanderers.

Vivienne's eyes were soaking in the horizontal universe. Space was time here. How could you convey that? Her quest had to do with perception. The small-sized photo of this would not get it across, because you had to feel much smaller than the desert to feel the desert inside you. No postcard of a huge Mark Rothko painting ever told you what standing close to a Mark Rothko painting told you: about colour, shine, light, eternity, degradation, paint itself. His paintings were painted shivas, joyous acts of mourning, or mournful acts of joy, and they put you in a glowing desert, and you did not get there by holding a miniature replica of mourning in your hand. You had to be small, next to the huge unforgiving world. When you strip the Earth and its water, you become the dry desiccation walking the dry desiccated land. Larger than a grain of sand, a human is still a grain of meat and bone. Before endtimes arrive upon us, the drought times will come, with Bonneville Salt Flats fire speed igniting our home lives down the canyons.

Vivienne could see a thing called *five hours away.*

You could see five hours away and walk to it, convinced it was surely only five minutes. Desert light was a species, a feral energy that came at you and bent you. Across the miles of sand, it looked like thousands of tent encampments had been set up.

The cold wind soothed their burned places. They started walking the dunes. The sand grew high and they walked it, climbing, sinking, pushing forward. The land taught them how to walk the land.

VIVIENNE TOOK SOME pics of their walking feet on re-virginalized sand, their rutted shoe prints, and here came a coyote print. Each of the four toe prints had a little line above it where a claw had landed. Below the toes was an interdigital pad that looked like a nose. The coyote's track was shaped like the letter *C*. This meant the coyote had come through at a lope. Johnny loved this stuff, here was the urban creature in love with scats and tracks, joyous to see footprints. He was standing and sketching the coyote track.

The coyote: First comes the *walk*, then the slightly faster walk called the *amble*, there is the *trot*, there is the *gallop* and there is the slower version of the *gallop* called the *lope*. Johnny adored the English language, it was the sea his brain matter swam in; words were the stars he steered by and they were the land below the stars at night. It thrilled him no end that a lope was a gallop, only slower.

He drew the coyote's lope track, with the one hind foot showing behind the other three feet and the characteristic *C* shape.

They climbed the next dune. There were lines down its wall of sand, long lines and dots on either side of the lines: a lizard. A thick herringbone track that looked like a tire tread ran up the side of the dune beside the lizard: a desert sand beetle.

When Vivienne Pink and Johnny Coma arrived at their dune, they used the far mountains off to the east as their guide. Vivienne recognized the notch between two of them. Their dune looked directly across to where the sun would rise between 07:05 and 07:10. They had fifteen minutes. They climbed up their dune, a nice thirty-footer. Vivienne rubbed out the ripples at the top of their dune, and the wind put the ripples right back.

The dunes moving in and out of each other, making glory shapes: the barchan dune, shaped like a crescent, *barchan* from the Arabic for ram's horn, with its steep slipface, its gouged eddy, downwind. The parabolic dune, upwind, was the same, only gouged and crescent in the opposite direction. There were the star dunes, with multiple slipfaces and wind coming in from chance directions. There were the traverse dunes, the classic ridges at right angles to the wind. Wind was a great artist. Wind erased your home, and the steel vehicle became the new encampment with wind-shattered windows.

They sat on wind's art. They held hands. Their four legs hung over the edge, two in khaki, two in blue cord. It was about freezing when they set out, and now they were feeling deep desert cold, colder at sunrise. Yet the burns burned. They touched icy cheeks together. Johnny kissed Vivienne with his warm tongue and his cold peeling lips. They had been married so long, they finished each other's silences.

They were just-me just-you in a space of three million square acres. They faced the Funeral Range.

The sun rose in the far mountain notch. Vivienne was ready to aim. The sun entered the notch. She shot it. Now it spread golden on the grey notch. She shot that. The sun beamed onto their faces, creating the first morning shadow behind them. Their bodies were projected down the sand dune where they sat, and along the sand beyond that. Alone, at the end of December, on their own planet. The early shadows of the morning were the best. You did not get shadows like this unless the land was open and clear and low and free of impediment.

Vivienne took Johnny's hand. They stood up. They turned around, letting the sun beam their bodies as shadows with heads elongated to the west. The long necks and long heads of the alien shadow invaders. They walked towards the Grapevine Mountains, zigzagging towards the highest dunes, the ones you see in the postcard of the Death Valley Dunes. Each dune was eighty to one hundred feet high. They climbed to the top of one, walking single file along a one-inch seam. Her day's work was almost done. There might be another picture.

She twisted her camera strap to her side. They sat with the etched mountains. It was 8:47 a.m. They slid back down the high dune, pushing through sand on a return route for a half an hour, way off course. Ahead was a mesquite tree shining in the risen sun. Like a crazy dried berry hairdo glowing rusts and golds. Vivienne saw the picture. She waved her hand at Johnny; he came close to her. He saw it now: the sun hit their backs, projected giant leg shadows in front of them, and their shadow heads were hidden inside the mesquite tree. This was the extra picture she had felt coming. She found it when they veered away from the straight path, by accident. The white sedan was way back east on the road, alone on the highway. They zigzagged to it, another half hour until the sand showed some low green, then gravel. They got in the car.

They drove back the short five miles to the motel, travelling in bright morning, which made the same highway seem like a different world than the dark secret highway of night.

They parked the car at 214, changed into fresh clothes and went to the restaurant. They each ordered a short blue stack. They dug into the pancake stacks, pouring on ample syrup. The coffee kept on refilling. They had not said a word to each other yet. The marriage did not care how the work went, the work did not care how the marriage went. It was 10:27 in the morning. Vivienne had finished her art day. Now came the hard part.

She opened her mouth: "Did she call you?"

Johnny looked up from his syrup and buttermilk blues. "I'm not getting into it."

"Did she call you? Because if she called you, I'm finished."

"Please, Vivi, it's been so good. No more aches and thunders. Please?"

"Did she call you? I want to know if she called you, because if she called you, I am going back to Baghdad. If she keeps calling you, and you keep letting her, then I am going to the Turkish border. Call me in Damascus. I may look up Dale. Dale, by the way, likes me. Nobody photographs Dale, but I photographed Dale. I want to know: did that anorectic lamp pole leave another sex message on your phone?"

"It's business, if I tell her not to call, we won't have the money. She's a fundraiser."

"She's a married fundraiser, Johnny."

"I know. I know she's married. I know I am married, too, by the way. Just by the way."

"For this, I stayed home?" Vivienne said. "For this I gave up war? 'Oh, it'll be great, you can take pictures of flowers.'"

"Stop with the Minnie Mouse," Johnny said. "I never said that. You love flowers."

"Flowers will wait, I want to go back to the story. It was you, not me, my dear husband, who said you were sick of reading books written by scaredy-cats who'd rather get all their details about the Middle East off the Wikiyenta than travel to see it with their own eyes. Please. What would happen if I went back to war, what's the big deal? I don't have to look Cairo up, baby; I've been there. I don't have to look up the Dead Sea, the Red Sea, I went diving in Eilat, baby, me and Moses, Moe and me, down with the fishes and the chariots, come on. I have been in Babylon, baby, Basra, Shatt al-Arab. Were we not in the Garden of Eden together?"

The waiter came by, with the handi-Pyrex of the hot stuff, and refilled their cups, and brought more syrup, and chose not to get involved with the Garden of Eden.

Vivienne pointed with a forkful of blueberry buttermilk pancake and syrup dripping on the wooden table. "How can I have been to the origin of the Torah, and now I am sitting here in Death Valley and I can't even remember why I came here? I should be back in the military grounds of Area 24, trolling for more pose boys. I have what is it? Two days to deadline?"

"We came to get Danny," Johnny said, scooping up the last of the buttermilk blue into his mouth. "To finally have it out with him. To get an apology on behalf of the people. So now I find out my own brother tortured you in Montevideo, and you told Val and not me."

"I told you. I had mercy on your manuscript. Isn't that what a lover should do? Spare the one she loves, so he can keep his soul intact and work?"

"I don't think they were talking about torture."

"I think they were precisely talking about the worst things you could imagine."

"I never imagined that," Johnny said.

"Sweetheart. Jojo. J. I've been living below the polite veneer so long, I don't know if you even ever see me."

"Look. We'll forget about Danny."

"I'm tired, J. I'm tired of wrangling your female fans. I'm tired of waking up on Sunday morning, and having one more woman who's never read any of your books on our front porch, asking for an autograph."

"Or stalking me. Glory hounds."

"There is that. I'm at my own front door, and there is a nice-looking, seemingly intelligent woman boasting to me that she knows you. She's trying to wedge past me into our home. Like I'm your assistant, or the maid. You know, maybe they're right. Maybe my life is as small as theirs is."

"Good job we've got them all on security cameras for the cops," Johnny said. "Look. We'll hang around here overnight, then we'll drive back to Vegas in the morning. You can be on your perch in the coffee shop by noon. How's that?"

She sipped and gulped her coffee. "If I had stayed away, if I had stayed in the conflicts, what would have happened?"

"I would have been articulated," Johnny said.

"What does being articulate have to do with it?" Vivienne stabbed a pancake.

"Not articulate, V. Articulated. Like how they get those ships in the bottles. They build it folded, and carefully insert it. Then they pull at it and magic! It unfolds inside the bottle. That would be me, if you went back to Iraq. You'd come back from Kirkuk, and there's your husband, articulated inside a bottle of Absolut Vivi."

"I asked you a serious question," Vivienne said.

"I gave you a serious answer. I can't live with the tension."

"But, I can, Jojo. I can. I feel alive with the dead."

"You've done those post-mortems, honey." He leaned forward. "Now it's time for *us*."

"But who is us, if I'm all knotted up inside? Peace gives me a headache."

"She didn't call, if that makes any difference. I told her if she keeps calling, I'm calling 52 Division. The cops know her big-time lawyer husband down there well enough, that might have worked. And Val keeps good dossiers on all of them."

"Thank you," Vivienne said, drinking more coffee, looking at the wagon wheel decor of the room: big, comfy, rustic, built with beams from a defunct mine. They paid and went their post-art-making morning ways.

Vivienne went into the room and got Andy's T-shirt from her suitcase. She put it on against her skin, zipped up her pink leather jacket and walked west on the narrow highway. She walked up a rutted side road, placed her camera on a rock, took off the jacket, took off the T-shirt, laid the white T on the pink leather and took pictures of it. When she got back to the room, Johnny was outside, drawing a palm tree with a water faucet at its base. She went in, got in bed, took off her jacket, laid it on her pillow and fell asleep in the T.

A LARGE WOMAN with a small dog on a long leash came walking across the parking area. Johnny sketched her. Walking towards her was a wobbly figure in bare legs and a big grey sweatshirt. Danny Coma in all his glory. Johnny put Danny in the sketch, and called out to him, "Hey Daniel! Welcome to Death Valley."

Danny, oblivious to the sound of his brother's voice, patted the small dog, and said, "Yes, Mr. President, chéri. I understand that it is understood that pre-eminent among the concerns..." The dog yipped a response, Danny nodded in agreement.

Johnny, feeling the invading passive voice infections, got up and went inside. Good. Danny had arrived under his own elvin steam.

22

ENEMY WATER

VIVIENNE, JOHNNY AND Val shepherded Danny through the first narrow entrance made of marine deposits left eight hundred million years ago, sedimentary rock called Noonday dolomite, rock that was one thousand feet thick. Once, down in quiet seas, there were vertical tubes through which the rotting algae at the bottom of the water sent up carbon dioxide, venting the marine rot upon the rocks. Now the quiet seas were quiet canyons. This first passageway was wide enough for only one person. It rose high on both sides, smooth and shiny, made of marble. The Noonday dolomite and the mosaic breccia had formed in a seabed, and under pressure the rock became a masterful mosaic, cliffs of it, and narrow dry falls you inched through, and climbed up and down rocks through. Whereas the testing grounds and the dunes presented as CinemaScope and IMAX views too big for the human eye to comprehend when standing in them, Mosaic Canyon in contrast presented as a narrow hallway through which an accused might be led, a spooky hallway with shiny sides reflecting back to him his bewildered face as he emerged from the hallway into an open amphitheatre. An open rock setting for the next stage of justice.

There was no shade in the amphitheatre. Danny hobbled in his loose boots to a big rock, hoping to get shade under the rock's slim overhang, sitting down, using the rock ledge like a slim-brimmed hat.

Val came over to Danny and did not sit down. "What do you know about the terrorist bomb set off at the supermarket in Barcelona?"

"Preposterous. One was never there," Danny said.

Val lit a cigarette. He walked back and forth in front of Danny. "June 1987? The Barcelona bombing?"

"One has not been in Spain, didn't I tell you that?" Danny said, with all the irritation of a man sending the tomato juice back when he had ordered tomato. Johnny and Vivienne were the audience.

"You were the Americans' point man for the Basque terrorists. Let me ask you again, Danny. What do you know about what happened on that day? They came down to Catalonia, far from their territory, and in order to demand their own parliament, which they already had, they bombed the Hipercor supermarket on Avinguda Meridiana. Can you tell us where you were that day?"

"One had things to attend to. The capital connections. Bad shellfish. One had been poisoned. There was no coverage. One had the youngsters to attend to, though it must be said they did supersede their poor father's graduate degrees. The plane was late. Intelligence had been reported in certain quarters of incendiary devices down in Barcelona, one has to cede that. Damn pilots and their unions. There was fog. Well, what else is new? Could one locate a rental car? They gave me a window seat. Ridiculous. The back went out, what else is new? Lumbago is no pile of peaches. There was a back molar acting up, absolutely impossible to locate a dentist. There was a service chinchilla demanding a ham sandwich and a kosher mouse demanding the chinchilla's ham be kept at a distance, plus when one merely goes to get the hand luggage out, my firearm discharged inside my diplomatic pouch. Very kind stewardess helped clean me up. One has immunity, extremely helpful. The damn fog. One had to circle, fly to San Sebastián, fly back, by which time the ETA had blown up the supermarket. Don't blame me. One will find no record of Daniel Coma in Spain. Not now, not ever. My retriever has never been to España. Can I get my gofer now?"

Vivienne saw that the fog was also a meteorological system inside Danny. He must have reached burnout, and then stayed on, in working embers, for another decade and a half. What happens to a man's brain when he soldiers on using muscles and synapses howling from exhaustion? Does he enter the whispers?

"Don't be a goon, Dan. If the thugs can't get the details right, don't be like a thug and claim to be a good guy."

"I am a good guy," Danny said. Like a lot of good guys, he had faith that bragging about being good was a good thing, and not bragging.

"Were you not in charge of the CIA's desk on the Basque terrorists known as ETA? Euskadi Ta Askatasuna."

"Very impressive. Five out of five. What's the point?" Danny reached down into his left Frye boot, losing half his skinny white arm down there, and pulled out an old cigar butt. His boot was his personal sidewalk curb. "I am semi-retired, leave me be." Danny put his hands on the rock rubble, tilted forward and did a handstand, his Frye boots waving behind him. "One yogas, one mini-marathons, one keeps up with the Ring Cycles," Danny said, his mouth close to the amphitheatre floor. "And yet, there they were, the trust-fund chums, them and their golf games. There they were," continued the mouth, looking like it was at the top of his head, his legs hanging in the air, "those smarty-pants. Daniel Coma got better marks than them. Daniel Coma beat his ass, then Daddy calls the dean and they are in like Flynn."

He pushed on his hands. The handstand was not bad. Maybe he had been looking for the terrorists in the yoga class. Saliva drooled down to his nostrils. "So things get taken? So a person says a thing, who cares? These people knew the machers; these people had lunch with the big machers. The children of Daniel Coma went to the lycée, and did it matter? They come from money. Daniel comes from Murray Coma's Furniture. So a person exaggerates. How else does one compete?"

More saliva from that *p* came down to Danny's eyelid folds, which in age had begun to fold back into his eye hollows. He lifted his booted legs a little higher to the sky. A nasal clearing came wet and meandering and coagulating in Danny's small forehead. "So I said I wrote some books. I madc a start, who has the time? Do I get any thanks from that big-shot brother of mine? Did he show any appreciation that I was trying to join him?

"Nothing but criticism from him and that one. Does he help me along? No way. He asks me for a loan, a bridge loan he calls it. For what? So he and his fancy friends can get on the cover of the book review again? Daniel Coma did not flaunt his modest scribbling, if I may, the way Johnny Coma and his kind do, they flog these *items,* TV, radio, whores, you won't find me doing that. Big deal so he has a website, I could have a website if I wanted, but these people." The *p* again drifted the saliva in twin rivers on either side of Danny's nose. His face was red from the handstand, the blood rushing down, the gravity.

Like many a man who used culture and art and its trappings to try and gain a foothold in a world they felt was looking down on them, Danny Coma was a man who mentioned and over-mentioned his regular normal museum visits or concerts, less as a note of his enjoyment than as a note of his being on the same playing field as the artist whose work he enjoyed. Danny made the internal mistake of thinking that the consumer of art and the producer of art were, perforce, colleagues. That he could compete with his sister-in-law, Vivienne, the internationally known photographer by telling a third party how he went to a photography exhibit.

Danny had made his heart lie.

Danny believed in fairness. Danny believed things should be fair. Danny felt this more than most folks, and he felt it so deeply, he accepted a job in which he was, legally, named as inviolate, and he was given immunity all over the world, and he felt this to be only fair. And when it turned out that this was fair and still he did not shine, he began to tell his story as a series of unfair acts against him. Danny Coma became a practiced schemer, and his mandate to lie was only fair to him. He felt agitated that his brother, Johnny, was independent and successful. It was unfair.

It did not matter that Danny had a regular salary regardless of the level of his work, or that he lived as a raja or a sri or a prince from the age of twenty-five on, or that he was guaranteed a full pension and his wife the cardiologist a full pension, plus the large cash-in-manila-envelopes she got from her Southern Cone "consulting," or that he got a handsome insurance payday from her death over the cliff. It did not matter that he owned three homes, and had spent his life with hired help and paid staff given to him. His internal fire was green. It did not matter that none of them deemed him small. Worse: they never thought of him at all.

And in his green flames, he believed, mistakenly, that wealthy people were all surface, because he saw them as all surface, and so to compete, he competed on the surface only: naming travel spots, exercise regimes, past academic degrees. But there was no Danny in the verbal meat. He was so fearful of being himself, while auditioning to be himself, he presented even his beloved choices as a regalia of bland, using the passive voice and a stiff cleansed diction more suited to tourist brochures from departments of tourism sent out during a military dictatorship.

Does the burned-out man speak at night with ghosts? What do the ghosts whisper about things done, about things that cannot be undone now? Do the ghosts excuse acts? Do the ghosts give the torturer's assistant a bye? Behold, the man sees spots in front of his eyes, the damn spots will not come out.

VAL PAID NO attention to Danny's handstand. "Let us talk of truce and blood, dear Danny. What do you know about the ETA's ceasefire of 1989, Daniel?" he asked. "The negotiated terror truces of 1989, 1996, 1998 and just this year, 2006. Did you or did you not get ETA to sign a truce in March? You know what? Every ceasefire you signed with ETA? They signed on the arrows, and began to kill again. You were their mark. The terrorists love truces. Truces are their drug, their high. A peace treaty is the jump powder up their noses. They're so elevated by the truce, they go out again and murder."

"Preposterous accusations. We saw daylight in San Sebastián. I took the waters at the La Perla spa on the Bay of Biscay. Gloria: fine masseuse. Never better. A kind woman's touch."

"Experience says liars lie," Val said. "Experience says – Okay. Let's switch to blood and art." Val went over to Danny, gently took Danny's feet down and kissed Danny on the cheek. Val sat down beside him, as if they were actors in act two of a play watched by Vivienne and Johnny. "So, then, murder in the museums. What do you know about the ice-blooded killing at the Bilbao Guggenheim, not long before it officially opened on October 19th, 1997?"

"One was," Danny said, sitting up straight on the sandy rock floor of the open-air amphitheatre of Mosaic Canyon. "One was an invited, if I may say, VIP guest. Frank said hi."

"You come from the same hometown, right? You and Frank Gehry?"

"Well and yes," Danny said, surprised that Val knew Danny was from Toronto, a basic fact, and that the architect Frank Gehry was from Toronto, a basic fact. He had hidden everything, been hired to hide everything, so that even the most basic facts of his life seemed like redacted secrets someone had broken into.

"And so, correct me if I am wrong, you and Frankie baby were having yourselves a little celebratory libation, there at the opening reception, is that right?"

"Of course, it was a great and splendid day. We had achieved so much together."

"Yet there was a murder plot at the Guggenheim to disrupt its opening to the public, Danny. Basque terrorists were planning to plant twelve grenades in Jeff Koons' *Puppy* and blow up the big dog made of greens and flowers in front of the museum, and kill VIPs, including the King and Queen of Spain."

"I heard the news that day."

"But, help me out here, Danny. Isn't it your job to anticipate the news? Isn't counterterrorism *professional anticipation?* To stop the news before it happens. We hired you to be prepared for terror, not be a consumer of the headlines about terror."

"If none of it had happened. How to stay the course, when blood becomes our heritage. The waters run red beside the museums, the cafés..."

"Now that you say it, dear Daniel, I have to agree with you. We have become so preoccupied with safety, we have forgotten our souls. The heart of art, you were hired to protect that, too. When the Twin Towers went down in fuselage flames, we lost so many beautiful paintings. Doesn't that grieve you?"

"I don't have time for grief, it is not in the job speculations."

"Danny. There is a price to pay, if public safety does not encompass inner security. We met about this, me and your other superiors: Danny Coma had become trapped in safe styling and sandpapered images. It wasn't always that way. We thought you'd be a tiger, out on the fringes, informal, vigilant. What happened?"

"You and my big-shot brother. Why don't you leave me alone and stop blaming me? My hands are dry, is there some water? My wife died, I'll have you know."

"I do know. Suspicious circs. We let that go. She was way off the grid. Your wife went rogue on us, but you did not have to follow her."

"That's how much you know. Who are you anyway?"

"If you knew, I'd have to kill myself."

"Do I see the gofer with some cleansing water for my hands?…Yes… No?... Ah, Mr. Gehry… He grew up on the same block of Cecil that my bubbie did. For all I know, his mother and my grandmother shopped in Kensington together." Danny picked up a smooth mirrored rock and threw it. Vivienne caught the shot. Danny's face had the blank petulance you sometimes see in photos of boys age ten or eleven.

"Did you know," Val said, "were you aware that the main mastermind behind the 1997 attempted bombing of the Guggenheim Museum is said to be hiding in Cambridge, England? Your old alma mater, plus you are an old hand at Spain. Did you know that it was Mister Basque in Cambridge who had the idea that the ETA terrorists would pose as gardeners, drive up with compost in a pickup and plant all those petunia pots in Jeff Koons' *Puppy* along with remote-controlled explosives?"

"That never went ahead," Danny said.

"Correct. You heard the news," Val said. "But no thanks to you. Three years before the terrorists tried to blow up the Guggenheim, the leadership sent out a communiqué saying, 'We will *tiralo todo con patas arriba*.' Topsy-turvy, Danny. Paws up. Shoot everybody."

"I don't speak Spanish," Danny said.

"*Digame* something I don't know. So the terrorists in Bilbao set out to make good their promise. But they were stupid two ways. One, they came with their manure, their gardeners' garb, their moss and petunias, on a Monday. But the actual gardeners building Koons' *Puppy* had completed their work on the Saturday. The police knew that. So they ran the plates of the suspicious-looking gardeners' vehicle, a Ford Transit, and found that, two, they were plates stolen from a SEAT Marbella. There was a shootout at the new museum between police and terrorists. A policeman was fatally wounded, and a massacre was avoided."

"What do you want me to do?"

"Your job."

Val's blood was boiling. He took incompetence personally. Vivienne was looking through the camera lens at Danny. Johnny, for his part, was shaking, with the kind of tremors and sick stomach only family can bring. He could hardly hold on to his sketching pencil, but sketch he did. Danny smirked his hidden knowledge, known to all in the open land. Johnny sketched Danny with a balloon coming out of his mouth: I WAS PROMISED.

"Here's us," Val said, thrusting a Polaroid Dan's way. "That is me, Johnny and Vivienne. That is Vivienne pointing to the actual blood of the policeman on the sidewalk, at the entrance to the Bilbao Guggy. Where were you? Getting a blow job inside Richard Serra's *Snake*?"

"Who said you were there?"

"I did," Val said.

"Well, check your sources."

They had walked that night, in Basque Bilbao, after the shootout at the Guggy, the Three Musketeers, in the exquisite shipbuilding fall dusk of rusty cordages along the inlet, the Ría del Nervión. The link between old Bilbao and Bremen and Pittsburgh was evident: it was the air of big work, and men who built the sailing vessels, big mines, big foundries; the air of a time and a place that in the States was now called the Rust Belt, but which felt alive still in Bilbao.

How they had walked that night the terrorists shot the Bilbao guard down beside Frank Gehry's titanium rebuke to terror. They walked in that Nervión autumn dusk, in its characteristic purpling over the hills, and the water was green and old and full of ship's hulls and algae. They walked over Santiago Calatrava's bridge, a magnificent lit up bridge made of turquoise glass, a marvel of swoop, called the Zubizuri – the "white bridge" that Johnny called the white bird. And Vivienne took pictures of them, high above the water, subsumed by turquoise lifting into the wet night and surrounding their bodies in the pic, and the Gehry Guggy in back, shining its own wet titanium silverization in the night. Maybe the Guggy was Marilyn Monroe, as the *New York Times* had it, maybe it was Elizabeth Taylor, stealth and northern, in violet and green. Terror hates beauty, because beauty always outlives terror, and especially when we remember the beauty we have known, which they have smashed to smithereens. Because terror has to make noise and beauty can be quiet. Because terror has to brag, and beauty can be modest. Terror knows in its heart that it is the one nobody wants to dance with, only the losers, only the bullies who look at beauty with flames so green they would destroy it. Franco is dead, but *Guernica* is forever.

"These ETA terrorists, come on, Danny. They're no more political than the old Mafia boys. You know what they say: these are not the sharpest knives in the drawer. Your pals were terrorists who never *started* high school, who keep killing people to get what they've already got."

Danny pushed up into another handstand and walked on his hands a few inches. A bighorn sheep up on the ridge might be forgiven for wondering what humans thought, or if they had thought at all. Two of them, legs crossed, huddled under a small rock overhang in a one-foot shadow for shade. A third, walking back and forth on two feet, with a white stick in his mouth, blowing smoke. A fourth who walked on his hands. Ta-da! An ovine against the sky might wonder about the awkwardness of this species in the canyon, a sense the humans had been brought to earth and did not know it.

Val urged Danny to his feet, then took him in his arms and began a slow dance with him, whispering in his ear. "What do you know about the Spanish terrorists' plan to come to the United States and coordinate bombings on one day, at one time, in major museums across the States?" He twirled Danny out in a slow jive move, then held him close again. "What did you know about the ETA plan to kill the King of Spain in September 2000 at the opening of the Chillida-Leku Museum in San Sebastián? What do you know about the plan to bomb the Met in New York, the Phillips in Washington, the Bass in Miami Beach, the Menil in Houston and the Getty in LA all on the same day?"

Danny looked at the massive open space he was in, as if for the first time. A fugue state can be a sly intention, then a habit of synapse. "Can anybody get a coffee around here?" he asked.

"Come on, Danny," Val said. "What do you know about Basque terrorists flying from Spain to begin bombings all over North America? What do you know about the emails intercepted between ETA members in Bilbao and ETA members in Bayonne, regarding ticket purchases on Iberia Airlines, to fly from Spain to Guatemala, and to make their way by land up through Arizona and Texas to start ETA branches in the US? What do you know about the terrorists' plans to come to Las Vegas and blow up major hotels this New Year's? Come on, Danny, cough."

Val lit another cigarette off the one still in in his mouth. He had one in each hand. "What do you know," he asked, "about Saddam Hussein electrocuting his own soldiers by dumping them in the rivers and sending electricity through the water?"

"I have heard it was done," Danny said.

"Do you know it was done?" Val took a puff from the right hand and then the left.

"It is a story told in the Middle East." Danny's eyes brightened.

"Tell me about the story." Val sat down at Danny's feet, giving a little haimish rub to Danny's right Frye boot.

Danny's back straightened. His body snapped even straighter, and his eyes lit out to a far memory. "Thank you all for coming here, today," he said. "We welcome the usual invitees, any extras welcome, wives, grandchildren, friends on tour, gather round, the expected list and *inter alia* and so on." Val wondered if Danny had gone back to the fugue-state Danny. Then Danny snapped back. "Ah, yes. Iraq. The draining of the great rivers. I understand that Saddam was hunting down the deserters from his army. They ran to the rivers so the rivers would hide them, and Saddam sent electrical wires through the water. He electrocuted his own soldiers. The waters were tortured. Of course, there was no reliable power; electricity was by no means secure – the blackouts! Then Saddam gave orders for the waters to be drained. Thousands of men lay where the ancient rivers ran. He had unearthed them at last."

Johnny and Vivienne came over and sat down. Vivienne put her head on Johnny's shoulder. He stroked her hair and kissed her head.

Danny saw he had a full house of three souls. He held out his right hand and spoke: "And so they said that those who lived by the crops near the water lost their economies, and so they said that the birds no longer had a home. The waterfowl was lost without water. Saddam called it Enemy Water, and he killed his own water to get at the traitors. The sky was full of electrocuted feathers, for they killed the waterfowl, as well as the uniformed men. And now the dry riverbeds were full of corpses and unexploded mines. And they sent more electricity through the riverbed, even though all the water was gone, in case someone was hiding in the water that was not there, and some of the mines exploded, killing the corpses twice." Danny stretched both his arms out, in grand podium style.

"And so did the dictator Saddam Hussein drain the grand biblical rivers. He called one river the River Mother of All Battles. And he called the other river the River Loyalty to the Leader.

"To save the *patria*, war kills the land." Danny pointed to the dry riverbed in front of him. He bowed. Vivienne, Johnny and Val applauded. Danny bowed his head again. Which Danny was this? Was it the Danny who had started out young and fresh and sharp? Or the Danny who became the underminer, the belittler, embarrassed by sincerity?

"And what Saddam Hussein started," Danny said, lifting his head, with moist eyes, "the fucking United States of America finished for him. They continued his work of destroying the Iraqi homeland. The great waters of the Shatt al-Arab down in the reeds and the rushes of the baby Moses, gone. South of Basra, Eden is gone. Goodbye, Eden. Gone. Blood and blood and blood. Adios, old pal. *Hasta Luegito*, Eden."

Val looked at Johnny. Johnny shook his head. Is this my brother, Danny? This man seems clear, heartful. The ambition was short, the fumes were long. Vivienne took a picture of Danny, who, despite the Speedo in the cold sunshine and the old kicked-up dusty boots, showed an aligned posture and seemed a man. His body had momentarily sloughed off its sarcasm, and that changed the body's look.

"And in the desert heat," Danny went on, "the corpses in the dry riverbed putrefied and filled with gases. The soldiers had been chased, electrocuted, blown up, thus murdered twice, and left to putrefy, dying a third time in the desert of Iraq. Then Pharaoh Saddam put the waters back in the rivers to hide the corpses, he returned the blood waters to the riverbeds, and the soldiers' decomposition went into the water supply. The people of Iraq were drinking the dissolved corpses of their soldiers. The land was buzzing with the murderous, and the earth was biohectic."

Johnny watched his brother. Danny could have been the contender-in-chief. Danny could have been a history teacher to remember. The last time Johnny had seen Danny show his tender self through words Johnny was fifteen and Danny was eighteen, and Danny was reading Ovid to Johnny. Forty years between open-heartednesses was a sick lonely desert stretch. Maybe Danny couldn't have had class. Maybe Danny couldn't have been a contender. Maybe Danny's passion was the passion of the man who lusts for the sidelines. Where you can know everything that the contenders do wrong. Maybe Danny couldn't have been somebody. Maybe Danny was a bum with a high-toned veneer.

Danny took one of Val's cigarettes and walked back and forth in front of his audience of three.

"And so the story is written," Danny went on, "that for the first time in five thousand years, the Arabs of the wet river lands of Iraq had to leave their fishing and wet *agrícola* life and be refugees fleeing the dry beds. The salt remaining became the oversalination of dry beds. Then, the Americans came in and destroyed the dykes and the Saddam-built canals. The over-salinated ancient riverbeds became flooded with sick salt and toxic war chemicals. Tortured were the waters of life.

"And mixed up in the poison soup were the bodies of our American boys in the rivers of old Eden.

"And so, my sons," Danny said, "in conclusion as we depart this morning, I say today: A country is not an idea, though politics would have you think so. I say this, as a student of history. A country is its land and its water. And war evens every hand. Thank you and good night. God bless and come again."

Danny took a bow. He pulled out his penis and peed on a rock. He said, "Can I go now? I want to get my gofer on the line to the White House. The President put me in charge of public security. I need to tell Georgie Porgie that he can downgrade to a yellow."

"Special Ambassador. Special Ambassador Coma, could I have a word with you?" Val was at Danny's side. "You must have had quite the life. Can we look forward to the memoir soon? Tales of coping in Copenhagen, or facing down photographers with your home appliances in Montevideo?"

"Yes, my lad. Come ahead." Danny shook his hand, having emptied his skeletal posture of the easeful teacher and the Sunday morning preacher, and letting the hail-fellow-well-met enter in. "So nice to see you again. When was it we last saw each other? Ceuta? No, don't tell me, Melilla. I heard in the wind it was those damn bastards from Morocco who bombed the Madrid trains, but one is never where one wants to be when one wants to be there, and so forth, so on, *inter alia*, pro rata and whatchamadiddle."

Whatchamadiddle, indeed.

23

FEAR FACTORIES

"THE PERSON OF a foreign service officer shall remain inviolate," Danny said, his right hand motioning to the sky, the canyon, the threesome of planes flying overhead. Daniel Coma who, if he had been born a generation earlier, say in 1910, and had wanted to have the job he had, dirty tricks hire under the cover of being an American foreign service officer, well, there would have been really no such work. The United States embassies, at first, were few and important. The United States was the new country, and abroad there were the first responders to the new hopeful country of 1776. The first responder was the Netherlands, then Paris (with Ben Franklin, yes, France), and Morocco. There was China, Japan, Siam. These were the legacy missions: Paris, the Hague, Rabat, Tokyo.

Danny dreamed of it: a small embassy station in an old elegant building. A Prague, a Libreville. He was going to sit with the cigar men and find them amusing and be amusing himself and feel distant from *Lord Jim* and know *Lord Jim* and love *Lord Jim* and talk about meeting up in London again, and facilitating trade routes and the trading of cultures, kimonos and kielbasa, Noh theatre and *No, No, Nanette*, explaining Torah to Thais, and exchanging anecdotes about learning to eat with chopsticks.

Slowly and carefully and with consideration, as if choosing a special house, it had begun, this thing they call diplomatic missions. Then it had grown, like the man with many houses, at home and abroad. Then with so many houses it did not know the number, something clicked in the brain of the executive function of the land, and impulse control quit, and the map ran amok with American embassy franchises. The map once devoid of US embassies was now full, and the country felt less secure, not more. So insecure with so many holdings, it began to hire staff to keep all its holdings secure. While nobody was looking, Ben Franklin in Paris became thirty thousand employees of the security firm whose job it was to protect US embassy staff around the world. About twelve thousand foreign service officers, about thirty thousand security staff for them.

It had become a bureaucracy of the dissatisfied put in to facilitate the imperializing of the ungrateful. For every one foreign service officer, there were three security hires to protect him. Fear factories, Val called them. Danny woke up and he was a bureaucrat in a bureaucracy, and there was no honour left in the lying.

And now, the biggest fear factory of them all was being built in Baghdad: the biggest embassy ever seen in the history of the world. Was this not further pharaohs?

How did Ben Franklin in Paris become the new embassy in Baghdad, Iraq, which would take up one square mile? The plan for the US Embassy in Baghdad was to have ten to fifteen thousand personnel there, half of which would be security.

And when the troops were gone from Baghdad, if there were eight thousand army and armed guards and "no troops," would the local Iraqis discuss semantics? How did the mansions of Paris and Rabat become a world where the word *mansion* became the word *fortification?* Time was a neutrino, the world was at speed, but Danny's heart beat slowly. He had wanted to get out of the shadow work at that nice twenty-five-year mark. But he had not. And again at the thirty-year mark. But he had not. And the thirty-five-year mark, but he had not. To leave, in Danny's eyes, would be to admit that Ben Franklin was not in Paris anymore, and neither was Marlon Brando in Indochine in *The Ugly American*. Ben Franklin was no longer living in the suburb of Passy, and neither was Marlon Brando, who rented a flat in Passy in *Last Tango in Paris*. The game changers were receding, replaced by the gatekeepers in contracted uniforms.

Like the anima, our shadow self, made into a holy bunker, like the part of us we did not want to know, writ large in other countries, denied but visible to all, a supersizing less about food than about a psychosis, the United States Embassy in Baghdad was an architectural monstrosity in progress. Its look – and the look was planned – was as totalitarian in appearance as anything Saddam Hussein had ever calculated when he himself razed his own Baghdad neighbourhoods, the shops, the souks, the riverboats, the alleys. The plan was to have the embassy area, ninety-six football fields in size, with AC in the desert land, with US food in the Arabian desert, with movie theatres where maybe the only sight of the emotionally tantalizing Arabia and its dust would be in the air-conditioned theatre inside the concrete walls so tall you could not even see great Arab Baghdad at all. Had the United States become the great imperial exporter of agoraphobia? Had fear become its main export? Had the USA outsourced *itself?*

The United States had out-Saddamed Saddam. As they were planning to hang him, the United States had taken up his totalitarian mantle, building a totalitarian monster's wet dream.

Danny looked at Johnny with fury, "For your information, I was born into a family of writers!"

"Dan," Johnny said. "You were born into a family of card sharks. Furniture salesmen, itinerant jewellers. Fur cutters. Shmatte workers. In the history of our family, I am the first writer. So far, the only one. Don't spin my life back to me, okay?"

"No wonder I have no confidence. Listen to him."

"Don't ride on my coattails," Johnny said. "I worked hard for my money."

"I have my own coattails, I will have you know," Danny said.

"Danny, if you thought my work was so easy, something you'd pick up when you got finished with a lifetime of your own, what did you think of your own job? If you thought writing was a little hobby, a little pastime your brother has been playing at all those years, if you had no real respect for my work, then is that why you screwed up so badly at yours?"

"You experts think you know everything."

"Yes," Johnny said. "We do. Because we don't. It's you ignoramuses who are the know-it-alls. You thought my writing life was all gravy, and you left out the *gravitas*."

"Or," said Val, "it's all a long con to get in your head, Johnny. A ruse to disrupt you, put Danny-static in your brain. It worked. So then, how be we continue our little tourist tour? Family on vacation, see the sights, Christmas holidays, natural wonders."

"Leave no trace," Johnny said to Val, giving him a pat on the back as they walked out of the amphitheatre into the marbleized hallway.

"Never do," Val said. He and Johnny walked ahead, followed by Danny, followed by Vivienne, who lagged back to take a picture of the backs of the three men.

Vivienne shot the back of her husband, Johnny: Johnny had class; Johnny was a contender; Johnny was somebody; Johnny used his hands, his forearms, his fingertips; Johnny was a workman; Johnny laboured; Johnny brought the world to readers; Johnny punched through the paper wall of the psyche. Johnny stopped. She took another quick pic of her husband. The back of a man in a long black coat, tucked inside a narrow shining canyon, under a blue so deep it reminded Vivienne that blue was a new colour, a found-hue miracle, an invention, which came after the original black and red of the cave drawings.

Val's body was open, elbows touching the close mosaic shine, the silver fox in the interrogation canyon.

Danny followed along, obedient, resentful, in a haze. Hunched, bowed, weaving. Saying, "I asked for water. Please. Is that a flash flood I see coming down the crevices? At last. At last, the fast knives of water will rush down to me. Have you no water?"

The droughts of ages provided no water to the guilty to wash the blood from their hands, even in mirage, even in madness.

24

TWO VIEWS OF MANZANAR

UP A HUNDRED feet on a promontory, Vivienne spotted the profile of that bighorn sheep, and she shot it against the noonday sun, its horns curved down, its head noble, looking down on its big rocky house and the four intruders.

The naturally tiled high walls made a canyon curtain.

"Hold up," she said. "I want a pic. You two stand on either side of Danny."

Val placed Danny against the ancient polished wall. He got on his left, Johnny got on his right. They each put an arm around Danny. They smiled, but not with their eyes. Vivienne liked that. Danny looked at the camera, stunned. "Let me have that," he said.

"You wish," Vivienne said.

"Call him Special Ambassador," Val said. "We named him."

"Oh good," she said, the camera at her eye, framing. "Now he can go back into Iraq and get rid of the non-army."

Vivienne climbed up and down a rock to get to the three of them, and she took Danny's chin and lifted it. "Good. Now you're going to look real pretty, Ambassador." She pushed Johnny in a bit, and Val in a bit, acting like it was a wedding photo, only nobody was asked to say cheese and the venue was about a foot and a half wide. A Western movie passageway.

"Remember that one?" Vivienne asked. "The one with, was it Jack Palance and Lee Marvin? Where they're in the canyon, and Lee Marvin says something to Jack Palance like, I may be a son of a bitch, sir, or something."

"I know, honey," Johnny said. "It was *The Professionals.* Lee Marvin and Ralph Bellamy. Lee Marvin brought the pretty Spanish Señora back to her husband, Ralph Bellamy. Remember? Bellamy hires the professionals. He wants pros to go out and find his kidnapped wife, taken back to Mexico. Then it turns out the wife wasn't kidnapped, the wife ran away with her lover. Bellamy told a lie to get his wife who hated him brought back to him by professionals. So there is Lee Marvin, yeah, sure in a canyon close like this, with Ralph Bellamy, and they let the Señora go, and Bellamy says, 'You bastard.' And Lee Marvin says, 'Just an accident of birth. But you, sir, are a self-made man.' Didn't you love that? They made it at Lone Pine."

Vivienne, still behind the camera, "One more, for insurance. I wish I were Lee Marvin. He is the woman for the nuclear age."

They finished the photo op, and walked further, and the open gouge appeared where they had entered, the wide entrance to Mosaic Canyon formed by ancient flooding waters. It was a source of endless fascination: in a place with no water, water had been one of the principal geological protagonists. Water and wind were the basin and range's ancestors, and only one of them remained.

Danny was sulking, shoulders down, looking smaller than small, an inviolate elf in violation canyons. The Honda sedan was the only vehicle in the parking lot. Strange. Foothill charcoal, upper pewter, then deep dark blue outlined the ridges and paler shadow pinks drifted on the belligerent blue California sky. "Aw, come on, Daniel," Val said. "Humour me, keep me company in the back, while these two humps drive."

Danny sat with Val in the back. Val took his hand and they held hands as Johnny drove down the dusty road from Mosaic Canyon through the space that used to be the deep coral sea. He turned right at the bottom of the hill, and carried on past the general store, the gas pumps, their motel and Stovepipe Wells. "You missed the motel," Danny said.

"I know," Johnny said.

"Where are we going? Help!"

"You'll see," Johnny said. "We planned a scenic exit."

"Don't kidnap me," Danny said.

"It's done," Val said, tickling Danny's hand.

The vehicle kicked up more road dust, going fast on 190 East, past the Devil's Cornfield, which was arrowweed on both sides of the road, spreading in land without signage. The sense you are on your own was once hardwired in humans, but modern humans have lost it. We make civilization to have surroundings, to orient us. The land alone scares us. Death Valley was the lonely margin that ran for millions of interior acres. Danny was in the hands of his captors, his brother, her...*that one*, Val, and the land out the window was a strangeness with shades and shadows of elsewhere.

Johnny turned left and drove up Scotty's Castle Road, through the valley, then up Grapevine Canyon Road to Scotty's. Scotty's Castle. "Let's stop at Scotty's," Vivienne said.

"I don't want to stop at Scotty's," Johnny said, "I'm taking us to the crater. As we discussed."

Vivienne put her hand on the back of Johnny's neck and massaged it while he drove. She leaned over to him and kissed his neck. She kissed his cheek, she turned his chin and kissed his mouth. He veered to the left.

"Watch it, man," Val said.

"Call Ma," Danny said. "You owe her twelve hundred dollars."

Vivienne did it again, kissing Johnny longer and harder, "Come on, honey, a little Scotty's? Five minutes." Johnny kept the car steady this time.

"You know," he said, "the biggest cause of death in Death Valley is not dying of thirst or being eaten by a snake, it's single car accidents. *Single car* accidents."

"Too much kissing," Vivienne said.

"She's nuts," Val said.

"I know," Johnny said.

"My brother never married," Danny said.

"Don't play the Pinochet card with me," Johnny said. "You are not getting off the hook because of age. What you did you did when you were young. Don't wait to get old to take a senility plea. Not with me, brother."

"See how he talks to me?" Danny said, squeezing Val's hand.

"I paid my debt to Ma by the way," Johnny said, turning his head from the wheel, veering to the right this time. "I paid it like twenty-seven years ago, which is also, by the way, more than I can say for some people, and society."

"See?" Danny said, investigating the mystery treasure down in the depths of his blue Speedo, comforting his family jewels with one hand, and smiling up at Val, holding Val's hand with his other.

They came to Scotty's Castle. Vivienne loved it. A magnificent folly in the middle of the desert. A castle built by Death Valley Scotty, whose real name was Walter Scott, a hard barking trick rider with Buffalo Bill's Wild West show, who then became a promoter, looking for backers for his separate and several schemes, including a mine he promoted which did not exist. And this Death Valley Scotty befriended the wealthy Albert Johnson. Scotty convinced Johnson to build a vacation home in Death Valley. This was in the 1920s. The two men built a monster mansion, with one man's money and the other man's bluster. Scotty claimed the mansion as his in his self-promotion. Johnson, who liked his privacy, did not mind having a holiday home that another man fronted with his blustering and self-promoting fun. When Albert Johnson found out that the mine did not exist, he did not even care. Scotty was the front man, while Johnson and his wife, the real owners, stayed low. Johnson enjoyed the BS of Scotty. The castle became a tourist site, a place to stop, Scotty's Oasis in a way, long after Scotty and Johnson and Bessie the missus had all passed away. Scotty was the third of the happy Death Valley castle trio, the publicity hound and it is his name that survives. The turrets, the porticos, in a photograph of Scotty's Castle, look like a castle in Spain.

The three men went into the snack bar. Vivienne went to the little bookstore. She had most of the books, the scats and tracks, the desert holes, the geology, the ranger tales, the survival tips, the maps. She asked the ranger at the counter if there was anything meaty, juicy, something she might not have read; what was his favourite book in the store? Without hesitation, he walked to the shelves and pulled out *Cadillac Desert* by Marc Reisner. *The American West and Its Disappearing Water.* The book was about twenty years old, the ranger said. It was the story of the mismanagement of water in California: the dams, the irrigation, the keening to the big hydroelectric projects, the killing off of the farmers' livelihood and land, and the growth of Los Angeles at the expense of the Owens Valley. When the ranger said the words *Owens Valley,* his face lit up, his eyes squinted.

"Do you mind if I take your picture?" Vivienne asked.

"Ma'am, you go right ahead." She had seen a light, almost a pilot light in its first low blue flame, in the ranger's eyes, coming higher in his eyes. He told her the story: His grandfather had farmed apples up north of Lone Pine when the first wave of the water crooks was finished absconding with the Owens Lake water and the Owens River water, and were making moves on the Mono Lake water, where large underwater tufa formations lay, part of the fragile ecosystem of the ancient heritage and drainage. But the bastards came in and took even the small fragile water the apple orchard farmers had. The ranger said he used to go to see his grandpa in the early spring when the apple blossoms filled the trees and they stretched for miles with their pale pink blossoms in the valley, "Almost like a Van Gogh, ma'am, do you know what I mean?"

Vivienne loved standing in an empty shop having an over-the-counter chat with a weathered regular guy who knew more, way more, than he let on to a passing stranger, but who had this knowledge reserve should a woman chance in, who was curious and liked conversation and was up for a couple minutes of intimate human speech, a small connection to remember, a moment of light in the pain. She did not have to ask him if he had served in the armed forces, if he was a veteran. She knew it. He was giving forth while maintaining a reserve, telling a story of his grandpa's farm going down, the apple blossoms he walked under as a small child, his enchantment with them, his shock when he saw a Van Gogh, when as a soldier he passed through Amsterdam, and the tree in the painting was his grandpa's apple tree in the Eastern Sierra. It gave him the same feeling. The ranger's air reminded her that men who have served tend to know and tend to emit that life is short. If life was short, chat was easy.

So, the ranger's grandpa's apple orchard went down, and the tiny community they had named Manzanar for the Spanish word for apple, *manzana*, became known not for farming, but for the rich open land the government took and made into a concentration camp for Japanese Americans. The ranger's eyes burned high and with a low fierce flame. His passions clearly were water, his grandfather, the long-gone apple blossoms in spring and the sick hateful move of the Feds in taking Americans of Japanese ancestry, the majority of them citizens, and incarcerating them during the Second World War. "It seemed incredible," the ranger said, "that they were making that movie with Bogart – what was the name of it?"

"*High Sierra*," Vivienne said. That damn movie had been stalking her since Vegas. Can you be on the lam from a movie about someone on the lam from the law? Do some movies pop up and peep at you, like true serial stalkers?

"*High Sierra*, sure," the ranger said. "Yeah, they're making that movie there right past my grandpa's old house, up 395, past Olancha and Lone Pine, and there's Bogey hanging that left to go up the mountain."

"Mount Whitney," Vivienne said.

"That's right, ma'am. If Mad Dog Earle had been driving up that way a couple years later, he might have seen the Feds out, paying no attention to him, but arresting Japanese Americans in the evening on the day of Pearl Harbor."

Vivienne had never heard of Manzanar. There was a Japanese internment camp near Lone Pine, where they made all the Westerns?

"Ma'am, there is an Ansel Adams photograph he took at Manzanar, oh yes." The ranger went over to the twirly postcard rack and picked out a black-and-white shot of rocks, big boulders, with mountains in the back. "You think this is just Mount Williamson like it says. But there's a story behind this." Vivienne was thinking how she wanted to just take this ranger along with her, gee he was swell. Well, that was her problem, she liked guys. She liked men. If you were looking for a man, it was nice to know there were men around.

"You come back and see me sometime, I'll show you a book we have on back order. Your friend Ansel Adams did with – maybe you might have heard of him – Tōyō Miyatake, one of the best-known Japanese photographers out of LA. They put him in the concentration camp, then he and Adams put together this sweet little book, *Two Views of Manzanar.* You see, Ansel could come and go, but Miyatake? He was behind barbed wire."

Vivienne was getting a one-on-one tutorial from a ranger, a book club for two.

The story was that Ansel Adams came to the Manzanar internment camp, and he asked to take pictures of the watchtowers, and they refused him, they did not want him taking pictures that would show this internment camp as an internment camp. So he went up in the tower, asking to take a picture of the landscape. But he managed to get shots of other watchtowers, guard towers, barbed wire.

"Ma'am, now this Mount Williamson picture is only of the rocks, but it could serve as a nice reminder. Mister Ansel Adams fought for the land, but he was always on the side of the people, he knew how to play the game is all. What's your business, honey?"

"I'm a photographer," Vivienne said, ignoring the *honey.* Every guy got one complimentary *honey.*

"There you go. You're all set. Would you like to take the *Cadillac Desert*?"

"I most certainly would," she said. She had a single Visa card in a secret zippered pocket inside her pink leather jacket. "I'll read it when I get home."

"Read it before that, ma'am. Read while you drive." He was chuckling, enjoying his own little joke, but with the proselytizing fervour of a genuine reader. Vivienne liked that.

"Where you off to today?" he asked.

"We're going to Ubehebe Crater, maybe Little Hebe, maybe even the Eureka Dunes. I once climbed them, whoa, that was like what? Three hundred feet?"

"Ma'am, I would say more like five hundred feet, some of them are eight hundred feet."

"You mean I climbed an eighty-story building? And I'm a slug, a slob."

"Ma'am, you look all right to me. You might want to get that psoriasis looked into, though." Her hands were scaly, with thick white salty areas, looking like half flaking cement, half chalk lines. "Ma'am, were you in a fight?" He reached out in a strange store intimacy between clerk and client, and touched the growing black growth on her cheek, now taking up almost the whole side of her face.

"Oh, it's okay," she said. "We were just caught in an atomic bomb test back at the Nevada Test Site."

The ranger gave her a quizzical eye. You don't believe me, she thought. But he was too nice and the book looked too good, and besides, she had more special rendition to attend to. "Any word on conditions at the crater?"

"Other than the wind, none so far today. Couple big fuel trucks overturned at 395, crazy wind. Go safely, ma'am. Leave no trace."

"I never do," she said. She came out of the store, and Danny, Val and Johnny were sitting at a picnic table under some cottonwood trees. It was considerably colder up here at Scotty's, downright frigid, the trees swaying. "Let's get going," Vivienne said, although she was the one holding them up. "Let's get Danny to the edge of the volcano."

25

THE UBEHEBE CRATER

THEY CAME BACK down the Grapevine Canyon Road, leaving Scotty's magnificent Moorish folly behind them and headed up the rough drive to the Ubehebe Crater. Partway up, they came to the Grapevine Ranger Station. It looked like a border-crossing hut. There was a woman inside. She asked them where they were headed. They said they were heading up to take a look at Ubehebe Crater, and maybe drive on to the Eureka Dunes. She leaned out through the station window and said, "I wouldn't advise that, folks. Not a great idea. You're on your own up there. Going up over that mountain pass…then there's nothing. I would advise taking a pass on the Eureka Dunes today."

"Is there any problem?" Johnny asked. "Anybody die?"

"Not that I heard of," the ranger said.

"Any avalanches or snow?"

"At Eureka? No, sir."

"I'm curious why a park ranger is advising us not to go to the most remote part of the park. If there is no problem, as you say."

Vivienne knew Johnny couldn't help it. He smelled a story. He was hard-wired to be curious. "Sir," the ranger said, "we've had some trouble. Nothing you need to worry about. It'll take you six to eight hours."

"It's only thirty-five miles," Johnny said, testing her.

She said, "Sir, that road to the Eureka Dunes is mostly a road in name only. We discourage visitors from going there."

"You trying to save the dunes from people?" Val asked from the back seat, patting Danny's hand.

"Something along those lines," the ranger said, peering past the sun's glare to see Val. "No trouble. Nothing to worry about. A professor out of Canada managed to get some *matériel* in the soles of his shoes on a flight to Vegas, said he was planning to blow up the Flamingo Hotel on New Year's Eve. So far, word is, he, well it's not for me to say, but the news is saying the professor was copycatting those Indonesian hotel lobby bombs. But no worries, folks, they caught him. No problem."

Vivienne said nothing. She bet money that it was the guy sitting across from her on the plane out of Pearson. The one with his white SUV shoes on top of his backpack.

"Okay," Johnny said. "We're heading to the Ubehebe Crater. We want to show Gramps back there the great explosion of when was it?"

"Oh, not too long ago at all, sir. Pretty recently. Oh, I'd say maybe two, three thousand years ago."

"Gotcha," Johnny said, and they pushed the vehicle on through the increasingly cold upsweeps of wind.

VIVIENNE AND JOHNNY got out of the car at Ubehebe Crater.

The wind was so strong everything flapped, from jacket collars to earlobes. Vivienne put her hands to her ears – the wind was so noisy she could not hear, the wind had G-force – and she walked to the edge of the rim. She tipped back and forth; the wind was trying to push her down the sides. She put her camera, which was hanging around her neck, to her eye; her arms were rocking back and forth. She planted her feet apart and dug her toes down to capture the ground. Johnny came up behind her and held her waist with a wraparound hug, to steady her for her photo. Val was still in the back seat of the vehicle with Danny.

The crater was a half a mile wide. The rim around it was thin. The sides of the crater sloping down looked like one large unfurled textile. White lines ran across orange-rust volcanic rock in chevron patterns, extrusions pushing up to the rim area where a band of purply brown ran around the giant rim. These were a type of alluvial fan deposits called fanglomerates. The floor of the crater, seven hundred feet down, was a soft brown with white pebbles or ghost growths leading to an orange centre.

IN THE CAR, Val pulled out an art postcard. It was *Pineapple and Anemones*, by Henri Matisse. A vase of pink, red, mauve, white anemones spilling over to a yellow container holding a red-orange pineapple on a yellow table. The colours in the card seemed like a revelation in winter; the anemones in a vase, which Matisse painted in a cold war winter, seemed a gift across time. While the Nazis occupied Paris in 1940, down in the south of France in Nice, Matisse painted a fresh pineapple in winter. He painted the everyday item as found desire, speaking to the other colours around it, the way a lover found alive might turn up, swaddled in wrappings, in winter, in wartime, alive, shining in a bright orange-red sweater.

Val asked, "What do you see, Danny?"

Danny was not paying attention.

"Fresh fruit, now that's a laugh," Danny said.

Val pressed a red button on his orange phone. This sent out a blue crackle. Even in the car, the desert air made any electrical device more effective. Val applied the phone (a radio wave device after all) to Danny's forehead. "What do you see? Look."

"It's a damn… I don't know what it is. A pineapple. Fine. Fruit and flowers. What do you want me to do with it?"

"You say you're a man of culture, Dan. Wagner, Harry Potter, *The National*, what do you see in front of you?" Val held the *Pineapple and Anemones* postcard up to Danny's face.

"It's a damn sun, some damn orange table, someone sent somebody a pineapple."

"You know what I see, Danny? I see a grenade. But maybe that's just me. I see an orange grenade. I see wheels. I see that yellow basket as a carry-on. I see someone smuggling an incediary device disguised as a pineapple on board a plane."

Danny understood Val was making chitchat. Val, however, was giving Danny one last chance to show he had a suspicious mind. And one last chance to show remorse.

"No tropical fruit on the plane," Danny said, off in his hospital ward in his mind, nursing all those bedded grudges. "I get bumped to steerage. What kind of world are we living in? A woman has her comfort bear. It's a real bear. I'm in business and a hairy bear is sleeping on my neck."

"Oh for pity's sake, Dan. I could fritz you from morning to night and all you would bleed is a bunch of straw men." He pushed the red button.

"No. Stop it. I will not have it... What is that?" Danny started hitting his own face. "Get off, get off me, why is the river green? Why is the river red?" Slapping himself.

"Danny, wake up, man," Val said.

Danny was rocking back and forth in the car, hugging his waist, saying, "I see the red rivers," slapping his arms, "I can't wash off the rivers. Is it her? Get her away from me… She told me what to do. Stop her voice." Slapping his own head.

Val was stumped. Val had promised Vivienne he would proceed.

"Daniel Coma, you have heard the charges. Your wife, Mrs. Coma put the juice to Vivienne Pink. She tortured an artist. You watched. You participated. Allocute now, Danny. Confess. Ask God to forgive you. Forget God, ask Vivienne to forgive you. Now is the time. What is that cute word you use – *reconciliation*? How about *repentance*. If you repent, you might live to see another begging bowl day."

"Oh get off the pot, you amateurs."

Val pushed the white button. He pushed a black button. A robotic cobra emerged from the orange phone. It wound around Danny's neck. Val pressed a blue button. The cobra applied even electricity around Danny's neck.

"Say you are sorry, Daniel."

"What did she tell you?"

"You heard her at Rhyolite."

"What else did she tell you?" Danny asked, closing his eyes, rocking back and forth again, speaking to someone not there. "Ah yes, my dear, I am coming. Not to fret. I have the up-to-date information for you. No, no. No need to do that…the beaches must be spared. There is too much blood already." Opening his eyes: "What else did she tell you? That one."

"She told me. The details. You did more than try out the electricity on her."

"I want to know what she told you." Like many an abuser who bonds with his subject in an odd belief that the two of them have been through something intimate together, Danny expressed himself in disbelief, a sense of disloyalty on the part of his victim, a sense that she had betrayed him by *speaking* of it. The utterance is the betrayal. The utterance to others. Because that brings others into the intimacy of the torture, reveals the secret of the act. The fear that binds private abusers and government torture-meisters is the fear of the storyteller. The story might be told in pictures; the story might be told in words. "What did she tell you? I want to know what she said." In lieu of repentance, the torturer will look for the feeling he was duped. Evil is not banal. Evil is evil. Men who torture do not, in fact, say *I was just doing my job.* They speak of the clear and present dangers. They say you cannot understand what the times were like. They say that to rout out the subversives, they had to keep almost-killing the artists. They will say the best of their lot had a fine hand. They will praise each other for the delicacy of their fingers. They will, as men, praise men who have the knack. They will speak of their brethren as the fine jeweller, the expert neurosurgeon, the heart surgeon, those who can bring the living to a state of almost dying, and yet never quite kill them. They will look down on torturers who kill their subjects as clumsy amateurs. The high bar of torture is not death, but rather the voyeurism of seeing the living suffer. And after all that, look at the gratitude. "I want to know what she said to you," Danny said. "Are there pictures?"

"Just say you're sorry," Val said. "She's right there, at the crater rim. Go to her, and tell her you are sorry for what you did. Ask her forgiveness." Vivienne was waving at them.

"I had no sleep. They told me I could sleep after the mission. I walked the Camino as a sorry pilgrim. Cannot we be nomads together, brother? It was, one must confess, slightly after the Tokyo Round that we began to – sham! Sim! Splat! Punta del Este, lovely for the holidays. One did most humbly accept the *credencial* on the Compostela Way. Pilgrim passport. Motivation: spiritual."

Val pressed a purple button. "Guess your thoughts on God left out the mercy," he said. The robot snake tightened around Danny's neck.

Danny said, "Why is the river red? No one will answer. Where is the river? I can't wash off the rivers." He pulled at his skin, lifting the loose flesh, biting it. "The voices told me to do it."

"What voices, Danny?" Val sent a full charge through him.

Danny rose up off the car seat. "The generals. Mrs. Coma. 'Mrs. C.' They said we needed to right the balance. The IMF was on our case. The hounds of banking said we had to cleanse the country of terrorists. No one takes pictures. That was certain. Mrs. C. said it would be all right; the work was authorized through channels. Fully compensated, come the day. 'Why sleep,' she said. We slept in red rivers full of electric wires… Is that her calling me? My missus on the crater…she speaks again of the need to shed the incarnadine…can I cleanse myself there…?" Danny opened the car door and fell on the gravel, missing by a second having his head cut off by the car door slamming in the wind.

Danny stumbled up. He looked like he had the famous medical *umbles: the mumbles, the stumbles, the grumbles, the tumbles.* He mumbled about the cleansing waters but there was only drying wind. Wind so loud Johnny and Vivienne at the crater edge couldn't hear anything. Val came out of the car and held Danny from behind. Danny saying, "I must go see her." Trying to wrestle out of Val's strong hold. "I see her at the crater. My love. You are forgiven!" Danny was granting merciful pardon to the ghost of his torturer spouse.

"Danny, just say you are sorry to Vivienne. Express remorse. Your wife is no more. The harmed one, Vivienne, is here. The reckoning is upon us."

Danny was struggling to break free. "No," he said. "Let us go see her.

She has a new mission. We fed them to the rivers. We took them to the beaches. We fed the wires into the Río de la Plata. We could not allow the Enemy Camera. Enemy Art knew too much. She took me under her wing, Mrs. Coma. The new mission, yes. In her coat may I find the fresh green river." Danny turned, put his arms around Val. He looked up at Val from eyes drained of the whole world. Age and acts were bearing in. "She put me in the crazy house. She dressed me like a bird and made me do things to those who threatened our nation."

Val pushed Danny's arms away. "Danny, it was never your nation or hers. You were foreign hirelings working for the Americans in other foreign locations."

"She took me to a nuthouse. I don't remember what she told them. She took me to the three corners, Paraguay. She came back, I don't know when. I said why don't we go hiking, like we used to. I had to push her off the cliff. Still the water ran red out of the tap. Still every household appliance seemed like a tool for the torturer. She was my mudlark. Yes! The new green mission…she is right there."

Danny ran from the car to the edge of the crater, spread his arms wide and jumped. Vivienne and Johnny rocked in the wind as Danny had rocked in his pain memory fever. Val hustled to the crater edge. Down below, Danny Coma was hanging from a narrow shelf of the fanglomerate, his fingers digging in. Johnny walked away. Val walked away. Vivienne took a picture. Then she knelt down, inching backwards to the crater rim. She stretched her legs over the side in Danny's direction. Danny called out, "Vivienne!"

"Yes, Danny," she said, "I'm coming." She landed her feet on his shoulders and pushed him hard. Danny Coma slid down Ubehebe Crater. "Good night, Ambassador." She looked up to the top of the rim. There was Val, reaching his arms down. He hoisted her up. She turned and took a pic of Danny falling to the Ubehebe Crater bottom, and another of him flat out on the orange core. "Let's go," she said.

"What a shame," Val said. "The sin of suicide."

They drove away from Ubehebe Crater in a low glowing pink through the corn-husk spectres flanking the road. The car curved past the dunes with their green shimmer at dusk. They rounded the final curve, hung a fast left through open parking and drove up to the walkway at room 214.

Four departed, three returned.

The walkway was full of feathers. Danny's bird suit was in a trash can, sticking out.

DANNY LAY AT the bottom of the crater. He had skinned arms and legs. His bare chest was ripped up. Nobody came to visit the crater. The sunset was a blink in time. No one reported Daniel Coma missing. It was December 28th. The day of reckoning. One of Danny's legs was broken. The temperature went down from a high of 62 to a low of 28 Fahrenheit. Danny rubbed his hands together to get the stains out, the bloody stains. His malfeasant dripping fog entered the textile pattern of the crater. He spoke to the ghost of Mrs. Coma. The next day, the man at the bottom of the Ubehebe Crater was dead of exposure. His wife was already dead, his two adult daughters were used to him disappearing for years with no contact. Nobody came to the crater the next day, sun to moonrise. On the third day, a turkey vulture with a six-foot wingspan took up the wind columns and rode the venting air with brown wings and a red head, making its characteristic grunt sounds, even SSSSSS hissings, having no vocal cords, but having a sense of smell from the sky for the carrion of a necrotizing mammal, and tore pieces of human flesh to carry and eat. Later, the low walking animals of fur made it down the slope and back up with rags of his skin and shards of his bones. On that day, December 30th, 2006, in Madrid, Spain, the ETA terrorists with whom Danny had negotiated a ceasefire in March bombed a parking garage at the Madrid airport.

26

DEATH VALLEY ODALISQUE

TWO DAYS WENT AWOL. Vivienne, Johnny and Val fell into an atomic shock lassitude in their motel room. From bed to door seemed like an insurmountable project. Val in his bed, Johnny and Vivienne in theirs, kept sleeping, kept prodding each other to get up and eat, kept falling back into the late December darkness. On December 30th, they woke up, three in a bed, got up, put on coats over their pyjamas and walked to the motel saloon for happy hour. They nibbled appetizers and drank cocktails. Johnny dubbed them sandtinis. They toasted Danny. Johnny spoke about how he was just a kid when Danny left home. How he kept a lookout for his older brother, an ear out, hoping to hear from him. But he never did. Once in a while much later, when Johnny was an adult, Danny would call from somewhere and speak to him on the phone in a stiff manner, like a condescending stranger talking to a clever four-year-old. And all that time, Johnny never knew the dark heart behind the twerp. Cain was no brother to Abel. Cain married a torture doctor; Cain's wife did inflict grievous harm on the wife of Abel.

IN A BRAIN fog, the Three Musketeers checked out of room 214 on December 31st. The Honda crawled up Towne Peak. Some wag had inserted a painted apostrophe *s*, making it Towne's Peak. Vivienne posed Johnny the writer beside the sign. They descended five thousand feet in ten minutes, their ears popping. They were travelling further west, in inland California.

They came to a massive salt playa. It looked like a lovely blue lake in the morning sunshine. They turned right, where there was no road sign. They were in the rain shadow of the Eastern Sierra now.

Ahead lay the legendary Panamint Dunes, rising behind Lake Hill. They were in the Panamint Valley. The wind had formed the sand, which had once been granite. The small rock mountains slid off other buttes through detachment faulting, the wind weathered the new limestone rocks. Once, this land was not protected, but now it was in Death Valley National Park, officially. The road they travelled was listed in the guidebooks as *Look for the sign to Big Four Mine Road*, but there was no sign for Big Four Mine Road or Small Four Mine Road or any sign at all; guidebooks were best used before or after a trip.

Along its sides grew creosote, bursage with its burrs, devil's guts – the parasite strangling the modest grey-green bushes with orange-threaded dodder nooses.

It was a zydeco road.

Men had played New Orleans Boozoo Chavis zydeco music on tin washboards smoother than this road. Vivienne in the suicide seat, with her camera trained out the window, bumped and jiggled; the under-carriage of the low vehicle jumped and hurtled, lurching. They drove down the desert road at the speed of fast rain, about one inch per hour. Jiggling like Jell-O down the desert gravel towards the Panamint Dunes until Vivienne called, "Stop!"

On their left in the desert scrub sat a car, rusted and abandoned, pock-marked, crushed, insides removed. Vivienne jumped out while their car was still moving.

The crushed and mutilated body, its fire stolen, had been sitting in the desert who knows how long, waiting for its close-up. Who knew how long the big sky had tended this old body? Who knew what the occasional flat-topped cloud saw looking down at the gouged and vivisected steel? Who knew what filmmaker chanced up the no-name corduroy and eyeballed the steel hobo in the deep Mojave?

How long had the rusting corpse been waiting in western isolation, dreaming the old CinemaScope and Technicolor dreams? And finally, here came the camerawoman who would make the car a star, and she got to work: *Ruined Coupe, Panamint Valley, Death Valley California, December 31, 2006.*

She came close, Vivienne Pink, the car whisperer.

There were bullet holes in the body, and she moved in towards them.

Below the three bullet wounds were four more in a rectangular pattern. The whole body had hundreds of wounds, it was shot full of them. A brown body with white patches and the greening patina of age. She moved forward on hard sand in her soft red-and-black leather sneakers, she did not want to disturb the dead.

The body's wheels had been amputated. There was nothing to carry it away, only rocks left. The steering wheel had patchy skin, brown peeling on the shiny white. Blue lakes pitted the rusty brown. The suicide door was frozen open, a paralyzed wing. She took small shutter kisses towards the capture.

Vivienne Pink, hunter, moved in to three feet, a sympathetic capture distance. She thrilled to know her prey in her scope, but the real thrill was the intimacy of the hunt. Transubstantiate the dead object, make it live in an art oasis. You could bring the dead to life by the empathy in the shutter.

Vivienne looked down at her arm as she hunted the car skin. Her arm was scalier, whiter, the patch above her wrist had risen, she rubbed it against her hip, white powder came off on her olive green pants. She saw her wrist bones inside the scaly skin. She shot her own degrading skin.

She turned and shot the car skin, a white patch on it. She shot the ground, patchy powder on beige green. She shot a cloud, one cloud in a cloudless blue field. She moved one step in towards the jagged blue patches of the car. She got dizzy, feeling like she had been lifted to that airplane window again, and she was looking down on herself: tiny white risen parts, tiny mountains beside snaking green water. It was the car.

She felt weak. The blue mountains were large surrounding her, shedding their dust. She looked at her arm. It too looked like the land as seen from a window seat. Fossil white patches, sinks, dips, thin hair trees, scabby epidermis. She felt a thickness under her right armpit that she did not remember being there before. She lifted her arm. A large bubbling was there, purple, grey, leaking black blood. She leaned forward and wiped her bloodied wrist on the car body, then shot a quick picture of this. She came around to the car front.

The corpse was filled with rocks. Who drove the body here, who shot the body full of bullet holes?

She got up and ran around the other side.

Inside a coyote lay in wait for her.

The coyote had been watching her from inside the car body, and she had not seen him. She had been ambushed by nature's own. Was it ever any other way? She might be thirty-four years in, in visiting Death Valley, but the wild coyote had desert ancestors older than the wandering tribes, in sand and indigo silks. Their manners and their morals went way back to when mountains walked without them, and sand dunes sang like Peggy Lee with no one to hear them.

Vivienne held her camera down at her side.

Without a camera, there was no picture. She had learned that, back in Vietnam. An idea for a photograph is an idea; a witness without a camera is a witness. She wanted to bring her witness to the world, in pictures. Hold that camera close, let it live and die with you. You and the coyote.

Vivienne Pink moved two feet closer to the coyote inside their shared corpse vehicle. She took a further half-step with her right foot, using it as a balancer, one leg forward, one leg back. The coyote had not moved one coyote furry hair. It had eyes like headlights as they stood inside the car that had none.

Vivienne had seen animals in Iraq used as decoys for Improvised Explosive Devices. The animals were murdered, slit open, the *matériel* put inside them and then they were sewn back up. Who was to say that this coyote standing so still was *not* a decoy, a perfectly sewn and stuffed taxidermic weapon? Who is to say that this was not somebody's idea of fun, or maybe they had stumbled onto a remote sensing area, where the coyote might be blown up at a distance. After all, China Lake was not far, other military grounds were not far, if you made it out to the main road and went in the other direction. Had the military been given permission to use national parks? This car corpse was an ark of sorts. Two by two, camera girl and coyote.

Vivienne locked eyes with the coyote. Come on, Mr. Fur, give me some angles. You are beautiful. Scrutinize my face, let's collaborate. No mellow here, baby, just you, just me, just Death Valley.

The coyote stared at her. Vivienne saw he had a ripped right eye, ripped like the steel peelings of the inside of the car. His fur eyelid had been cut. His gold-red skin was bare of fur, she saw now, in a few flank spots. He had one metal bolt in his side. He did not look wild in a fresh way, he looked wild in a wounded way. Damaged, the way the rabid can be. Her empathy was disciplined. There were great pictures here. She was mute as the desire to use only her eyes impulsed her. The coyote had the characteristic bent back legs. The front legs stiff, straight. He had that marvellous thick tail, though it was cut halfway up, indented, as if for fun someone had semi-scalped it.

Her camera was at her side, still. She was all eyes.

She was on the coyote's turf. Dig that long nose, so steady, dig how the nose is the prime visual feature. Dig those ears, their sharp points. Big ears, all the better to hear your soft night prints with. All the better to make a mess of your laughing, those ears, the original desert mountain surveillance. Furry echo chambers, fur canyons, those pointed ears of the coyote. There was no companionship here. This was not friendship. This wild was the ring, this desert was the agon, this coyote was her enemy, a valuable enemy, a valued one, maybe this was her golden combatant. This coyote could roam with the wild dogs of slum alleys, and be regal, and rule the gang. He could enter the ring, in charge, and she was the underdog, and she could take away his image but leave his soul, and he could be intact and she could win and he could win, as long as he did not eat her.

He could win, even if he ate her.

Vivienne lifted her camera, now in a quick clean move. She took a shot of the coyote. The coyote did not attack her.

He was the perfect posing model, showing his angles, showing parts of himself at the same time, articulating his limbs. He was the Fur Pharaoh. He received her in the rubble of his ruined kingdom. In his vast mesquite country he received her, amidst the wintering berries. He was trim, battle-hardened, fearless, curious. She was a stray mutt with her own battle scabs. He was staking his claim, as a creature who ruled this desert dominion moment; he ruled even the ruins. Here was evolution indisputable, the soft fur scape and the hard red eye. *Come to Daddy, let Daddy tear out your eyes.*

His nose smelled her camera lens. His eyes took in the smell of her scarred parts.

She took two more shots, three was a good number. No even numbers, even numbers were bad luck, stay with the odds, stay with the good luck wild coyote. The coyote moved. He moved towards her. She did not budge. He stopped. She dared raise her camera, leaving her stomach exposed, her crotch, her legs, her precious photographer's feet. He was full face and torso in her frame. His eyes had history. That was his story. He invited her back into her genes. He invited her into the feral chain. Yes.

She was jealous of his four legs. Oh, to have two extra legs to rush up the dunes and see the world from on high, and prey at night into tents, to come down from the avalanche cities into the urbanscapes and terrorize exurbia with your professional silence.

Come on, baby. Do something.

The coyote moved to the side of the car carcass, towards one of the emptied windows. But just a foot. Vivienne could now see a black box on his left side, facing her as he came alongside of her, tied to his flank, like a Hebrew phylactery box that contained the Torah you davened with every morning. What was it? Was it a bomb? Her gut said bomb.

Get out of the car, coyote. Nice and easy. Her heartbeat lowered; it did that in emergencies. Like an athlete.

She took a pic of his side, with the box on it, his Torah box on his damaged desert fur, a desert ancient as she had suspected and known.

Carrying the Torah and the sand ark, a desert nomad. Get that pic. Get it as easy as if it were your last one.

The coyote climbed up through the window. Vivienne shot his ass with the mysterious black box sticking out of his fur profile. She shot him going through the window. Then he – marvellous – turned and looked back at her. He jumped out of the car towards the salt playa. Vivienne followed the coyote with her telephoto. The coyote reached the playa. Its fur shone regal orange in the high crystal sunshine on the salt, simply sensational, a fur ghost in the promised land of playa. The coyote blew up. The coyote exploded. Someone, somewhere, had set off an explosive device that was either in the black box or in the metal bolt Vivienne had seen on him. Vivienne shot the explosion out of instinct and because she was in the middle of shooting.

She shot the explosion as the shock wave lifted her up, rattled her brain, shook her, filled her mouth with sand, threw her against the car, banged her against the car, beat her up, let her down.

Johnny and Val flew through the air and fell down, hitting gravel and animal bones that had been lifted from hidden areas and flown, forensic material weaponized by the shock wave.

The car had a new small dent in it, from Vivienne's head being pounded on its side, and Vivienne had small mulches of rust and green patina from the car on her. Who knows which photograph of us will be the last one ever taken?

Val and Johnny stayed back. Vivienne ran to the playa and found the coyote in pieces. Cars, humans, mannequins, lab pigs, plane wings, coyotes, it is one world, one gigantic scientific experiment. Vivienne located the coyote's heart under a length of golden fur. The heart was still warm, still beating. She held it like a baby to her own heart.

Val and Johnny were standing about fifty feet away.

DEEP IN THE heart of nowhere, where the land was a beautiful rootless rogue, Val Gold watched Vivienne Pink. She was all passion, plus the discipline to unfold it in art labour. He adored her. Why wasn't she his?

The years had slipped away. Val left Brooklyn during the Vietnam War. He moved to Toronto, saying he was a draft dodger as his cover story. But Johnny and Vivienne were his prey; the US government wanted to know more about these Canadians, and they had hired Val to do it. Then, as the years went by, as Val provided intel on the writer Johnny Coma and his wife, the photographer Vivienne Pink, to Washington, he began to realize that he was in love with Vivienne and that Johnny had become his best friend. Val's secret was his very presence in their home in Annexia. He believed – as did many a man whose work becomes his life, whose country becomes his wife – that someday it would all sort itself out. Surely he was not going to live until he died without someone of his own to love him? *This drought inside me.*

Who knew that when Val Gold, the other man, finally made his move to get Vivienne, he would do it by trying to kill her husband? Kill the opposition, rather than adore the homeland.

In one move, Val got a flick knife out of his pants, a custom Italian stiletto switchblade that his pal Dale had given him on the night train from Baghdad to Mosul. Val and Dale had been travelling north to Erbil, in Kurd country. An intruder had come into their compartment when they had dozed off. Val had grabbed Dale's stiletto out of Dale's jacket and stabbed the intruder. Val dumped the body in the corridor. This was Iraq, during the Iran-Iraq War.

After the Mosul train stabbing, Dale had given Val his stiletto. Dale called it a flick knife, as a Brit might from the Teddy Boys era. Or as a man might, if he wanted you to think that.

Val pressed the little button and the seven-inch blade flipped out.

Val loved the intimacy of the knife. No drone would ever replace the feeling of being close enough to slow dance with your adversary and slip that sharpened blade right into his rib cage, pulling with just the right amount of pressure to crack that rib, and if you were lucky in the same insertion get through to a lung. If your karma sat proper, you could move in with the blade retracted and *flick* it out right through bone and skin.

Vivienne did not like the way Val was moving towards Johnny.

Vivienne stayed with her telephoto lens. She watched Val fold the blade back into the holder. She breathed with his movements, snapping a pic as Val flicked the blade out again. *Whoosh.*

It was one in the afternoon. The shadows were long. Val put his arm around Johnny's shoulder. Vivienne kept taking pictures.

Val was thinking: If I make a small war, I can be at peace again, with the beloved of my murdered best buddy. *This drought will end.* Val flicked the switchblade clinically into Johnny's right side, under his breastbone. Vivienne heard a crack. Johnny was bleeding. He tried to wrest the switchblade from Val's hand. Val pushed against Johnny, using Johnny's rib cage as a fulcrum to push the blade in further to Jojo's liver. Johnny twisted Val's hand and pulled the blade out of his own body, then stabbed the bloody knife into Val's right palm. "You fucker," Val said.

"Me fucker?" Johnny said. "You're trying to kill me and I'm the fucker?"

"I deserve her. You've had her long enough. It's my turn now." Val came at Johnny with his hands, one bloody and bleeding.

"You'd better see to that hand," Johnny said.

"No, you'd better see to it," he said, punching Johnny square in the jaw on the left side. They both heard Johnny's jaw bone crack.

"You've got no claim to her," Johnny said, crouching, his tush back, his legs well planted. "You think we don't know who you are? Vivienne takes pics of you when you're sleeping, you two-bit government gumshoe. Even if I die, Vivienne would laugh at you; you're her art pet. 'Oh, Vivi, let me tell you about Van Gogh.' Kill me. Go ahead. Marry the Pentagon."

"You don't own her. She's free to choose," Val said, swiping at his knife, which was firmly in Johnny's right hand.

"She chose twenty-four years ago. You're RSVP'ing a little late, Valerie."

Vivienne was behind them with her camera, with coyote guts and coyote amber fur on her arms, shooting the scene. "Don't take my picture," Val said. "Did you take photos of me when I was sleeping?"

"Oh, grow up, Val," Vivienne said. "Did you think my marriage meant nothing?"

"You're a parasite," Val said, turning his head to look at her. That mistake gave Johnny the advantage. Johnny lunged at Val, slit Val's thick belt, jumped down, slit his two shoes open, jumped back up and laid a full knife cut across Val's forehead.

"There," Johnny said. "A souvenir of your love for Vivienne. Right, Vivienne?"

"The two of you are so damn stupid," she said. "You make me miss those sick dictators. At least I knew where I stood with them."

Val wiped the blood off his forehead. He was looking at Vivienne who was moving closer with her camera.

Vivienne's face was red, peeling. Her eyes kept blinking. She had lesions on her neck. She had coyote fur in her scalp. Her wrist had rust from the car on it and still warm bits from the coyote's lungs, bowels.

A freight train–like sound pumped their ears full of high-rolling sound waves. A plane buzzed fast and low over them, leaving its tail showing as it raced down between mountains. One more haircut free from the US military.

Vivienne picked up a long piece of the coyote's corpse, would you call it a carcass already? When the wild become tame through the forced agency of humans, they will become tame enough for humans to tie explosive devices on, domesticating wild animals for the purpose of human cruelty.

It starts with the human, and you call the human not a human, for your dire purposes. You call the human an animal and he becomes an animal to you. You enact your dire darkness upon the animal, and you call the animal not an animal with breath and heart, you call the animal a thing. You enact your dire self upon a thing, a car, and you call it what it is, a car, and you mutilate and torture the car and you rip off the car door. The car door is as an animal, as is a human. Then you mutilate and torture the human, you burn the human alive, and beside the human you burn the car alive, and it is all the same thing. The human is as a car door, his arm is as a car door, the car door is as the human, in the dark fires of rage. Then you go to the human bridges over the human rivers, and you hang the car door by its noose, for the people to see. Then you hang the decapitated torso of the human over the river, for the people to see.

And this happened in Fallujah, Iraq, in March of 2004. And Vivienne Pink was there. I am not human to them, I am a car door. I am rust on fire, from the river.

She carried the side of coyote down the scrub sand to the car, also a corpse, but of steel. She hunched her body through the doorway on the driver's side. She laid the coyote behind the metal springs coming out of the bottom of the car. Moments ago, he had been defiant and gorgeous; the photos she had taken of the coyote's magisterial defiance were now ancient archival material. The coyote was a fur city that was no more. She stroked it. How could it still be warm?

How to do a coyote odalisque? Vivienne looked down at herself. The pink leather jacket, the green khaki pants, the red-and-black shoes of Spanish leather, ah – the python vest.

What a trip, that was the idea. Clothe the coyote, even part of the coyote, in Vivienne's own snakeskin. Fur against reptile. Mammal and squamata. She took off her pink leather, draping it on the skeletal steering wheel. She took off her vest; she laid it on the coyote. She bent down and lifted the elongated side of the coyote, the side that had turned and caught the light. The coyote might have known it was going to die, but if it did not, if it did not have that human knowledge, it knew in its animal heart it had been brutalized by men.

She wrapped the reptile skin around the mammalian warmth. There was blood on her vest. She got low, immersing herself in available light. Down at the level of dogs. Shooting like a bloodied stray dog, feral with a camera. A stray dog ready to shoot her brethren, when they got thrown through the air and landed, broken.

The coyote was full of dust, mesquite winter berries lifted off far trees, along with dry winter sage, resin and burn. BOOM! The deafness.

Her ears could not hear, so the photographic eyes in her head were sharper. Ever so seldom the wild brutality, shaped in art, can begin to heal the pain. Ever so rarely the angels are present just this side of the frame. Down in the car bowels, the skin of the coyote thrummed. The python diamond skin shone on top of it. Vivienne lay down on the rusted coils. She pulled the coyote skin over her stomach, with the reptile skin covering it in part. She held the camera up to shoot a self-portrait, a female-identified head, with hair resembling the lower hairy shredded ripped parts of palm trees; the face covered in boils, black carbuncles, the right side swelling up with black bruising; a fur and snake body, white human breasts protruding, the nipples high and red, with blood and gold glowing coyote fur drifting down on them. Her eyes were indigo in white turning yellow. Ever so seldom, the choices conspire to make chance marry intention.

Death Valley Odalisque, December 31, 2006.

You could grow carrots in her hair, and offer radioactive sides for the dinner party. Her skull was a holiday decoration for the new nuclear age.

THEY DROVE DOWN the corduroy road in bumpy silence. Vivienne had a coyote heart in her hand.

They drove up the pavement road to a verandahed eatery on a rise in the pines.

27

ARROGANT BASTARD

ANDY SAT WITH his back to the road, high up on the restaurant verandah of the Panamint Springs Resort, a rustic eatery with a fading old motel out back, set at elevation between the sand dunes and the badlands. He was the only customer. He amused himself reading the list of beer on the menu: Big Sky Moose Drool, Descartes Inversion, New Belgium Fat Tire, Pliny the Elder, Monk's Blood, Consecration, Salvation, Defenestration, Sanctification. The Abyss. He ordered an Arrogant Bastard.

He nursed his Arrogant Bastard, waiting for his ribs and smashed potatoes.

He stretched out on the wooden bench. The dust from the salt playa was blowing across the grey road, covering a white sedan coming up, nose to the sky.

THE WHITE CAR made a sharp left in front of the verandah. Johnny parked the vehicle. Val, Johnny and Vivienne came up the wide wooden stairs. "Let's go around the side where we can have some privacy," Vivienne said.

"Anything the lady says," Val said. He rubbed his forehead where Johnny had slashed him with the knife, a bit of blood came off. He was clomping in his stabbed shoes.

"Right you are. Perfect. You lead, we follow, *mi reina*," Johnny said. He was holding onto his side, where the stab wound Val had made was leaking a bit of fluid.

Vivienne's hair looked like singed bamboo. She was moving with wobbly exaggerated purpose along the verandah, like a dipso in the wee hours crossing Lonely Avenue. The three of them plopped down in a tree-shaded corner, on a long bench.

Vivienne scanned the space. To her left down the bench fifteen feet away sat Andy, a cigarette dangling from his lips. Wearing the gold suede jacket.

He looked over at Vivienne with blank eyes.

She was disarmed. Her camera hand started trembling.

A waiter appeared. Cowboy boots black, dark jeans, medium dark hair, black T-shirt with red lettering: SWISS CHEESE SANDWICH. "Can I get you folks something?"

"Mercurochrome," Johnny said. "Anything Mexican in a *cerveza*, inform me about the burgers, no names please, and if you have some heavy-duty tape for wounds that would be swell."

"Any specials?" Val asked. He held up his blood-smeared palm, drying and leaking. He wiped it on his grey pants.

"We've got our house ribs on today," the waiter said. "Sweetbreads on Monday."

"When's Monday?" Vivienne asked.

"Tomorrow," the waiter said. "Hang on. I'll go hunt down some menus."

THE WAITER WAS back, without menus. "Anything to drink?"

"Rubbing alcohol on the rocks," Johnny said. "How's that Mercurochrome coming? Okay, make it a blue burger, double side of onions. Give it a whirl."

"And for the lady?"

"I want a Red Truck," she said. "You guys want to share a Red Truck with me?"

"Bring the lady her Red Truck," Val said. "Everything depends on it."

"Wasn't that a red wheelbarrow, sir?" the waiter asked.

"Another independent scholar heard from," Val said. "One Dos Equis. Two. Four Equis."

THEY SOUNDED HIGH to Andy. But was it her? By what means had she appeared to haunt him? Was it truly Vivienne, who had unhinged him when she induced his shoulder blades to confess their grief story, as she photographed him? The pink jacket, the red bits in the dusty hair. It was her. Buzzing around with other men.

"Just the Red Truck, darling," she said. "The bottle works." This voice had smoke, chocolate, tannin and notes of photographic fixer in it. Had she come from inside him to be incarnate, a hex radiating her damn grace vortex?

THE WAITER WAS back, again without menus. He sat down beside Johnny, as if in a consultation. "Sir, do you mind if I ask you, you look injured, is that a stab wound I'm seeing? Do you know if the wound was penetrating or blunt?"

"He stabbed me," Johnny said, pointing to Val.

"Man, you shouldn't be doing that," the waiter said to Val.

"Stay out of it," Val said. "I want to marry his wife."

"You shouldn't do that either." And to Vivienne: "Is he having any trouble breathing? Is his breathing compromised?"

"Your breathing will be in trouble," Johnny said, "if you don't bring me a cerveza. Any brew works."

"You're the boss, sir. Was that a mozzarella omelette with a house salad? Ranch or Italian? Sir, do you know if you've had a tetanus shot in the last five years?"

"Lord in his mercy. No omelette, no mozzarella, no *ensalada*, no house, no ranch. I asked for a blue burger. Extra onions if you have them. Any Swiss in the house?"

"No, sir, sorry. No Swiss," said the man wearing a T-shirt that read Swiss Cheese Sandwich. "Do you mind if I take your pulse?"

Johnny put two fingers on his wrist, looked at his watch. "My pulse is fine, my breathing is slightly shallow. You do feed beer to shallow breathers, don't you?"

"Yes, sir. But you do know your liver is exposed."

"Good. Perfect. Go fry it."

"Sir."

"An extra side of slaw and Percocet will do fine."

"Coming right up, sir," the waiter said.

In the bright high chill, the dry carnal geology inched along. Vivienne's brain was bouncing back and forth in soft sea jelly against the hard carapace of her skull.

ANDY CHUGGED Arrogant Bastard number three. He watched Vivienne. Johnny put his arm around Vivienne's neck, kissing her neck, whispering in her ear, kissing her neck at the back. Andy turned away, watching her more intently in his mind that way. He put his head down on the table, seeing the sharp images of him and her; her photographing him in that hotel room in Vegas; the two of them on the bed, confidential, touching each other slowly; how she spoke to him of walking down the steps of Tudor City across to the UN, and there was a young Quaker burning himself alive for peace. How she knew the confusion of his intentions in enlisting. How there was something about her, and if he named it she would for sure disappear. A very white man picks you up in a night alley and takes you in early dark to the heart of marginal America, and the deeper you go to the outskirts, the closer you come to your own uncouth centre. Andy could see her, like predatory gratitude, on that bed, letting him be the prey who stroked the hunter, murmuring tender lullabies. He lifted his head from the table: she was there. She needed to be with him. He needed to shelter in with her aromas.

THE WAITER TOOK a fourth tour to their table.

"Sir, here's your burger, your duct tape, double onions, no Swiss, Percocet on the side – you said slaw, didn't you? – the two Coronas," putting it all down on the table. "What else have we got here? Here's that gauze you wanted, a little gauze and goat, we threw in some sweet potato fries. Do you mind if I palp you?"

"Go ahead," Johnny said. "My best friend tried to kill me down on the playa. Palp away."

"Let me have her," Val said.

"Judas. Disloyal putz. Spy." Johnny was doubled over.

The waiter came around beside him. "No need for name-calling now."

"But he is a spy," Johnny said. "He entered our house and our garden under the guise of friendship."

"Forgive and forget," the waiter said, touching Johnny's wound area. "You have to divide the abdomen into four quadrants to do a proper palp, sir. Okay, are you feeling pain?"

"I've been feeling pain since Angola, 1986, son. Your Cold War really put a hurt on me. I hitched a ride on one of Reagan's arms shipments, in a pretty pale blue plane. I got shot up in that Cold War. Yup. If they nailed Angola, that would take care of Cuba and the Soviets, wouldn't it? Hey, I got a book out of it. Can you get me a new liver?"

"I'm sorry, sir. We have bison next week."

"Ow. Oh. Whoa. Not there."

The waiter was pressing into quadrant number three. "Numero tres, right there, sir. I think I see some coffee grounds coming out of your wound, not a good sign. Have you been vomiting yet?"

"Son, I haven't even had a bite."

"Waiter? Could you kindly get me some portobello and goat?" Vivienne asked.

"I have some leeches in the kitchen, ma'am. He has a serious stab wound. His skin is clammy." He was holding Johnny's hand. "Would you like me to put on 'Madame George' while I bleed you?"

Johnny took the waiter's hand away. "Just get my wife some food, will you?"

"Coming right up, sir. Ma'am, that was a small Caesar and was it cranberry juice for the lady? And no worries on the spy front. I had a friend who turned out to be DEA. Things pass."

"Thank you for your psychiatry," she said. "Just the mitosis and the curds, doctor."

Blood had dried at the wound. The waiter wet the napkin, wiping the Mercurochrome over it. Johnny winced and howled, "Oh living Jesus." Val took the napkin from the waiter. Johnny had his Moleskine out, as he was being treated by Val he was sketching the very thing that was happening, drawing in real-time pen lines: a goofy bellied guy with an open wound and a big-haired guy with a big cloth and a big wacky grin and a bottle with an *M* on it, and the bellied guy going, Yipes! Yips! Eek! Awk! Gawk! Yiperama That Hoits!

When in distress, Johnny went to the place of routine, where he made things. Back to his atavistic roots, where the ancestors took the burnt pieces and drew on the walls of caves.

ANDY GOT UP, walked the length of the verandah, turned and walked right back to Vivienne. She took her shades off and looked with hard twin beams at him. What did Andy do, follow her? He walked back down the verandah and around a corner. His back was like old times in fervour to her. She did not have time for memories. Memories kill you. Memories hang you up. Literally. Her hands kept shaking.

The pain of war had not broken Vivienne Pink. The broken places had not made her stronger either. What did not break her, made her persevere. She was not stronger, she was more determined. The world breaks you and makes you stronger in the broken places. People who misquoted that line from Hemingway tended to be people who never had a bad break in a bone, or ever saw war. It was much more *fuck you* than any sentimental *makes you stronger.* Quoting it gave them the glow of the chicken-hearted. It was your animal part that powered your art, not some literary quotation. Then, of course, there was good old Friedrich Nietzsche and his *That which does not kill us makes us stronger.* Men: so squishy, so sentimental. No, baby, it was much more, in the field, You fuckers, you will not win, I will beat you. I will walk into the sun, I will walk into the minefield, I will face down the acid-gut vultures. It did not make you stronger, it made you *live.* You learned to love Death Valley. You began to love to walk through Death Valley, the valley the geologists called a graben, walking through your own quilted blood and the split rocky lobes of your head. What does not kill you makes you go to Death

Valley. The world tries to break you, but you make a deal with the world. If you don't kill me, I will tell more stories in my work.

Work lust moved into her bone marrow. Here is where art is made, in the studio of your body. She said to Johnny and Val, "Back in a minute. Washroom."

She walked through the atmosphere that Andy had walked through, the belligerent, the war resister. As she turned the corner, she saw he was not there. Down a soft gravel area sat a short row of motel rooms. Rustic, peeling, no one around. She was, in fact, at the washroom, a wooden addition at the side of the building. The mirror inside was cracked, rusting at the edges, with rainbow stains. Vivienne took a pic of herself in the mirror: pink leather, long camera snout, cheeks as blotched as a bad mirror face.

She peed, and opened the door. Andy stood outside. "What are you doing here?"

She stepped close to him. "I had a funeral to attend."

"I wasn't aware there were any funeral homes in the vicinity."

"It's Death Valley."

Andy sat down on the ground. She joined him. She offered a cigarette from the Pink cigarette pack she had carried from Nevada. They inhaled old Okinawa tobacco together. "Are you going back to Canada?" Andy said.

"It's my home. I don't know. It's base camp, anyway."

"Come with me to Baghdad."

"Are you crazy? And what? Sit somewhere and wait for you?"

"Embed yourself." He chuckled. "In my bed." He put his mouth at the end of her lit cigarette and inhaled the smoke.

Vivienne shook her head, saying, "Does being AWOL give you the giggles?"

"I don't know for certain I am actually AWOL, ma'am."

"Oh, with the *ma'am* again."

Andy was afraid to say her name. He had not said her name out loud since he left her. He was scared to say it, even to her. The Vivienne in his mind had kept him going. He took her hands, kissed them. "Vivienne. Then let me come with you."

It was too much too soon and she liked it. She had liked it in Nevada and she liked it in California. The drought made their kisses spark with tiny blue.

Andy could be the road taken. As soon as you take that road, the other roads drift back in the rear view.

You stand too long at the crossroads, ghosts eat you.

"Stand over there," she said, pointing to the jerry-rigged loo door. Andy, with the small leavings of his smoke, stood against the door in profile. "Talk to the cigarette like you used to," she said.

Instead, he put something starlit into his cheekbones, held his smoke down beside his left leg and looked right at the camera lens. He whispered, "Vivienne."

Vivienne saw the misfit heart coming at her. There was something of the damaged man unafraid to humble his strength.

Andy came over to her. "What happened to your head? Your hair. It's white."

"I think we were in an A-bomb. Bu it might have been two miles away, so…but I think I got a concussion… I don't know. Then down at the playa an IED went off inside a coyote." She rubbed her fingers on her pink leather shoulder, where the coyote blood had dried.

"Do me a favour," he said. "Kindly take off your jacket, Vivienne."

She slipped her jacket sleeves down. Andy removed the jacket, draping it around his shoulders. Vivienne's arms were stippled with white scales, black-blue buboes rising, blisters near her shoulders, other buboes under her arms, the blisters nearer her wrist, her left hand had a lake of red, the white-tan skin had come off entirely. An inch of her right wrist bone was sticking out. Andy kissed it.

"You have to see a doctor," Andy said, stroking her face.

"How did you get here?" she asked.

"I met a man in an alley who brought me here, I think. He left me on the other side of the mountain. You know, I actually do not know how I ended up here."

Vivienne reached into a pocket of the pink leather jacket, and pulled out Andy's white T-shirt. She took off her python vest and put the T-shirt on. "You kept this," he said.

She kissed his cheek. "Your T-shirt saw a man jump into a crater, and a coyote rigged with a bomb explode. Your T-shirt has volcanic ash and coyote gut bits on it."

"My T-shirt smells like you," he said. He was shy to show her the small piece of her green jersey he had cherished. If he brought it out, would all his feelings for it go away?

Andy walked towards the small motel. Vivienne snapped his back, walking away, his gold jacket with her pink jacket draped on top. He sat down in a white vintage-metal round-back chair at room 15. The 1 above the 5, the numerals metal. She moved towards him, from fifty feet to twenty feet to eight feet to four feet, then she kneeled down and shot his body from below.

Vivienne's arms looked like a perverted extension of the python skin vest she was wearing. Her bare arms were another family of reptile skin, they were burns like Nagasaki. The photographer had changed more than her subject had. What happens when the photographer is a victim of the war? Who takes the picture-taker's picture?

They went into room 15.

"I'm burning up," Vivienne said. She took off the vest. She was topless with her back to him. She turned. Andy had a hard eye, she snapped that face on him. He did not move. She snapped that too. She turned away. He came over to her, he put his palm on her back. He reached out and took her camera, she did not resist. He walked backwards to the door; he snapped multiple shots of her back.

"Do you know what's going on?" he asked.

"If you're not AWOL," she said, "you might be a deserter; we'll take a couple pics, and then get you back. Johnny might be able to help. He's counselled deserters."

"You're tattooed," he said. "Vivienne." He snapped the two of them in the mirror. "Look at yourself. Look at your back."

"I can't see it," she said. She craned her neck and got a partial view. "Holy cow. What? There I see something. What is that? That's not me, can we wipe it off? Fuck me, you're right. Oh my God. How did that happen?"

"Take off your watch," he said.

She did. The analog face of 11:02 was burned into her left wrist. What had happened? Like a little piece of pie branded at her wrist bone inside a circle with dashes on it. This must have been the exact hour they stood at Sheep Springs in the Divine Strake's light, which burned the python pattern into her flesh. She had seen her bones inside her body, it is true that a thermonuclear explosion lights up your bones like a full-body x-ray. Then she remembered. She had taken a couple pics of her arm, lit up like an internal x-ray light. Thank goodness. She had taken an actual photograph not of the bomb in the sky (although that too), not the aftermath (although that too), but a human being at the exact moment the bomb blew. A human who became an x-ray light, a human who became python tattooed, in the moment the branding sizzled her flesh. God saw how the shanda was another magnet to us humans. The shame drew us to want it, and want it in epic proportions.

"Why are you here with me?" Andy asked.

"I want some insurance pictures," she said. "I have a deadline for a book. I've got no money coming in. I do not need you. I want to take your picture is all."

This all was true, yet it was not the reason. The reason was the need. It could be a sudden fire in her eyes, it could be the hairline crack in her composure. The fissure, the rimose in her art heart. Back around the corner, at a table in this remote eatery, her husband and her best friend were sitting. She had up and walked away, saying nothing, to sit and kiss, to kiss and reminisce and camera-schmooze with a man she had known in a hotel room back in the blur earlier in the holidays. And that seemed not crazy.

The thing about Crazytown is this: you never feel crazy in Crazytown. In Crazytown you have never felt more sane in your life. You feel clever, alert, super-sane. That's Crazytown's trick. Outside of Crazytown, they are all nuts. "Forget the A-bomb and let me photograph you," Vivienne said.

"Look," Andy said. "Last time we were flying over to Iraq, we're in the plane, somebody left some old camera magazine from wherever. I'm flipping through it, and I come across this picture of a woman from Japan who had the pattern of the kimono she was wearing burned into her skin from the bomb at Hiroshima. You look like her." Vivienne's lower back was tattooed with intricate snakeskin diamonds.

"You can't see what I see," Andy said. "*Guapa*, I hate to see you this way." Using a Spanish endearment: gorgeous, pretty thing, guapa. "Come. Lie down with me. Let me stroke your hair." He took her in his arms. Her hair was full of metal bits. Andy tossed the hair like worn feathers from a wounded avian, a small crushed thing down in the cobbles who sipped from a rain puddle, who sipped from the nuclear rain. He stroked the woman he had known as a redhead with a thick short mane, an older woman with olive-tinted skin in lovely condition, with choice lips who knew how to use them, with a smooth back dotted with a decent number of beauty marks and moles. Now, a few days later, this woman looked ravaged, as if she had had months of radiation and chemo; as if she had suffered months of starvation, paltry feeding, no bathing, dirt work; as if she had walked the refugee trail of world deserts. Heavier blood had pooled under her blue eyes, shock wave bruisings, and the hair of the radioactive dove girl came off, as Andy, soldier-nurse, stroked her. The green filigreed light outside the motel room waved in the high elevation breezes. She had the body of a nuclear winter. It is alive with us, in our life. It is alive, on the newborn fledgling winged planet. Andy took her to the bed.

He stroked her back, pausing at the raised python pattern tattooed into her spine's skin. She was part bird, part reptile, part woman. Vivienne Pink, photographiste.

ON THE VERANDAH Val was saying again to Johnny, "Let me have her."

Johnny said, "Val, don't try me. You stick a knife in me and demand my wife? Is this what you spooks call protocol?"

"I put in my dues."

"Dues don't get you the dame."

"Cute. You're buried half the time in your writing. I take care of her."

"Val. You're the other man. That's your job. If you had wanted the job of husband, when there was a clear opening, you should have taken it. You let your chance go by a lifetime ago. Find yourself a nice Jewish girl and move back to your homeland."

"For your information, we're in my, as you call it, homeland."

"Oh yeah. I forgot," Johnny said. Fully aware of it.

"I am the boss of your brother."

"Late brother."

"I am the equivalent of a chief of mission."

"So you're the chief CIA spy for Toronto. It's not a points situation, Val. You don't build up years and then cash them in for another man's life. Listen to yourself. 'Equivalent.' Are you the equivalent of a husband? Are you the equivalent of my buddy?"

"Johnny, I am your friend."

"At a distance. With qualifications. I'll give you a pity B-plus at faking friendship."

"I can't believe you're saying this."

"Sure you can. That is exactly what a fake friend would say. I bet your bosses in Washington told you to write a fake memoir in which you trash V and me. You're a tenant. You keep my wife company when I'm away. Tell me this, Val, has Vivi ever photographed you?"

"Of course."

"No. Really photographed you. Got you alone, in a place. Did she ever come into your room with her camera and close the door? Don't you ever wonder why Vivienne spends so much time with you, but she has never made you a subject? You don't appear in any of her books."

Val had never thought about this. Johnny and Vivi had befriended him. Had they been on to him from the beginning? Had their friendship been fake? Val felt ambushed. They might have been watching *him.*

VIVIENNE AND ANDY were on the bed of room 15. The door was open. She was wearing his white T-shirt. He had on her python vest. He had her wounded head next to his neck, in a close nest. In Andy's keeping,

Vivienne was a wreck, feeling lightness in her limbs.

Where there is no water, Earth's creatures will feel the former riverine life, how we miss our gills, our scales fluorescent magnificent, how things own us when we own things, how winter douses the light to let us rest in our emotions.

In a small room, you could pretend it was dusk with each other.

VAL WAS GRILLING Johnny about Vivienne and Andy.

"So how does this guy turn up out of nowhere?"

"Beats me," Johnny said.

"Hang on," Val said, getting up and walking down the verandah and around the corner. In the distance was the open door of room 15. Entwined legs were moving on a bed. Why him, and not me, Val thought. She's known him two minutes and she goes with him. Just when I decide to make a move on Johnny, this guy reappears out of nowhere to stand in my way.

Val walked towards the motel room. Vivienne got off the bed. She motioned to Andy. He got up. Val watched Vivienne stroke Andy's hair, and them kissing. Vivienne picked up her camera; she walked to the open door. She waved to Val. Naked, she took his picture, him reaching his arms out to her. She closed the red door.

Val was sweating in the cold. His spy electrolytes were spiking and dipping in his body. He stepped into the rustic washroom. He pulled his special orange phone out of his pants pocket, pressing a green button on it. "I'm married," said a voice from the phone. Vivienne's voice. Val pressed a blue button to rewind the tape. "I could love you," said a voice, then Vivienne's voice, "I'm married." *I could love you.* The soldier, Andy, talking to her in the hotel room in Vegas. Good job I put the bug on that bed, Val thought. She needs protection. How the hell does she know who this Andy is? Val pressed a purple button, fast-forwarding the tape. He leaned against the wooden door, with his eyes closed. "Let me nurse you… Let me take care of you…hush now, hush now…down, down, ease your wings down…" Val, hearing Andy's voice, could picture Vivienne back in that hotel room. Val put himself instead of Andy with her on that gone and done bed, saying those things to her. In the bivouac of the tiny facility of the small motel, the world had gone trespass on him. The agencies of love had passed him by. He replayed the part where Andy was cooing to Vivi, and Val whispered along with the voice on his phone, "Hush now, hush now, let me take care of you..."

He wiped his wet face with rough paper towels. His long lined face with the knife slash on his forehead looked like hell in that dying mirror. He came out into the cool wind. The red door that held her was still closed tight. Val walked back to the table and said to Johnny, "Do you think she knows?"

"Chances are he'll keep his mouth shut," Johnny said.

"Why should he? He's got the cash. He's got no loyalty to you."

"He has no reason to be a rat."

"He's overplaying his hand," Val said. "I don't like it."

Johnny laughed. "It's not up to you. You still don't get it. It's none of our business."

The waiter appeared. "Ribs and smashed potatoes for the tall guy," he said.

"He's naked in room 15 with my buddy here's wife," Val said.

"No worries," the waiter said, setting the food down at Andy's empty table.

"You're a laugh," Val said to Johnny. "You set up a guy in a coffee shop, so our Vivienne would have someone to snap. You basically *hand-pick* who your wife will pick...and you say it's none of your business? Man, when she finds out."

"She's not going to find out, I told you. This Andy fellow is solid. He has the cabbage. Chances are he won't talk." Johnny turned the notebook page to a fresh one and drew a toothpick with a squiggle thing on it, then wrote *#21* beside it.

Val glanced down at the line and squiggle, raised an eyebrow, "What's that?"

"That, my friend," Johnny said, tapping his silver space pen on the page, "is *número veintiuno.* To you, number twenty-one. To the fly on the wall, maybe an hors d'oeuvre or a toothpick. But that, my friend, is a marriage."

Val looked at Johnny with a mixture of contempt and total enjoyment of the absurdity. Val's shoes were dog flapped, slit, cut, Johnny's left side was blood-dried, his face hanging off-kilter.

Johnny pointed to his sketch. "To the innocent, that is a tapa, a toothpick with calamari. If I told you it was grilled, would you believe me? If I told you Vivienne and I like it, would it make a difference? If I told you I could leave this page anywhere, anywhere she might find it, and when she saw this line and this squiggle and the #21, she would know immediately, instantly what it meant." He tapped the page. "That, my Valerina, is love. That, my friend, is marriage. That is the ultimate spycraft. The secret signs between marriage partners. Do you know what Vivienne would say when she saw this?"

"Do I care?" Val's eyes looked at the #21, and at the verandah space where Vivienne might return.

Johnny leaned back on the red leatherette. Their lit cigarettes sat in the black plastic ashtray, burning to ash. "She'd go,' 'Oh. Aw. Gee. He left a little love note, he left me a note that said:

Dear V, my Vivienne, darling Vivi, let me remind you, you are the star I steer by.

Remember how we used to go to Txapela in Barcelona up the Passeig de Gràcia at two in the morning for tapas at the counter? How we had to sit on the west side, how we had to sit right by the part open to the street, how it had to be the fourth and the fifth stool in and the first order was Dos Numero Veintiuno, and then Veintiuno, dos mas. Before we even sat down, when we still had one leg in the street, we would say, 'Two Number 21,' and then, with the melting squid in our mouths all olive oil and tender, we would say, 'Number 21, two more.' Number 21 meant the order number on the tapas menu of the Basque tapas joint where the fresh squid, which had walked up from the Mediterranean a moment ago, was off-the-cuff sizzled in the wee hours. We solved all the world's problems with squid and Rioja. Number twenty-one also meant we kept doubling down on the grilled calamari in the place we learned it was swell to drink the best wine in the best place, Barcelona, where the protocol is informality, and to drink it as the locals do, in short unstemmed flat-bottomed three-inch-high round glasses. The wine tutored us in how to drink the wine. The squid taught us how to eat it.

"All that, huh?" Val said. He knew it was true, and he hated that it was true. If Val wrote down #21 on a piece of paper and handed it to Vivienne, she might think it was a motel room number, or an invitation to blackjack.

Johnny ripped out the page from his Moleskine. He got up and went inside the restaurant. The waiter was schmoozing the lady at the cash, who was snapping rolls of coin into the till. Johnny folded the piece of paper. "You see a woman and a guy go around the corner a few minutes ago?"

"A man and a woman around the corner a few minutes ago?" the lady at the till asked.

"Yeah. She's in pink. He's tall; gold jacket. A few minutes ago."

"A few minutes ago? Gold jacket, tall, she's in pink?"

"That's it. Can you knock on his room door?"

"Knock on his room door, sir?"

He gave the mirror-talking woman the folded piece of paper with #21 on it. "Pass this in. When they're done."

"Done, sir?"

Johnny did not like how *done* rhymed with *fun*. "Done?" he said. Now he was doing it. "Yes. And tell her Johnny loves her."

"Johnny loves her, sir? Will that be all right with Johnny?"

"It will be all right with Johnny. I am Johnny."

"Oh. I see, sir. You're Johnny? Good. I will be sure to pass the note to her, when she's finished." As forecast by the therapist-doctor-waiter, Van Morrison's voice came on the loudspeakers. "Madame George."

Van singing about how Madame Joy saw them to the train. Johnny was joyful in a small way to have a message in the wind to her. Maybe she didn't know how much he loved her, maybe she didn't know he relied on her love to stay alive.

The waiter said to the lady at the till, "Lauren, bear with me. I gotta make an adjustment." He reached into his black Swiss Cheese Sandwich T-shirt and after a series of squeaking sounds, he pulled out an arm. He laid the wooden arm on the counter. "Not the best, but it was all I could afford, you see, sir. The VA is trying to see if they can get me an arm that fits."

Lauren said to Johnny, "Billy is good people. He lost his arm to the Taliban."

Johnny was feeling dizzy. His ears opened to hear more of the wildcast mumbles of Van Morrison and the dilating doom of a velvet judgment day.

28

ATOMIC PYTHON TATTOO

THERE WAS RUIN here. The word *lush* was not a word you used here, you used *stark*. In a small motel in a beautiful stark nowhere place just shy of the badlands, a man and a woman in the afternoon winter sun had retired inside a small nondescript room. When the duende is humming, you need no luxury digs.

"Let me kill your husband," Andy said, easy, Vivienne in his arms in bed. He could have been saying *Let me drive you to my mom's house.* Johnny was still her husband, Val was still the second guy and Andy was still the promised air of springtime. Vivienne looked at her left arm: not as mottled as the right arm. She put her camera into her left hand and, with that weaker hand, she shot her right arm, forensically, the living autopsy of bomb damage. She had always wanted to go to Japan, but hey, Japan had come to her another way. Tōmatsu, the great Japanese photographer she so admired, who took the great photos of Okinawa, of Hiroshima, of the American sailors and the Japanese teens emulating the American sailors, why, Shōmei Tōmatsu could put Vivienne Pink in his photo gallery of the skin of America, which had become a dermatological landscape of damage. Hey, baby, I'm a mess, let me be your model. I've got Atomic Neck. I've got Nevada Arm. I've got me a Holiday Atomic Tattoo. An A-Bomb, the ultimate hack of my body.

"Are you game?" Andy asked. "But what about that other guy, what's his name who stuck his face in our business back at the Flamingo?"

Vivienne was wary of the way this Andy was talking. He sounded too sane. "I'd like to spend my life with you," he said. "I'm going to sit outside for a bit." He put his gold jacket on over his bare chest. He had his jeans. He was still barefoot.

Vivienne lay on the bed, frantically immobilized. The red door was open. She crawled to the end of the bed, taking pictures of Andy's back just outside the door, his left arm in that gold suede jacket, his arm bent the way a long-time smoker bends it, solicitously, politely, enjoying it, an intimate story with his hand. A story of how you make the endless time pass.

Vivienne knew she was in shock, and she kept being in it. She kept playing through the skill set of knowing the danger she was in, and staying in it. Of recognizing it the way a marathoner might recognize his hypothermia or his dehydration and keep on going. The way he might know his cramps as not ordinary cramps and keep on going. Know injury and know the payment coming, having paid that payment before and kept going, using that now-familiar skill set honed when you have said, *I cannot go on one more inch,* and you do. And it is a kingdom of incremental inches, and then glory comes, and you know it came only because there was a choice: go ahead, or turn back, or stand pat. And you could not look yourself in the mirror if you stood pat or went back, so you inched on, and then you looked yourself in the mirror, and more glory: your damn face had been blown to a distorted fuck up. You did not, however, give up. If you gave up, there was no story.

Vivienne framed Andy in the golden Western doorway, his arm in the gold jacket, his cigarette shorter, his hand – Yes! – about to flick the ash down and she got that drooping arm, the ash falling in the air, and her own left arm she lifted into the frame, a skin object that resembled the shingled roof of the eatery in the distance. The subject was a clothed man, the photographer a nude woman.

Andy, not turning around, said from outside, "I can use my gun. I can go around the corner and put two in him, and you and me can hotfoot it over to Lone Pine, maybe up to Independence, Mammoth Lakes. Are you game?"

"Are you nuts? I told you this is not a movie. Stay away from guns." She moved closer to the door, then she decided she had to take the shot another way. She walked backwards to the bathroom and took a pic of the ordinary modern nondescript twin beds and the TV on the plain particleboard bureau and the standing lamp with the pink accordion shade by the doorway, and the doorway framing Andy's arm, which he had threaded through the white metal arm of the chair, and which was, sans cigarette, gripping the bottom of the chair. His tense arm and hand told a story.

Once in a while, the gift of the gods, those tumbling sparkles, the charismatas, get lit on fire out of the embers of their own atomic memory base. Once in a while, what a woman made a man feel, he feels again, how roiled up and unsettled she made him feel; how she made his soul seep out to the surface of his skin, and show itself to the lens of the camera; how they entered a conversation together, between the maker of art, her, and the materials of her art, him. How he felt vulnerable as her plasticity. How he loved it – as if she were forgiving him for something he had not done yet.

"Your husband loves you," Andy said, not moving from his chair outside the door.

"What do you know about my husband? Leave my husband out of this. Not your concern, honey. Buzz off about him, okay?"

"He is looking out for your welfare," Andy said.

Vivienne did not come to the doorway, or go outside. One minute Andy was suggesting killing Johnny, next minute he was talking like he knows him, like they're pals. One minute he was her soldier-nurse, next minute the nurse would be a killer. She sat down on the bed, seeing an old bicycle wheel leaning up against the trunk of a tree. She got a shot of that, saying, "You want to kill my husband, then you say he is looking out for me, he loves me. Which is it?"

Andy craned his neck back, leaning through the motel room doorway.

"Both," Andy said. She saw smoke curl around his head, a new cigarette, a new shape to his fingers. "Jojo loves you very much."

"What did you say? Jojo? Jojo?! Where in God's name did you get *Jojo* from?" She did not say, *my husband's nickname, my name for Johnny,* because she had trained herself in being secure. After all, Johnny was a well-known writer and many a man, and many a woman, wanted something from him: glitter dust, glitter semen, glitter blurbs, the taste of labour by association, Johnny Coma's glitter name. Johnny called them glory hounds. This kid could have gone and Googled her, and found Johnny, but her names for Johnny and Johnny's names for her were not on any website. In fact she and Jojo planted false information about themselves, which their closest friends knew was false, in order to follow it, and see who among the poseurs passed on the, as Johnny called them, wiki-winks J and V had inserted themselves.

So how did this soldier boy on his way to Iraq, who she had encountered in the hotel coffee shop, know her nickname for Johnny? Calm down, Vivi, she said to herself, no doubt you dropped it, said it in the room back there, after all, you did gender-bend with this guy twenty-six stories up, the night before he was due to deploy.

Still. It bugged her.

She came to the doorway. He did not look up at her. She tapped him on the shoulder. He still did not look up. "What else do you know about me?" she asked.

"You?" Andy said. "Plenty." He flicked his cigarette into the dirt.

"You fucker. Stop talking to me like that. You know my husband is just around the corner. Johnny is. Johnny, to you, if you do not mind." She crouched at the door, duckwalked forward, rested her right arm on the arm of his chair. He moved his arm. He got up, walked past her into the room. Vivienne stayed outside and took pics of him through the doorway with the dark inside and the light outside, Andy a shadow figure, a phantom, the TV on, colour flashing out, a good pic of his shoes at the end of the bed and the colours off the TV screen in profile.

"You want this book finished, don't you?" he said when she came in.

"I do." She searched his eyes. There were flecks of hurt in there, discipline and light.

"I know you are married," Andy said.

"Good," Vivienne said.

"I am not going to get all hung up on you."

"Good."

"Or see you and me fixed up together."

"We are agreed," she said.

"I am not going to come back from Iraq with you on my mind and look for you."

"Honey, you will never be in that position."

"If I had a picture of you beside my bunk, I would never look at it in the middle of night. I know what you look like, don't worry, I won't come after you."

"Same page," she said.

"Jojo won't let you go," Andy said.

"Shut up about him or I will..."

"You will what?" He sat up straight, shaking the headboard.

"Stop it," Vivienne said.

"He has you on a leash. I thought you were better. J does."

"This is a one-minute warning," she said. She wanted his head and the wall to meet cute, real cute, cute as a motel wallboard concussion. No one had ever called J by that one initial but her. You do not come into a marriage and start using the private names of the lovers. Who does that? This was *way* over the line. Woe betide the stranger who uses the tender names of lovers from outside, to them.

"The J-man, yeah I bet that's it," Andy said. "Do you write him letters, 'Dear J-man, Dear J-ster. My little J.'"

"Thirty seconds." Fight or flight? Her adrenaline had one highway: fight. The adrenaline surge had already shut down her peripheral vision. She saw Andy in a focused lit circle. "I would not advise it," she said. "You have ten seconds."

"J. Oh *J*." Talking high and mocking.

"Nine."

"J, J, J, J. Oh J dear, would you?" The letter *J* was not a word, it was not a symbol, it was hardly a sound, it was the strangled sound of love, performed only for those in the private cave.

"Five," she said.

"Oh, darling J-ster."

"Four."

"Mister J. Coma. Is it V and J?"

"Three."

"Do you call him J when you do it? Was it the J-man who banned you from going back to Baghdad?"

"I am warning you." Her blood was boiling, her hands were shaking, her thighs were shaking, her hand was her weapon, her power, her art. She stood over him, feeling the blood in her bicep. And the rush to her open hand, and she slapped him hard. Her hand lay on his cheek in a print, deep red. "You shut up about me and my husband, okay?"

"No. No I won't. I met you, I thought you were a feminist, but you have to check with him before you can work?"

She put the power of her gut and her eye in her fist and gave him a hard one on the jaw. Jaws were on special today. They both heard it crack. He was on his feet with his hands around her wrists. She kicked his nuts. He let go of her wrists. She punched him hard and precisely in the skull. "If the bomb does not get you, Vivienne Pink will. You dare." She put her hands out, palms open, fingers urging him, *Come on, come on.*

"I told you a girl like you always hurts a guy like me." He socked her in the solar plexus.

"Is that what the military teaches you?" she asked. They were both crouched in animal attack position, bums out.

"Maybe." He was holding his right wrist with his left hand. "You're solid," he said. He rubbed his head where she had cracked him one.

"What did you think?" she said, unsmiling.

"You seem too sweet to be that solid," he said.

"That is a man's way of thinking, honey. How's your jaw?"

"I think it's broken."

"Good. Teach you what to say."

"He does love you," Andy said.

She looked around the room. Nothing to denote a visitor. "Where is your luggage?"

"I don't have any, somebody dropped me off."

"Oh, great, are you that loose? Who was she?"

"Only with you," he said, stepping to her, kissing her tight.

She backed off. "You insult my husband, then you think you can kiss me?"

Andy got his wallet out of the secret zip pocket inside the gold leather jacket, unfolded it and showed Vivienne a thick neat pile of bills lining the black wallet. "Guess where that came from? Five thousand dollars. Five. Not one, not two, not even a handsome three. It was going to be two on layaway and three when I delivered. But I convinced the guy to give me the full five on faith."

"Good for you, baby," she said. "I just bet you did. What was it? To kill someone? To service the next girl? Blackmail? Oh I know, surveillance. You could surveil your subject up here in Joe Schmo's Motel up nowhere's ass on a mountaintop just out past the backside of deadwater lakes. Man, you must have some real grift gene in you."

"That's true, I do. My dad did his fair share of mah-jong tiles with the boys back at Boulder Dam. He had to hock his sax once, never mind, yeah, I convinced the guy I could do the surveillance, so he gave me the full five thousand. Meet Mister Benjamin Franklin and his little Benjies. Cast your eyes on fifty Bens, Vivi."

"Jesus. Do not call me Vivi. That is my husband's name for me. I do not even let Val call me Vivi. And nobody but me calls my Johnny J. What are you, educated slime?"

"Harsh, ma'am, if I may say so. You are right about the surveillance, nice mission, surveil the subject up a mountain. What would you say if I told you he said it was okay, that he gave me the A-okay to call you that?"

"Who? What? Call me what? Where? Who, why, what in the holy hell are you talking about, sonny?"

"Your husband. Johnny Coma. *J*."

"You say J one more time you will be picking teeth out of your nostrils and that jaw will be so glass they'll melt you down for sculpture."

"He gave me the five thou and said, 'She likes to be called Vivi.'"

"Bull. Total BS. I never heard such bull in my life. If you know my husband so damn well, which you do not, why did you not even blink an eyelash at him when we walked up the stairs here? I have had it with Crazytown, get me to Peaceful Acres, Lord, I am ready."

"Doesn't that prove it? You didn't say hello to me, and you had me half-naked as a prisoner in your room," Andy said.

"Is that your story?" Vivienne asked. He was getting weird, creepy. Was he really going to retail these lies? Others had. How modern to agree to photos and then to say the photographer forced you.

"Oh excuse me. Not half-naked," Andy said. "All naked. You forced me to take a shower with you, you threatened me and got me naked." He liked how he must look when she got mad at him. Good enough to get her going. How she was getting that pre-aura look in her eyes, how she wanted to take his picture, how they were dancing in anticipation together.

"Forced *you*?" she said. "A soldier? Look at me. I am not even five foot four, I weigh one twenty-five, I have small feet, look at my hands." She knew she was vamping for time, situating herself in its small variations. "I forced you? A soldier, built, please." She came over to him, took his hands, put her arms around his waist, held him back to admire him the way lovers do, admiring his body, then laid back and socked his jaw in the same spot again, harder. "Is that what you want? Because I am sure that is what you ordered off the woman-hating menu."

ANDY WAS IN the bathroom, looking in the mirror, holding a wet towel to his jaw. There were no face cloths in a motel this one star. His bone structure was at a slant, his perfect cheekbones receding. The swelling had come quickly on his lower jawline.

Vivienne looked in the mirror. Her face looked like limestone, mixed with pink rhyolite, mosaicked with shine and bioturbation. The black lake on the left bubbled away like a birthmark branded by the birth of atomic power. The largest organ in her body had been compromised thoroughly, her skin, this organ of organs set on the outside of our bodies. There were peeling patches on either side of her nose, as if the skin were rice paper. The largest organ in your body turns to paper. Along the top rim of her lip, blisters had come up black, but now the black hard bubbles were shining green and spotted with yellow pus. She took a picture of herself: *George W. Bush Loves Me.*

The two of them had gained an air in the last twenty-four hours of one of those couples you see when you travel, whose story you wonder about and invent. She – getting up there in years, but must have been pretty, even beautiful until recently – was it illness? Did he beat her, did she drink, time on the street, cancer? Her arms looked plague stricken, sarcoma ridden.

His eyes were deep and spooky; he looked like bar fight central.

It came on Vivienne like a thought photo: the pics she had taken of her and Andy in the Vegas hotel room? Those pictures could never be taken again. Health is a mirage we review in old photo albums. She had aged ten years and gone down the class-appearance ladder two notches overnight. She looked like a ruin, *stark*.

Her visage and air in the mirror was rough, ferine. Andy looked like a beaten-up human with his pet creature.

Her neck scar from the electric collar torture was there when she had met Andy. He had never asked her about it; she'd never told him the story. Yet he had stroked her neck when he called her his dove.

"Your husband loves you," he said. "He wants you to finish this book."

"Leave it alone already, you do not know him, you do not know me."

"He told me." Andy picked up the wallet. He riffled the Benjamins, all fifty of the one hundred dollars bills. "He gave me this green."

"Baby, do not play me," Vivienne said.

"We were having a drink in Margaritaville, back in Vegas. I was having a quiet drink at the bar. He comes in, he sits at the bar and he orders food, I noticed that. People who come in and order food right away at a bar have ordered food at a bar before. I made him as travels a lot for work. He orders a Sam Adams, the coconut shrimp, the garlic mashed potatoes, sound like him?"

Vivienne was feeling antsy, alert.

"We got to talking. He asked me if I would like to earn a couple thousand dollars doing some work for him. He called it a subcontract. I told him I was shipping out in the morning. He said perfect. He said, *perfect.*"

"I heard you," Vivienne said. She put her arms around Andy's waist, tight, she put her head on his shoulder, she took a pic in the mirror. Tentatively titled, *Betrayal, Panamint Springs Resort, Death Valley, California, December 31, 2006.* She did not let go of Andy. He did not try and loosen her grip. She did not say, *What else did he say?*

"I said I doubted I could get it done before the morning. He said, 'Give it a whirl.' Does that sound right, *Give it a whirl*? I said, 'I think if I understand you correctly your woman will be mighty upset, sir.' He said, 'Chances are. Call me Johnny.'"

Vivienne took her arms away from his waist. She walked to the bed, sat down, lazily scoping the outside through the lens of her camera, seeing nothing. Yeah, I heard you.

"He said, 'Two thousand now,' and didn't he up and hand me two thousand bucks right there at the Margaritaville bar. I'm listening to 'Sea of Heartbreak' so loud I could barely make out his proposition, and this guy I do not know from Adam is handing me cash on the barrelhead if I go sit in the coffee shop, in and out all afternoon, starting when he gives me the signal, and all I have to do is make sure the lady in the pink jacket makes me an offer to go upstairs with her."

"You make it sound dirty. You ungrateful little twerp. I ought to spank you."

"I won't say no." He had the upper hand so he was laughing, he could afford to. Power likes how things are cute and funny, little amusements are power's shiv weather. She did not have to ask him to wipe that smirk off his face, she could do it for him. And then make him immortal in a photograph, beaten and smirkless.

Johnny. Sure. He did love her, he did cherish her, he would do anything for her, he had told her multiple times there was no one like her. "My Johnny did that?" She was standing now. "Jojo hired you to what? Seduce me?"

"To be present for you. To get in your way. To help you finish your book."

"That fucking fucker. That fucking control freak. I hope he is counting his balls, because in one minute he will not remember he has two."

She was out the door of room 15 and steaming her body down the scrub area past the washroom, around the corner right up to Johnny and Val's table where she slid in beside Johnny on the bench, put her hands around his neck and did her move, the one that Marty Hirsch had taught her when she was a teenager: how to kill a man by crushing his hyoid bone. She expertly pressed in on the horseshoe-shaped hyoid, which supports the muscles of the tongue, finding it between Johnny's chin and his thyroid cartilage. Johnny was choking, as Vivienne intended him to be choking. Talk now, my love. Talk now, my sweet, talk darkly, make plans to run my life, go ahead, control me. Talk now, writer. Give me a reading.

Val watched, doing nothing.

29

THE NEW DRONES

VIVIENNE FELT THE edges of the eatery fade to fog. She felt a disjunction in her arms, a flash flood of energy. She pressed down harder on her husband's neck. The jugglers had arrived. Behold the re-entrance of the jugglers. Who mock your tidied-up soul. Who arrive in big military vehicles bringing blackouts to your existence. She was in a blackout inside a blackout. She had come back from shooting with conflict-zone eyes, and she had kept her same outward face, and that was the lie. Her unharmed face had been a cover. She came back, and she did not recognize her own thoughts. She seemed, on so many days, to be speaking the implanted words of somebody else. Yes. Somebody timid, too polite, not even shy really, worse. Genteel. Her coarse war-weathered voice seeped in the smoke of the celestial true began to squeak, to get lodged high in her windpipe. Every night she dreamed the same dream: she was down by a river washing a photographic print of its chemicals, the print was six feet by ten feet, many beautifully clothed women washed with her. Then in a sweat, she woke up, every morning, at the lucid edge. There was no river. She was bathing the photographic paper in the dust of an arroyo. Yet she cleaved to the vividness, the truth of the dreamscape. Days passed with her answering Johnny's fan mail, sparing him so he could write, pretending to be him, flirting online with the ladies, feeling smug about how they crowed they knew him, but they had never known him, only his wife, the war photographer giving them e-thrills as her pastime.

How had she, the dirty dog of Saigon, come to feel so smug in her little art time cons? At night in the deeper part of the Earth's molten core, the world asked for her, Baby Pink, Queen Moxie, like a lonely lover, asked why she had deserted the hot spots of the suffering world – the refugee camps, the war huts on a border, the hideouts embedded with guerillas – only to roam in stasis with the satisfied, as the corrosive grace of history marched on without her. Making art is stray dog work. Her gut was the rotgut truth of rough womanhood. The conflict peaks and the war-shredded jungles aligned her; why else was she alive? She was meant to be a wild witness. Johnny was trying to domesticate her. He was trying to steal her eyes!

She pressed her fingers even harder on Johnny's neck, putting her back into it now. He had set her up! She could feel ropes binding her eyes, making fluorescent green shine back into her retinas. Her eyelashes closed into the bindings. Light pink danced at the edges. Pounding hooves kicked up dust in her brain. She heard the clicks of shoeless feet. And this the jugglers did implement.

In the green and pink blindness she saw her Original Child Eye spinning. Why be safe? Was she safe in El Salvador, when phone voices spoke of her death to come? Was she safe when Mrs. Coma put the electric screws to her neck, in Montevideo? Her life intention had roamed until it found her. She was meant to be a photographing mutt down at curb level, watching with x-ray eyes the aching pulse of the morphic planet and its distressed representatives walking. Let the horses' hooves pound her. She would be the rough shepherd to their wildness.

She felt the rope on her face fall away. The tight lime cotton fell away. The blackout was clearing. She had gone out to war to chase starlight, even in the darkest ditches. And to keep her home, Johnny had tried to be the puppet master of starlight, putting her together with Andy, as a one-time thing. But he was dealing with the girl from the North Country fair and the boy from the far West. Vivienne and Andy – starlight. Do not mess with starlight.

"You set me up with Andy, my darling husband," she said. "Tough titty. Those atoms fell for each other. Step back, puppeteer. The chemistry lives on without you."

And this she said, as the small metal buttons on her scalp grew into metal seed pods, a metal Medusa at Panamint Springs. The broken parts will rise, sprouting empress steel bulbs of glory, the broken brain will erupt as a rogue headdress, a radioactive tiara full of snapping eyes. She loosened her thumbs. She took her hands off Johnny's neck.

"Fuck your little names for me, Johnny," Vivienne said. "Fuck our little love codes. Fuck your drawings, and you know what? Fuck your novels."

Johnny went back to sketching a cartoon woman with giant eyelashes on giant eyes, a big luscious mouth and fire hair. He was smiling.

She picked up the plate with Johnny's half-eaten burger and dropped it on the verandah floor. She poured the remains of his Corona on it. "Are you prepared to die?"

"Oh please," Johnny said, taking a slug of Val's beer, a drag off of Val's burning smoke. Val continued to say nothing.

"And you," Vivienne said, pointing at Val. "Do not blame me, because you've lived a life unloved. What did you expect? That a woman would live your life for you? Not me, brother. You. You. You fucking...*American*."

Val wasn't listening to her. His mind was on the orange phone in his pocket, which held her voice and how it sounded when she was taken by someone who was her thrall. He did not want to hear the sound of the actual Vivienne speaking to him.

She walked back to room 15. "Get your gun," she said to Andy.

"I have it here," he said, patting his jacket.

"Kill my husband. I'll sit in the car," she said. "You kill him, we'll go to Lone Pine. Okay?"

"Yes, ma'am," he said.

ANDY WALKED OUT the red door of room number 15, headed in a straight line to the corner, rounded the bend, walked to the table where Val and

Johnny sat and aimed his pistol with his arm straight out, his eye firm. The story the gun was following said that Andy San Diego shot the legendary writer Johnny Coma right in the heart, one late December day in '06 at Panamint Springs in the desert.

As Andy aimed his weapon, though, Vivienne's eye was there first, at Johnny her beloved one and only, then at Val, and her arm pushed the pistol in Andy San Diego's hand and, as Lady Luck would have it, the soldier shot the spy Val Gold. Vivienne pushed Andy's arm, so the gun took aim at Val's heart, instead. Val Gold held his heart and called, "Vivienne."

Johnny Coma's best friend, Val, had been shot by one of his wife's photographic subjects, a man she had not even known existed back east in Toronto on Christmas Day. Now, as they closed in on New Year's Eve, Vivienne was taking off with him. Andy the soldier she met in the coffee shop, and her husband, Johnny, was sitting there with a look of fury. *You changed.*

"Bye-bye, J," Andy San Diego said. "I'm your wife's man now, Mr. C."

Val was doubled over onto the table. Johnny said to Vivienne, "You do want war, don't you, any other way."

Vivienne said, "Goodbye, Val," as she pivoted on the stairs, and one-handed got off another shot of Val, of the waiter just coming out to the verandah, looking at her, looking at them, looking at her, another guy at the edge of the frame. What had just happened in this picture? The lady from table one was running away with the guy from table two.

The waiter stood there with a Corona in each hand, and a box of Band-Aids in his mouth.

VIVIENNE PINK AND Andy got in the white Honda and left, zooming up the incline to the badlands road. The time elapsed from when she said, "Kill my husband," to when they drove off was three minutes, one hundred and eighty seconds. You could take one hundred and eighty thousand photographs and more in that time. Vivienne took one.

Behind them the Panamint Range and the Panamint Valley moved back as they rode west along Highway 190 with the Argus Range on their left. On their right lay a gorge and Rainbow Canyon. Rimy snow, looking like the twin of desert salt, lay on the dark brown volcanic rock of the road where low purple hills carried the snow into the blue sky, and frozen snow danced down the volcanic badlands, melting below in the sun. They stopped at Father Crowley Point.

At the outlook at Father Crowley, where the world was rough and empty, and there was no railing or any security down into the deep canyons, they got out of the car.

She was not sure that she even liked him.

On the edge of the canyon, a man sat. His head was wrapped in a long red shawl that blew in the wind, its long fringed tendrils lifting and falling. He was sitting with his legs stretched out in grey pants, ballooning below a rug he had wrapped around them to his waist against the cold. The rug, Vivienne could see as she came closer with her camera to her eye, was soft, velveteen, a type of rug she had seen plenty of in Baghdad in the souk and also in Herat, Afghanistan. It was woven in the traditional motif of one of the Turkmen tribes: a repeated animal like a llama in deep blues and orange-reds and brown-purples. The sun was bathing the rug as desert suns do. This was the natural process of what many rug dealers back East did, sent their rugs to the Southwest desert to have them laid out, to be bleached and reach that ancient Middle Eastern look in authenticity, what sun does to animal wool. The man saw Vivienne and Andy, he beckoned them come to him, he unwrapped the rug from his legs. It was about six feet by seven, an instant wilderness room shape and it was, instantly too, a place to sit, a table to put things on, a social space defined on the rock, a little floor lacking a roof, the floor, the table, the seats, as rugs carried on pack animals have always been. If it is cold in the desert you wrap the floor around you.

They stood in a strange courtesy at the edge of a Death Valley cliff, a stranger in woven goods their improvised calm host.

Vivienne watched erosion behind the man down in the striated folds of basin and range. She watched the opposite of photographic time, yet what she the photographer yearned for: the moment is short; the photograph forever.

"My burro broke," the man said. He lifted his red scarf from his head. His hair fell down in cascades of grey. He wore a long wool coat on his upper body, in a Southwestern motif of dark brown chevrons, woven arrows on tan wool with orange threading. Peculiarly and wonderfully, his lower-than-hip-length coat with wide lapels and his lap rug went together, the way a stylist might put together woven desert classics of different patterns but similar provenance and shades for a fashion shoot in which the photograph told a story the viewer was intrigued by. This man was the mystery narrative encapsulated in a melancholy composure with the tablelands setting off the wonderful textiles he wore. His grey dried hair was perfect, woven by disuse and bad grooming and the punishing dry air. Vivienne felt her hair, while looking at his, and a matted clump came off in her hand. Andy had his arm around her waist. Vivienne showed him the clump. He took it from her. It was the size of his palm. "You look like you've been scalped," he said. "Let me see your head."

The robed gentleman came over. He looked down at Vivienne's head. "I lament," he said.

Andy said, "Baby, your scalp is singed." He touched her head. "There's a big clot. I need to get you to a doctor."

"No doctors, I have a book to finish."

"Let me help you, baby, take all the pictures you want, we'll finish it together."

Not since Martin Hirsch in Vietnam had anyone offered to help her. Her primary lesion was Vietnam when she was fifteen, turning sixteen that November, and just getting started. After that, they admired her, but she waded in close to death and that scared some souls who felt Vivienne's close-up shots of the morbid might infect them. People *not* in the photographs thought their souls might be stolen. Andy offered to partner with her; he was touching her burned scalp with the care of a combat medic.

And the strange gent wearing the velvet rug around his legs pulled the wide lapels of his chevron wool coat around his neck, threading the red scarf through his hands like a rosary.

He placed the red scarf on Vivienne's head. He put one hand on the scarf, and he spoke: "I lament the end of the nation. I lament the end of the free people. I used to stand behind a camera, I shot their movies for them, I walked into the fire of the storm, I was invincible, I owned planets."

He turned his head down towards them. One of his eyes had been badly damaged. It looked like it was glass, or blind. This left eye had a drooping area under it, which made his face longer on the left than the right. He walked to the edge of the cliff. Andy said to Vivienne, "You're hurt. Let's get you to some help."

"Later," she said. "After New Year's. There's something here." She was not addicted to danger, or violence, or war, she was beholden to her eyes. She had pledged to be faithful to witness. "I can feel a story."

The robed man bent his two legs into a lotus position. He put his head down in his lap, suggesting that his back was supple, despite the old robes and air of destitution.

"*And they said, There is no hope: but we will walk after our own devices, and we will every one do the imagination of his evil heart.*" He straightened his back. His closed his eyes. He took the coat off with ease. Life had happened to this man, he knew how to get out of a coat quickly. On the velveteen soft Baluch rug of orange and grey-green from the Middle Eastern territories, he was in a perfect lotus, his shoulders amazingly aligned here on the tableland volcano edge where a nominal highway cut through the grand nowhere.

The man said, "I am Jeremiah. I come to say to you my lamentation for the people. I lament the nation, please return to us our land. I see them with their banks, I see them with their riches, they are crooks every last one of them; this boom has to go down. I own three houses, I think I own a fourth. I left my wife, I abandoned my daughters, I have nothing but money – it has to go bust. Now therefore go, to speak to the men of Judah, and to the inhabitants of Jerusalem, saying, *Thus saith the LORD; Behold, I frame evil against you, and devise a device against you: return ye now every one from his evil way, and make your ways and your doings good.* Go back to your station, your camp awaits you, son. Evil is the only road ahead that way. But back you may have a chance to redeem the spent chances. Do not crush the brush. Pack it in, pack it out. Leave no trace."

The Jeremiah man got up from his lotus position and went to the edge of the canyon. He looked down. "Don't jump," Andy said, coming to his side. He pushed Andy away.

"Leave me to my solitude. I know my future… And lo, even those whose land suffered Nagasaki did remove Chernobyl from their textbooks. And lo, those in receipt of bombs did say nuclear power is safe. Jerusalem is no more; now it is Alice in Wonderland." He leaned over the edge, looked over it. Vivienne grabbed his shawl and put it over his shoulders. Moths flew out of the shawl, and off his coat, a swarm of them into the canyon. She stepped back, and shot a pic, the man's profile making a triangle shape of his back in the woven wool item, bent at the waist. He touched his toes, he made pinwheels with his arms going in opposite directions from each other, he moved into a tai chi position and slowly, ever so slowly, he rotated, doing soft leg and arm damage to invisible opponents. He put his hands together in a prayer position and bowed to the canyon, and all of God's world below, a gouge in deep burnt rock brown. "Let me toss you little hummingbird moths out into the world, go well my hoverers, go in the wind like the sand."

A line of bikers came around the badlands bend. They stopped, pulling in closer to Vivienne and Andy at Father Crowley Point. Six bikers got off six Harleys. In black leather, top to bottom, and the characteristic blue or red bandanas. "Hey," the first one said to Vivienne, "How's it going?" He was friendly, white, sunburnt, beefy. His darker complected, acned second came over; he had longer darker hair, a moustache and a gold tooth when he smiled, also friendly. Each of them had one gold earring.

The darker haired biker looked at Vivienne's camera. "Nice rig. You want me to take your picture? You and your son?"

Vivienne laughed, Andy did not. "I'm in the service," he said. "I'm going to marry her."

"First I heard," Vivienne said, not to Andy, but flirting with the biker.

Andy did not take the bait. "She's been in a bomb test," Andy said to both bikers.

"Ain't it the story," said the ponytail. "Can't live with 'em, can't afford the chemo."

"Take a shot of us," Vivienne said. She came close to Andy. They put their arms around each other. "I'm already married," she said, as the biker aimed the Olympus and pressed the shutter, holding it as if he knew something about cameras. He did not take too long to line the shot up – the sign of an amateur these days, over-importantly lining up mom on some city street in some foreign land, as if the casual informal shot for the family was the key shot in a major motion picture, oblivious to locals and traffic, not at all how a pro on vacation shoots a candid shot – with fun and offhand skill, holding the camera with one hand. The biker turned the camera vertically to get her and Andy in, the way travellers later wish they had done.

"Let me get an insurance shot," the biker said. He wore a grey feather in his red bandana.

"Sure, honey," Vivienne said, opening her arms wide, waving her hands to motion him closer.

"Your son got a stick up his ass, ma'am?" he asked, from behind the camera. Andy was smiling for the camera, but the biker could sense that Andy was jealous, wanting the badlands to be his and Vivienne's alone. Vivienne did not want to betray Andy's tender jealousy.

"Yeah, sure, as a matter of fact," she kissed Andy's cheek. "It's called –" she made eye contact with the biker who was holding the camera down at his side, just as she did "– it's called the military."

The biker smiled, but less a laugh smile than a smile of been-there shot-that. "Oh, yes," he said, keeping the camera at his side, "they got their hands around my neck back in the day, I can tell you. I got back from Madame Nhu and Diem. I got a good job working for CBS News. They saw I had a knack for the film, so they put me to work, where?" He took a couple steps towards Vivienne. "I got out of Hanoi and I got to work in Central America. They put me into El Salvador. I was a war vet and I was back shooting another war, this time my camera was my, well, you know."

This biker had those war eyes. Vivienne knew that look, she had seen it set in her own eye sockets in the mirror.

"You ought to get that arm to a doctor. Or at least a vet," the biker said, smiling, his eyes brightening from the dark blue back to a brilliant sea blue at his own small joke.

"You mean," Vivienne said, "one of those like in the movies where the guy says, 'You are the first patient I ever had who talked back.'"

"I've seen a few of those." He took a pack of smokes out of his leather jacket, a box with a dancing skeleton on it: WOODEN-KIMONO NAILS. "Care for a coffin nail?" he asked Vivienne, who said, "Don't mind if I do." He had nice fingers, silver rings on seven of them.

"There used to be a place out on the Pan-American Highway, outside of San Salvador, during the war, called Jimmy's," the biker said, curving his body, using the black leather folds as a quick leather grotto against the wind, lighting his smoke not with a lighter but with a thin match from a small box. Sure, weatherproof matches, that was what you wanted out here. His five fellow bikers were smoking too, standing around, taking a leak, schmoozing, using their bikes as tables, chairs, bar counters.

"Jimmy's. Jimmy was Chinese," the biker said, lighting Vivienne's Wooden-Kimono Nail off the same match. "Everybody knew Jimmy. You got caught in a bad invasion, you could hole up at Jimmy's, spend the night. Jimmy looked out for the reporters. I could leave my rig with Jimmy, no problem. So anyway one night we get the word from Jimmy, we had stopped in for a beer on the way out to the war, there was going to be a big attack, maybe we didn't want to chance going back to the capital. The Americans, yeah, my people. Chinese Jimmy and his Jimmy rooms on the highway knew what the guerrillas were doing and the damn American generals did not. Far as I ever heard, Jimmy did not ever tell a one of them about any damn guerrilla attack. Let them make their own way out. But he warned us, he warned the press. There are guys like that everywhere.

It was the dry season, everything was real dusty on the Pan-American. The guerrillas had their own radio station." He inhaled.

He looked at Vivienne the way a man in a bar in the dark looks at a woman on a bright August afternoon. He was making a nice little corner of the badlands widescreen. He was acting incidental, the way a confident man can. Man, Vivienne was feeling that itch. She wanted that look captured inside her camera, which he himself was holding. Those eyes had known war. The brotherhood of baby blues with explosions etched around the war irises. "That was the thing about El Salvador, the guerrillas had their own radio station."

"You mean their own radio frequency. Their band?" Vivienne said. Well, here was the thing. She knew of Jimmy's. She in fact knew Jimmy's. She knew *Jimmy*. She had been there, in El Salvador. She had holed up at Jimmy's more than once. She had a photographer's crush on this biker guy, but stronger still was her long-bred suspicion of new people getting too close. Better not to say she knew Jimmy.

The biker came closer into her personal space, but he blew the smoke away, sticking his tongue through it, making perfect smoke rings. His tongue had a tiny turquoise stud in it. "That's right, little lady. When they were going to make a guerrilla raid on some town, say Berlin or out in the farmland, they would broadcast the plan so the people could evacuate before the battle and the cameramen could decide in or out, do I want to die today."

"I have seen that day," Vivienne said. Not lying, but not forthcoming.

She was ignoring Andy. He walked out to the dividing line on the highway. He lit a smoke, as easy as a guy leaning against a closed store window. A big oil tanker truck came at him. He nonchalanted out of the rig's way, watching Vivienne flirt with the biker. "Now I know how that husband of yours feels," Andy said, just loud enough for Vivienne and the biker to hear him.

"He talking about Dad?" the biker asked.

Vivienne stepped closer to him, about two inches away, put her hand on her camera's neck, which they were now both holding. "Yeah, that is right. Dad. Is that not right, darling, you and Dad never could get along, could you?"

"I knew there was something about her," he shouted to his buddies who were yanking up their pants, buttoning their leather against the weather, and getting back on their bikes, kicking them into noise. "Gotta go," he said. He handed the camera to her, the lens pointing to him. She took it from him, her right hand feeling at home with it close to her muscle memory flesh again. He fished in his jacket, and handed her a card: BARRY KATZ, Freelance Cameraman, Fotógrafo, Sansen, 444 Columbus Ave, San Francisco, California.

"*Yo tambien fotógrafo,*" she said, walking him to his bike.

"*Fotógrafa,*" he said. "The lady with the camera, good luck, *buena suerte, que vaya con Dios.*"

"*Ojalá,*" she said. "Shalom," looking down at the card, "Barry."

"Look me up if you're ever in the city." He was revving the bike.

"Got a pen?" Vivienne said to Barry, who put a foot down in the dirt.

"Always," Barry said. He went into a black leather pocket, taking out a slim silver pen. "You can use it underwater, or when you're travelling to the moon, honey. My buddy Marty Hirsch gave it to me. He's been on the street for years, lost his hands to diabetes."

You hear a thing. It cannot be. So you do not hear it. Vivienne pulled a scrap of paper out of her pants pocket. She wrote #15 on it. "You get to Panamint Springs, ask for this room. It has good pics in it." Miniature shock waves changed the air pressure in her brain. Her body was a propagating disturbance. Hirsch? No way. Marty Hirsch homeless in San Francisco? She would not hear it.

Then the echo insists back into you. "Is your buddy Hirsch..." She could not say it.

"Marty Hirsch," the biker said. "My old buddy. I was his second-in-command, or as Hirsch used to say, I was his wing-nut wingman. Here." The biker unzipped a side pocket on his leather jacket. He showed Vivienne a photograph. The man in the photograph was wearing a dark olive pullover. It was frayed at the boat neck, the cuffs were soiled, the hands coming out of the sweater sleeves were wooden. The man was standing in a wonky way, jolly like an alky. His pants were grey, sweatpants. The sweater was tucked in, the pants tied by a rope. The man was deeply tanned, scorched in the way of the homeless on the street. His feet were bare. He wore a piece of cardboard around his waist: JUNGLE ROT. NO LOOKING. Behind him, a couple walked, wearing parkas with the hoods up. "We're talking one mother of a cold day in the Tenderloin. I found Marty at the corner of Eddy and Leavenworth, I took him to the Elm Hotel, got him a homeless single. We tried to get him into rehab. No dice."

It could not be the same Marty, not her Martin Hirsch. Her MH was sleek, handsome, hilarious, fearless. He followed the story until the story followed him. Her Marty taught her everything. He treated her young pretensions as if they were the sincerity of an adult. Her Marty made her the photographer she was. Her Martin Hirsch led her to see her first human being setting himself on fire. Her Marty gave her the gift of being in her destiny at the tender age of fifteen. Marty was her mentor in everything. He tendered her into how love could be. With the flesh war outside their rickety red door of luck, he took her into the gauze drapery. Marty was her first love. His deep knowledge had become part of her DNA, the way it is with mentors in our lifetimes. The man in the photograph Vivienne held was disfortunate. He had nowhere eyes. He was in the jolly gone place a Vietnam veteran might go, when alcohol is his new wife, and the sick things he has seen in war eat him bad as a snake uncoiling in his insides, the wickedness of the world feasting his goodness to a soul husk. Her camera felt like a lie around her neck. A thing born in fire and solace had become a thing that brought Martin Hirsch to amputation and addiction. They come for your scars, they come for your early young lesions, they rip them off like skin and they pour alkali rivers in them.

"We got him off meth," the biker said, "but no way the booze." He flapped the photo. "At least he's got feet here. No feet, no hands. There was some total fuck-up at the VA to get him some feet, last I heard. I haven't seen him since I don't know when."

"Can I have this?" Vivienne asked.

"I don't… Miss, why would you want a picture of this bum? He's my buddy."

"Come here," she said. She took him to the edge of the canyon. She whispered in his ear. He took her two hands. They sat down at the rim. He put his arm around her shoulders. Vivienne Pink wept at Father Crowley Point, solaced by Barry Katz, the leather-clad biker. Then he began to sob and she solaced him. He got up.

He got back on his bike. Vivienne stood beside the bike; a sudden bonding had made them old friends for a moment. "That is the most fucked-up fuck of a thing I ever heard of," he said. The line of bikers stretched back east in a curve around the badlands.

Vivienne came to Andy. "That guy? His name is Barry Katz. He was Martin Hirsch's best friend in Vietnam. I missed meeting him, he was off in Laos, he just told me." She was sobbing. "My Marty. Remember I told you about the guy I met in Paris, I was fifteen, it was late May? He took me to Vietnam."

"Guy picks you up at the *Venus de Milo*?"

"The very one."

"I was jealous when you told me," Andy said.

"I'd just met you."

"What does that have to do with anything?"

She laughed. "That man, who took me that week I met him in Paris to Saigon to be his camera assistant? My mentor? The man who changed my life? He is homeless in San Francisco. He is a boozehound with no hands. This man took photographs for the ages. He took pics that were on all the covers. He has wooden hands. They cut off his feet. I do not know what to do."

"Marry me," Andy said, cradling her head to his chest. She pulled back.

"Oh, for pity's sakes. What is it with you men and marrying? Can you not just listen to a woman for a change? Are you going to end up just like all the rest?"

"No," Andy said. "I'm sorry to hear about your friend Martin Hirsch."

"Oh fuck off. What do you know? Stay out of my world."

The things that cannot be, already are. All these years, the young Marty Hirsch, Vietnam photographer, was in her mind, frozen in 1963, 1968, 1972, 1974. But that man had been kidnapped by distress, that man had been made a street person by berserk circumstances, that frozen man in the frozen photographs had ceased to exist, that young shining eye was a drunk, wearing rope-tied pants, and the barefoot alcoholic now had no feet. All bets were off. Anything, now, could happen. Care had deserted her.

"Here," Vivienne said, handing her camera off to Andy. "This is a total lie. I do not want to ever touch this thing again. You do it. You go lie with this. I want to jump into that canyon."

Jeremiah spoke into the canyon. "*I will scatter them as with an east wind before the enemy; I will shew them the back, and not the face, in the day of their calamity.* Jerusalem is no more. I will send for their many fishers and I will send for their many hunters and I shall hunt them from every mountain and from every hill and out of the holes of rocks."

He shook the rug with his feet and moths flew out.

"*And first I will recompense their iniquity and their sin double; because they have defiled my land, they have filled mine inheritance with the carcasses of their detestable and abominable things... Surely our fathers have inherited lies, vanity, and* things *wherein* there *is no profit.*"

The moths flew back to the chevron pattern of his rug. "These are the new drones. The new Moth Drones." He took the turquoise stud from his ear. "The turquoise is dug at Fallon, near Reno. I refashioned it to do surveillance." He threw the turquoise up in the air. It flew to Vivienne's nose. It turned back and forth, robotically. "Dragonflies, moths, flies, bees. They are all government weaponry now. I engineered them. People," he stood up, he put his arms out, folded ailerons, and he spoke to Rainbow Canyon. "People, Jerusalem is over. Jerusalem is never come. Jerusalem will never be."

Andy got in the car, passenger side. Vivienne got behind the wheel. Her mentor, Marty, who held cameras high to witness the wicked, the humble, the war prism of berserkers, he was a quadruple amputee on the streets of the city. In a portal with a paper cup. They come for your broken parts, and amputate them.

The toxic veil of the chemical empire covered them as they drove.

30

SWITCHEROO

THE SKY WAS a felted underbelly. The air was full of lithium.

Back about a million years ago, give or take ten or twenty thousand years, there was plentiful water and runoff down past lakes in the Great Basin. Here beaches receded and land popped up, and the thin white line of the beach border still lies on the ancient falling valley rocks, and down from later-named Owens River water flowed to later-named Owens Lake, which was a beauty.

Here, the first white man came in 1843. Joseph Walker walked and took a wagon train through Owens Lake, and for fifteen years until the California Gold Rush, Owens Lake and this part of the Northern Mojave was quiet and lonely and wet. There was time yet for water to live.

But there was a faraway town on the west coast, far from Owens Lake, a small settlement, San Pedro, described by observers of the day as a fetid inward swamp, a place contrasted with San Francisco, which was a booming cosmopolitan port, but the fetid swamp had ambition. It was a nowhere place, and unlike San Francisco, it was hot, tropical. It had been compared by the local wags to Guayaquil, Ecuador, or Veracruz, Mexico, but without any of the charms or industry of those hot swampy places. A hot swamp facing the Pacific, its rear to the desert, it had little drinkable water. But its ambition was monstrous. *Want water. Need water. Give. Me. Water.* Oh, back around 1900, the monster climbed up hills, looked down on mountains. *Water, give me water.* The monster saw Owens Lake, its blue Owens Valley waves, the boats carrying ore from shore to shore, its river irrigating fruit trees popping apple blossom orchards in the spring, manzanas up the road. The monster needed water to live; the Owens Valley needed water to live; the monster invaded to kidnap the water by pipeline.

By the time of the major water felony in the year 1913 the monster was known as *Los Angeles.* To live and grow strong, the municipality of LA literally sucked the farming Owens Valley dry. Locals detonated parts of the pipeline named the Los Angeles Aqueduct. Locals kidnapped the LA politicians who came by train to sell the locals on their campaign that Los Angeles needed to live, and they did not. Trains of army men came up to quell the Owens Valley. Mule teams of fifty-two hauled the steel pipe (which in photographs looked like nuclear bombs) up the valley, and natural gravity siphoned the water down to the mouth of Los Angeles. DRY LAKE on the map means, in translation, Los Angeles invaded this land, Los Angeles stole its resources, Los Angeles became an imperializing empire. Los Angeles was the conqueror; this dry lake was the ecological scar the invading army left behind. A white mummy blowing the highest level of particulate pollution in the lower forty-eight states.

Most years, 300,000 tons of dust blew off this dry playa. Was Los Angeles in 1913 the model for the United States in Vietnam? In Korea? In Vietnam, in Iraq? Was LA a fractal of its entitled federal parent?

Vivienne and Andy inhaled the toxic air, which included arsenic.

Once, empires conquered lands, and paper treaties sealed the deal. But when we conquer resources, we remove the land from the land.

Martin Hirsch was the model of men; Owens Lake was a model of water. Vivienne looked out across the miles-long white winter corpse. The wind blew dead rotted matter into her eyes. Martin Hirsch was homeless. It could not be. Untended, sunburned. His skin in the photograph the biker showed her was peeled. It had old, unhealed exposure. Living on the street gave skin the look of disease, the look of bomb survivors, the look of prison. Our blue planet, its space, its air, had become the giant planetary prison. Trapped here, to inhale the arsenic off the once beautiful wet waters.

She held out her arm. "Here," she said to Andy. "Shoot me." He took a picture of her arm. She pointed to her eyes. "I can't see. Shoot it."

Vivienne was always the shootiste, never the subject. Now, screw it. Martin Hirsch lived on the street. What had happened to his cameras? To his archives? What happens to the picture file of a great war photographer if he heads down the methamphetamine highway and becomes a toothless smell with a paper cup?

You could take a paper cup and cut the end out, and bellow to the world that America had been an environmental army, attacking itself. The heavens, troubled, could not breathe anymore, man's acts made even heaven above a polluted danger. The oversalination of the dried-out lake sent the birds away, and the sky could be forgiven for begging better health care options.

For a local Owens Valley resident to see his ancient heritage water, he would have to visit a water tap in municipal Los Angeles.

They lied to the Martys, they lied to the armies, they lied to the birds, the water, the lakes... Was democracy really an elected form of lying?

Vivienne took off her leather jacket. She took off her python vest. She put them at the soft side of the hard playa. Unknowing pale orange mutant grasses grew into late afternoon. Masses of soft grey-blue blew up and down. Here was the forensic evidence of poison. America conquered itself, experimented on itself, ravaged its own land, bombed its own western desert back to the Stone Age. America weaponized its own air, which for years concussed its citizens. The land was too big, the space was too large, America's house was supersized, America busyworked into ruin, calling it love of country.

Vivienne Pink, photographer of others, stood, topless, here at Owens Lake. "Shoot my tits," she said to Andy. The thought of ever touching her camera again made her brain bounce her eyes around...her camera? It, too, was a lie. All bets *were* off.

Her right nipple had sunk down into her breast, becoming a declivity with sloped brown edges, flat at the bottom. It was pebbly and orange on the flat part.

No cars came. Vivienne took off her pale olive pants. He had first met her in the pink jacket and olive pants.

A Christmas holiday week souvenir photo: a war photographer, two days after being in the vicinity of an atomic bomb exploding, stood in front of a lake whose lifeblood water had been sucked away to kill it dry. The photographer was naked. Her legs were apart, defiant. She first held up a finger but folded it back in. She put her hands on her hips. She made love to the lens. She had never done this before. Not with full intention. She had never been the model.

Andy, her subject, shot her. He did not speak. She had made love to him with this camera. He had played the role of her. Now, she played the role of him.

Vivienne could feel he wanted her, somehow, to bring the grief about Marty – Marty homeless; even her, young in Vietnam – out through her skin and bones. To use the agency of her cheekbones, her eyes.

They both knew that here, now, the first time she posed, truly, with intention, adopting the art moves of the material for a camera, she looked like a ruin. Her glossy thick red hair was now dry whitened bloody patches. Her cheeks bloomed black blisters. Her eyes were still concussing from the bomb's shock wave.

They both knew there never had been photos of Vivienne Pink in her prime, in her glory. Once, she was young and beautiful. But there were no photographs to show it. But there were photos of them in a mirror with other misfits in similar deserts on the TV in the background. There were reflections of Vivienne remaining as ghost evidence.

They both knew her book had changed. They both knew the agencies of this change were outside them, and within them.

She posed with the feeling she might include some of these pics in the book. *How the soldier-subject picked up a camera*. The strange ways men come to art. Maybe by the end of the book, the soldier-subject becomes the soldier-photographer, showing his photos of Vivienne.

Back in the Vegas hotel room, her camera had made love to Andy's grief, and asked him to use his body to tell the story. Now Andy had the love camera. Now, he the subject was using the camera to make love to her ruination. He might be forgiving the world, while still hating it.

Photo: *Atomic Moxie, Owens Lake, December 31, 2006.*

Inside the car, Vivienne pulled on her pants, vest and jacket, closed her eyes, put her right hand flat on the window. Andy reached across her and did up her seat belt. He stroked the leaking black blisters on her cheeks. He called her Baby Pink, Baby Pink. He gentled her dried bird's nest hair. Black matter was falling onto Vivienne's pink leather jacket. The photographer had become nuclear evidence.

She took the photograph of Martin Hirsch out of her jacket pocket. She handed it to Andy. He tapped the photo. "I saw this guy." He leaned his chest against the steering wheel. Vivienne said nothing. "I saw this guy in Vegas last week, by the Marlboro Man, before I went into the homeless alley. He had that same Jungle Rot sign. The wooden arms."

Beyond the sadness that your mentor was a beggar now was the unbearable notion that you had been in the same city, by chance, where he was begging; that you might have walked past him; that you shot pictures in a high-windowed room, and your handsome visionary teacher was down there, one of the flashes on the edge of sunshine. Her camera, the lying rat.

They drove away from Owens Lake, old California crime scene, trying to escape the new trick of the Divine Strake bomb. The air is a mean stalker.

Along Highway 190, they passed the Olancha Dunes, where the movie *Bagdad* was shot in 1949.

They arrived at the junction of 190 and US 395.

Civilization was a small diner set in pines and willows at Olancha. Vivienne got out of the car.

A line of newspaper boxes stood outside the diner in the dust. To Vivienne's eye they looked like strange artifacts, odd bodies with something to say in their eye windows.

They sat in a red leatherette booth, reading the *Los Angeles Times*.

Saddam Hussein to be hanged by the neck on New Year's Eve or earlier.

The wind had knocked over transport trailers on the 395. Those Santa Anas were brutal.

James Brown's body was to be transported, the newspaper said, from Atlanta, Georgia, to New York City. It would be driven by the Reverend Al Sharpton, due to the coffin being made of pure gold and too heavy to fly. The gold coffin would be driven to the area of Harlem by white horses in a caisson, and James Brown's body would lie in state to be viewed by his fans at the Apollo Theater, where they could pay their respects through the New Year's weekend.

President Gerald Ford had died on Tuesday, December 26. The normal long weekend of New Year's Eve falling on Sunday, and Monday being New Year's Day, the holiday would be extended, the paper said, and Tuesday, January 2nd would be a national day of mourning.

Vivienne got a Cobb salad, Andy got a turkey club. They sat eating and reading, saying nothing to each other, like a married couple or old friends or long colleagues.

Vivienne dove into a feature on Lynette Fromme. Wow, yeah, "Squeaky" Fromme. Of course, no wonder the *Times* had a piece on her: she had tried to assassinate President Ford. Squeaky Fromme of the Manson Family. Born as a good Santa Monica girl. On the *Lawrence Welk Show* at age eleven. A popular cheerleader type. Lynette had moved to Redondo Beach with Mom and Dad and not long after high school graduation was into booze and drugs and was on the street homeless. She moved to Venice Beach, where she met Charles Manson. She was nineteen. She and Manson teamed up, and well, will you look at that, Vivienne put her finger on the article, Squeaky and Charlie had lived together in the desert in Death Valley. She was twenty-one at the time of the Tate and LaBianca murders. She had carved an *X* into her forehead. She had agreed to participate in Manson's deal with the Aryan Brotherhood: that in exchange for the Aryans giving Manson protection in prison, when any of them they got out Manson would have women waiting to service them. Squeaky had agreed to be one of those women.

Vivienne read on: then Squeaky decided to approach the President of the United States, Gerald Ford, on September 5, 1975, in Sacramento. She was twenty-six at the time. She had worn a long red robe. She'd carried a Colt M1911A1 .45 semi-automatic pistol. She had pointed the pistol at Ford. A secret service agent had restrained her. The news cameras caught her protesting, "It didn't go off." Decades later she claimed she came to wave a gun at the president to get life. "Not just my life but clean air, healthy water and respect for creatures and creation."

Vivienne looked out the window of the Olancha diner to the Sierra highway. That was the thing about California, wasn't it? It was so hard to tell the environmentalists from the mentally disturbed. Everyone inhaled the holy rhetoric along with the pollution.

Yeah, here was the evidence, Vivienne saw, of just that thought. Just when you thought the assassination attempt was the deranged act only of a Manson Family member, another person tried to assassinate President Gerald Ford, seventeen days after Squeaky. On September 22, 1975, in San Francisco this time, outside the St. Francis Hotel, Sara Jane Moore did in fact get a bullet out of her gun. Ms. Moore was a forty-five-year-old former nursing school student and accountant. The day before the assassination attempt, police had arrested Ms. Moore on possession of an illegal handgun, but had released her and taken away her .45. Next day, with a .38 in her hand, she stood in the crowd forty feet from the President of the United States. The new gun was unfamiliar to her. She had a deadeye aim but the .38 skewed six inches off, and the bullet whizzed by six inches from the president's head. She put up her arm and tried again, but this time a disabled ex-Marine standing by tackled Ms. Sara Jane Moore and took her down. A chance gun, a chance Marine and in the fall of 1975 President Gerald Ford lived to see another day, in fact, thirty-one more years of them. And Ms. Moore was sentenced to life. And Ms. Moore, the quiet middle-aged accountant, said, "I didn't want to kill anybody, but there comes a point when the only way you can make a statement is to pick up a gun."

All the pretty assassins, from the nice white suburbs.

Who is a pod, who is a politician, who snatched the bodies, was it all the gun-toting accountants?

Vivienne looked at Andy. "What day is it?"

"It's on the paper," Andy said, not looking at her, keeping his eyes on the newspaper he held up unfolded, large enough to cover his face and more.

"It says the 31st, it can't be the 31st, did we lose some days there? Did we have a blackout? Andy, honey, are you on the lam?"

"I might do time," Andy said. "Listen, Baby Pink. I've done time. They won't give me more than a year and a half, nine months, six, maybe no time. Fort Sill, maybe Miramar brig, maybe San Diego. I can still move out."

"But they'll be gone," Vivienne said.

"Not yet."

"But…did you lie to me?"

"What lover isn't a liar, my love? Remember when you first sat down at that counter? If that couple had stayed a little longer, I might never have met you."

"You talked like you meant it. I mean, you flirted, then you ignored me, but of course I saw right through it."

"Oh you did, did you?" he said.

"Yes. I did," she said. "I could feel you wanting to say hello to me. You wanted company."

"Not by a fuck of a long shot. I didn't want company, I wanted you."

"You wanted the money to pretend you wanted me."

"The role started feeling real. I was falling for you." He got up, came to her chair, sat on her lap and kissed her. The café applauded. "Much obliged," he said, and went back to his seat, not at all embarrassed.

Remember when we first met, so long ago now, why just back at the middle of this week…when you colluded with my rat of a husband…?

A MAN WALKED into the diner carrying a large baby. "Hey, John, how are you today?" the waitress asked. Apparently-John sat down at a table, placing the large baby on a chair beside him. The baby turned its head towards Vivienne: it was not a baby; it was a man whose feet were curled under his body, his right arm looked fused to the curled feet.

A man about fifty came in, bushy eyebrows meeting in a *V* on the bridge of his nose, and a gnarled beard with dark brown, dark black, dark blue and green in it. He had on a little round cap, embroidered. He made a *HFF* sound like a hello with breath expelled only. The waitress brought him coffee. A regular.

A plain-looking man with a wide sad face came in. On second glance his face was not sad, it was surprised. The surprise looked permanent, just as the fused feet and hand of the man in the chair did. He sat down, the plain-faced man, in the booth back of Vivienne and Andy. Andy returned the paper to its broadsheet folded state. "So, where now?"

A pretty woman walked in, caught Vivienne's attention. She had eyelashes six or seven inches long, like little hairy dogs on each eye. A man came in with her, his head was on sideways. The waitress said hi. They sat down in the booth on the other side of Vivienne and Andy.

"You said you wanted to go to Lone Pine," Vivienne said. "We're in Olancha."

The waitress came over, "You two okay? Can I get you anything you need?"

"How far is it to Lone Pine from here?" Vivienne asked.

"Lone Pine, John, how far to Lone Pine?"

John looked over from his table. "You folks visiting? Where you from? Not from around here I'll wager."

"You just won your bet," Vivienne said. "Canada. We're Canadian."

"Canada," John said. "Nice place. Nice place, nice people, good luck, you're going to need it in this wind. You and your hubby there might want to stop the night somewhere, heard there was an oil truck blew up near Bishop. Where you two from in Canada?"

"Toronto," Vivienne said.

"Toronto. Nice place. I was in Vancouver once. In the army. Very nice people. Good luck to the two of you. Newlyweds?"

"Peggy Sue got married," she said.

"Buddy Holly," the man said. "A personal favourite of mine."

Vivienne went into the pocket of her pink jacket where there was a secret zip compartment. She took out a piece of newspaper, folded many times, black and white and yellowed. She unfolded it. Andy was curious.

"Honey," she said. "Remember the day we first met, when we were lying on the bed in the hotel room? I was telling you about the Quaker who self-immolated under the Secretary of Defense's window, during the war in Vietnam?" She read from the clipping: "'Baltimore Quaker with baby sets self afire, dies in war protest at Pentagon… Pacifist releases girl as flames engulf him in front of building.'" Vivienne looked up. She knew the next part by heart. "His daughter was a year old. Her name was Emily. In Vietnam a poet wrote an homage to her, 'Emily, My Child.' It became a well-known poem in Vietnam. They named a street in Hanoi after him. They issued a postage stamp to honour Norman Morrison. They called him *Mo Ri Xon.* His name is legend, he is a hero. My cousin Jeff in Chicago, he got hold of one of the Vietnamese stamps honouring Morrison, the FBI came to his house and seized it. It was illegal in the United States to own a stamp showing an American Quaker, because the Vietnamese issued the stamp. Okay. So, remember a couple years later, when protestors occupied the Pentagon in '67?"

"I wasn't born yet," Andy said.

Oh Jesus. Oh, okay. "Well, protestors were holding a sit-in in May of '67 at the Pentagon, you know, about the war, and they occupied the Pentagon for four days. But at the start, they kicked it off with a vigil for Morrison. So, he was still a name to know eighteen months after he lit himself on fire under McNamara's window."

Andy's eyes asked, Why are you telling me this? And she did not know.

Who knows? It was windy in the dry land, so she thought about fire.

There was a new three-year war, so she thought about a new baby. They were heading to one more hideout of the minor walk-on cameo Carlita Manson, so she thought about the major hero, Norman Morrison. Somewhere there was a forty-something woman named Emily, whose father sacrificed himself for the love of country. She put the clipping back in her jacket's inner compartment. That *Baltimore Sun* clipping, November 3rd, 1965.

Andy waved for the bill, doing that air-signing Vivienne remembered from the coffee counter in Vegas.

They drove out of Olancha on the 395, through Cartago, towards Lone Pine. The grey strip of highway stretched through the open soft low tumbles on the right, and the mountains rising and shrinking and etching deeper with more snow cover accompanied them on the left as they rode north. They passed a ghost gas station near Cartago, and found one alive near Lone Pine. Vivienne and Andy got out and stretched their legs in the chilly temps. The gas guy, as he filled the tank, said, "You folks heading up to Mount Whitney?" He pointed west and up. "The highest point in the lower forty-eight."

Vivienne said, "We're going to the Alabama Hills for our health." Andy took a pic of her saying this, with her droll smile, and her hand riffling the metal buttons growing in her hair.

"That's the idea," the gas man said. They drove on. Mount Whitney was up there amid its posse of grey jags of prominence against the winter blue.

They entered Lone Pine. They drove fast down Main Street, and hung a left at Whitney Portal Road, Vivienne saying, "A half-hour before I first met you, I was watching *High Sierra* in my hotel room; Bogart was on the lam from the law, speeding right here through Lone Pine, beating it up to Mount Whitney right there to make that fated escape."

"I was trying to escape you," Andy said.

"I was trying to escape you," Vivienne said.

"How're we doing?"

As they climbed higher, just like Bogie, they entered the Alabama Hills. "We're at the movies," she said. Barren conglomerates of rocks stood tall and pointed, clustered like evolutionary teeth. These pinnacles had entered the minds of moviegoers through the hundreds of movies made here, shaping our dreams of American cowboys. That archetype of the American West, which blew into the minds of moviegoers, that rock canyon DNA, those modern canyon lobes, had their origins here, in the Eastern Sierra just up from Lone Pine.

They hung a right at Movie Road, passing the ghost of *Yellow Sky*, which had been constructed as a ghost town for *Yellow Sky*; passing the Lone Ranger Canyon, just in from Gene Autry Rock and just shy of *The Charge of the Light Brigade* a little bit south of *Gunga Din* bridge, Stuntman Canyon and *High Sierra*. Vivienne and Andy got out of the car at *Rawhide*. "I know these rocks better than my cousins," Vivienne said. "Look. Here's where the Rawhide Station stage pulled up. Here's where Jack Elam was going to shoot the baby girl." Andy took a picture of her with her arms wide open.

"Let's go up Movie Road to Bogart Curve," she said. The movie was over, but the movie never stopped showing Bogart climbing the rock face and falling.

31

FALLOUT ALICE

ON BOGART CURVE, a large cat with a brown bowler hat stood alone by the pinnacles. She had big mascaraed lashes, two little red dots on her cheeks and she wore long ginger robes. She was waving to Andy and Vivienne.

They got out of the car.

The cat waved them closer. From behind one of the classic western rocks an item dollied forth: an orange toadstool with a green-coloured baby reclining on it, smoking a hookah. "I like to lie on the Big Lie," the green baby said. "How about you?"

On closer examination, the baby looked more like a caterpillar. The legs did not exist. It had multiple shortened hands, stubs. Its face was lined, leathery. Its eyes were rheumy. "The plutonium?" the caterpillar said. "Dude, nothing but Pluto with some knee 'em." He, she, it pressed a button, and out of the orange toadstool popped four yellow sunflowers in plastic, each with a written message. The first sunflower said Safe. The second sunflower said Nuclear. The third read Progress, the *o* made into a smiley face. The fourth read Power. The sunflowers sang in unison, "Nuclear Power, Our Safe Progress."

Across the Alabama Hills, a white rabbit came hippy-hopping, decked out in a blue naval uniform. He carried an item on a chain, which Andy and Vivienne first thought, using the classic *Alice in Wonderland* story, was the White Rabbit's pocket watch, his guide to running late.

But in Andy's telephoto, it showed itself to be a dosimeter, smaller than normal, used to measure radiation. "I declare, the future is with us, the future has arrived," the Naval Rabbit said, coming to them. "I was there when they dropped the bomb on Nagasaki. I am a double survivor. I saw Hiroshima, I saw Nagasaki. What man could do! We were late! We better get moving, otherwise the rest of the world would own progress, and we would be left behind. There is a saying promoted in Japan: 'Nuclear energy: a correct understanding brings a prosperous lifestyle!' We face the sea; many plants face the sea. We have another saying, 'You must never speak of the harbour waves!' If the schoolchildren learn not to say the words, you would be surprised how little they will worry.

"Once upon a time, I heard my ancestors speak of Cat Dancing, crazy cat suicides into the sea, Minimata disease; Mr. Eugene Smith who came and took pictures of the new babies, the old people crazy from mercury. That was a very bad idea. We removed the pictures. No need to worry young girls with tales of sick fish. Now our Alice will take you at your earliest convenience to a scale model of Unit One at our Shika nuclear plant, located on the Sea of Japan. Alice was trained at the Shika publicity building. She will give you a pill, and you can join her in touring the scale model."

"I think they're making the big movie," Andy said to Vivienne. This was, after all, a long-time movie location. But if it was a movie, where was the director? Where was the camera? If a bomb falls in the desert, did it happen if they hide the pictures? Vivienne's lungs were breathing into a photo. Her arms were feeling the phantom organ her camera had been at the end of her fingers, its delicate shutter.

She looked at Andy, the new recruit to camerawork. The model had fallen in love with the camera. Like the actor who begins to direct, Andy seemed a natural. He was close up to the rabbit, asking, "Is this some kind of Western-in-Wonderland going on here? I bet you're the Nuclear White Rabbit. Kind of kooky. The sidekick, right?"

"We saw the power," the Rabbit said. "We could be a player on the big stage. No more Emperors! Cast off the past! Nuclear power is clean and efficient."

"So," said Andy, "if you think negative thoughts, bad things will come your way? That the idea?"

Alice in her pinafore came over, she tipped her brown bowler hat, and said, "All is well." She held out her school-style pinafore at the edges, as if to curtsy with her clothes.

The green caterpillar called from his toadstool, "Anybody got a doobie for the Dude? I hear there's some fierce Purple Haze coming out of Bogotá." He seemed content, however, to put his hookah in his mouth, and to lie back, and let the bubbles roll. "Tell them, sweet Alice."

"Wow!" Alice said. "Absolute Safety! We do not speak of earthquakes or tsunamis. If the nuclear plant goes rogue, we have the water trucks standing by; no worries. Situation aces! The police are ready to water bomb the rioting leakage."

"You know," said Andy. "If you put me in charge, I'd get those robots I've been reading about to do all the work. You get a plutonium spill, what's it to a robot?"

Andy shot a pic of the giant White Rabbit, in his waistcoat, looking at his pocket watch, saying, "Poor Mooty. We thought Mooty the Robot was the way. We had to admit our own mistake. Mooty went moot." He walked over to the caterpillar, who handed the White Rabbit the joint. He took a toke and handed it to Alice, who sucked in the marijuana. "Ah, we had to lay off Mooty," the rabbit said. "The sight of a robot at a nuclear plant could make the people think an accident could happen. Since no accident will ever happen, why build robots? Why hire those Mootys? We put Mooty on the dole and we built exhibits and hired guides to explain to the people what the zero risk of nuclear means. We hired adorable Alice."

Vivienne's eye caught smoke coming up from a far dusty patch.

"You see," the White Rabbit continued, "buying insurance for the nuclear plants encourages the growth of fear. We prefer to grow an economy, right, Alice?"

"I am proud to be a plutonium princess," Alice said.

The White Rabbit handed Vivienne the joint. She inhaled. "Hey, Alice, baby," the Caterpillar called from his toadstool. "Need another toke?"

Alice came to Vivienne and said, "After Chernobyl, we began our education progress. You will find no Chernobyl in our textbooks now. Only positive thinking. If children hear the sad tales of the misfortunes of others, it makes them want misfortunes of their own."

"Yeah, that pretty much sums up my days in school," Andy said. "I had to learn about nuclear fallout from this pretty lady, right here." He let the camera fall by the strap to his chest. He put his arm around Vivienne. "She was in a bomb blast, when was it, Vivi?"

"I can't remember," Vivienne said. "A few days ago, I think."

"It is safe for the fertile women," Alice said.

"I think it's probably real safe for the fertile mannequins," said Andy.

Vivienne felt altitude ill. Her hometown genes from TO on Lake Ontario were set at around three hundred feet above sea level. The Alabama Hills were about four thousand feet above sea level. She had exchanged low for high, wet for dry, married for separation, camerawork for eyes burning in the vivid pictures not taken.

The White Rabbit said, "We do not speak of anti, we speak of *for*. We do not look back, we look *forward*."

"I'm all for that," Andy said, kissing Vivienne's cheek. She wandered off, using her eyes without a camera. She scanned the Eastern Sierra land. How many giant rabbits of different dimensionality and breed had the nine hundred nuclear explosions in the Western States created? What gene jive happened? Were any of the grand mountains left unaffected? Were any of them pure rock anymore? Did rock climbers endanger their health by breathing in the plutonium and the dead hand radiation dust drifting off them, for decades? Did the atomic age leave even basin and range as dangerous dust-emitting nature?

Under the sight of Mount Whitney, the highest point in the contiguous United States at 14,495 feet, it was only eighty miles to Badwater, the lowest point at two hundred eighty-three feet below sea level, back down in the heart of Death Valley. Charles Manson had had his shack back near Badwater, and Manson had run right here to the Alabama Hills, where he was finally captured.

The White Rabbit smiled with cheesy buckteeth at the camera. "My dear boy, if you hold a full emergency measure test, the people will become alarmed. It is best to relegate emergency measures to the back office. That way, you do not show the public any fear. You spare the public the unnecessary hysteria of seeing their leaders in a panic."

"You mean," Andy said, speaking from behind the camera, "as the Zen sensei of FEMA might say, 'When in doubt, do nothing.'"

"Exactly!" the White Rabbit said.

The moon face and the sun face of Mount Whitney rose and fell in copper and granite. The rock pinnacles of the Alabama Hills began to meld, in the early part of dusk.

Invisible miscreant rain kept falling, falling. Who knew that the muscles of fish, the glands of humans and the rocks of the planet were everlasting collateral now? Who knew that movie set rocks emitted zombie poison? Who knew that the beloved hoof dust of Westerns was now forensic bad fortune? Who knew a nation of empire could be an ecological disrupter of pharaonic proportions, and not even know it? The planet knew it. We had disturbed the Earth. We played with hot stuff, the earth got hot, the passengers flying overhead in a plane looked down on the heated Earth, they flew through the disturbed air. And we say to ourselves, If the earth is so overpopulated, why do I stand here, so alone? We are glandular magnets to the iodine as we walk through Earth's stuff.

The green caterpillar crawled out from the cowboy rocks. He tried to straighten his off-kilter middy blouse and smoothed his Black Watch kilt, leaning forward to Vivienne, "You got any dirt from *The Conqueror*?" Vivienne ached to take the caterpillar's picture. Her life was a habit she was finding hard to break.

The green caterpillar took off the kilt and put it around his shoulders over the middy blouse, a nonchalant négligé cape. He sucked on a desperate end of a roach.

"I had a guy down here once on one of the tours, claimed he had the original Howard Hughes suitcase with that dirt from *The Conqueror*. I heard that Howard Hughes shipped sixty tons of the radioactive dirt out of the location of *The Conqueror*, west to Hollywood, to have the same look back on set. The movie workers on location in Utah got cancer, and the guys back in Hollywood got to breathe in the authentic nuclear ground dirt. A guy came to work, a gaffer or a dolly grip, and he went home with embryonic cancer. Who knew? What did Howard Hughes know? What did anybody know? All on the down low I pass along the rumours. I don't want the suits coming in here to Aliceville to mess with the larva, you know what I'm talking about?"

"The story goes that everybody who worked on *The Conquerer* got cancer," Andy said.

"Handsome," the caterpillar said to him. "Let us not exaggerate. Not *everybody*. Just like I don't know like maybe totally massively, you know, like 50 or 85 per cent."

The White Rabbit put his paws together in a steeple. "Dick Powell, the director, got cancer. John Wayne got cancer. Susan Hayward got cancer."

Andy was holding Vivienne's camera she had given away to him. His back looked straighter to her, his feeling towards the camera something like the soldier-nursing he gave her back in the high piney air of Panamint Springs in room 15 of the small oasis hotel. He held the camera in one hand, the way pros do, cradling it like a preemie baby. "They shot *The Conqueror* near St. George, Utah, right near the Nevada border. They were shooting the movie at the same time they were setting off one of the biggest nuclear tests in history."

"Series," the White Rabbit said. "Sir. No, sir. It was a series. A miniseries of tests."

"The Rabbit is right," Vivienne said. She swallowed a blockage. "The Nevada Test Site. Sixty miles from Vegas. The test, yes, *series* was called Upshot-Knothole. They did eleven nuclear tests, set off eleven bombs between March and June of 1953. Each one of the bombs was the equivalent of Hiroshima or more. Some of them were three times as powerful as Hiroshima. John Wayne and Susan Hayward, Pedro Armendáriz, Agnes Moorehead. They say that of two hundred twenty people who worked on the film, ninety-one got cancer, forty-six died of it. The experts said they had three times the usual percentage of cancer. Actors died for their art, the government killed John Wayne. America killed America's symbol."

Mount Whitney, snow topped in the glints of pre-sunset, shone and looked down.

"You ever see *The Shootist*?" the White Rabbit asked.

"Love it," Vivienne said. "Love Lauren Bacall."

"John Wayne was dying of cancer in that movie."

"I know, he put up at Lauren Bacall's boarding house. He dressed all fine in his Sunday best, in the morning he went out to kill himself. Great character."

"The character was dying of cancer," the White Rabbit said, "and the actor playing the character was dying of cancer. Left wing, right wing, cancer is the ultimate agnostic. You can see John Wayne dying in *The Shootist*. Beautiful movie."

"I love Richard Boone. I would never kick that man's voice out of my bed," Vivienne said. "He wore those turquoise gloves. It takes a real gunslinger to wear turquoise leather. He wore turquoise leather and spoke Spanish without subtitles."

"I would call them more of a teal," the caterpillar chimed in.

"All right, not kill himself," the White Rabbit said. "Get into a saloon shootout, suicide by Richard Boone. I liked his name: John Books. Books in his cover finery."

"I think you are a poet," the caterpillar said, sucking hard on his rolled weed. "You ever write for Sonny and Chernobyl?"

Alice came close to Vivienne. She whispered, "Wonderland is not well. Wonderlanders were downwind." She lifted her pinafore skirt. Below her waist was a giant balloon-sized growth. "I must go back underground, to safety. May I conduct you to the sanctuary?"

32

LASCAUX IN CALIFORNIA

ALICE LED THEM to an area of soft cottonwood and low willow, like new baby hair on an open space. Alice tapped her foot three times. The ground opened: a small hatch of earth rose, a cottonwood door. "Come down to the secret," Alice said. "No worries, it is non-atmospheric."

Vivienne and Andy stepped into the hole and fell down to the bottom, where they were in a long narrow tunnel. Alice fell down beside them, gathering her pinafore skirt.

"We don't have long," Alice said. "Welcome to the sanctuary. Try not to breathe too much. Maybe fifteen minutes. They say you can't come down here. They say it does not exist. This is your lucky day." The hatch above closed. They were in darkness. "Close your eyes," Alice said.

"Ma'am, it's totally dark already," Andy said.

"No it isn't," Vivienne said. "Alice is right. Your eye doesn't know the real dark. You have to sit in the dark to know how much light there really is." They closed their eyes and held hands, each of them with one hand in Alice's hands.

"Okey-dokey," Alice said. "Open your eyes. Walk with me down the tunnel." Alice had a small flashlight. She shone it on the rock wall: horses. Beautiful horses in red and black outlines. A small foal, it had to be, nuzzling a larger mare. "They brought the horses, when the tunnel space was larger, they took a certain number of wild horses, to save them from the radioactive air. That foal, who is no longer with us, was born down here. A blind albino. Too bad his mother did not escape the fallout."

"I was once at Lascaux," Vivienne said. "The real Lascaux. These look like ancient horses."

"Horses are ancient," Alice said.

"Then they raced in the Westerns in all that radioactive hoof dust," Vivienne said.

"Safety first," Alice said. "Chin up. Use your time in the gallery." It was the close-up tenderness that Vivienne could feel coming off the rock walls to her. The materials had dictated their own purpose. The small foal had been drawn with its tiny belly on the curve of a rock that looked like a belly. The walls had sculpted in organic evolution the shape of the art to come, once the artists went underground.

"They were working down here while they made *Bad Day at Black Rock* up above," Alice said. "The new artists of the nuclear age. There is a door you must not go in, far in the tunnel. That is where the Deserter Community is. When they left the war they came to the sanctuary. I must not tell you; I have been told they will find me; look, while we have time."

Vivienne was two inches from a horse's eye. She could see how the eye, like the foal belly, had been in the rock, and the artist drew the eye outline in red, and the horse around it. Was it possible that when the bomb tests went underground, and the bomb testers said "No worries," because there was no longer fallout in the atmosphere, that there was a whole natural world living under the Earth's surface – the geology kin of the old marine seas, and still kin of the marine seas – which was being bomb-tested back to caves?

Andy was a foot onward. He was stroking a red cow and black bull. "No touching," Alice said.

"I couldn't help myself," Andy said.

"Yes," Alice said. "The desire to touch them is overwhelming. We must be intimate, and leave. If we visit one half hour, we take three hours off the cave paintings' lives. Our carbon dioxide degrades their existence."

Alice in the sanctuary had lost the cartoon voice. Alice shone her flashlight closer to the drawings of horses, cows, sheep, dogs, cradles with baby faces. There were creatures with vertical antlers, smudged snouts. Their heads were bowed, they walked in concert. The three-dimensional rock presented the chance for invention on the veined ochre undulations. A horse-looking creature with a deer nose and toes for feet moved on the undulating rock face. It looked like the origin of the horse species before they had hooves. Veins, eyes, mineral ruts, tsunamis. Sanctuary in a quarry.

On the other side of the cave was a large grey blotch on the ochre: the thing with smoke hair. A sketched prayer, a form of salvation, etches as a way to make silent cave music. The original storyboards of the cave. Vivienne ran her hand over a space where there were no drawings. She felt it curve under her own scratched up hand. Here and there, a heart was drawn with a long cord, here and there a stick or device had scratched over the animal faces.

When science goes on a manic jag, and elected officials become fall-out spinners, the people will go to their underground Sistine Chapels, the humble rock tunnel locals, their souls like sheep dogs herding them to safety, to art, to oasis. The oasis may not have palm trees, or water, or be a shimmering mirage. It might be Lascaux-in-the-Desert.

If you could recoup Earth now, would you do it?

Marty Hirsch could not do it. He was monogamous with the bottle. Vivienne took a sharp stone at her foot and scratched on the tunnel wall: MARTY. Let the ages figure that one.

Her shoulders felt right. She held onto the stone. She pulled it across the rock: a long face, crazy lines for hair, crossed out eyes, caterpillar body. She looked down at her shoes. A dark rock. She picked it up and wrote LIE, then CROWD, then BONE. Alice did not stop her.

Vivienne ran her hands along the rock tunnel. She thought, What would it be like to work with stone, as a material?

Alice turned off her flashlight. "Close your eyes again," she said. Vivienne reached out for Andy's hand. She could hear his exhalations. "Open your eyes," Alice said.

The Cheshire Cat in ginger robes appeared, holding a stoneware jug with the word MILK in blue paint on it. The Cheshire Cat shone a flashlight on the milk jug. Alice sat on the floor of the cave. The Cheshire Cat said, "We warned you: you must never say the word *tsunami*." The Cheshire Cat poured milk on Alice. The milk was clear. The Cheshire Cat's pitcher contained gasoline. The Cheshire Cat walked down the cave tunnel into the darkness.

Alice went under her skirt and took out a long wooden match. She struck it on the cave wall and lit the clear accelerant. Alice in Wonderland self-immolated, hidden underground at the Alabama Hills on December 31, 2006. The tunnel filled with smoke. When the Buddhist monks in Vietnam burned themselves alive to protest the war, they did it in the understanding that this was heart privacy forced in pain to make a burning scandal in public. Alice, in the new age of publicizing every nano of emotion, had made the act of heartbroken suicide private again, in the cave of the mountain sanctuary. Here, with an audience of Andy, a war veteran, and Vivienne, a war photographer, Alice burned to char. Alice was gone. We radiate our tribulations out in our calls to exalted nowheres, yet the world radiates its harm back to us, in turn, by way of begifting us its mangled grace.

Andy knelt down and, in available flashlight light, took close-ups of Alice. They will tell other versions, and even if there are photographs, they will say it did not happen. Alice's hands were like mitts of clotted ash. Her face was made of embers. Alice promoted safety. Alice was never safe.

Vivienne took some of the ashes from Alice's eyes; she smeared them in their charcoal endeavour on the wall of the ochre cave: ALICE WAS HERE. Then Vivienne took a stone and ran it through that, crossing it out in a whitened line.

The White Rabbit stuck his head into the tunnel. "Hurry, you're late. Important. Get up here."

The White Rabbit hopped down with a long hose. He sprayed water on Alice. "Best leave now," he said. "No problem. She was not pregnant. Keep worries under your hat."

Vivienne and Andy climbed up the delicate rope ladder at the hatch. They were back in the Western movies location, the pinnacles in place, mute protagonists. The hatch closed. The entry to the tunnel was back in camouflage as part of the endless soft rock land at elevation, under the Alabama Hills pinnacles. Perhaps a jet nomad at a window seat on a plane looked down and saw two dots moving across protuberances.

Andy and Vivienne wandered to a movie set rock area. They sat down in a narrow space. Andy unzipped Vivienne's pink leather jacket. He unbuttoned her python vest. He put his hand on her left breast. She put her hand on his crotch. He unzipped his gold jacket, inched it off, covered her shoulders. He had on a black crewneck sweater. She lay down on his lap. "I remember how we watched *The Misfits*, the day I met you," he said, whispering in her ear. "You could be Monty, resting in Marilyn's lap."

"I think I've spent the better part of my life travelling through Montgomery Clift," she said. She fished down in a pink jacket pocket, pulled out the white T-shirt. She lay back with the T-shirt on her face. Andy took a picture of Vivienne: who is this woman? Is this a woman? A human figure with a white garment covering her features, reclining in a Western passage with a gold jacket over a pink jacket over a scrap of reptile skin. Wild sagebrush hair.

IN THE HILLS of the Eastern Sierra of the place they call California, as the crow flies nine miles over 395, there once was a concentration camp, not too far from where they filmed the epic Western films. And they called the camp by the name Manzanar, in homage to the apples that once had grown so flourishingly there. Where white and pink apple blossoms sent pretty clouds falling in the juicy spring. And when World War Two had begun, and when the Japanese bombed Pearl Harbor in old Hawaii, and the federal government of those United States made the wounding decision that they must *concentrate* its Japanese Americans, it scouted concentration locations. And Los Angeles, who had become the landlord of the apple orchards it devastated by siphoning off their water, offered them up for lease, becoming the landlord of Manzanar, as the story has come down to us, in legend. Just a hop north of *Hopalong Cassidy* and Rawhide Station.

In March 1942, population began arriving. At its peak, Manzanar had ten thousand people. Ten years later, Manzanar was a ghost spot with old watchtowers, old barbed wire, and the gardens that the camp citizens had created were also over.

Water, orchard, greed, no water, desolation, real estate, concentration camp, museum.

There is a photo by Dorothea Lange, which she took in 1942. The photograph is of a young man called Eddie, president of his high school senior class in sunny California. Eddie, all ready in his thick-cuffed rolled-up denim jeans, his coolly crushed fedora, his thin crewneck sweater, his sartorial sport jacket; Eddie sitting on his luggage, waiting for the train, at Los Angeles Union Station. But wait, Eddie is waiting for the train in May of 1942. Is school finished? It doesn't matter. Eddie is waiting to be taken to a concentration camp. All-American Eddie is Japanese, and they are taking the class president away. They are taking all-American Eddie to Manzanar.

There is a photo by Ansel Adams, which the ranger at Scotty's Castle showed Vivienne: *Mount Williamson, Sierra Nevada, from Manzanar, California, 1944.* Sly, subversive, in black and white, taken from a concentration camp watchtower, it shows a mountain peak almost as high as Mount Whitney below brilliant white clouds shafting sunlight down. Most of the photograph is of rocks on low ground. The long view of history, the rocks remained.

If Ansel Adams had been Japanese, if Dorothea Lange had been Japanese, in 1942, and 1944, they would have been arrested – for possession of a camera. The United States of America made it illegal for anyone of Japanese origin, in the United States, to possess a camera. They could legally come into your home and arrest you if they discovered your act of treason, having a Kodak Brownie in your dresser.

When the state is a berserker, what happens to the citizenry?

BY THE TIME it was legal to own a camera again for those released from the American concentration camps, the nuclear age was in full swing. The winds, ordered in plans to blow west into what were called, officially, low-use populations, decided to blow east as far as the high-use Midwestern and Eastern cities. Like Rochester, New York, home of Eastman Kodak Company. When atomic test Simon went off in late April 1955, the winds carried the radioactive rain and dust into the forming muscles and brains of newly born and elementary school–aged boomers and also into the Kodak film. Shutterbugs and pros noticed their film was all fogged. Yes, said Kodak, it's from the bombs. So Kodak sent out regular updates to film aficionados, letting them know where they could buy unfogged unradiated camera film.

If it fogged the film, what did it do to the fetuses?

BABY, COME HOME to me, we say to the planet. The sky is filled with *vanitas*; the sky is filled with our own vainglory.

Besotted with the thrill of the atom, married to the bomb, off on toots of reckless environmental abandon, intoxicated by the nuclear spree feeling, supersizing vain hallucinations, the paranoia of the state bloomed like helter-skelter impulse control on a cocaine-fueled spring break that never ended. In between bombs tests, the atomic DT's set in, and again came the blackouts that lit up the skies with iodine makings, with cesium drift. The deciders all tanked blotto jagged ruination upon us, then shaking, went stinko again and high; slow-motion speed bums made mock of elegant curiosity that brings us to science. The delicate insolence of the desert climate sat lonely. Scorned as marginal, the desert was our lonely heart in the middle of drought land. Lonely Avenue was where a ewe, born with its heart outside its body, wandered, hairless.

Sweet Van Gogh pear blossom cloud trees rise again. Dust the turquoise Aprils with bee pollen and hive buzzing. Rocks erode in granite, mica, silica, pinks. The modest fence of stakes is not done yet in the golden dusk, and our final sundowning has not hit us yet, we are alert to the powder the rock the shine, in words, in pictures. Tell it.

33

FIVE DAYS

"'DESERT – DESERT, DESERT. And a cold wind is blowing and the sky is grey with furious clouds. I feel like an atom off in space between the moon and Spica!!'" Vivienne Toronto said to Andy San Diego, quoting Ansel Adams who wrote that in a letter in 1936 while he was travelling in New Mexico, a man in his thirties, long in thrall to the look of the Southwest, its radiance. And Ansel Adams made the trees and the rocklands emblematic in his photographs, and gave us a gift even he, Ansel Adams, did not know he was giving – how could he? He showed us what the sky of the Southwest looked like, what the rocks and shields and forests and badlands and tablelands and sierras and, yes, Death Valley looked like and how light loved it, before that light was radioactive. He had been born at just the right time, 1902, to be a tiny child in a 1906 earthquake, and to go forth with his musical imagery, his note perfect sightings, to show us the land before the air drifted into all things with its cesium: the paint of paintings, the skin of humans, the photographic paper you print on. The grapes, the wine you drink. Canvas and epidermis. Ancient redwood forest; basin and range; the species origin in its new atomic lesions. And that is why he is the essence of the human in photographs: he gave us the gift of longing and missing the land itself before we knew it was such a blessing; he made us fall in love with the planet's wild body. Here it is, it will never come again. We will never come again to see it.

Henri Matisse painted a swaddled pineapple in 1940 while the Second World War warred on in his country; Ansel Adams, in 1944, just down the road from a California concentration camp, went out at dawn in Lone Pine, and caught the majesty of the Eastern Sierra with fierce bright light coating the winter peaks, and below, hardly discernable, the bare-bright stick trees so tiny against the sierra, and tinier yet, a small horse grazing. Winter dawn alone when conflict poisons all things – this can save you.

The escarpments at the end of day gave that last glint before dying. Andy and Vivienne rode across Horseshoe Meadows Road past the ancient site of the *Gunga Din* temple. They turned left, nodding to *Along the Great Divide* on the right, and almost in darkness past *Tremors,* and down Tuttle Creek Road to meet the Whitney Portal Road. A few scattered lights pulsed down below in the town of Lone Pine. The temperature was dropping. The cold rocky vacancy was moments from darkness. They drove down to the Mt. Whitney Restaurant at the juncture with Main Street. They had bowls of beef barley soup, Vivienne Toronto her usual Cobb salad and Andy San Diego his usual turkey club. They had been together a few times only. They had been apart more. They had entered each other's heads and organs; they had crawled under each other's skin. The time apart etched the time together, like photographs you have never taken but which remain present, the ghosts that etch your dreams when the days get dark and the cold sets in, and you try and get back to that feeling of the photo not taken. The cave scratch withheld. One of them had shot with intent to kill a man, but they had not stayed to check if he was still breathing. She was married, but not to him. He had been married, but his wife died in that night crash. He was a soldier, maybe absent without leave. They ate their food, and listened in on two men sitting at a table by the window, looking out on dark and empty Main Street.

One had long grey-blond hair and a beard, the other had close-cropped medium brown hair. The beard spoke extra slowly about how he couldn't remember what used to be there in the store across the street from way back when they were growing up. Did the other one know? The short brown-haired one put his arm around the long-haired beard and helped him with his soup. They both looked about fifty. The beard was saying he thought there had been a flower shop there. Short brown hair said, "No, Pauly, that was the old art gallery."

A quiet night on Main Street, early dark on New Year's Eve. Andy looked at Vivienne with such desire, throughout the nosh. He did not seem to understand that he had a skin over his heart.

They paid the bill for the food in the town restaurant and rode out into darkness, which used to be dark waters. When worlds swam and rocks protruded into water and soft things waved their antennae and glitter fish swam on by.

Andy steered through the darkness, looking straight ahead. Night was the pharaoh of winter. Night owned December, night owned January. They were unguided explorers on the road without corners, with only a light beaming ahead from their voyaging wagon to guide them through the new mysteries. The clock on the dash was an ornament, a thing with scratches or dials or Mayan numericals. Time had been infinite and time was infinite and it was a lie to say it had been between Christmas and New Year's, for that made their connection terrestrial, and the feeling they had between them was that it was extraterrestrial, not of this Earth. They were aliens to each other, and beloved. They might have come down from dawn clouds, or they might have risen with magma cools from the ocean. They did not know if the blowing dust was moonlight off the reflected fallen stars in an egress of birds and Eden, or the residual evidence of chemicals at the water acreage of the moonlit crime scene, or a kind of thickness of your heart expanding in a loneliness with someone else in a car at night alone on a backcountry highway, with the night cadavers above your only light, your only lumen.

Vivienne looked at Andy, radiant at the wheel. He was humming an old blues tune, something all melded in shotgun events, public pain, breathing acoustics dragged by rope behind the devil's pickup, through the dank scenes of men in pinewoods and the hope for retribution from the pine coffins. The camera was the third passenger, sitting between them. Andy drove with his left hand, picked up the camera with his right hand and shot a shot of Vivienne looking at him. She was framed by the window and the flying dark.

She felt the dark joy of looking.

Night rode towards them, pulling them forward.

Vivienne Toronto and Andy San Diego drove in solitary grandeur through the Eastern Sierra night crossing back into Death Valley. They had never imagined it would be so regal, this crossing. Even Charon arrived in brine, taking your coin across that thin black line.

They passed along the northern edge of Owens Lake. Only a small shack with a small gold pin of light shone, and night and the lake passed on by, seamless. Just one more night in the great capsule through the velveteen.

They travelled for a long lie of dark until they rose in elevation three more times, and travelled back down to the level of the sea.

They kept moving east from the night called California into the night called Nevada, and under a waxing gibbous moon, Andy stopped at the Death Valley Sand Dunes.

Andy had a plan. He took Vivienne in by foot to a high dune. He set the camera up on a dune seam. The wind was merciful, and stayed low for them. "Vivienne Pink, will you marry me?" he asked. "Baby Pink, would you do me the honour of becoming my wife?"

"Yes," she said. Though she was already married.

The camera on a timer under the moon between new and full, clicked as Andy bent on a dune, and Vivienne took his hands, *yes*.

She had gone rogue in her heart, and it felt good. Andy was the cure for peace. He pleasured her by his existence. This could last a long time, especially if you'd lived two-thirds of it already. The past was frozen, the future ephemeral. Andy was pure now. Vivienne felt elevated, just to see his face, in available dash light. They came onto the big night highway, and still there were no lights on the highway and there were no signs at all. It was a nowhere land, paved in many grey lanes. They came to a cliff looking down into yet another high mountain valley. And there, twinkling in its red gas streams, was the hidden city. Area 24. They drove down into the metropolis with dry desert all around and high planes mixing with ancient starlight. They came low into the bright lights, gold with the red, blueshifting like heart-shaped Doppler effects all down Las Vegas Boulevard. They had known each other five days.

34

BIGHORN

JOHNNY COMA RETRACED the path he had taken west as part of a threesome. Now he was one.

There was a sweet MGB roadster, in ebony green, which had been sitting down the slope at the Panamint Springs gas station all day and into the morning. Hey, dibs. Johnny came down to examine it. The keys were in the ignition. Hey, double-dibs. Johnny Coma in his sweet two-seater all shiny took off at a nice curve-hugging speed back east on the 190.

He drove in a blind fugue. He was racing the sunset.

He left the higher green and gained warmth, dropping down to the salt playa as it shimmered in his rear-view mirror. Vivienne had worn coyote skin there.

Johnny climbed to Towne Peak – the sparkling black-green car close to his body, nice handling – and down at sea level Stovepipe Wells appeared, glints of roof in the sunshine. He stopped at the general store, a ghost in his own life. A day or so ago, he had walked over a couple times a day to the store, the way you do, making a base of a remote location, making a little nest of a couple wayfarer's buildings. A little stage set.

Now he was passing through, with no roots or room. He was the anonymous man who used to be a two-day local. He got gas and Clif bars, hot coffee and cold water.

He drank water passing the Death Valley Sand Dunes, where he and

Vivienne had climbed tall towers of sand. She was his North Star. What do you do when your North Star is gone from your eyes?

He ate the cold and the hot, driving past the masses of rusty green arrowweed of the Devil's Cornfield. He'd come past here with Vivienne and Val, and Danny, on the day they turned left to Scotty's and Ubehebe Crater and dumped his brother out of their lives.

Johnny took the opposite turn this time, curving with the 190 down into the land below the sea. The sea was salt and he sailed with elbow room for giants in his tiny ebony green skin past the road into Salt Creek where the fingerling-sized prehistoric fish, the pupfish, here for twenty thousand years, still swam in their salty pockets. A vehicle in the distance threw up a dust cloud. There must be a road there. Down past Harmony Borax Works on his right, whose name seemed to Johnny like lovely miners' found poetry. Up on his left, set in the purple mountains, was the Furnace Creek Inn, all Spanish pale yellow stucco and red roof tiles. Johnny kept going, aiming to circle back for a drink at the inn.

He decided to take a look at Artist's Palette, a favourite spot of Vivienne's. He drove up Artist's Drive, a one-way road, one car wide. He drove through the powdery alluvial fans of the Black Mountains.

He walked into the washes of this most beautiful of Death Valley sites, Artist's Palette, variously Artists Palette and Artists' Palette on road signs, where the shades and hues had been a palette formed long before cave art beetle red or charcoal black. This was the palette of seven million years ago, this was the palette of fourteen million years ago, this was the palette that had sourced and survived all things. Red from iron oxide, the manganese purple, the pale white-pink ash, the mica green.

Johnny walked out of the wash to the parking. A biker had a radio on: ETA terrorists had broken their truce, bombing the Madrid airport last night. The biker asked Johnny to take his picture with his phone, so he took one of Johnny.

He drove back up to the Furnace Creek Inn, the luxe digs on the hill, built in the Spanish style, in the first big tourist boom to Death Valley, in 1927. He ordered afternoon tea and ate homemade scones, mini pizzas and smoked salmon, and sipped Earl Grey tea, brought in a proper pot, with a pot of extra hot water on the side. He and Vivienne had loved this spot, had eaten those things. The sun cut out early behind those mountains. He realized he wanted to be inside the scene he was watching from the window.

He was out the inn door and down to the MGB; he zoomed down the road to Badwater, just as the bright blue sky was beginning a thick purpling. Badwater was a couple hundred feet below sea level; the thick salt crust saturated the air as the blue lowered down in a curve. The salt playa was as enormous as a salt planet. Wet indigo seeped into the dark purple sky and into the indigo Johnny Coma walked. The word *beautiful* returned to him. And then he saw the creature: it was a ram. A ram with its legs stuck in the salt.

Johnny saw the rump of the ram, shining white to match the ram's white muzzle, as the air glinted a last light but only slightly. Johnny already had his Moleskine sketchbook in his hand, sketching the ram, not ten feet away. The ram stood in its characteristic frozen position. This was a desert bighorn sheep, come down from the rocky cliffs and escape paths away from predators and bothersome beings. The ram had come down to the source of water. It was deep in the absence of it. Johnny had seen the creature in books and paintings, but never so close in person. Johnny sketched the ram, making arrows to the outline for its colour, a pale chocolate, almost a chocolate-grey, as if arisen from the more dusty outgrowths of the desert. *Majestic* was a true word for the bighorn. Its horns looked like two majestic dominating curved bone parentheses. Its eyes had brains, Johnny could see that, even in the gloaming. Each horn was massive and turned back in a curve coming out the bighorn's skull. This was a cliff dweller, and they said that it had bodily susceptibilities similar to human susceptibilities, that the bighorn sheep is a thing we should know, a creature we should save, because it is a horned litmus test for the state of our human environment.

The sky inked Johnny, the salt basin, the ram. How little he had known this intimate planet. Winter lowered its cold skin. It was December 31st.

How little he had known the wild ones. The horned ones, wearing trumpets on their heads, shofars we could blow to sound our regret and our joy, on the Jewish New Year. How little he had known his Vivienne. She had spoken to him, but he was too busy with words to hear her.

Johnny inched out on the salt, which cracked under his feet as he walked. The salt playa had the ram's tracks in it. Johnny sketched the tracks in his notebook. The classic track of the bighorn sheep: the side parts straight, three and half inches by two and half inches, the footprint looking like a double teardrop. In the buff and grey of the original palette times, the old Pleistocene times, these Russian bighorn sheep had walked over the Bering Strait land bridge from Siberia, they had been in the country for at least 350,000 years. Johnny closed his notebook and just looked. The ram stood alone, an isolate in the vast salt fjord, its feet sunk in salt.

The ram must have set out when the mountains were pale yellow in earlier hours of the day, and come down from the mountains to walk uncommonly in search of the water places, and now the granite night had returned. He was a vision of glorious pelt in ruin; atonement was in the air for all things in nature, and man had reckoning with the beasts. Lightning struck Johnny's heart for the things he had done to the beasts and how he did not atone, and how content he had been to be apart and how he had so rarely seen the beasts. And the desert was the first surveillance. The desert watched Adam and Eve, the desert watched Abram and Abraham, the desert watched Isaac be born to a man one hundred years old, the desert saw it all. Humans left far too many traces. Johnny was at Badwater, the lowest place in the United States of America. He looked up to the far snow peak of Mount Whitney, the highest spot. The ram stepped out of the gloaming salt. The ram came close to Johnny with its shofar horn. This ram might be the ram of the Book of Leviticus.

But the goat, on which the lot fell to be the scapegoat, shall be presente alive before the LORD, to make an atonement with him, and to let hi for a scapegoat into the wilderness.

The land is lonely for its emptiness. The land is sick with th

How little he had known the wild ones. The horned ones, wearing trumpets on their heads, shofars we could blow to sound our regret and our joy, on the Jewish New Year. How little he had known his Vivienne. She had spoken to him, but he was too busy with words to hear her.

Johnny inched out on the salt, which cracked under his feet as he walked. The salt playa had the ram's tracks in it. Johnny sketched the tracks in his notebook. The classic track of the bighorn sheep: the side parts straight, three and half inches by two and half inches, the footprint looking like a double teardrop. In the buff and grey of the original palette times, the old Pleistocene times, these Russian bighorn sheep had walked over the Bering Strait land bridge from Siberia, they had been in the country for at least 350,000 years. Johnny closed his notebook and just looked. The ram stood alone, an isolate in the vast salt fjord, its feet sunk in salt.

The ram must have set out when the mountains were pale yellow in earlier hours of the day, and come down from the mountains to walk uncommonly in search of the water places, and now the granite night had returned. He was a vision of glorious pelt in ruin; atonement was in the air for all things in nature, and man had reckoning with the beasts. Lightning struck Johnny's heart for the things he had done to the beasts and how he did not atone, and how content he had been to be apart and how he had so rarely seen the beasts. And the desert was the first surveillance. The desert watched Adam and Eve, the desert watched Abram and Abraham, the desert watched Isaac be born to a man one hundred years old, the desert saw it all. Humans left far too many traces. Johnny was at Badwater, the lowest place in the United States of America. He looked up to the far snow peak of Mount Whitney, the highest spot. The ram stepped out of the gloaming salt. The ram came close to Johnny with its shofar horn. This ram might be the ram of the Book of Leviticus.

But the goat, on which the lot fell to be the scapegoat, shall be presented alive before the LORD, to make an atonement with him, and *to let him go for a scapegoat into the wilderness.*

The land is lonely for its emptiness. The land is sick with the noise of people. The land does not know what it looks like anymore. The land has forgotten it is so beautiful.

And we have brutalized it, and we have not shown remorse yet.

Earth, soil, ram, salt, reconsider me. The ram butted Johnny's hand, pushing its horn through Johnny's hand, severing the fingers in one clump. Johnny backed up, slipping. The ram pushed him into the sharp-edged salt. Johnny Coma's arms were bleeding from the salt that cut him with horizontal stabs as the ram stabbed him right where Val had stabbed him, up under his breastbone, this time absolutely exposing his liver, impaling it as it sat exposed. The ram kept impaling Johnny Coma with its atonement horn. Johnny longed for the voice of his wife. He said, "Vivienne," longingly, regretfully, lonely, in ending, until Johnny Coma, novelist, was dead at sundown on New Year's Eve, at Badwater. Johnny Coma, writer, bled out into the blue. His body imprinted its presence on the salt, like a creature leaving its outline, its meuse, as it departs. On high promontories and in low holes, the aching angels wanted back on level Earth, to feel purpose again, as humans. The ram picked up Johnny Coma's Moleskine notebook in its mouth.

And the nuclear mountains kept on buzzing.

And so shall our atonement be drawn to them, as magnets to the inland sea.

And the night fell in its granite enclosure, and the old ram was the colour of granite and returned to its mountain high to watch over the desert.

Off in a corner on the main floor, off anonymous, off entrained, enchained to the death moment, off on a piece of wood, off modest, off humble, off as death on a sidewalk, lay the painted bird in a small frame. Painted on wood in 1890 approximately. The bird like an old man, the bird not human but how humans in age become like old birds. The bird, simple in his grey feathers. The bird with his clawed feet curled. The bird as an adored wonder. The bird as a silent thing, a found wonder. Death as the freak. Death as the freak show. Death the unpretty. Death with no dignity, or with dignity. Death does not know the word. Death the oasis. Death in your feathered unglory, on a simple piece of board. The adoration without frills or advertising. This is what Val wanted, this is what he had achieved. He did not, as the saying goes, need or even want someone to share this moment with him. He wanted Vivienne Pink, and she did not want him the way he wanted her to want him, with no strings, and this was known the very first day. On the first day, there was darkness and then came the terrestrial life, and the firmament was her, and the light came from her eyes.

The bird in the painting was so humble; the dead bird of the world, on every sidewalk.

He left the bird and went upstairs to the Klee Room. He sat with his favourite Paul Klee, *Arab Song*. After Klee was in Tunisia in 1914, he painted *Arab Song* in 1932. It was a masterpiece of humility, on burlap. Pink and turquoise paint, an abstract figure that could be sand, or a monolith, or a woman peeking out from behind a chador. This painting was older than Iraq, as named and mapped by the British. Hell, Dennis Hopper was older than Iraq.

Val left the Klee Room and went to visit the Rothko Room. He sat with *Green and Maroon*, painted in 1953. The nuclear spring of eleven tests in three months occurred that year. Yet Rothko lasted. He painted the truth of doom so heartening, he made a living shiva of a canvas, so you came and sat and you grieved the world, and the offering lasted. Even as our necks drew the radiation to us, our souls drew the paint to our hearts. Forty-one Januaries ago, the Broken Arrow accidental nuclear bombs rained on Palomares, Spain.

Val went back downstairs to visit one more time with Ryder's *Dead Bird* and say goodbye. He was a corner man with a simple dead avian on wood. He hoped the dead bird missed him.

He left the Phillips Collection and he walked up 21st and one block over to Connecticut, where he went into City Lights of China. He sat alone against the sky blue padding, on the turquoise leatherette chair on the blue-tiled floor, and thought of Vivienne. He sat alone in the country he came from, which he worked for, in some other place. It was cold and clear in the capital and Val Gold in his dusty silver fox hair and his charcoal grey sweater and charcoal grey jeans and ripped-up suede slip-on shoes looked, to the casual General Tso's chicken-eating observer, like a foreign man on business in the nation's capital.

It was a quiet Tuesday in early January of the year 2007, in Washington, DC.

He was as lonely as a man can be. A day ago he had been in the far reaches of the desert, in the inner heights of Death Valley, where no water flows to the sea. No one could see the desert on him, but they might wonder about the hollows in his cheeks and the set of his plump lips and the look in his eyes, staring as he ate as if he were facing the final boat boarding to the end. He lifted a cup of green tea in a toast, "Vivienne."

In the morning, Val flew to Syria, and Dale picked him up in Damascus. They rode in from the airport in Dale's bright green Austin-Healey much like the one that picked Val up back in Death Valley, back a billion years ago in the drop of water we call two days. But Dale's car was painted flat, and it did not show your face.

ACKNOWLEDGEMENTS

The team at Wolsak and Wynn, gems all – Noelle Allen, Ashley Hisson, Emily Dockrill Jones – have been professional, detail oriented and open hearted.

If you're a lucky writer, you work with an editor who feels the intention of your book, and desires to bring that intention into better focus. Paul Vermeersch has been that editor. His smarts, sense of play, work ethic and artist's eye raised the level of *Death Valley* many notches.

There are people who believe you, and people who believe in you. My husband, Dennis Lee, believed in me, and the book, as I ghosted along in the work. I am grateful for his bedrock love.

I first laid eyes on the American Southwest desert area known as Death Valley in 1994. I trekked there on eight hiking and photography trips, letting the desert tell me how to tell its story.

Two photography exhibits, early in the game, fed into this quest. I saw *American Ground Zero,* the photographs of Carole Gallagher, at the International Center of Photography in New York in 1994. Gallagher spent years photographing downwind victims of the Nevada atomic bomb tests and collecting their stories.

In Barcelona in 2004 I saw an exhibit of photos by Michael Martin, *Deserts/Desiertos,* which galvanized my sense of the desert as soul oasis.

As I wrote, my desk companions were the photographs of Shōmei Tōmatsu, who documented life in Japan, especially in Okinawa, and in Hiroshima and Nagasaki after the bombings.

I have used quotations from the King James Version of the Bible in chapters 3, 10, 15, 20, 29 and 34. They are in italics.

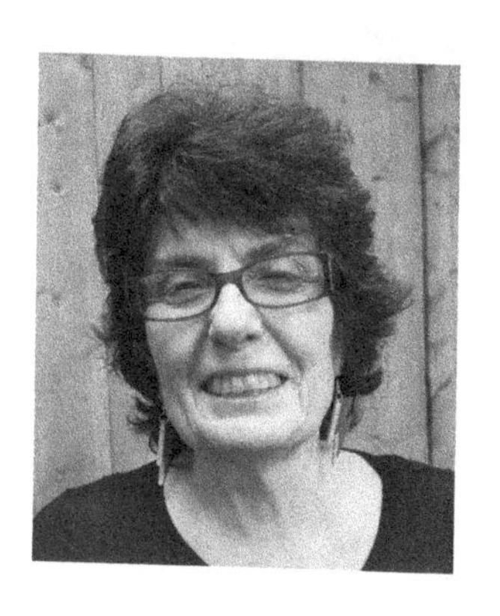

Susan Perly has worked as a journalist, war correspondent and radio producer for the CBC. In the early '80s her Letters from Latin America for Peter Gzowski's *Morningside* reported from locales such as El Salvador, Guatemala and Chiapas. During the Iran-Iraq war she broadcast Letters from Baghdad, and she produced many documentaries for the weekly program *Sunday Morning*. Perly is the author of the jazz novel *Love Street*, and her short stories have appeared in numerous magazines and anthologies. She lives in Toronto with her husband, the poet Dennis Lee.

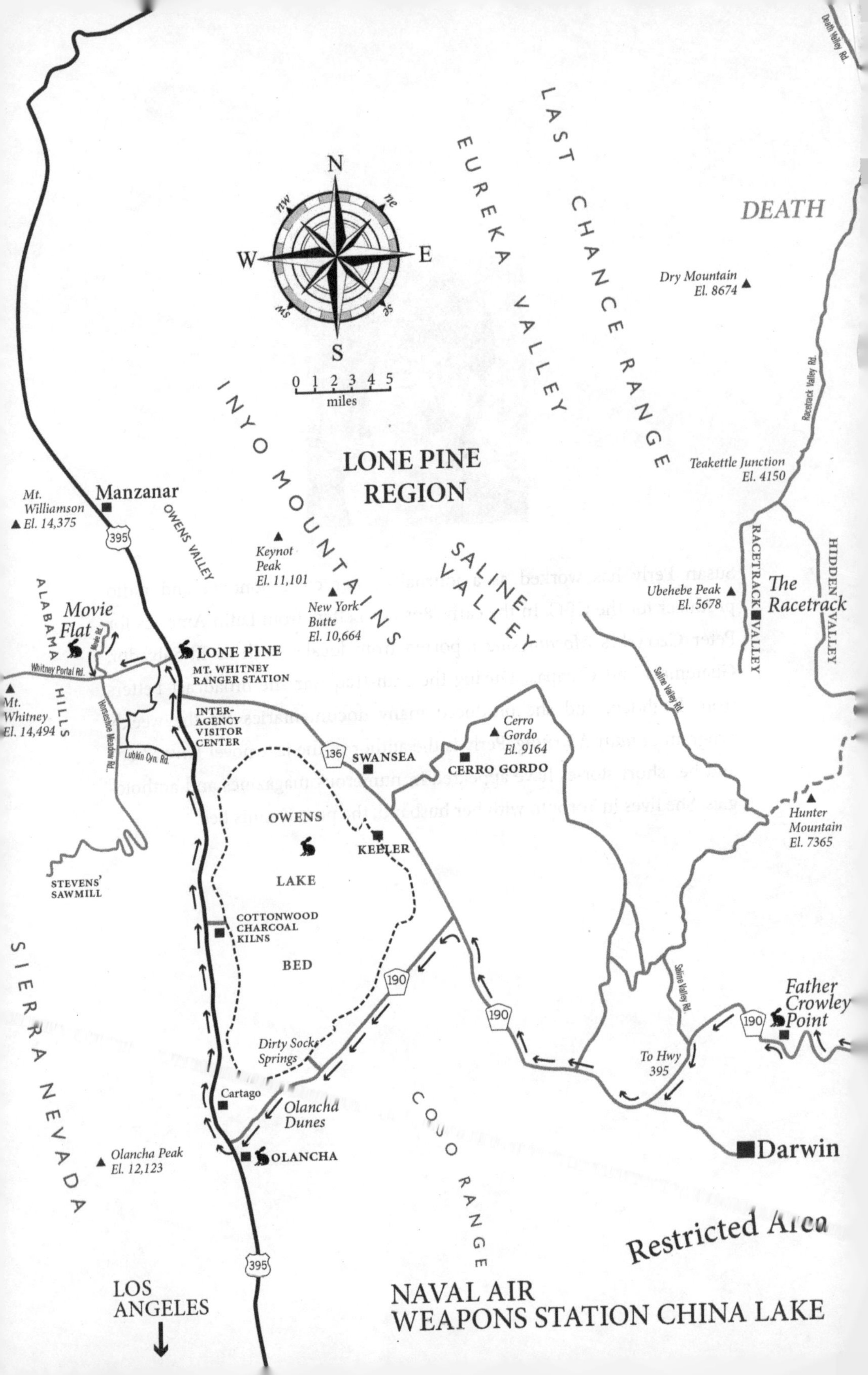

LONE PINE REGION
N
E
S
W
nw
ne
sw
se
0 1 2 3 4 5
miles
LAST CHANCE RANGE
EUREKA VALLEY
INYO MOUNTAINS
SALINEY VALLEY
DEATH
Death Valley Rd.
Dry Mountain
El. 8674
Racetrack Valley Rd.
Teakettle Junction
El. 4150
RACETRACK VALLEY
HIDDEN VALLEY
Ubehebe Peak
El. 5678
The Racetrack
Manzanar
Mt. Williamson
El. 14,375
395
OWENS VALLEY
Keynot Peak
El. 11,101
New York Butte
El. 10,664
ALABAMA HILLS
Movie Flat
Movie Rd.
Whitney Portal Rd.
LONE PINE
MT. WHITNEY RANGER STATION
Mt. Whitney
El. 14,494
Horseshoe Meadow Rd.
INTER-AGENCY VISITOR CENTER
Lubkin Cyn. Rd.
136
SWANSEA
Cerro Gordo
El. 9164
CERRO GORDO
Saline Valley Rd.
Hunter Mountain
El. 7365
OWENS LAKE BED
KEELER
STEVENS' SAWMILL
COTTONWOOD CHARCOAL KILNS
SIERRA NEVADA
190
Father Crowley Point
To Hwy 395
Dirty Socks Springs
Cartago
Olancha Dunes
COSO RANGE
OLANCHA
Olancha Peak
El. 12,123
Darwin
Restricted Area
LOS ANGELES
NAVAL AIR WEAPONS STATION CHINA LAKE

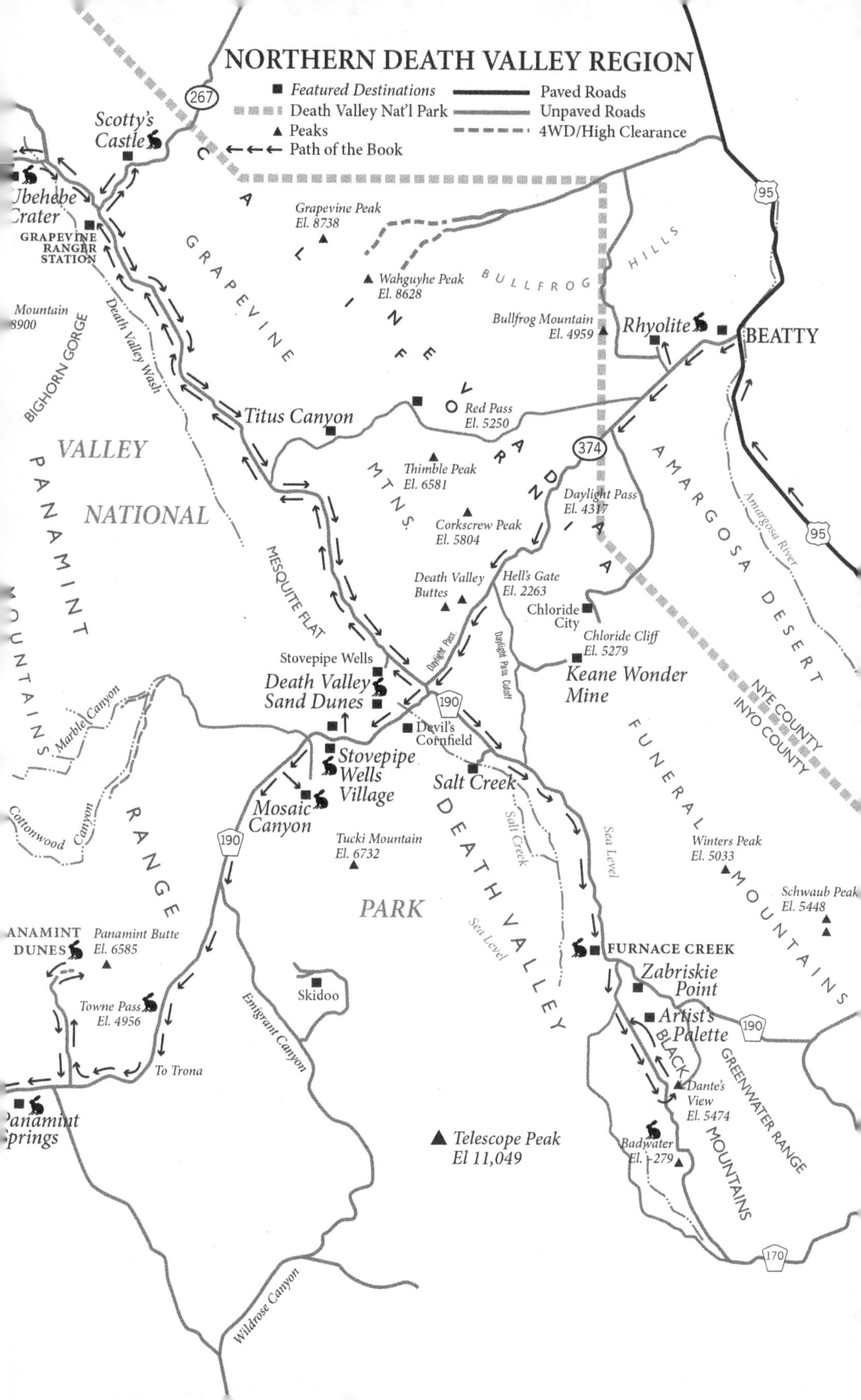
NORTHERN DEATH VALLEY REGION
Featured Destinations
Death Valley Nat'l Park
Peaks
Path of the Book
Paved Roads
Unpaved Roads
4WD/High Clearance
267
Scotty's Castle
Ubehebe Crater
GRAPEVINE RANGER STATION
CALIFORNIA
NEVADA
GRAPEVINE
Grapevine Peak El. 8738
Wahguyhe Peak El. 8628
BULLFROG HILLS
Bullfrog Mountain El. 4959
Rhyolite
BEATTY
95
Mountain 8900
BIGHORN GORGE
Death Valley Wash
Titus Canyon
Red Pass El. 5250
374
VALLEY
NATIONAL
PANAMINT MOUNTAINS
MTNS.
Thimble Peak El. 6581
Corkscrew Peak El. 5804
Daylight Pass El. 4317
AMARGOSA DESERT
Amargosa River
MESQUITE FLAT
Death Valley Buttes
Hell's Gate El. 2263
Chloride City
Chloride Cliff El. 5279
Daylight Pass
Daylight Pass Cutoff
Stovepipe Wells
Death Valley Sand Dunes
Keane Wonder Mine
NYE COUNTY
INYO COUNTY
190
Devil's Cornfield
Marble Canyon
Stovepipe Wells Village
Salt Creek
FUNERAL MOUNTAINS
Cottonwood Canyon
RANGE
Mosaic Canyon
Tucki Mountain El. 6732
Salt Creek
Sea Level
DEATH VALLEY
Winters Peak El. 5033
Schwaub Peak El. 5448
PARK
PANAMINT DUNES
Panamint Butte El. 6585
FURNACE CREEK
Zabriskie Point
Skidoo
Emigrant Canyon
Towne Pass El. 4956
Artist's Palette
BLACK MOUNTAINS
GREENWATER RANGE
To Trona
Dante's View El. 5474
Panamint Springs
Telescope Peak El 11,049
Badwater El. -279
170
Wildrose Canyon

35

THE DEAD BIRD

VAL GOLD HAD been wearing his Kevlar-lined leather jacket at Panamint Springs when Andy shot him. Val was taking no chances. He did not trust Vivienne. Val did not see that his mistrust of Vivienne came through to her, and since she did not have his confidence, she mistrusted him as a result. When the bullet came, it tore the leather but not the lining. He watched Vivienne drive away with Andy. He went into room 15 and slept in the sheets where she had played with her new man. Her musk was embedded in the pillow slips. He woke in pale light the next afternoon, near sundown. Val knew it was time: he went out to the highway, waiting to go wherever the first car was going. It was going east. A grey-blue low-cut Austin-Healey, early days of Vietnam vintage, 1963, Val was guessing. The guy was putting on some speed, like the old kamikaze grounded pilots who wanted to fly their wheels on the pavement, after the war was over. The guy was planning to make Vegas in a hurry. Val said that was fine with him, drop him at the airport. He figured there might be a spare seat on a red-eye to DC.

THE DRIVER DROPPED Val at McCarran. In the airport washroom, Val sponged the dust off his pants and sweater, poured the sand out of his shoes into the trash can, cleaned up the slash on his forehead, wet his hands and pushed them through his thick silver hair. One more bruised holiday man making an exit from the desert.

Val knew Vivienne was not in love with him. She had never been. He had signed up, he had enlisted, not for war, but to be the other man. Nobody made him do it. She did not lead him on (except with her smile, except with her smell, her laugh, her thighs, her lips, her wit, her bravery, her refusal to say the word *brave*). On the plane, he sat at the window, in homage to his Vivienne and how she did not want him. When he met her she was not yet married to Johnny, and Val asked her many times, "How come no one ever asked a fine woman like you to marry him," and Vivienne always said, "Ask me," and he never asked her, and then Johnny one day said to Vivienne, "Will you marry me?" and Vivienne said, "Yes." And Val never knew for sure if she might have loved him like a wife, but he saw marriage as an option, and Canada as an option, and he liked to keep his options open, and the man who keeps all his options open and believes there is always time can end up sitting on a plane alone, married to work. Val Gold, American citizen, single, counterterrorism expert, watched the lights of the gaming valley coalesce into an amber clot, a resin for the ages, the lost city, the last city. They banked up over the mountains, and flew over desert darkness, where only occasional glitters told there was secret activity but mostly it was darkness. The plutonium Buddhas sent off their secret flames.

At Reagan National, he got a cab to the New Hampshire Inn on 21st Street where he routinely stayed in Foggy Bottom, so as to be low key and not posh, have a kitchen and be easy-walking distance to the Phillips Collection. When Val Gold was low, and he was low now, he found solace and a rebuke to the noose by going to sit with paintings. Right here in DC, right up 21st Street, between Q and R, was the Phillips Collection, the first modern art museum in the US, and one of the best still. It was a secret haunt of artists themselves. Artists and writers came here, keeping it to themselves, finding the small rooms in the personal mansion of Duncan Phillips to be a place for quiet, for sight, for thought, for reflection, for meditation, for examination, a rest for eyes and heart. There was the Rothko Room, the Klee Room, but first off, Val wanted to see *Dead Bird* painted by Albert Ryder.